**Outstanding praise for the novels of
Daniel Palmer!**

DESPERATE

"Fans of well-crafted Hitchcock-like thrillers
will enjoy *Desperate*."
—*Associated Press*

"Palmer's best book to date."
—BookReporter.com

"Palmer has a way of telling the story and
making it fresh."
—*Winston-Salem Journal*

STOLEN

"Unrelentingly suspenseful."
—*Publishers Weekly*

"He already exhibits the skills of a master craftsman.
Fans of Harlan Coben or Lisa Gardner
will adore his look into the lives of an everyday couple."
—*RT Book Reviews*

"A twisting, suspenseful chiller of a book."
—William Landay, *New York Times* bestselling author
of *Defending Jacob*

Books by Daniel Palmer

DELIRIOUS

HELPLESS

STOLEN

DESPERATE

CONSTANT FEAR

FORGIVE ME

Published by Kensington Publishing Corporation

FORGIVE ME

DANIEL PALMER

PINNACLE BOOKS
Kensington Publishing Corp.
www.kensingtonbooks.com

PINNACLE BOOKS are published by

Kensington Publishing Corp.
119 West 40th Street
New York, NY 10018

ISBN-13: 978-0-7860-3385-0
ISBN-10: 0-7860-3385-1

First Kesnington hardcover printing: June 2016
First Pinnacle mass market paperback printing: June 2017

10 9 8 7 6 5 4 3 2 1

Printed in the United States of America

First Pinnacle electronic edition: May 2016

ISBN-13: 978-0-7860-3386-7
ISBN-10: 0-7860-3386-X

For Matthew, Ethan, and Luke
Thanks for having my back all these years.

And for the team at NCMEC and people
like Nadine Jessup.
One victim is too many.

PROLOGUE

She sat at her writing desk in her home's spacious first-floor office, dreading this moment that came every year on this date. The dainty desk was a replica of a *bonheur-du-jour*, a piece of furniture from the eighteenth century made specifically with a woman in mind. The name, "good hour of the day," referred to the time of day when women took pleasure from opening, reading, and writing letters. She was there for that purpose, but took no pleasure in the task.

Gazing out a bank of windows, she saw the empty garden beds. They would blossom beautifully in springtime, as they always did. But spring was several weeks away. The grass around the beds was brown, and her mood was somber and gray as the overcast sky.

From one of the desk's lacquered panels, she removed her checkbook, then fished a ballpoint pen from the desk's main compartment. Out of habit, she checked the balance in the check register—plenty of money in the account, as there always was. The simple observation summoned a familiar feeling of guilt, followed by profound sadness.

She wrote out the check for the same amount as always. Her handwriting was impeccable. The loops, curves, and lines formed perfect, beautiful letters, properly spaced, neat and elegant, almost like calligraphy. She'd loved writing in school, and dreamed of one day writing a novel. She felt she had so much to say about love and relationships, the big questions of life. But that was a long time ago, a different lifetime, and she had since become an entirely different person.

From the living room next to the office she could hear the television. The sound of some sporting event in progress—basketball, she thought. What did she know? Watching sports on TV was her husband's pastime, not hers. And yet, this was her dream—a husband resting on his lazy chair; a child reared and off on her own; a fine house kept tidy and organized, thanks to her fastidious nature; gardens in need of tending—everything as it should be.

But some dreams come at a price.

She knew that now.

From one of the little drawers across the back of the desk, she removed an envelope and addressed it from memory. Her tears began to fall. The words turned to smudges. She crumpled up the envelope, took another, and started anew. From the same drawer, she got a blank piece of paper and wrote *With gratitude for your efforts*. She signed her name and folded the paper around the check. Then, she slipped both items into the envelope and licked it closed. The glue tasted extra bitter on her tongue. She slipped the envelope into her purse. She would drive to a mailbox tonight, so it would go out first thing in the morning. She closed her eyes and took inventory of all she had, all her good fortune.

In a whispered voice, she uttered the same phrase she spoke every year on this day, at this exact moment. "May God forgive me."

CHAPTER 1

Nadine had thought about running away for years. She lived in a nice colonial house in Potomac, Maryland, but home was hell. She was supposed to be the child, so why was she the one taking care of her mother? It wasn't fair. No, not right at all. Her mother had always loved to drink, but it was different after Dad left. Wine used to make her giddy, but now it just made her slur her words.

Nadine had begged her father to let her come live with him, but he was too busy with work to look after her, or so he'd said. She'd be better at home with Mom, he'd said. Ha! He should come and see what Mom had become since he'd left them for that bitch.

She tried to tell her father what it was like living with Mom. Weekends spent in bed. Often there was no food in the refrigerator, and Nadine would have to do all the shopping (driving illegally, but always carefully, on her learner's permit) and the cooking, not to mention the cleaning. Mom walked into walls, tripped over her own feet.

Somehow her mother still had a job. She worked for Verizon, doing something in customer service. How she got to work each day, given her evening's alcohol consumption, was nothing short of a miracle. Her get-ready ritual involved a lot more than a shower, some makeup, and breakfast. Her mother needed half the Visine bottle to get the red out. She often turned on bathroom faucets full strength to mask the sound of retching.

She'd come downstairs, cupping what looked like a handful of aspirin in her palm, and bark something unpleasant at Nadine. "Turn down that TV. I have a headache."

Of course you do, Nadine would think.

"Is that what you're wearing? You look like a tramp." It never failed. Mom's mouth would open and something cruel, something cutting, would spill out.

"I made the honors list," Nadine announced on the fifteenth day of March, the day she finally ran away.

Her mother rubbed at her pounding temples as she poured a cup of coffee flavored with Kahlúa. Something to take the edge off, she would say.

"You better, for what we pay that private school," was her mother's reply.

Nadine's chest felt heavy, throat dry, while her eyes watered. She would not give her mother the satisfaction of seeing her cry again. Her mother would pounce if a single tear leaked out.

"Toughen up, Nadine," she'd say. "The world is a brutal place, and you'd best have a thicker skin."

Her mother's jabs always held a hint of truth, which made them hurt even more. Nadine's school was expensive, that was a fact. But her father paid most of the tuition.

Money, it seemed, was the only thing that wasn't a problem in Nadine's life. Dad sent them plenty. He said he was happy to support them, but Nadine knew the truth. He was assuaging (an SAT word she'd recently learned) his guilt.

He didn't want her in his life. He wanted his new, young wife and no kids to hassle them. He wanted to travel and go to all the fancy restaurants he posted on his Facebook feed. One look at her dad's profile page and it was obvious a kid didn't fit into the picture. After the divorce, her father had moved to Philadelphia—Bryn Mawr East, to be exact—with a new executive position at an insurance company and a new woman in his life. He posted a few photos of Nadine, but those were all recent. No "Throwback Thursday" posts (#tbt in Facebook parlance) on her dad's page. No pictures of Nadine aged infant to tween; no evidence of his former life, aka his great mistake as he'd called his marriage during an epic pre-divorce blowout.

That was how he viewed his family. That was all Nadine was to him—a great mistake.

Apparently her mother felt the same way.

Nadine's last meal at home was chicken casserole, which she prepared using a recipe she got off the Internet. Her mother downed a bottle of wine with the meal. In her drunken stupor, she failed to notice the shoes Nadine had left in front of the closet door. Her mother tripped over the shoes and fell to the floor, twisting her ankle on the way down.

Nadine apologized. She had meant to put the shoes where they belonged, but was preoccupied with school, and dinner, and her too many responsibilities.

Her mother was hearing none of it. She went to the couch and applied ice to the injury, then poured herself another glass of wine, allegedly because it helped with the pain.

"Sorry again, Mom," Nadine said. "Are you okay?"

Her mother's eyes were red as her nail polish. "You're so thoughtless, Nadine," she slurred. "How am I going to go to work now? I can't even walk. Sometimes I wish your father would let you go live with him. I know that's what you want."

That was it. That did it. Enough was enough. Her father didn't want her. Neither did her mother. The choice was made not *by her*, but *for her*. Nobody wanted Nadine, so nobody had to have her.

After her mother slipped into drunken sleep, Nadine took all of the money they kept in the house—400-some dollars—and her mother's jewelry and walked out the door with a school knapsack filled with clothes instead of books. She walked to Montgomery Mall, about four and a half miles, then took a Metrobus downtown. She had plenty of money to spend, plus whatever a pawnshop would give her for the jewelry.

Pretending to be her mother, Nadine had called in sick to school. It was that easy. Her mother would take the day off to nurse her injured ankle—she'd already sent the e-mail to her boss. She'd wake up late and hung over, and think Nadine was at school. She'd think that until five o'clock rolled around.

Then she'd wonder. Maybe she'd call some of Nadine's friends. It would be seven . . . and then eight . . . and then panic. Maybe panic. Or maybe not. She'd probably be happy. Relieved to be rid of Nadine once and for all.

Nadine didn't know what her mother was thinking. She'd been gone for three days without calling home. She'd found a motel on the far side of the city that didn't bother to check ID, didn't care that she was a sixteen-year-old girl out on her own.

The question was what to do with all the time on her hands. She enjoyed school and did her homework diligently. She loved English especially, loved to escape into other people's happy or miserable lives and forget about her own for a while. She found a used bookstore off Dupont Circle and bought several books, including the entire Testing Trilogy by Joelle Charbonneau. She devoured all three volumes in the span of two days. But something was missing. Idle time to read had in some ways diminished the pleasure.

She was wandering aimlessly in Union Station, admiring the shops and all the things she had no money to buy, wondering how to pass the day, when a man approached.

He was tall and good-looking for an older man, with a nicely round head sporting a buzz cut like Jason Statham's, and a clean-shaven face. His most notable feature was a pair of piercing blue eyes. He carried a bag from Heydari Design, which Nadine knew sold women's clothing and accessories.

"Can I ask you something?" he said to her.

He had a foreign accent, Nadine thought. But it was subtle. Something distinctive—*sophisticated* was the word that came to mind—something like a count would use. He was dressed sharply in a tailored navy suit, blue oxford underneath, no tie. His shoes were polished black loafers.

Nadine gazed at the man, unable to speak before finding her voice. "Yes," was all she said. *Why is he talking to me? What could he want? Did Mom put out a missing persons report? Does he recognize me? Am I in trouble? Will he call the police? Will they take me to jail? Worse, will they take me back home?*

"I just bought something for my daughter. She's about your age. But after I left the store, I was hit with doubt. I could use a second opinion. She likes the color blue, if that helps any."

From inside the Heydari bag, he removed a twilight blue linen-blend scarf, fringed at the ends for a touch of sophistication. It was lovely, something Nadine would have bought for herself if she had money to spend on such purchases. Books and food were all she could afford to buy. Plus she needed money for her motel room. Where else was she going to sleep? There was a lot more to running away from home than she had contemplated.

"I think she'll love it." Nadine meant it, too. To her surprise, her chest suddenly felt heavy. Here was a dad doing something lovely and thoughtful for his daughter. Her father gave her birthday presents, but always mailed them. It was never anything she wanted because he didn't take the time to get to know her tastes, her color palette.

Her father was nothing like this one, she decided.

"Thank you. I feel a bit more confident now."

That accent, where was it from? European? "You're welcome," Nadine said.

The man nodded his thanks, turned to leave, but stopped. He seemed to be appraising her in a way that made her feel vulnerable. "This is going to sound odd," he said as he took out his wallet.

Does he think I need a handout? Nadine was mortified to think she looked so bedraggled (another SAT word) that he suspected she was homeless and in need.

To her great relief, he took out a business card instead of cash. "I run an entertainment agency, and I'm always on the lookout for new talent. If you don't mind my saying, you have a great look. Almost like a Jennifer Lawrence type."

Nadine had to suppress a laugh. JLaw? Her? *Come on.* Nadine didn't think herself exceptional in any way. She was average at everything—height, weight, academics, sports. Name it, and she fit smack dab in the middle, undistinguished and indistinguishable from her peers. Her hair color was brown, eyes brown, and that's what it would say on the missing person posters if her mother bothered to file a report. Weight 118, height 5'3". Average. Perfectly average.

She blushed.

"I'm not saying you look like her exactly," the man explained. "But there's something about you that's very compelling. I'm not kidding. I find talent for TV, movies, reality shows. It's a booming business these days with so many places for content."

Nadine shrugged. She didn't know what to say. She looked down at the card. STEPHEN J. MACAN. MACAN ENTERTAINMENT. No address, no phone number, no website or e-mail. It felt secretive, which made the business seem more exclusive. He had to find you; you couldn't find him.

"Have you ever had headshots done?"

Before Nadine could answer, the man's cell phone rang. A smile came to his face as he answered the call. "Hi, honey. I'm still at the mall shopping for Megan." He pulled the phone away and mouthed the words *my wife* for Nadine's benefit. He held up his finger, an indication he wanted her to stay.

For some reason, she did.

"I'll be home soon. Want me to pick up something for dinner? I could grill up salmon, if you'd like."

A pause while his wife said something in response.

"Great. Oh, and I got the opinion of a girl about Megan's

age, so I think I did well with my gift. We shall see." He gave a little laugh.

Some inside joke about how difficult Megan could be to shop for, Nadine supposed. The joke was made with love, not malice. It was so obvious Megan's dad adored her.

Nadine's heart turned. *Why can't I have the same sort of relationship with my father?*

"I'll be home soon. Love you. Bye." The man's attention went back to Nadine. "So are you interested in becoming famous?" His smile was warm, genuine.

Nadine wondered if his daughter Megan had the right look. The man, this Stephen Macan, seemed so certain *Nadine* did.

He wouldn't lie about something like this.

It was all happening too fast for her to process. A little tickle in the gut told her to be cautious. She handed the man back his card. "I don't think so."

The man looked resigned and a little disappointed, but offered no hard sell. "Just so you know, there's no second chances. This business is too hard for any self-doubters. We look for people who think they were meant for something more. I thought I had it right with you." He shrugged. "Maybe all this shopping has dulled my instincts. Anyway, I wish you the best of luck." He stuck out his hand.

As soon as she shook it, Nadine felt numb all over her body. She wasn't sure what she was feeling. Ashamed? Disappointed in herself? What were his words exactly?

People who think they were meant for something more.

That struck a chord. Despite her parents, she thought she was worth something more. She could make something out of her life and show them all. That's right. Become somebody and get on *Ellen* or *Good Morning America* and have a tear-filled reunion on live TV while her parents apologized to their celebrity daughter for years of mistreatment. Wouldn't that show them!

She watched Stephen Macan walk away, swinging the bag that contained a beautiful scarf for his daughter, who wasn't pretty enough for a movie career of her own. He wasn't creepy at all. She got no vibes like that from him. He had a wife to whom he spoke sweetly and a kid about her age. It was happenstance that he saw her and asked a very reasonable question about the gift, and then luck that he saw something *in her*.

It was the real deal, Nadine decided, a genuine opportunity that she let pass by. And think! The next time her mother might see her could be on TV or in the movies. She tried to imagine her expression. It would be priceless!

The man was a good distance away, almost out of sight.

Nadine took a determined breath and went running after him.

CHAPTER 2

Four weeks later

Angie DeRose arrived on foot at the Columbia Fire-house to have lunch with her parents at the scheduled time, on the scheduled hour, on the scheduled day. Given the fluid nature of her job, that was a minor miracle.

Angie loved the work, though. A good thing because it was all consuming. The phone rang day and night. No one took vacations when kids ran away, and run they did, twenty-four by seven by three sixty-five.

The calls varied. Sometimes it was a crisis with a child custody case, or surveillance work that might require her to spy on a cheating spouse, or follow a lead on a possible parental child abduction. Maybe an irate spouse had gotten wind that their ex was headed off to party—and who was going to watch little Joey while Mom or Dad did the Harlem Shake with a shot of tequila in one hand and a beer chaser in the other? An anxious parent didn't care one iota what time of day it was, whether or not it was a holiday, or if Angie had plans to meet her parents for a meal. Thus was life as a private investigator. She wouldn't have it any other way.

The restaurant, a renovated fire station with exposed brick walls, served quality American eats. It was a favorite of the DeRoses. Angie and her mother Kathleen ordered salads and soda water with lime, while her father got the salmon special. It was easy to meet for lunch because her parents lived near her office, still in the same house in Arlington, Virginia, where Angie grew up.

Having lunch with her parents grounded Angie. Since founding DeRose & Associates at twenty-eight, five years ago, she had struggled with orbiting so closely to the dregs of humanity. She had gone into the business with a purpose, but had been naïve about the depth of human cruelty. The deplorable ways parents could treat each other or treat their precious children were too numerous to count and endlessly gut-wrenching. Each case was like turning over a rock to see what sort of horror might slither out.

Most difficult were the surveillance gigs to get proof of child abuse. Those hit her the hardest, but they were also the best way to get a kid out of danger. Some of her colleagues—the men, mostly—could shut it off, go to bed without seeing the cigarette burns dappled on a young kid's arm. Not Angie. She took it all to heart, carried with her the emotion of what she saw every day.

When it was a runaway or a child custody case, she went overboard to get results, to get proof, in order to protect the child. She lived and breathed it. Her wheels were constantly going, just like her office phone. Hell, somebody had to make sure the kids ended up safe or with the right parent.

Over the years, Angie had seen squalor that made a

cardboard box on some desolate street corner look like an upgrade. Malnourished children. Beaten children. Children terrified of abuse. Neglected children. Drug-addicted parents who preferred the pipe to their kid. Out-of-control teens who raged against authority and railed against their terrified and despondent parents.

For the most part, Angie saw the world as a broken place that could never be properly fixed. In the presence of her parents, that world shone a little brighter.

She knew she was one of the lucky ones. Not many of her clients wanted to meet their children for lunch, or surprise them with a spur-of-the-moment visit. Her parents' support and friendship over the years had made all the difference, especially during the hardest period of her life.

Her best friend Sarah had vanished without a trace. It was senior year of college at the University of Virginia, and they were a few months shy of starting their lives. That semester Sarah got hooked on something—Oxy, the cops thought. Then she was gone, just like that. Gone. And that was how she stayed. Missing.

What had happened to Sarah Winter? Might she still be alive? The questions haunted Angie. She'd longed to do something to honor Sarah's memory, her spirit. Opening DeRose & Associates Private Investigators, she'd hung a picture of Sarah on the office wall behind her desk. That picture served as an ever-present reminder of Angie's mission—find the runaway kids and take them back home.

"Daddy, you look tired," Angie said as they waited for their meals. "Is everything okay?"

Gabriel DeRose's thinning dark hair rested high on a broad forehead. He kept in shape by walking on the treadmill and doing some weight training, but over the years he had developed a noticeable paunch. The lenses of his black-rimmed glasses magnified the dark circles around his eyes. The skin around his neck was looser, his full face a bit wan. Still, he looked distinguished and poised in his blue pinstriped suit.

He returned a thin smile, and Angie's heart warmed with love. "I'm fine, sweetheart. Just busy at work. That's all."

Always busy at work, Angie thought. Like father, like daughter—and like mother. The DeRose family was a kinetic bunch. Her father ran DeRose Financial, a well-respected financial services firm that specialized in investing for high-net-worth individuals. He had two employees, hundreds of millions under management, and in Angie's opinion, too much stress. She worried constantly about his health. She wished he would take more time for himself, but he had worked so hard, for so long, he was either too afraid or had forgotten how to hit the off switch.

Kathleen had never worked full-time, but she probably outpaced her husband and daughter in effort and hours worked.

"How's the committee going, Mom?" Angie asked.

"Which one?" Gabriel said with a laugh.

"You pick, Mom," Angie said.

"Well, the Lupus Foundation is doing another donor drive, if that's any indication, and I'm up to my eyeballs in mailings." Kathleen was one of 1.5 million Americans living with the disease. She'd been diagnosed when Angie was an infant. Kathleen had hidden little about her disease as Angie grew up, often talking about her fatigue and blinding headaches, and showing Angie her swollen feet, legs, and hands.

Angie was sure lupus was the main reason she grew up an only child, though her mother said otherwise. "One is enough for us. We have everything we need and want with you."

It made Angie feel better, though never lessened her desire for a sibling, especially a sister.

It took years for Kathleen's doctors to prescribe the right course of treatment. During that time, lupus episodes had required many trips to the hospital. In addition to an anti-inflammatory regimen, Kathleen took a number of other medications to treat conditions commonly seen with the disease. Lupus had no cure, and although it was an inheritable disease, Angie had never experienced any symptoms.

"I'm sure you'll surpass last year's effort," Angie said.

"Perhaps. I'm assuming I can count on you for twenty-five dollars?" Kathleen said this only a little playfully.

Angie always gave what she could. "I'll make it fifty this year. I did a transport yesterday that paid pretty well."

Transport meant Angie had entered a sleeping teenage boy's bedroom with an ex-law-enforcement agent at her side. They woke the startled kid, and his parents had to explain that he'd be going away for a while, right then and there, non-negotiable. A car was waiting for him downstairs. Angie escorted the parents out of the boy's bedroom while her partner made it clear who was in charge. They drove the teen a few hundred miles to a wilderness therapy program in southwestern Virginia, and Angie pocketed a thousand bucks for the effort. It was no problem donating fifty to her mom's committee. She'd give more if she could.

"How is business going?" Kathleen asked.

"Busy," Angie said. "Runaways and craptastic behavior seem to be recession-proof."

"Any time for yourself?" Kathleen's face showed concern.

Angie resisted the eye roll she had perfected in puberty. "Mom, are we doing this again?"

"Just look here." Kathleen took out her smartphone and showed Angie a Tinder profile she had made—for Angie.

"Mom! What are you doing?"

"Well, I was curious, that's all. I saw something about Tinder on *20/20*, and it looked promising."

"Please, stop."

"Just look for a second. It's fun. It uses your location so you see people who are near you. You swipe right if you like them and left if you don't. Couldn't be any easier! Oh, he's cute." Kathleen swiped right.

"Mom. Mom! No. We do not need to do this."

The phone made a *ding* sound. Kathleen looked, and her face lit up. "He thinks you're cute, too! And he's just three blocks away."

"Mom!"

"Well, it's true. You are cute."

"Dad, don't encourage her." Angie didn't have trouble getting dates. What she had trouble with was keeping relationships. Any guy in Angie's life had to play second fiddle to the phone. Out to dinner and a case came in—*sorry, gotta go.* In bed after a lovely wine-and-dine and a kid runs—*sorry, but gotta go.* Some guys would put up with Angie's unpredictable workday for a time, but none stuck it out for the long haul.

So just as with Match.com, and eHarmony, and every setup Angie's friends had arranged, some Tinder guy would invariably find her long legs, raven hair, and green eyes attractive. They'd come up with some tactful (or not) way to compliment her sculpted figure and commend her for rocking jeans and an evening gown with equal aplomb. They'd appreciate how she could tackle a teenager twice her size and then cry at the end of *Pitch Perfect*, a movie she'd watch any time it was on. But they'd always, always, get tired of her phone.

The right guy was out there. Angie didn't think he was on Tinder.

"Well, I'll e-mail you your username and password. Just give it a try."

"Your mother means well," her father said.

"I think I'm a little jaded because of the job," Angie admitted. "It's eye-opening to see how much bad there is in the world. Between divorce and fighting over children, infidelity and cheating left and right, it's hard. And it hasn't gotten easier."

"Maybe change careers."

"I can't walk away. I love it."

"You love what's hurting you," Kathleen said. "Sounds dysfunctional to me."

"Yeah, Mom. Well, love hurts."

"Whatever you do, we'll support you, you know that," her father said.

Kathleen took hold of Gabriel's hand. The gesture warmed Angie's heart. This was what she wanted for herself someday. She'd been raised in a traditional, old-fashioned family, and after thirty-seven years of marriage, Angie's parents still held hands. They were always touching, or laughing, or looking at each other in a loving way. They argued, of course, but not with the sort of rage common among Angie's clients. Gabriel and Kathleen DeRose had pedestrian disagreements, but nothing that caused lasting bitterness or resentment. As with lupus, there could be flare-ups followed by long periods of calm.

"Let's just change the subject. How about that?" Angie said.

"Well, then, ask me about the Arlington County Fair,

because that's another story entirely," Kathleen said with a roll of the eyes.

"You're still doing that? I thought you resigned from the board last year."

"They begged me to come back. How could I say no?"

"And she's still teaching swimming," Gabriel said. "Organizing registration now for when the pool opens in May."

Angie did not look at all surprised. Swimming was something her mother had done for years to help lessen certain lupus symptoms. But Kathleen being Kathleen, she couldn't just swim on her own. She had to do something on a larger scale, so she volunteered to teach swimming to disadvantaged DC youth every summer at a city pool.

"Guess Dad's not the only one I'm worried about. You sure you're not doing too much, Mom? The Arlington Fair board has always been such a headache."

"I'm fine, sweetheart. It's just nobody can agree on a theme for this year's competitive exhibits. I've suggested 'Expanded Horizons' to celebrate all the opportunities Arlington has to offer, but of course Bill Gibbons has to object to just about everything."

"I'm just thinking that maybe you should slow down a bit, that's all."

Even with lupus in the picture, Angie was more concerned about her father's health than her mother's. Kathleen looked splendid and healthy, stylish in her short, graying haircut. Her skin had a radiant glow, with wrinkles that implied more wisdom than age. At sixty, Angie's mother was still a strikingly beautiful woman, with a kind face and blue eyes the color of the sea.

After the meal, Gabriel slid an oversized white envelope across the table in Angie's direction. She could see it was unsealed and had no address.

"Dad, is this another prospectus? I still have a few you've given me that I haven't had time to look over yet. Not that I don't appreciate your financial advice."

"No, it's not that," Gabriel said.

Angie caught something in her father's eyes—a glimmer of concern, perhaps. She felt uneasy and a little bit nervous. "What is it?" she asked.

"Just open it, dear," her mother said.

Angie took out the papers, and her chest tightened. "Mom, Dad, why this now? Are both of you okay?"

"We're fine. We just need to have this talk, and your father thought now would be as good a time as any to make sure you know our wishes."

"We're the medical proxy for each other," Gabriel said, "but if something were to happen to us both—"

"A car accident, for instance," Kathleen tossed out.

"Okay. God forbid."

"Just say, if it did, Angie," Kathleen went on. "You're an adult and it's important you know our wishes."

Angie glanced down at the sheet of paper that had the words ADVANCED HEALTHCARE DIRECTIVE splayed across the top of the page in bold lettering. Her parents had never discussed their end-of-life intentions with her. She skimmed the document. "No CPR, no mechanical ventilation, no tube feeding. What *do* you guys want?"

"Read it more carefully. It's only if we're brain dead, sweetheart," Kathleen said.

Angie looked aghast. "Mom! Please."

Gabriel spoke up. "You're our only child, so we're counting on you for this. Walt and Louise did this with their kids, and it's high time we did it with ours."

Walter and Louise Odette were her parents' neighbors,

but Angie had grown up calling them Uncle Walt and Aunt Louise. The Odettes were the closest thing she had to blood relatives. Her mother and father no longer had contact with their extended families.

Gabriel said, "I also have a will I want you to look over, and instructions on where to find our assets and how to claim them. That sort of thing."

Angie wasn't a child. She understood her parents would die one day, but she hoped that day would be a long time coming. She was adult enough to have this conversation, but that didn't make it any less sad or awkward. "What I want to do is talk about you two taking a trip to Bermuda or someplace warm and fun. Maybe a cruise. Hell, maybe I'll join you."

"You know I think those are just petri dishes on waves," Kathleen said.

"That's not the point, Mom. This is a little depressing, and I already have a lot of depressing things to deal with back at work." Angie slipped the papers back inside the envelope. "I'll look this over tonight and call you with questions. But what I want is to not need these papers for a long, long time."

"Yes, agreed," Kathleen said.

"Now, how about dessert? Who's with me?"

Angie's phone rang. It always rang. She spoke in crisp, short sentences, every word purposeful and to the point. Her eyes narrowed while her parents waited in silence.

Angie got up from the table and slipped her phone back into her purse. "Got to take a rain check on that dessert, you two," she said, coming around the table to kiss her parents on their cheeks. "It's a runaway."

CHAPTER 3

Angie worked in a modest but respectable space, with walls painted eggshell white, a dropped ceiling, phone, Internet, and a plug-in kettle so she could sip green tea whenever the spirit moved her (which happened often).

Carolyn Jessup sat across from her, gazing hopefully at the framed photos lining the walls. They were pictures of the many families whose children Angie had helped to reunite. Well, first she found the runaway kids, and then she reunited the families. Not all her on own, either—better-trained resources helped handle reintegration, from organizations such as the NCMEC—National Center for Missing and Exploited Children. Angie wasn't present in all the photographs on her wall, but she was a major part of every operation.

Among the many pictures was one of Angie and Sarah Winter, arms draped around each other, goofy smiles on their faces, looking as if they'd have a million tomorrows. Unlike the other photographs, Sarah's picture would stay on the wall until the day she was found.

Carolyn had supplied pages of biographical details on Nadine and her family. Angie carefully read through them all. She knew right away she'd need help on the case. The sign on Angie's office door read DeRose & Associates, Private Investigators, but & *Associates* was an exaggeration. Angie's tax return did not list any additional employees on the payroll. She did, however, have an extensive network to tap whenever she needed to farm out jobs or required a skill outside her area of expertise.

Angie's specialty was finding runaways, but her office also handled computer forensics, transport, and surveillance work—all areas where she called on her network of colleagues.

Despite the proximity, people from Maryland seldom crossed the river to Virginia. DC was fine, but they typically didn't go any farther. If the police had given Carolyn a referral, it was probably to a PI based out of Silver Spring or Bethesda. Carolyn must have done her homework, ignored geography, and gone with the investigator who had the best reputation for finding runaways.

"Where do we start?" Carolyn asked. "How do we do this?" Her nervousness was as evident as her drinking problem. According to her driver's license, she was a decade older than Angie, but looked twice that. Most of the luster had been squeezed out of Carolyn's straw-colored hair, and a strong odor of booze—gin, something hard—seeped from her pores. Broken capillaries spread across a reddened complexion like a road atlas. Her face was unnaturally bloated. What looked like blushing was probably alcohol-triggered rosacea.

Drugs and alcohol were corrosive as acid to the parental bond. Angie suspected they had played a role in this case. Nadine wouldn't be the first. Four hundred thousand kids ran away from home each year, many to escape the ravages of addiction.

"What makes you think your daughter ran away and wasn't taken?"

"She took her clothes. Her backpack. What abductor lets a girl pack before she's taken?"

Angie curled her lip and gave a nod. Since she'd opened her agency, the number of children reported missing had increased each year. While the numbers were staggering, only a fraction—perhaps as few as 100 cases annually—fit the profile of abduction by a stranger or remote acquaintance. Family members represented the largest percentage of the abductions, well over 200,000 going by last year's figures.

"Is there any chance Nadine is with her father?" Angie asked. "That he's hiding her?"

Carolyn scoffed. "You think he took her? Ha, that's a good one."

"Why?"

"Because Greg loves Greg, and there's not much room left for anyone else." Carolyn made eye contact.

Angie saw no nervous tics, nothing to indicate deception. "According to you, he's paying my bill."

"And he was too busy with his work to be at this meeting," Carolyn shot back. "Need I say more?"

No, you don't, Angie thought.

"Did you have a fight before your daughter ran away? Was there a specific incident that upset Nadine?"

"Nothing really." Carolyn scrunched up her shoulders and scratched at her nose.

"Please, Carolyn. Let's just be honest here. Lying won't help us find Nadine. So let's try again. Was there a fight the night before she ran away?"

Carolyn dabbed at her eyes, and the gesture seemed authentic. "I wouldn't call it a fight. It was just her stupid shoes. She left them in front of the closet and I tripped over them."

Angie wondered if Carolyn had been too drunk to notice they were there.

"I sprained my ankle and had to miss work the next day. Maybe I used harsh language. I don't really remember."

"Was it the first time?"

The question hit Carolyn like a slap across the face. The anxious mother shrank into herself the way a hermit crab retreats into its shell. "We've had issues since Greg and I divorced."

"What sort of issues?"

"You know, typical mother-daughter stuff."

"Can you elaborate?"

"Nadine could be disrespectful, you know. She doesn't understand how hard it is to be a single parent. How much pressure I have on me."

"What about Nadine? Did she feel like she was under a lot of pressure?"

The distant look in Carolyn's eyes suggested that it had never occurred to her to ask that question. "Maybe. I don't know. Look, the past is the past. I don't know why any of this even matters. What I want to know is what you're going to do to find my daughter. She's been gone a month."

It mattered on many levels, Angie knew, but she wasn't about to debate the point. Nadine was well past the danger zone. More than three quarters of kids who ran away returned home after a week. The longer Nadine was missing, the less chance they had of finding her.

The technical difference between a runaway and a thrownaway child meant nothing to Angie. One left voluntarily and stayed away from home for consecutive nights, while the other was told to leave the house—alone and without money. Runaway or thrownaway, both types of kids were on the streets, where they attracted dangers like wounded fish in a sea of hungry sharks. Drugs, gangs, human traffickers, muggers, rapists—a gallery of perils loomed every minute a runaway stayed away from home.

"Are you still in regular contact with the police?" Angie asked. "I saw that Nadine's been entered into the FBI's National Crime Information Center database. Sometimes this can be difficult because of bureaucracy and backlog, but it's done and that's a good thing."

"The police haven't been helpful at all," Carolyn said with venom in her voice. "Especially after they figured out Nadine packed her belongings and called the school pretending to be me."

"Not really a surprise," Angie said. "They're working murders, serious crimes. Runaways are not treated with the same urgency as, say, an abduction case."

"I'm sure the level of urgency from the police would have been higher if it had been one of their kids who ran away."

"I don't disagree," Angie said. "But the problem is too many kids go missing. I promise you, it's not like they forget that for a parent, a missing child is a very big deal. It's simply that they don't have enough resources to track all the kids down. That's where we come in."

It was a constant complaint from parents of runaways and hard for Angie not to get frustrated and vocal. She needed law enforcement to be a friend. At the same time, as Carolyn had found out, they could do little to help.

"When did you last speak with your contact at NCMEC?" Angie asked.

"Sometime last week."

"So you know they printed new posters? The old ones typically get taken down after a while." Angie reached behind her and peeled away one of the posters from a printed stack. She'd gotten a copy of the poster from NCMEC when she'd learned of Nadine's disappearance. The word *missing* atop the poster in bold red lettering caught the eye. A QR code on the side would connect anyone who scanned it with a smartphone to the NCMEC website. Below that were two recent photos of Nadine. She was a pretty girl with straight brown hair and a friendly smile. Even with Carolyn's drinking, Angie could see that someday Nadine would grow up to be the spitting image of her mom.

Carolyn studied the poster intently but did not seem impressed. "So basically I have an entry in a database and a damn poster I could have made myself."

Angie had heard this response before. "She's part of the system. It's a start."

"What's next?"

"Have you been to your daughter's bedroom? Gone through her belongings? Did she leave behind anything that might tell you where she'd gone? A cell phone, a camera, a notebook, something that might detail her plans?"

Carolyn winced. "The police searched her room but said they didn't find anything useful. I trusted them. Honestly, I was glad they went through her things and not me. It's hard to go in there now. It's just too painful."

"I understand. The bedroom is where we're going to start."

Carolyn's face brightened. "We have plenty of money to pay you. I heard you were the best at this."

"I'll do what it takes to find your daughter. I want to meet Nadine's friends if at all possible. Chances are she's not hiding out with one of them, not for this long anyway, but they might know where she's gone. Did Nadine have any relatives she was close with?"

Carolyn shook her head. "I don't keep in touch much with them."

"You haven't shut off her phone, have you?" Angie grimaced slightly, hoping the answer would be no.

"No. I'm still paying the bill."

"Good. I need you to keep calling her phone. Don't shut it off. That's the worst thing you can do. We'll monitor Facebook, Instagram, Snapchat, and other social media sites where your daughter may have a presence. Meanwhile, I want you to write down any places where you think she may have gone. I want every one of them. Places you visited that she liked or someplace she's talked about always wanting to go. Think hard on this, because we're going to search them all."

Tears flooded Carolyn's eyes. "It's my fault—my damn fault. You must think I'm the worst mother ever."

"I don't think that for a minute," Angie answered.

"I should have come to you sooner. I just thought the police—" Carolyn could not finish her sentence.

Parents' responses to a runaway child were as varied as the circumstances. Some blamed themselves and were consumed by guilt. Others were defensive. Some were openly angry, and all too often Angie heard plans to punish the child after all was resolved.

"What about the posters?"

"Well, I've got a stack, and I'm making my own with my contact information on them. Between my team and the team at NCMEC we'll see that they're in as many spots as possible. They will be geo-targeted too, based on the information we supply." Angie reached across the table to take Carolyn's trembling hand. "Trust me when I say I'm going to do everything possible to find your daughter."

CHAPTER 4

Four weeks earlier

Nadine caught up to Stephen Macan after a brief sprint. In a semi-breathless voice, she explained her change of heart.

He seemed genuinely pleased. "Can you come now?"

"Now?" Nadine replied.

"Well, I have some time and we can get the headshots done. This is a very fluid, fast-moving business. You have to be able to stomach that sort of thing."

Nadine barely gave it a thought. It made sense that things happened quickly in this business. She'd heard the term *overnight success* plenty of times, and now it had new meaning.

"Sure. I guess."

"You have nowhere you have to be for a few hours?"

Nadine shook her head. "No. Nowhere." *Really nowhere,* she thought.

"Well, let's get going then. Time's a-wasting. Is your car here?"

Nadine wanted to place Stephen's accent, but it was hard, something she'd never quite heard before. "I don't have a car."

That was no trouble at all for Mr. Stephen Macan. "Fine, then. Mine is nearby. I'll drive you to the studio and get the headshots done, then take you wherever you want to go."

He was all smiles, but Nadine felt uneasy. *Where exactly is this studio?* Her mother certainly wouldn't approve of her getting into a car with a strange man. A ripple of anxiety coursed through her body, but what could she do? She didn't want to offend Mr. Macan. She had already said she'd do it. She felt committed. Besides, he looked so pleased, happy with her—finally someone was happy with her—that she hated the thought of disappointing him.

Nadine pushed aside her doubts. She would have the stomach for this sort of thing, just as he asked.

They walked in silence to the garage where he'd parked his Cadillac Escalade. It was an impressive car, but even more impressive was the tall man who emerged from the driver's seat. He was a lot younger than Stephen Macan—Nadine put him in his mid-twenties—but he had that same star quality. Not just handsome, but beautiful. He had chocolate eyes and gorgeous olive skin. His hair was dark, thick, and lustrous, cut over the ears, and his chiseled jaw was splendidly accented by the perfect amount of scruff. He wore a blue blazer with a white oxford shirt underneath, dark pressed blue jeans, and expensive-looking cowboy boots on his feet.

"Nadine, this is Ricardo. Ricardo, Nadine. She's getting the full workup. Headshots, marketing package, glossies, the works."

"Sounds good, boss." Ricardo opened the rear doors of the Escalade, and Stephen motioned for Nadine to get inside.

He has a driver? She felt even more relaxed about her decision now that another person was present—a driver, no less. Mr. Stephen Macan was indeed a very big deal.

"Mark my words, this one is going to the silver screen." Ricardo slipped Nadine a conspiratorial look that said she was lucky, and his boss was seldom wrong.

Soon enough, Nadine was seated beside Stephen in his roomy and plush Escalade. It was a luxurious ride, something her father might drive, or at the very least, envy. A bottle of water was in the cup holder, and the console held a bag of peanut M&Ms that she devoured.

Stephen was looking at his smartphone. Nadine took out her phone and did the same. She went right to Face-book and her stomach turned over as she read the posts her friends had written on her wall.

Nadine we miss you and love U!! Please come home. Xoxo
It's not the same with you gone. Where u @
girlfriend?

One of her friends, Sophia, even wrote a poem.

My heart is broken
My friend is gone
To where I do not know
I miss her so

The short poem got seventy-eight likes and a bunch of really sweet comments.

Tears came to Nadine's eyes. She missed her friends terribly. Hard as it was to read all the posts, she still believed she had done the right thing by leaving. She couldn't stand one more minute in that house and didn't want to burden her friends with her problems. Leaving was better. Leaving gave her a chance to get back at her mom and dad. She wanted her parents to feel guilt, shame, sadness, and regret. She wanted it to hurt.

Her plan was working, to some extent. To Nadine's surprise, her mother had miraculously figured out how to use Facebook, and had taken the time to write something. It wasn't the most incredible message ever written, but it was something.

> Honey, please come home or call and let us know you're all right. We miss you and need to hear from you. Love you so much, Mom.

Nadine checked twice, but her father hadn't written anything. No surprise.

"Do you mind if I ask exactly how old you are?"

"Eighteen, almost nineteen," Nadine said, answering Stephen Macan, finding the lie came easy. Her shirt was tight-fitting against her chest, and even with a jacket on she looked developed, mature—maybe almost nineteen instead of sixteen, her true age.

"Are you in school?"

"No," Nadine said.

"Did you drop out or something?" Stephen's curiosity came across as genuine.

"Or something."

"Just not for you, eh? Wasn't for me, either. But look at me now—never went to college, and I've done all right. Hey, you won't even need to get a GED if I think what's going to happen to you happens."

Nadine caught another flash of Ricardo's million-dollar

smile in the rearview mirror. She was more than inclined to believe Stephen.

With Ricardo driving the speed limit in the middle lane, they got onto I-695 heading south. Nadine wondered where they were going. She wanted to ask, but worried that it might sound pushy or unsure. She wanted Stephen (and Ricardo) to think she was confident and fine with whatever happened next. That was how she was going to play it, how she wanted to come across.

Instead of asking questions, Nadine went back to her phone and those messages on her Facebook wall. It felt good to read them. It felt so good to be missed. Nadine was glad she was gone.

At last they left the highway. They drove through a business district, then through a residential neighborhood, and then into a quieter, darker business district. The coming sunset was a rich tapestry of pinks and yellows stretched across a faded blue sky.

Nadine thought about getting back to Washington in the dark. Where was she going to sleep that night, and the next night, and the next? She'd left nothing in the motel room, and didn't have a reservation to return. She was living day-by-day. Everything she owned, she carried on her back.

Brick buildings and warehouses made of corrugated steel cast tall shadows on quiet streets. Most people would think twice before walking alone in that part of town.

They kept going. Nadine was relieved that Stephen Macan did not keep his photography studio there. She was completely turned around, and wouldn't have known she was in Maryland if it weren't for the GPS app on her phone.

"Are you hungry, Nadine?" Ricardo asked from the

driver's seat. "We got sandwiches up here. Turkey and Swiss. It's good."

Stephen looked upset with himself. "I have good instincts for talent, but I sometimes miss the mark on the obvious. I can't believe I didn't offer you something. I'm sorry, Nadine. Please. Eat."

From the center console Ricardo produced a small portable cooler and passed it back to her. She was famished and ate the sandwich in a few large bites.

"So how are you feeling about this?" Stephen asked.

Nadine's eyes went to her phone. "I guess I'm a bit nervous," she admitted.

Stephen gave Ricardo a nod. The next thing the driver handed Nadine was a flask.

"Take a few long drinks. You're going to want something to help take the edge off before your shoot."

"Thanks," Nadine said, taking the flask from Ricardo's hand. She took a hard swallow and felt the burn rip down her throat. It was straight vodka. She had been unprepared for the sensation, but managed to keep it down. She didn't even cough, and felt proud of the accomplishment.

"Can I ask you something?" Stephen said.

"Yeah?" Nadine liked how he spoke to her, like an adult, like she mattered. She took another swig from the flask. They were on I-295, still headed south.

"Are you a runaway or something? Be honest. In my many years of doing this business, I've seen it all."

Nadine bit her lip, unsure how to respond.

"Look, you don't have to talk about it if you don't want to. But there's no judgment here."

"Thanks."

"It's just that it's hard out on your own. I mean, if this

doesn't work out—and I'm not saying it won't—I can be your friend. You look like you could use one."

"Thanks." *Do you have any other words in your vocabulary, you moron?* Nadine couldn't believe how idiotic she sounded, how juvenile.

"You're really pretty," Ricardo said from the front seat. "I think he's gonna be right about you."

"You do?"

"Yeah. I do."

They drove for a bit in silence. Nadine gazed out the window at the unfamiliar landscape. She'd never been to that part of Maryland before and still had no idea where they were headed.

"I ran away," Nadine said.

Stephen's full lips crested into a pleased-with-himself smile. "I knew it. Mom or dad?"

Nadine understood the subtext of his question. "Both," she answered.

"Yeah, well, you'll show them, right?"

"Right," Nadine said.

"You got any talent, like can you sing? Done any acting?" Ricardo asked.

Nadine gave a shrug. "I can sing some. I wanted to audition for *American Idol*, but my mother wouldn't let me." *You'll embarrass yourself* were her mother's exact words.

"Yeah? Let's hear something," Stephen said.

"What? Sing?"

"Yeah, do what you were going to do for your audition."

Nadine could hardly speak, let alone muster up the courage to belt out a tune.

"Take another drink. Work up to it."

Nadine did just that and another. She was feeling more

courageous with each sip, but also a little sleepy. Just a little.

"You tired, Nadine?" Stephen asked. "You can close your eyes if you are. We've still got a ways to go."

"Yeah," she said. "I'm a little tired." Her voice slipped out dreamily. Her words sounded far away, as if they had bubbled up from a deep well. She put her phone in her backpack, shut her eyelids, and that was that.

When her eyes opened, she felt woozy and disoriented. They were in some city neighborhood with brick stores, plenty of neon, lots of people. White skin was the minority—nothing like Potomac, that was for sure. Nadine's mouth felt dry. Her stomach roiled, but she wasn't going to puke or anything.

They had stopped in front of a three-story brick building, an apartment building perhaps.

Stephen saw she was awake and gave her some water. "We're here"

Nadine's legs felt heavy on her way up the front stairs. Ricardo unlocked the outside door and she followed him into a dark foyer with Stephen close behind. The floor was covered in tile with inlaid geometric patterns. Nearby a wood staircase snaked up into the darkness.

Ricardo unlocked a door at the end of a narrow first-floor hallway. Nadine didn't notice a sign for a photography studio, but that didn't mean anything. Studios could be anywhere, even in apartment buildings like this one.

She still wasn't feeling herself when she followed Ricardo into the apartment at the end of the hall. It was a relief to see a camera set up and some kind of a lighting rig. But it was also just an apartment with a leather couch, some IKEA-style furniture, and a kitchenette. A short hall-way led to a bathroom, with a bedroom off to the side.

"You okay?" Stephen asked. "You look a little funny."

"I think I drank too much vodka," Nadine said.

Stephen Macan did not look surprised. "Look, I have some work to do nearby. Ricardo can do the shoot after you take a nap. There's a bedroom, nice and comfy. You need to feel fresh and perky for the camera."

Nadine's head was buzzing. She needed to feel better than this, that was for sure. "Is this a studio?" Her tongue felt thick in her mouth, swollen, and she could hardly understand her own question.

"Yeah, it's one of them."

Ricardo escorted Nadine to the bedroom. Shades were drawn. It was dark at first, but Ricardo turned on a light.

To her relief it was a nice-looking bedroom. It had a small TV, an area rug, and a couple well-cared-for house-plants. Hanging on the walls were framed posters of pretty girls with the words *Macan Entertainment* at the bottom—publicity shots, she assumed, like they were going to do for her.

Ricardo lowered the futon and got a blanket and pil-lows out from the closet. Nadine was so tired she wanted to vanish beneath that blanket and sleep for days. She slipped off her backpack and went right to the bed.

Ricardo covered her with the blanket. "Sleep it off," he said as he closed the door behind him.

Nadine was going to do just that, but after she checked those Facebook messages once more. She wanted to see if any more people missed her, not that it would change anything. She wasn't going home until she had a reason, until she was somebody. But it still felt so good to know she was missed.

She unzipped her backpack and rummaged through the contents, looking for her phone. Her hand felt around the main compartment. Her journal and pen were there, some clothes, but not what she was looking for. Then she checked all the zippered pouches. Panic welled up. She emptied the contents on the floor. Nothing.

Her phone and her wallet were gone.

CHAPTER 5

Angie had spoken with Greg Jessup by phone, which completed a piece of the puzzle. She had asked all the questions of him she had planned to, except for the one that troubled her the most. *Why didn't you take the time to drive down from Philadelphia to Virginia and meet with me in person?*

He'd said he would do it, of course he would, but something came up at work and, well, he just couldn't seem to get away. He'd made it sound as if Nadine needed a wake-up call. He said it would build character for her to learn how hard life on the streets could be. She was always coming down on him for never being around, but that was because she didn't understand what it meant to have a work ethic. She'd come home, he believed, a changed person.

Angie didn't deny that, but she doubted it would be changed for the better. It took restraint not to call Greg Jessup an asshole, but speaking the truth would do nothing to help Nadine. Over the years, Angie had been exposed to all sorts of dysfunction. It never got easier to understand or accept.

Disgusted as she was with Nadine's father, Angie didn't press the issue. If it were absolutely necessary, she would drive up to meet Mr. Jessup in his home, where he was living with his new young wife and printing money thanks to a new corporate executive job. But it wasn't necessary, at least not yet. And while it was comforting to know Greg's checks would clear, Angie cared a hell of a lot more about finding the missing girl.

Bryn Mawr was a very affluent village and home to many of Philadelphia's business leaders. Angie figured Greg Jessup was nesting, getting ready for Family 2.0. That could have contributed to Nadine's feelings of abandonment and her decision to run away. Daddy's lack of compassion aside, Angie trusted her radar. She didn't get a creepy vibe from Greg. That didn't mean he had never sexually assaulted his daughter. It happened plenty of times, in plenty of cases. Any evidence of it would turn up in Nadine's bedroom, in a journal, on her computer. Angie didn't get a list of Nadine's closest friends because Daddy was too out of touch with his daughter to know them.

From elementary school right through college, Kathleen DeRose could list everybody Angie had been close with, including the posse who'd hung out with Sarah Winter before she'd disappeared. Being a good parent took more than just a checkbook. It took caring enough to ask questions and get involved even when your kid couldn't think of anything worse you could do.

Carolyn more than compensated for Greg's deficiencies. Her drinking problem aside, Nadine's mom compiled a list of her daughter's closest friends, boys and girls, including Sophia Kerns, who was apparently the best friend. Angie had names, addresses, and phone numbers. She would speak to each kid on the list. But first she had to go through Nadine's bedroom.

Angie was in a spitfire mood—cranky, short-fused, and jacked up as if she'd had Red Bull in her coffee. It was the energy of the hunt. Her blood buzzed and she felt all her senses come to life. No detail could be overlooked, no lead ignored. It was day two of Angie's investigation and already new cases came in—the phone didn't stop ringing on account of Nadine—but she farmed out those jobs to her *& Associates*. Finding Nadine would take focus and a team effort.

Accompanying Angie was a Vietnamese semipro skateboarder and computer expert named Bao Johnson. He was twenty-two, had long dark hair, plenty of piercings and tattoos, and wore flannel as if grunge was still the music of the day. Angie had met Bao when she'd tracked him from Washington to Boston after he'd fled his foster home. She'd met him again after she'd tracked him from a new foster home in Delaware to a rundown motel in Jacksonville, Florida. She'd met him again when he ran from a foster home in Maryland to a skate park in Newark, New Jersey.

He'd stopped running at age fourteen when Angie introduced him to a couple she knew who later agreed to adopt him. The dad was an accountant, mom a schoolteacher, and the perfectly normal home life provided Bao with what all these kids wanted. Bao had run because the foster families Child Services had placed him with wanted the payday more than they wanted the kid. Didn't happen all the time, but it happened with enough frequency to make Angie's business a profitable one. Truth be told, she'd gladly give up the income to make the problem go away.

Bao's adopted family had rules, of course, and expectations he'd had to meet, grades and such. They'd asked the hard questions. They didn't change a *no* to a *yes* just because he got angry, just because he told them that he hated them and was going to run again. It wasn't easy, but Bao's parents knew every kid he hung out with, where he went, who he went with, what time he'd be home—and surprise, surprise, he never made good on that threat to run.

A few years later, just after he'd turned twenty, he went to work for Angie as a certified computer forensic consultant. He was incredibly helpful, not only because of his skills and expertise at the keyboard, but also because he knew how runaway kids thought.

Sitting at Nadine's desk, Bao was looking at her PC, mumbling to himself, which Angie took as a good sign. While he worked, Angie scoured the bedroom, looking for a journal or anything that might reveal more about Nadine or give a clue where she might have run.

As far as bedrooms went, Angie didn't think anyone would pin this to a Pinterest board, but it was nice enough. Compared to a lot of the bedrooms runaways abandoned, this one was practically palatial. The color scheme was white with a splash of fuchsia. Cutouts from magazines of the "it" celebs of the day were taped to poster board, so they could be replaced with a new contingent of "it" when the fashions changed. Books stood in the bookcase, clothes hung neatly in the closet, a collection of stuffed animals too precious for the trash lined the bed.

She was rummaging though Nadine's dresser when Carolyn entered carrying a laptop computer. It used to be, long before Angie's time, that the photographs she had asked Carolyn to gather would have been put into a shoebox or displayed in photo albums. Now they were mostly in pixel form.

"I made a digital album of all the recent pictures of Nadine that were on my phone. Some of them Greg sent me, but he didn't have a lot."

"This will be helpful," said Angie.

"I did get a bunch e-mailed to me from Nadine's friends."

Angie stopped what she was doing to sift through the collection of photos. She ignored the booze on Carolyn's breath. Finding Nadine would be only half the battle. Angie might locate the missing girl, but without big changes in the Jessup family, Nadine might not stick around.

If the photos were any indication, they had a lot of fence mending to do. The pictures of Nadine with her parents were somber, her brown eyes heavy with sadness, but not all the photos were gloomy. Some showed Nadine laughing with her friends, making goofy expressions, looking like a kid who had a place in the world, who fit in, who wasn't lonely and alone.

Angie began to believe that life with her alcoholic mother and disinterested father was the main reason, if not the only reason, Nadine ran. It was a show of defiance, a way to teach them a lesson. On the poster board of cutout celebrities, Angie recognized one of Anna Kendrick from the movie *Pitch Perfect*. The "Cup" song from that film featured the line, "You're gonna miss me when I'm gone." Angie wondered what those lyrics meant to Nadine.

"What are you going to do with these, anyway?" Carolyn's words came out a little sloppy. She wobbled slightly on her feet.

Two in the afternoon and the woman already had her drunk on. This job made it easy for Angie to appreciate her good fortune, to be ever grateful to her parents for her upbringing.

"Bao is going to create a Find Nadine Jessup Face-book page," Angie said. "We'll list my phone number, but we need as many recent pictures as we can get. This goes up today. Then we'll e-mail all of Nadine's friends and ask for their help linking to the page."

Bao was hunched over Nadine's laptop, but listening. "I've already created the e-mail address, Find Nadine Jessup at gmail dot com," he said without peeling his eyes from the screen.

"Not saying it will go viral," Angie added, "but it could, and it's an important step in the process."

"Have you found anything helpful on Nadine's computer yet?" Carolyn asked.

Bao spun around the small wooden desk chair to face Carolyn. "She wanted to cover her tracks. She deleted her browser history before she ran. This was a planned event."

Carolyn looked crestfallen.

"Don't worry," he said, pushing his long black hair from off his face. "Nothing is ever deleted on a computer. She must have read something about deleting the cookie file, but there are other ways to get at the data. Right now, I'm running a system restore and I'm also parsing the log files. We'll know soon enough what she was looking up online. Chances are, that's where she headed."

"How do you know?" Carolyn asked.

"Because that's what I would have done."

"Most runaways don't go far," Angie said. "From my experience, the ones who leave foster care are more likely to leave the state. Others stay close to home, crash with friends, people they meet. Few leave home thinking the street is their ultimate destination."

"But I've already called every one of Nadine's friends and all my relatives, like you asked," Carolyn said. "She's not with any of them."

"That's why I'm going to talk to each person individually," Angie said. "Maybe one of them isn't telling us the truth."

Bao returned to his efforts while Angie spent some time cross-referencing the list of friends she had compiled with the pictures Carolyn had collected. Angie was clicking through the photos, taking in every detail of Nadine that she could. Was there a boy online she'd been talking with? Somebody who had lured her away? Somebody who made her feel special and loved? Bao would find that out soon enough.

"Bao, any luck with the Facebook page?"

"No, she logged out and her Facebook profile is set to as private as can be. I'm working on getting access, though."

"What about social media accounts? WeChat? Vine? Twitter? Instagram? WhatsApp?"

"Checking them all and the logs," Bao said. "No activity on any of her other social media accounts."

"What about any kind of tracking on Nadine's cell phone?"

"Like a Find My Phone app?" Bao answered. "I wish, but we're not getting that lucky."

"Carolyn, whatever you do, do not turn off the phone," Angie said. "I'm assuming it's in your name."

"It is."

"I want a call log history," Angie said. "I'll need your help for that. Your cell phone provider should be able to assist. Get on that right away, if you can." *And no more booze,* she wanted to add. "We need the last few hours of calls, every text, every call coming in and out of that phone."

"What's that going to do?" Carolyn asked.

"We're looking for patterns. Who was she talking to

around the time she went missing? Had she made other calls to that person? Who was she texting?"

"You think somebody lured my daughter away?"

"It's a possibility. It happens more often than you think. We need to compile a list of key people and then we'll head to those locations, hang up posters, start asking questions. That's how we get information. Once you get a few answers, it usually snowballs from there. Then we can figure out which way we need to go."

"Or I get into her online accounts, browser history," Bao said. "That might help, too. Unless you've found a diary, Ange."

"No, I haven't. I don't think she kept one."

"The police have to do this work," Carolyn said with venom. "I can't believe they're not doing this for my daughter! She's missing and they're not doing anything to find her. She might be dead for all I know!" Carolyn sank to the floor, tears streaming, her body convulsing as she sobbed.

Angie went to her, knelt down, and brushed away some of the tears streaming down her client's face. "I know this is hard, beyond hard, and it's so frustrating. I know you want the police to do more, but unless we can prove there was a crime, they're going to be limited in what they can do for us. That doesn't mean they don't care. They want to help, and we're going to help them. We're going to keep them informed every step of the way."

Angie's phone rang. DAD, the display read, so she let it go to voice mail. Carolyn needed and deserved her full attention right now.

"It's just not right," Carolyn said, no longer crying, but her hands still shaking. "God, I need a drink. Can I get you two something?"

Angie bit her tongue. It was not the time or place to confront Carolyn's drinking.

Angie's phone buzzed as a text came in. **Sweetheart it's Dad . . . call me ASAP 911. It's Mom.**

Angie's breath caught, and her hand went to her mouth.

"What is it? What's wrong?" Carolyn asked, taking notice of Angie's distress.

"Hang on, hang on." Disoriented, Angie dialed her father, her hands shaking violently.

"Daddy? Daddy, what's going on?" Angie said as soon as her father answered.

"Baby, I'm so sorry. I'm so very sorry." Her father's breath came in spurts. He was crying, something Angie had never heard him do before.

"Daddy, where's Mom? What's happened?" The tremor in Angie's voice made it hard to get the words out.

"She's gone, sweetheart," Gabriel said. "Your mother had a massive stroke this afternoon. She's gone."

CHAPTER 6

Kathleen DeRose wasn't gone, not exactly. Angie was completely shocked at the sight of her mother motionless on her hospital bed, even though she knew that the brain damage from the stroke had been extensive and catastrophic. They had shaved the front of her head and made a hole to alleviate the pressure. A thin plastic tube drained blood from the brain while machines clinked and hummed and breathed for her. Kathleen did not have enough brain function left to breathe without mechanical help.

Her mother's eyes were perhaps the most disturbing sight of all. They were milky gray, gazing at nothing, vacant. The eyelids fluttered in a reflexive way, as if dust had gotten stuck underneath.

The doctor on call explained the situation as best he could. Other doctors who'd treated Kathleen when she was first admitted would have to fill in details later. Still, a picture formed in Angie's mind that was devastatingly easy to understand.

Kathleen had suffered a hemorrhagic stroke, the least common but most often fatal of the two types of strokes.

An aneurysm had burst, causing blood to spill into places blood didn't belong. The result was tremendous swelling and pressure that damaged most of the cells and tissue in the brain. The aneurysm could have been related to the lupus, but chances were they would never know.

Angie's mother was alive, but dead. She had a heartbeat and lung respirations, but it was all because of the machines. The staff at Virginia Hospital Center had been incredibly solicitous, and answered every question Gabriel and Angie could think to ask.

Hours went by. Nothing major happened, because the major thing had already occurred. Angie had nothing to do but wait at her mother's bedside.

Night turned to day and the doctor who first treated Kathleen finally interrupted the all-night vigil. Gabe and Angie were alone at Kathleen's bedside. Because of a long-standing feud and an unconventional upbringing, Angie's family was her father and her mother—no siblings, cousins, aunts, or uncles were in the picture. They'd never been a part of Angie's life; instead, Walter and Louise Odette had served as honorary aunt and uncle.

The doctor, a thin, kind-eyed man with graying hair, led them to a room where the reality came into sharper, grimmer focus. Kathleen's heart was failing. They would need to put in a PICC line to give her medicine that would prevent a fatal heart attack.

"But she's brain dead already," Angie said.

"Yes, she is—ninety percent, we believe, but technically she's alive as long as her heart continues to beat."

"Ninety percent?" Gabriel said, hope coming to his voice.

"Well, it could be closer to a hundred percent," the doctor said, "but to test we'd have to put in the PICC line.

However, I've read her advance directive, and this is an invasive procedure."

Angie flashed back to the lunch that had foreshadowed this tragedy. Hadn't her mother used this exact scenario?

Her father was crying again. "She doesn't want any extraordinary measures," he said, choking back tears. "Ninety percent or one hundred, what's the difference? We have to let her go."

The doctor's empathic look made it clear he concurred.

They had to wait for the respiratory team to arrive before any of the machines keeping Kathleen alive could be disconnected. In those tense, tear-filled hours, Angie and her dad passed the time singing some of Kathleen's favorite songs to her. Paul Simon, James Taylor, Cat Stevens, The Band. Neither Angie nor her father were decent singers, but the music came from the heart and the performance quality didn't much matter.

Angie went into "handle it" mode. She started to make calls, arrangements, dealing with logistics of dying. She always operated at a higher level during a crisis. This fit that category. She was not frozen by grief, but propelled by purpose. She wrote an obituary while her mother's heart continued to beat without that PICC line in place. The funeral home offered sympathy, but ended the call by asking her to phone back when her mother "officially expired."

"Officially expired?" she repeated for her father's benefit. "What do they think, Mom's a carton of milk?"

In between, Angie spent a lot of time talking to her mom, telling her all the things she loved about her, the memories she'd always cherish. She sat on an uncomfortable chair, drinking coffee, holding her mother's hand, talking like a daughter who never had enough time to properly catch up on all she had to say.

She spent some time going over Nadine's case. When Angie left Carolyn's house, she'd called another private investigator, Michael Webb, to come in and continue the hunt with Bao. Webb ran a bouncy house business and did PI work on the side as part of Angie's & *Associates* contingent.

She was in the middle of explaining her strategy for locating the missing girl when the respiratory team arrived.

Angie went to the waiting room to get her father, who had fallen asleep on a thin-cushioned couch that was too small for his tall frame. "It's time to let Mom go." She had nothing more to handle, she realized, and the tears came.

CHAPTER 7

Exhibit D: Excerpts from the journal of Nadine Jessup, pages 7–12

Let's start here. This is so screwed up! Date unknown. Place unknown. All I have to get down my thoughts is my journal and a pen I brought from home. My phone and wallet are gone and I'm totally freaking out. When I finally woke up, I felt sick, not like I was going to puke or anything, just really weird. My head was fuzzy and it was hard for me to stand. I don't drink much, so I guess I took too many swigs of that vodka in Ricardo's flask. I don't even know how to feel except for stupid. I thought this was a good idea, but now I'm not so sure. Where am I? Who am I with? And I don't have a phone or my wallet!! I'm such a moron (lol just ask my dad).

I needed to get my stuff back, so I walked to the door, more like stumbled, turned the knob, but it's locked! The door is effin' locked! Now I'm really freaking out, so I turned the handle some *more, but it doesn't budge. So I banged on the door really hard and nobody answered and then I think I screamed, but nobody came. My mouth felt funny. My tongue was like a sponge sucking up every bit of water. And the room was spinning around so fast I couldn't stand anymore. I went to the futon and just fell down and the next thing I knew my eyes were closed and when I opened them again I saw Ricardo hovering over me.*

Ricardo stared at me and for some reason I wasn't scared or grossed out. I liked how he's looking at me, like he's really seeing me. Somebody is finally seeing me! His eyes are beautiful, big and brown, and his smile is something you can't imagine. Like it warms you from the inside. He's not touching me or doing anything creepy, he's just kneeling on the floor beside the futon, hanging out, watching over me like he's my protector or something. He's wearing jeans and a tank top white undershirt and you just know he works out. His body is really amazing. Strong arms with really well defined muscles.

I've always wanted to be someone's special somebody. There was this boy at school, I'm not naming names, but I had a wicked crush on him for so long and I smiled so hard every time we talked my mouth hurt. But nothing ever happened between us because he already had a girlfriend, or I think he did. Either way I wasn't going to say anything because I didn't want to get rejected. But I loved that feeling of a guy caring for me even if it was only in my imagination. Why can't I have a

*real boyfriend? Somebody who really cares
about me IRL? Ya know . . . in real life. I always
wondered what it would feel like and I can see it
in Ricardo's eyes.*

*My phone. This is my biggest worry. I asked
Ricardo about it and he tells me he doesn't know
anything about it. He tried to help me find it. We
looked all over the room. Maybe I dropped it
somewhere because I was drinking. I try to
remember. Did I have it in my hand when we were
going into the apartment? Ricardo thinks I did.
Or more specifically he thinks I had them both in
my hand when I got out of the car. That's what he
remembers anyway. It's possible because I was
looking at my phone. Maybe I wanted my wallet
for something. I don't remember. But Ricardo's so
certain of it that now I'm certain
of it.*

*I feel sick because I must have dropped it or
something and I remember a little bit about the
neighborhood. It's a pretty rundown part of a city.
God, which one? Where the hell am I? Right?! I
ask Ricardo and he says we're near Baltimore,
that's where the studio is, he tells me. Then I
remembered the photo shoot (How did I forget?
How much did I drink?) and suddenly I'm
worried about something completely different.
Ricardo tells me that Stephen Macan had to go
home. Probably to give his daughter the present I
told him to buy, probably to have cake and ice
cream with his perfect family, and then he'll post
pictures on Facebook or Instagram, which is*

*something my father would never do for me. Now
I've really screwed up. I'm always screwing
things up. The photo shoot got cancelled because
I got too drunk.*

*Get it together Nadine! I'm more worried
about upsetting Stephen Macan than I am about
my damn wallet and phone and Ricardo feels
terrible about both things. He's also being so
super sweet to me. I told him I didn't feel that
great and right away he got me a glass of water. I
asked him how long I'd been asleep and he said
all night! ALL NIGHT! I guess I really did drink
too much.*

*I don't know if we're doing the photo shoot or
not anymore. I'm not sure I even care. I've spent the
whole day talking to Ricardo. He's AMAZING!
Really amazing. He's older. Twenty-three I think,
but he thinks I'm almost nineteen and that's not
too big a difference. That's totally normal. We
could go out together and nobody would think
anything of it. Not like he's sixty and I'm twenty-
five or something. To prove my point we did go
out. Ricardo took me to this restaurant that serves
Mexican food, but it wasn't like the Mexican
restaurants near my house. This was a lot, I
dunno—more authentic, I guess. Everyone spoke
Spanish and they talked really fast. Ricardo did,
too, but it was really hot to hear him talking
Spanish. Anyway, he ordered me this burrito thing
and it was great, but I was soooooo hungry I
would have eaten the aluminum it was wrapped
in. I drank a big glass of water and I was starting*

*to feel a whole lot better, a lot more like myself.
But I still didn't have my cell phone or wallet. I
had no money and maybe that's why my stomach
was in knots. Or maybe it was Ricardo who kept
looking at me and smiling at me but in the sweet-
est way imaginable.*

*He asked me about my mom and dad. I'm
thinking "you don't want to hear about them," but
really I was worried if I talked about home I
might cry. Guess what? I talked about home and I
cried. Not the ugly cry, but I definitely needed
some napkins and people looked at me and I got
really embarrassed. And all I could think is "oh
my God, I'm such a loser." But you know who
didn't care? Ricardo, that's who. He moved his
chair closer to mine and brushed a strand of hair
off my face. Then he wiped away one of my tears
with his finger and told me it was ok to cry. He
didn't have a good relationship with his parents
either, he said, and it made him really sad. He
understood.*

*I asked him if he thought I was stupid to
run away from home. He said no, they didn't
understand me or appreciate me and you know,
he's right. They didn't. I feel badly leaving my
friends, but they'll get over it or maybe they'll see
me in the movies! Ha! That'll be so awesome.*

*It still can happen, too. Ricardo told me that
I'm really special. There have been a lot of girls
who have had photo shoots at the studio and
there's something unique about me. Me! Ricardo
told me that's what Stephen Macan said after I fell
asleep (Ha, fell asleep, lol. Passed out is more
like it). Anyway, Ricardo said he's been instructed*

*to look after me because I guess I'm really
important to their business. I'm going to make
them all a lot of money! Can you believe that?
The most I ever made was a few hundred dollars
working as a babysitter.*

*Ricardo touched my hair again and he didn't
have to because I wasn't crying and it wasn't in
my face. But I liked it. And I wanted him to do it
again, but he didn't. He did say I should get used
to the idea of being famous and that I shouldn't be
Nadine anymore. It's not a famous name. Can you
think of one really famous Nadine? I can't. He
called me Jessica. I liked it. There are a lot of
famous Jessicas out there.*

CHAPTER 8

The home of Angie's parents (now just her dad) in Arlington was crammed wall-to-wall with mourners who represented the varied interests and activities of Kathleen DeRose. It was difficult to move around among so many bodies, so Angie stayed rooted in one spot. People found her, one after the other, each offering their sincere condolences. There were people from the Lupus Foundation, of course, and the Arlington County Fair, as well as kids Angie's mom had taught to swim, and the parents who had driven them to the service and the reception.

Angie wore a loose-fitting black dress, accented by an understated strand of pearls. She'd tried to cover her pale and waxy complexion with a generous application of makeup. She had washed her hair, but didn't give it the treatment to make it look pretty. It didn't feel appropriate.

She felt strangely detached from the moment, an observer more than a participant in both her mother's memorial service and this reception. She would hug whomever approached her, thank them for their support and condolences, and assure them she was doing all right, hanging in there best she could, but she was numb, and had been since the hospital.

The reception, especially, was too much for her to process. Too many bodies, too much noise. She wanted to be alone with her father, to grieve privately—but right now, it was about her mother, not Angie. Kathleen needed to be celebrated, appreciated, and memorialized.

The service was lovely, or so people said. Angie had delivered a eulogy, one of three presented to a room of more than five hundred mourners who filled the church and spilled out into the hall. She'd talked about her mother's unconditional love and support, her passion for helping others, her loyalty to causes she championed. Kathleen DeRose was, in Angie's words, a road map to a life well lived. "Be kind, love fully, and embrace the moments as they come."

Angie felt a hand on her shoulder and turned. Walter Odette was standing behind her, smiling at her. He had broad shoulders and a square-shaped head topped by a thin covering of hair that still had plenty of brown. At five-foot-nine, Walter was taller than Angie by only a few inches, but his barrel chest made him an imposing figure at any height. He had the kind of eyes that sparkled and laughed even when he wasn't telling jokes as old he was.

Today the glimmer was gone. He smiled, but his teeth were yellowing, and Angie took note of how much older he looked. He had more creases on his face than she remembered. Everyone looked older to her, including her father and her mother's friends. Even her own friends looked older. In this regard, Kathleen's funeral was a celebration of her life and a wake-up call to the living that death was coming for them all.

"How you holding up, kiddo?" Walter asked.

Kiddo. Angie liked that he still saw her as the little girl who grew up calling him Uncle Walt. She returned a wan smile and gave his hand a squeeze.

"Hanging in," she said. "You?"

"Numb," Walter said, his voice warm but a bit more gravelly, a bit tired.

"Yeah, me too."

"Louise has been crying her eyes out for days. She can't believe your mom is gone."

Angie looked across the room and saw Walter's wife of forty years at the buffet table talking with a group of Kathleen's friends. Over the years, they had become Louise's friends as well. They all sort of looked alike—women in their sixties, early seventies, put together, hair kept short but styled, bodies kept in decent shape by frequent visits to the health club, friendships maintained through book, movie, and bridge clubs, as well as various charitable endeavors.

"I haven't been able to get over to her," Angie said. "I actually haven't left this spot."

"I know you've heard it a million times," Walter said, looking Angie in the eyes. "But if there's anything I can do to help, don't hesitate to ask. I'm here for you."

"You always have been, Uncle Walt."

They hugged as a familiar voice spoke. "Any room for me in there?"

Angie's face lit up. She broke from Walter's warm embrace to give her good friend Madeline a hug.

"Hey! I've been looking for you," Angie said, her smile genuine and bigger than any she had made all day. Tears stung her eyes. She hadn't realized the importance of having her friends there until they began to arrive. Paying their respects were a dozen or so people from various facets of her life—some she knew from high school, others from college, a few from the PI biz.

Of all who had come, none was more important to Angie than her dear college friend, Madeline Hartsock.

Back in college, Sarah, Madeline, and Angie had been an inseparable trio—the Three Musketeers some had called them. When Sarah vanished, the tandem of Angie and Madeline led the search for their missing friend. They'd seemed to merge into one over the many months they hung posters, managed the website, fielded leads, and worked with law enforcement, all to no avail.

The experience altered the trajectory of their lives. Angie became friendly with a private investigator hired by Sarah's mother. Angie searched relentlessly for Sarah. Her alertness and situational awareness impressed the investigator so much he offered her a job with his well-established firm, The Kessler Group, right out of college. "You have a mind for this work," he'd told her, "and you don't slack off. Stamina and a sharp eye, that's what you need to be a PI."

She worked five years for the firm, earning her master's degree in criminal justice at night. Her time with The Kessler Group gave her the confidence she could run an agency of her own. Her mentor not only agreed and supported her transition, but had made his own firm part of Angie's *& Associates* network.

Madeline, who was pre-med at the time of Sarah's disappearance, gave up medicine to become a sex crimes prosecutor in Washington, DC. She always believed Sarah had fallen into drugs and somehow got swept up in the sex trade, a theory that was never proven. Her research into human trafficking, however, opened her eyes to the prevalence of predators, and she'd found her calling putting the bad guys behind bars.

"One of these days, I'm going to get the guy who took

Sarah from us," Madeline had said. Angie had vowed to be the one to bring her that prize.

"Madeline, you remember my Uncle Walt."

"Of course." Madeline hugged the man she didn't really know. Funerals made for fast friends. "I'm sorry about your loss. I know you thought of Kathleen as a sister."

"I did," Walter said, his eyes misting. "The DeRoses are like family to me."

Madeline, who was tall, thin, and naturally blond, looked nothing like Angie, but called her friend a sister from another mister. She understood Walter's point completely.

"I was wondering if any of your mom's family might have come to pay their respects," Madeline said. "Now seems like a good time to put that feud to rest."

Angie had been thinking the same, but she recognized everyone who was there by face if not name. She had asked her father if he planned to include her mother's family in the services, and the answer had been a definite no. Despite that, she held out hope some of her mother's relatives whom she did not know, whom she had never met, might come across the obituary and show up unannounced.

Her father was never going to have any of his family there. He'd spent his childhood in an orphanage and when that closed, moved to a series of foster care homes. Like a lot of kids who entered the system at a more advanced age, Angie's dad did not get adopted. All she knew of her father's mother, her paternal grandmother, was that she was a drug addict who didn't know who'd gotten her pregnant. Despite the extraordinary obstacles presented to him, Gabriel persevered, avoided the temptations of the streets, and made something of his life.

While attending University of California, Berkeley, on

a full academic scholarship, Gabriel met and fell in love with Angie's mother. She was Kathleen Tyler back then, young, pretty, and fiercely intelligent. Gabriel and Kathleen had an instant and undeniable chemistry. They knew after two dates they wanted to get married and announced their plans the day after graduation. Not everyone was thrilled by the news. The way Angie had heard it, her mother's family had serious reservations about her father. They didn't want the couple marrying so young, nor did they approve of Gabriel's sketchy background.

Harsh words were spoken, words that escalated and sowed the seeds of acrimony. When Kathleen, unmarried, discovered that she was pregnant with Angie, the anger came to a boiling point. Kathleen and Gabriel decided to cut off all communication with her family and go it on their own. At some point, Angie's grandparents had died. She had never once met them.

The reception continued, the hours passing, brief conversations expressing the same sentiments. *We're so sorry for your loss. Such a tragedy. So young. Too soon. Your mother loved you very much. She was so proud of you.*

Every one of them rang true to Angie, and the words of sympathy provided a degree of comfort. The hard part, she suspected, would come later, after everyone went home, after the sympathy cards and Facebook posts stopped coming, when she and her dad had quiet time to contemplate the enormity of their loss.

Madeline stayed to the end. Along with Louise and Walter, she helped with the cleanup. Angie checked in with her father. She didn't like seeing him in this new way: frail, old, and sad. Her heart ached for him, for them both.

Tears came to her father's eyes, but he managed a strained smile. "Well, that was hard."

"We'll get through this together, Dad." Angie gave her father a big embrace.

Nearby, Louise and Walter joined the huddle for a group hug, with Walter calling the play.

"As long as we stick together, we'll be all right. Anything you need, Angie, Gabe, anything at all, you don't hesitate to ask."

Walter and Louise lived down the street from the DeRoses. They had been in that house since Angie was a baby. She had fond memories of rolling down the hill in their front yard—Odette Hill, she called it—and exploring the variety of flowers that Louise grew in a small greenhouse out back. Walter was retired law enforcement and Louise was a homemaker who had raised two children, both of whom were off on their own.

Louise was a master cook as well as a gardener. "Angie, don't worry about your dad. I'm going to make sure his fridge is fully stocked."

But Angie did worry. She worried about him being alone and lonely. Kathleen was her father's life. They had many friends, but most of those friends were tethered to Angie's mom. Her dad had his work, his daughter, and his wife. Now it would be easier for him to devote even more time to crunching numbers. Perhaps Angie could get her father to try fly fishing, a hobby Walter enjoyed, or some other pursuit to keep him from vanishing into the protective shell of his work.

That would come later.

They needed to grieve and keep busy, so Angie helped with cleanup. She had washed all the extra tablecloths and put them back in the plastic bins where they were stored. She turned to her father, who was washing some platters. "Dad, I'll take this up to the attic."

"I'll come with you." Madeline had stayed longer than Walt and Louise and the catering staff. She followed Angie to the second floor, and then up the staircase in the master bedroom to the attic.

It was organized up there. Kathleen had been fastidious about boxes and labels and things of that nature. It was also easy to maneuver about. The walls were sloped, but the space was wide and the flooring completely hid the insulation. Angie's father had talked about converting that attic into an office, but it would mean moving all the boxes of things Kathleen had accrued over the years.

Angie put the carton in its appropriate place while Madeline went exploring.

She opened a cardboard box labeled ANGIE ART and pulled out a headband adorned with beads and colored feathers. "Museum quality," she said, holding up the object for Angie to see.

Angie returned a laugh. "Second grade, I think. Mrs. Ferguson. I remember I used to sit next to a kid who ate crayons."

Madeline made a face. "Sounds like pica."

"Whatever it was, he was a cute kid with a blue smile."

Angie opened a nearby box and found a photo album she had not looked at in ages. There were pictures of family vacations, time spent at the lake house with Walter and Louise, other photos of other trips with friends who had kids Angie's age. A pang hit her as she thought about how complete and happy her small family looked.

Angie and Madeline took their time rummaging through boxes, looking through clothes, books, crafts, letters, various bric-a-brac. Kathleen DeRose, fastidiously organized, did not easily part with anything, so there was much to explore. One box held an odd assortment of old magazines, another a carousel filled with slides. Without a good light source, it was hard for Angie to see what was on those slides.

"Maybe there's a projector in one of these," Madeline said as she went looking.

Dozens of boxes and plastic containers were neatly arranged and stacked in varying heights. From one cardboard box Madeline removed a small wooden music box made of burl maple with a burnished finish. A violin and horn carved from mother of pearl were inlaid into the wood and accented by a very subtle, light-colored border.

"Wow, look at this," she said, admiring the box. She lifted the cover and then stroked the red velvet interior of the top compartment, which was divided into two sections. The right section contained the mechanism for playing music; the section to the left was empty. Underneath the main compartment was a drawer for storing valuables.

Madeline handed the box to Angie, who turned the wind-up mechanism. The chimes, like metallic raindrops, plinked out the recognizable melody of "The Blue Danube."

"I've never seen this before." Angie turned the box over in her hands, admiring it from all angles. "It's so beautiful."

"Was it your mother's?" Madeline asked.

"I don't know."

It was a bit stuffy in the attic. Angie wished she had changed out of her dress into something more comfortable. When the song finished, she wound the mechanism once more. Again those notes chimed out, sad to her ears.

"I love the song," Madeline said.

"I wonder why my mom never had this out?" Angie pulled open the bottom drawer, tugging just hard enough so the drawer came out entirely. She was about to put it back in when she noticed a slight gap in the bottom panel. Removing the panel revealed yet another compartment.

Something was inside.

Angie's long fingers removed a color photograph of a young girl—four years old, five at the most—wearing a pink short-sleeve dress decorated with white polka dots, with shirred detail at the waist. The brown-haired girl had doleful eyes but a sweet albeit sad smile, and a strangely deformed right ear that was almost nonexistent.

Angie tried to the place the girl, but she was certain she'd never seen her before. The picture was taken outside, in some cityscape that Angie didn't recognize.

Turning the photograph over in her hands, Angie gasped aloud. On the back, in her mother's impeccably neat and distinctive handwriting, were words and a code that made no sense.

May God forgive me
IC12843488

Angie studied the message, then handed Madeline the photograph with the message facing up.

Madeline turned the picture over and studied it for some time. "What the hell is this all about?"

Angie couldn't answer. She didn't know.

CHAPTER 9

Exhibit D: Excerpts from the journal of Nadine Jessup, pages 13–22

I did the photo shoot today! Oh, wait, before I go into that I should re-introduce myself. I'm Jessica Barlow. Whadda ya think? Pretty sexy, huh? It's got that Jennifer Lawrence ring to it I think. I mean, it's the same number of syllables and everything. So no more Nadine Jessup. Ricardo now calls me Jessie and I think that's super cute. Jessie Barlow. I like that.

Oh, and here's the update on my phone and wallet. They're gone. Like gone for good gone. Ricardo and I walked up and down the street and he asked a bunch of people but nobody had them. And they would have given it to him, too, if they did because he's really respected out here. People looked at me different just because I'm with him. One gross guy actually tried to grab me and said something like how much for this fresh meat, something disgusting like that and Ricardo went off on him. I thought he was gonna rip the guy's head off. But the bad news is my phone and wallet are gone and I'm not getting them back. I don't have my license yet, but I did have a credit card, a student ID, all my money and now I don't have any of it. FU*K YKWIM?

Ricardo took my jewelry (well, my mom's jewelry) and he's gonna sell it for me so I'll have some money again. And then I should make money once I get an acting job, or something. And Ricardo says I'm DEFINITELY going to get hired.

And about Ricardo . . . here's the big news on that. We kissed last night!!! It was incredible. He's the best kisser, I swear. It wasn't like I was expecting it or anything. It just happened. We were on the futon in my bedroom (yes, it's my bedroom now), just talking. He's so sweet the way he talks to me, how he looks me in the eyes. I was telling him something about my mom, I think. About how much she drinks and how I think she's really messed up. Ricardo's dad drank too much, too and he really got what I was trying to say. Then all of a sudden we were kissing. At first I was totally freaking out because he's like way older than me, but my mom was like five years younger than my dad and I'm only seven years younger than Ricardo so that's not such a big difference.

Anyway, the kiss was awesome and I know he wanted to go further but he held back, I could tell. And I'm glad he did, too. Not that I wouldn't, you know, do more, but I don't think I'm ready for that. I'm ready but I'm not ready. HELP I'M SO SCHIZO!

*So the photo shoot, right? I think it went
really well. Stephen Macan wasn't there. I dunno
where he was and I haven't seen him since that
first day. But that's ok. I'm staying in the apartment
(wherever this is, somewhere near Baltimore,
remember? Crazy, right?!) Sometime last week I
was sleeping in my bedroom and now I'm crashing
at this studio. But it's nice here and I don't have to
go out for anything. Ricardo brings me takeout
and there's a TV and I write in my journal (which
I hide btw) so I'm not bored or anything. But I
miss my phone. Ricardo says he's gonna get me a
new one and I can't wait.*

*Anyway the stupid photo shoot. I keep
rambling! It was just me, Ricardo, and some
guy named Buggy there. Yeah, you read that right.
Buggy. He hardly said a word. Kinda creeped me
out. He was this really thin guy who wore one of
those hipster hats, sunglasses and a plaid short-
sleeve shirt with a white undershirt underneath
and ripped jeans and he smoked lots of cigarettes
which I think is gross. But Ricardo says he's cool,
so I guess he's cool.*

*Ricardo took the pictures and Buggy watched
and that was fine. All I had to do was sit on the
stool and smile. My eyes started to hurt from
flash stuff but after it was over, we looked at the
pictures and they were nice. I actually have a
good smile. Even Buggy agreed.*

*Today Ricardo and I just hung out on the futon
kissing and drinking vodka straight. We talked for
hours about things I can't even remember. Bands,*

*TV shows—just stuff. The TV in the room isn't as
big as my TV at home, but it's big enough.
Ricardo had a Netflix subscription so we binged
on a bunch of shows. We did a whole season of
Lost, which I had never seen. It was so awesome
because I was snuggled up with Ricardo the
whole time. I could have been there with him for
hours like that. We kissed a lot and we did a bit
more, ya know? I don't need to write it, but it
happened. Not IT, but stuff, things.*

*Is he my boyfriend? I don't know. I like that
he's taking care of me. He treats me like I'm his
girlfriend. He feeds me pretty well, too. There's a
pizza place nearby and a KFC and other places to
eat. I made a salad with him one night in the
kitchen. It was incredible to just do something so
normal like cut vegetables. Go figure! It felt to me
like we were a couple. Kinda weird, I know, but I
liked it. We just got along. He never calls me
Nadine. He calls me Jessica. Jessica Barlow.
That's who I am now.*

*I still don't have any money, or my wallet, or
my phone. Ricardo went to sell my jewelry, but he
said his guy was trying to rip him off so he's going
to wait. That's fine with me. I don't want to get
taken. Ricardo looks out for me. Last night we
hung out together. We drank and I got high for
the first time. Now THAT was awesome. I felt so
free. It was just weed (I think LMAO) but I was
free of all the bullshit. Ya know? Free of everyone
judging me. I've been missing my home, my room,*

my stuff, but all that went away. I felt light. Does that make sense?

Ricardo and I made out for who knows . . . hours. It got pretty intense. I had my shirt off and he did too. (AH-Mazing bod!) I'm almost there. Almost ready. I want to do it with him, but I'm scared I don't know how it will feel, but I trust Ricardo. He's looking out for me. He says he loves me.

I got high again. High high high and I liked it. When I'm stoned I don't miss any of my friends. I don't miss Sophia, or Hannah, Madison, or Brianna. I don't think they really get me. At least that's what Ricardo says. He takes his time to really listen to me. People don't listen anymore. Ricardo says that, too. They just want things. It's all about them. I told him about the time Sophia called me a complaining bitch on Facebook. She hurt my feelings but later said it was a joke, and I was cool with it. Ricardo didn't agree. He said people write online what they really believe. It's like weed. You're free to be yourself. You have to think about what you're going to say before you write it, and that's true, you do. So Sophia had to think long and hard before she called me a bitch.

Ricardo has a phone so he looked up my Facebook page. He read a lot of my posts, the comments and stuff. And I see it now. In one of them Brianna called me fat. Well, she said, "what did you eat before you took this picture?" That's saying someone is fat. And another post where I talked about my mom being drunk again and my dad not giving a shit about me, Madison wrote that I should jump off a bridge. That would show them. Ha-ha-ha, she wrote. I thought she was being funny but Ricardo saw it differently. That's what she really wanted me to do. Jump. Off. A. Bridge. A real friend would never say something like that. I never thought about it until Ricardo opened my eyes. I asked if I could use his phone to send a message to Sophia and Brianna. I wanted to find out if they missed me at all. Ricardo said no way. They didn't give a shit about me. Nobody did. Except for Ricardo, of course. He's watching out for me. He's the only one I trust.

CHAPTER 10

Gabriel DeRose sat at the kitchen table and studied the photograph intently. Angie sat across from him, while Madeline heated water in the freestanding kettle for tea. The mood was tense.

"Tea," Madeline said. "It will settle us all down."

"You've never seen this photograph before?" Angie asked her dad.

Gabriel shook his head. "No, never."

"And you've never seen this music box before?" Angie picked up the burnished maple music box, opened the lid, and again "The Blue Danube" plinked out. It was a lonely tune that warbled with all the energy of a last breath.

"No, never." Gabriel rubbed at his temples, fatigue really showing. His eyelids seemed to grow heavier the longer Angie watched him.

Gabriel took the music box and held it in his hands, turning it over, examining it from all angles same as she had done. "All of your mother's jewelry is up in our bedroom."

"But that is Mom's handwriting on the back," Angie said. "You agree with that."

Gabriel turned the photograph over and studied it carefully. "I mean, it could be," he said, but not with assurance.

"Do you have anything of Mom's we could use to compare?" Angie asked.

Gabriel didn't have to think long. "Look in her desk drawers in the office. I'm sure she has a bunch of notes there."

Angie left and returned moments later with a box of papers. They were notes her mother had jotted down on various types of stationery, scrap paper and the like.

Looking through them was surprisingly emotional. They were frozen moments of time, innocuous events of little consequence, but remnants of the past like footsteps that marked a life's path. Angie's mother had these thoughts, these ideas. She'd written them down, never thinking her daughter would go through them after she was gone. Never thinking Angie would use them to try and match the handwriting on a photograph her mother had wished to keep hidden from everyone, her father included.

The first note was a list of things to do. It included calls to the Lupus Foundation and her friend Tracy, who had been at the house a few hours ago. Angie studied the handwriting. The similarities were unmistakable. The words, *May God forgive me* and *Call Tracy* were written in the same neat cursive. The letters were of average size, with narrow spacing between them.

From her PI work, Angie had learned something of the science of graphology, the study of handwriting. She used it on occasion to get a better sense of the people she was assigned to track. It took a bit of unpredictability out of the equation. Kathleen's handwriting slanted to the right, which was suggestive of somebody open to new experiences, someone who enjoyed meeting new people. Both were true of Angie's mom. The *i* and *e* were formed using wide loops indicative of openness, spontaneity, and a willingness to try new experiences. This was true of her mother as well.

Angie flashed on a memory of a family trip to Annapolis maybe twenty-five years ago.

Kathleen sat in the front seat of the family car studying a map. An idea struck her. They should continue driving east and go to Bethany Beach for the afternoon, she said, then asked, "Why not?"

"It would be a three-hour drive home," her father said. "That's why not. "

It was late spring, and the sun beat bright, and the air was warm and inviting. The next thing Angie knew, they were off with no suitcases packed, no plans for an overnight.

Soon they were splashing in the ocean, laughing as they raced to beat the waves that crashed against the sandy shore. Mother and daughter dared each other to venture out into the low tide as far as their bodies could stand the cold water, while trying not to get their clothes all wet. Kathleen wore a long dress that she hiked up above her knees. She twirled and danced on the sand while Angie ran circles around her mother, laughing under the call of the gulls that circled lazily overhead.

*Behind them her father, his pants hiked to his knees,
leather shoes in his hand, watched his wife and daughter
frolic on the empty beach.*

*Afterwards, they went out for ice cream—before din-
ner even—and her mother pleaded with her father to
spend the night, to not make the long drive back to Virginia. "Do it in the morning," she said.*

*After much cajoling, Gabriel relented and they found a
decent enough motel—not a chain, but a family-run business. They bought pajamas at a Walmart, and while her
father snored beside her, Angie snuggled against her
mother's side, basked in the television's flickering glow,
and fell asleep to some program.*

She'd long since forgotten what program. The pajamas
were probably in one of the boxes in the attic along with
all the other bric-a-brac her mother couldn't bear to throw
away, but some memories hadn't faded, like the pine-
scented smell of that motel room and the sound of her
mother's laughter as she'd twirled on the beach.

Angie gazed across the table at her exhausted father
and thought of his childhood memories. Of the orphanage
he talked about only on occasion, of the mother he never
knew, but whom he believed was a good person, a woman
in crisis who did her best in a difficult situation. In that
moment, Angie felt blessed beyond measure to still have
her dad in her life.

Her heart swelled with love as she pushed the box of
notes over to her father. "You can look through them, but
it's definitely Mom's handwriting on the back of the photograph."

Madeline returned with the tea. Everyone spent a few
quiet moments taking tentative sips as the drinks cooled.

Then she took the photograph in her hand and examined it more closely. She was a prosecutor, accustomed to evaluating evidence. "What do you make of this poor girl's ear?"

Angie glanced at the young girl's smiling face, focusing on that misshapen ear. "A birth defect, perhaps."

"Or maybe she was maimed and that's how it healed."

"Like a dog attack or something," Angie said. "Possible."

"What city do you think this was taken in?" Madeline asked.

"That would be helpful to know," Angie said.

Gabriel had gone silent. He was shuffling through Kathleen's notes, perhaps conjuring up his own memories of his life with Kathleen. Angie moved her chair closer to Madeline's so she could better see and study the photograph. The buildings were made of brick and fire escapes were affixed to some of the exteriors, suggesting that people lived in apartments above a row of shops. It was morning, Angie believed. Many of the shops were shuttered with heavy-duty roll down metal doors.

Because the photo was taken from street level, Angie couldn't tell how high the buildings were. Could be three stories or could be just two like a strip of row houses in Philadelphia. Angie didn't know if any of them had stores on the first level like this street did.

The shop signs were all for mom-and-pop type businesses. BEAUTY SALON. PATSY'S PIZZERIA. TONY'S PASTRIES. The street was peppered with bits of trash and a nearby mesh barrel was filled to the brim. A poster had been plastered to the side of a building, but a figure blocked out most of the letters. What Angie could see meant nothing to her.

> *000*
> *DS*
> *THS*
> *'m I*
> *IN'?*

It looked as though there was some additional text between *000* and *DS*, but it was written in a much smaller font and too blurry to make out. The photograph's main subject, the girl with the sweet sad smile, stood in the foreground near a fire hydrant that had one of its caps missing but no water shooting out. Meaningless graffiti marked up the staircase to one building entrance. It was a hard landscape, an urban one.

Angie thought of big cities like New York, Chicago, but it could have been the North End in Boston or a neighborhood in Detroit, Philadelphia, even someplace in DC. The milieu was gritty and old in a way that made her think it was an East Coast city, not some newer place such as Dallas or Columbus. The picture included no cars with identifying license plates, and the phone number on the sign to the beauty salon didn't include an area code.

"Any ideas?" Madeline asked.

"Yeah," Angie answered. "Lots of them. But I need the right one, and for that I'm going to need some expert assistance. I need Bao."

CHAPTER 11

It was the twenty-first day of April, and Nadine Jessup had been missing for a little over five weeks. Bao was sitting at Angie's desk when she arrived at the offices of DeRose & Associates. He sat in her chair gazing at his laptop, Beats by Dre headphones snapped in place, white canvas sneakers on the desk, fingers feverishly tapping away at his keyboard to what seemed like the rhythm of the music. His skateboard, his only mode of transportation, leaned against the wall and gave Angie a good view of the scuffed-up wheels and stickers plastered on the bottom.

Bao wore dark, loose-fitting jeans and a maroon T-shirt with a panda pictured on the front. He was one of the few people she knew who could rock a panda bear T-shirt without looking like an eight-year-old boy. His dark hair was free-flowing and his piercings were plentiful but not overdone. Whatever Bao put on, Bao owned it. He could make Izods look like a new trend in skater fashion.

Angie had on a low-cut black shirt and gray slacks, fairly typical attire for her. She always dressed comfortably. The day could be unpredictable. With a phone call, she might go from the desk to her car on a stakeout.

"What's the latest?" she asked.

Bao said nothing as he continued to type.

Angie waved her arms in front of him until she got his attention. He slipped his headphones off and she could feel the vibration of the music in her own ears. "You realize that's going to permanently damage your hearing, don't you?"

"What?"

"Funny, Bao. Where's Mike?"

As if on cue, she heard the toilet flush and the faucet run. A moment later, Mike Webb emerged from the only other room in her office, buttoning his pants while he pressed his cell phone to his shoulder with his ear.

Mike Webb was in his fifties and looked every bit that age. His neatly trimmed beard had gone gray, but specks of dark hair remained peppered throughout. The hair on his head, silver at the temples, had retreated from the front like glacial melt, but a respectable amount remained so he could still rock a side part. His face was kind. If he added padding to an already decent-sized paunch, Mike could easily pass for Saint Nicholas at any mall in America. He always wore button-down shirts with pattern designs (checks and plaids) and khakis, the uniform of a hardware store manager—which happened to be one of his many previous careers. Now he was part of the *& Associates* team, along with his other job.

He talked into the phone. "Okay, how about this, Mrs. Walker. I'll do the Bounceland Ultimate Combo, dunk tank, and I'll throw in an obstacle course. Same price."

Angie looked at Mike aghast as she quickly shut the bathroom door. Whatever he just did in there needed to stay in there. Mike Webb, not being the bashful type, probably couldn't care less that he had fouled the office with his business, nor did he seem to mind conducting another type of business while on the can.

"Okay, fine. What about the cotton candy machine? Is that still a go? Great. Thank you, Mrs. Walker, for choosing Bouncy Time Funland Rentals. We bounce for you. Have a great day."

Angie glared at Mike, hands on her hips.

"What?" he asked.

"That's just gross," Angie said.

"What is?" He really didn't get it.

"You. Talking to Mrs. Walker on the phone while you're doing"—she pointed to the bathroom door—"that."

"I had her on mute. And now I have an eight-hundred-dollar rental for this Saturday, thank you very much."

Mike had started Bouncy Time Funland Rentals with one bounce house in his inventory. Now he had a warehouse full of bouncy castles and obstacle courses that covered the spectrum from Dora the Explorer to Spiderman.

"What's the latest on the Nadine Jessup case?"

"I interviewed—um—hang on a second." Mike crossed the room and fished a little black notebook from his laptop bag. He flipped quickly through the pages as he scanned them. He lived and died by that notebook. His handwriting made chicken scratch look like calligraphy. How he could read it was a mystery to Angie, but he was a copious note taker, even as he digitally recorded every interview.

A few years back, he had come to Angie as a client. He had separated from his wife of ten years and suspected her of neglecting their two young children. He had married late in life. His wife, twelve years his junior, still had some giddyup left in her party tank. He'd wanted evidence that she was leaving the kids, eight and six at the time, to hit the bars in Old Town Alexandria.

Angie took Mike's case, no problem. She had a license to carry a concealed weapon, but rarely did. Her weapon of choice was a video camera. It helped that she could blend. Who would think the girl walking behind was recording your every movement using a camera hidden in her eyeglasses? She knew her way around the firing range, but men didn't come to Angie because they wanted a tough-talking Sam Spade type. They came because they specifically wanted a female PI.

Women's intuition might be a cliché, but the saying came about for some reason. Angie trusted her gut instinct. She could usually pick the cases where something shady was going on. Male clients, who made up a significant portion of her business, often felt a woman could best understand what they were going through. She respected the therapeutic aspect of the job. She understood that plenty of referrals had come because of her empathetic nature. Empathy was vital in cases of runaway children and affairs of the heart.

Many men had broken down in tears after seeing irrefutable evidence of their cheating wives. What they didn't want was to blubber in the office of another man. Most male PIs would say things like, "Screw her," and "You're better off." Angie was different. She would give them a hug. She would say, "This must be so hard for you. I'm sorry for what you're going through. You're a great guy and you deserve better." It was just a nicer way of saying, "You're better off," but it was what these guys wanted and needed to hear.

In the case of Mike Webb, his concern about his wife proved valid. Angie had recorded the party gal out at bars with several different men while the children were home with a babysitter. At least, she had the decency to get a babysitter. The judge did not take kindly to the mom coming home sloshed late at night when she should have been with her children.

Mike had been so impressed with Angie and the work she did that he got his PI license and became a damn fine investigator. He was the first person she had thought to call to keep momentum going on the Nadine Jessup case. He had also been fielding Angie's phone calls; in her time away from the office, he'd landed an insurance fraud investigation and two new cheating hearts. Since Mike's focus was Nadine Jessup, the new assignments had gone to other & *Associates* members. Angie would oversee those investigations and collect a fair share of the fee, but her attention needed to be on Nadine.

"So I spoke with Sophia," Mike said as he read from his notebook.

"Who is Sophia?" Angie asked.

"A friend of Nadine's from school."

"And?"

"And she hasn't heard from her, and I don't think she's lying."

Angie was inclined to believe him. She wouldn't be speaking with Sophia herself. She might have a gut instinct about cases, but nobody could read body language better than Mike Webb.

"Anybody else?"

"Five other friends, two boys, three girls. All interviewed. Nobody had anything super revealing to share. Whatever issues Nadine faced at home, she kept tight-lipped about them at school."

"Anything new from the mother?"

"No. Just that she needs an intervention at some point. My ex could be her AA sponsor."

"We'll mention it to her after we find Nadine," Angie said. "No need to put Mom on the defensive."

The judge who'd granted Mike full custody of his children had ordered the mother into alcohol rehab. She'd been sober three years, and the turnaround had earned her joint custody.

"What about you, Bao?"

Both Mike and Bao had come to the funeral, but since her mother's death, Angie had not had time to catch up on the Nadine case. They'd certainly had no time to discuss it at the reception. If there had been any big breaks, they would have called.

"The Facebook page has about two thousand likes," Bao said. "Word is spreading."

"My phone hasn't rung with any tips, but still that's a good number," Angie said. "Anything else?"

"Yeah, the parse on the log files gave us something."

"What?"

"New York, Philly, DC," Mike said. "Nadine was on TripAdvisor. Yelp. Thrillist. Checking out those cities."

Angie's face lit up. "Well, that's something. Keeps it to the eastern corridor. Makes sense. What did we do about it?"

"Mike's been a hobo," Bao said.

"And this is the busy season with bouncy houses, Ange," Mike said.

"Bonus to you if we find her."

"Hey!" Bao said. "Don't I count?"

"Okay, each of you. Bonus. What did you do, Mike?"

"Basically, I canvassed. Three days. Philly to DC. I hit the malls, the big shopping areas, places that I know we can poster."

"NCMEC hooked you up?"

"I had so many Nadine Jessup posters with me, you'd

think she was going on a world tour. Plus I made some of my own. It was a good thing I went, too. A lot of the initial posters NCMEC put up had been taken down."

"So we've chummed the waters. Good. Let's follow up with the police in each city. Maybe we can narrow this down. NCMEC can help there, too. Mike, can you take point on that?"

"Sure thing."

"Nothing on Nadine's cell?" Angie said.

"No. That's been quiet," Bao said.

"I'm going to go," Mike said. "I'll get over to NCMEC and start working the phones."

"I've already adjusted the Facebook page to geo-target those cities," Bao said, getting up from his chair. He slipped his computer into his bike messenger bag, slung the strap over his shoulder, and kicked his skateboard to the floor. Just like that, he was ready to roll.

Angie leaned against her desk and looked behind her to make sure Mike had left the office and was well out of earshot. There wasn't any big secret here, but Angie kept her personal affairs on a need-to-know basis.

This trait was something passed on to her from her parents. The DeRose family was notoriously private. Kathleen had had a large turnout at her funeral because of her community involvement. By contrast, Angie's father kept just a few close friends, with Walter Odette being the closest of them all.

Over the years, Angie had had it drilled into her not to overshare. A shrink might have a field day with her career choice. Her job was to unlock other people's secrets, shine light into dark corners, and reveal hidden truths. All children had a rebellious side, she believed, and at times she wondered if her career was a form of that rebellion. Was it her way of being a runaway?

"Can you stick around a second?" she asked Bao.

Angie fished out the photograph from an unmarked white envelope, camouflaged by the clutter of her handbag. Her bag was almost the same size as the one Bao used to carry around his computer. Angie knew she could be more fashionable with her accessories. She also knew that Target wasn't a handbag brand name, but that they had great prices and fine enough merchandise.

She showed him the photograph.

"What's this?"

"I found it in the attic in my parents' home. My mother hid it in a music box. Look on the back."

Bao read the inscription.

"That's my mother's handwriting."

"What's it mean?"

"I have no idea."

"Who's the girl?"

"That's my question."

"Well, where was this taken?"

"I don't know."

"How about when?"

"Bao, those are all the questions I have. Now, I need your help getting the answers."

"That's not all the questions," Bao said, studying the back of the photograph. "Why does your mother want forgiveness?"

CHAPTER 12

Exhibit D: Excerpts from the journal of Nadine Jessup, pages 25–30

Just a normal day of hanging out. It's so much fun having nothing to do. School, my life, it all seems so far away now. Ricardo says just wait until it starts happening for me. My acting career. Ha! That's so funny to even think about. But he believes and so I believe. When it happens I won't be so relaxed so he tells me to enjoy the downtime while I can. We'll be jettin' from film set to film set. Maybe go to France for that big festival . . . whatever it is, Cans or something.

It feels like my old life happened to somebody else. Ya know? I think of this apartment as my home now. It's nice here. Well the shower is a little gross. Drips of water and yellow stains around the drain kind of gross. And the bathroom isn't the cleanest. The kitchen is super small but I imagine it's the kinda kitchen I would have in my first apartment, so it's cool by me. But it's not the best money can buy. It's not like my kitchen at home. A kitchen worthy of Potomac, Maryland. Say that with your nose in the air all snooty like! This is real life out here. Ricardo takes me out for walks around the neighborhood. HA-HA-HA I sound like his dog. But I have to go with him because this neighborhood isn't the best. That's what he says and I believe him.

Buggy came over. He brought weed and we sat around smoking. Buggy freaks me out. He just looks at me and doesn't say much. He's creepy. He watches me and I think he's thinking gross thoughts. I dunno. But Ricardo likes him so he comes over a lot. He always wears a fedora hat and bowling shirts with a wife beater tank underneath. Last night Ricardo and I watched Jaws, the shark movie. I had never seen it, but there was this scene were the old fisherman guy (whatever his name was, Quint, right?) he's talking about being in the water with a bunch of sharks and he says something like a shark has lifeless black eyes, like a doll's eye. I thought about that when Buggy came over this morning because that's what his eyes look like to me.

So Ricardo opened up to me tonight. I want to cry for him. I feel so bad!! How can people be that cruel? WTF is wrong with people? That's what I'm saying. WTF people! And I thought my father was an asshole. Ricardo's dad used to burn him with cigarettes, lock him in a trunk, and beat him with his belt. He said he once spent three weeks locked inside a closet. He got water and food sometimes but he had go to the bathroom in the closet. So gross. So wrong. Anytime he did something wrong his dad would put him in that closet. Then . . . get this . . . his father killed his mother. He stabbed her to death in front of Ricardo! Ricardo went to live with an uncle who abused him as well. He hit him and beat him and Ricardo made some references to sexual abuse, but he wouldn't go there with me. I feel SOOOOOOO bad for him. He's such a sweet guy. How did he turn out so great? He ran away from that sicko uncle of his and lived on the streets hustling. Why do young people sell drugs? Because they have to, that's why. What other choice did he have? He used money to buy a cheap digital camera. He took pictures with it all the time, but didn't have a computer so he just looked at them on the little display and when it got full he deleted the old ones to make room for new ones. Now he has a computer and he saves his best photos. He showed me some of his favorites and they are INCREDIBLE!! Totally amazing. He took this one of a homeless guy that would just break your heart. The guy lives in a cardboard box and moves his stuff around in an old shopping cart, but honestly he looks so happy to me. This whole experience has really opened my eyes to the world. I've learned more out here than I ever did in school. I think about that card-

*board box picture a lot. I had a nice house and
everything, but I felt so alone. The guy with the
box has nothing, but he looked so happy in that
photograph. Explain that one to me, will ya?
Xoxo world! J. Barlow!*

*Totally freaked out. OMG freaked out. The
craziest thing happened just now. My heart is still
pounding. Gotta catch my breath.*

*OK, I'm better now. OMFG heart is still
pounding. Here's what happened. I passed out
after getting high and drunk and when I woke up
Ricardo was kneeling over me. Straddling me.
I've never seen him look so angry. He scared the
sh-t out of me. His face was this horrible scowl.
He dropped tons of shredded paper on me like it
was confetti or something. I didn't know what it
was at first, but a few bigger pieces fell and I
could see it was my face. These were the pictures
from the photo shoot. Ricardo had cut up all the
pictures into little pieces and he made them rain
down on me. What's going on, I asked him? He
said that he showed the photos to Stephen Macan.
He'd been busy and hadn't had time to look them
over. When he saw them he freaked out, or so
Ricardo said. She looks like a scared little girl.
That's what Stephen Macan told him. She's
supposed to be sexy. She's supposed to be the next
JLaw! J. Bar, right? I'm Jessica Barlow now.
"These pictures are crap." Those words are di-*

rectly from Stephen Macan. Ricardo tells me he's going to lose his job if I don't take better pictures. They invested a lot in me, he says. This apartment isn't free. The food. Photo expenses. All the booking calls Stephen has been making, setting up appointments, all that stuff. Everything depends on these pictures coming out right. But how can I make it come out right? I didn't think I was any good at this to begin with. They did, not me. But Stephen still thinks I have it in me and he told Ricardo to get it out of me or he'll find somebody else who can.

Everything is such a mess now. What am I supposed to do? You should have seen him. He was screaming and yelling, hitting the walls. Like totally panicked. I have to do better. If he loses his job it's going to be my fault. Where is he going to get another photography job? He kept saying to me, do you think photography jobs are easy to come by? Well do you?? I told him we could go away together. He said if he gets fired because of me he won't go anywhere with me. He won't want to see me again. This job allows him to do his art photography. Ricardo is a real artist! He's not just a hack. I can't let that happen! Then he called me a weak little girl. He said he's wasting his time with me. He says he's going to get fired for sure. He's right. I am a weak little girl. But I'm going to do better. I'll do whatever it takes. I need to go talk to Ricardo. Back soon.

☹ *So sad right now.*

* * *

I told Ricardo I would do anything to make the photo session work. Anything. I don't want to lose him. I can't. He's the only one who's ever cared about me. He doesn't think I can do it though. He was a lot less angry this time, so it was easy to talk with him. I had to be innocent looking but experienced at the same time if that made any sense. I said I wasn't experienced and he knew what I meant by it too. So we fixed it. I mean we did it. By it, I mean it. I wanted to do it with him, too, but as soon as he got on top of me, and started moving, I felt so weird. It didn't hurt, but it didn't feel good either. We didn't have any music playing or anything like that. The soundtrack to my first time was Breaking Bad because that's what he was watching on Netflix when it happened. I was too embarrassed to look him in the eyes. So either I closed my eyes tight, or I turned my head and watched the TV while Ricardo ... . well, you know. Guess what show I'll never watch again? I was so freaked out and my heart was beating like crazy. After it was over I asked him if it was any good? He said I needed a lot of work. Just like with my photo shoots.

Ricardo says my friends may be right about me. We took another set of photos and they're getting worse. I look fat in them. I don't look anything like Jessica Barlow should. He says I'm plain and dull and boring and nobody is going to give these a second look. It's not even good enough for my Facebook profile pic. He said he thinks he understands now why my father doesn't give a crap about me. I'm so damn forgettable.

Something is working at least. The sex is getting better. We've been doing a lot of I&I, that be Intercourse & Inebriation. I can't have sex if I'm not drunk or high. It relaxes me. Anyway, I won't lie—I like it. A LOT. Ricardo tells me he loves me. He tells me he loves me everyday. All the time. He says I'm his girl. I'll do anything to make him happy. I mean anything. He's the best thing that's ever happened to me. He gets me like nobody else. When I'm with him I feel like I belong. I want to make him happy. Yesterday he said he's getting a little bored with me. He wants to try new things. I asked him what and he showed me a lot of stuff online, things I never saw before and I'm trying it out with him (I'm also trying to scrub it from my mind). He makes me watch videos (ok, it's PRON—ya know, the code word for P.O.R.N., and some of it's nasty too). He likes to watch and I try to do it like they do it in the videos. I'm trying to be what he wants me to be. I'm kind of grossed out by a lot of it to be honest, but I'm getting used to it now. He says we should buy stock in Trojan. HA-HA! Now that's funny.

I wouldn't do this if Ricardo didn't love me, didn't want me. And I love him. It's not some puppy dog thing either. We get each other . . . really get each other. He tells me he'd do anything for me and that's what makes it ok for me to do anything for him. I'm not going to get into all the

*details. Cause it can be nasty. This isn't some
smut diary. Get your mind out the gutter
PEOPLE! This is my journal and I don't want to
write about it because, I dunno, maybe someone
will find this someday and I'd be super
embarrassed about what I've done, but trust me
I've now seen it all and done it all and well, at
least I'm good at something.*

*Ricardo says that I'm amazing in bed.
Amazing. He's used those exact words. That's
something, right? I'm not grossed out that he has
so much more experience than me. I mean he is
like seven years older or something. But I'm
flattered he thinks I'm getting good. And I really
need the confidence boost because none of the
pictures are working. We've tried everything.
Makeup. Hair. We used all the money from my
jewelry to buy me new clothes and new makeup.
None of that worked. I asked if I could have a new
phone and Ricardo said no. I can't talk to
anybody again. To make this work I have to
forget about Nadine and become Jessica. But it's
NOT working. We even took some pictures
outside and those came out the worst. I look like I
belong back in Potomac. I have no edge! A real
actress can belong anywhere and can look like
anything. I look like a scared little girl from the
suburbs hanging in . . . in . . . in wherever I am. I
don't talk to people, so I don't ask them. Ricardo
doesn't want me to.*

*One time I started a conversation with a guy
in line at the pizza place down the street from the*

apartment and when we got home Ricardo got really mad. Smashing walls with his fists kind of mad. Like the day he cut up my pictures mad. I asked him what was wrong and he said I had made him jealous. He said if I ever talked to another guy in front of him again, he'd hit that guy so hard he'd kill him.

And then he'd hit me.

CHAPTER 13

Angie lived in a one-bedroom apartment at Seminary Towers on Kenmore and Van Dorn. It was an older complex but nice, with good light and easy access to I-395. Plus it was affordable and in a safe neighborhood, easing her father's worry. The Papa Bear thing was a little endearing, but it also wore thin and quick. She was no longer his little girl to protect. She could handle herself just fine. Just ask any instructor at the gun range, from her self-defense class, or her gym.

The weekend had passed in a blur and still no sign of Nadine. It was almost eight when Angie got home. She had been at the office doing paperwork and would have arrived sooner had Mike Webb not called to offer a recap of his time with MCD, the missing children division of NCMEC. He would meet regularly with the team from MCD until they found Nadine or the missing girl's parents pulled them from the case.

MCD had two units of case management. The Critical and Runaway Unit (CRU) took point on the Nadine Jessup case. The information CRU gathered would have been confidential, but Carolyn Jessup had authorized access for Angie and any of her associates. Mike and the assigned case manager worked the phones all afternoon and made contact with police in the targeted cities. They also reviewed all the tips—there were plenty—and made sure the police knew which ones they thought were most promising. They hoped for a break in the case soon.

Tomorrow, Nadine will be six weeks gone. She could be anywhere. Alive or dead. Hooked on drugs. Hooked on survival, which could mean any number of things, none of them very good. Making money under the table on the streets often meant under the sheets as well.

Angie had farmed out three new cases to other trusted & *Associates* members. Two of them involved runaways and one was a transport job. It was a busy time for the DeRose agency, but she was fine with taking her cut of the referrals instead of a much larger payday. She wanted to focus on Nadine.

Focus meant the job and little else, which was why she'd arrived home carrying a plastic bag with takeout Thai food from Rice and Spice on Duke Street, five minutes from her apartment. Cooking required time, and time was something in perpetually short supply. She enjoyed cooking, and collected cookbooks like paperback novels, but she couldn't remember a time the oven got used for anything other than reheating. The veggie pad thai would probably be tomorrow's dinner, as well.

Most nights, she preferred to eat lighter meals. Stakeouts had a way of packing on the pounds, and her mother's healthy eating habits (doctor-recommended on account of the lupus) had become Angie's as well. But the day had worn her out, and the strange photograph continued to weigh heavy. She craved carbs.

Hanging on the kitchen wall was a large framed poster of Tuscany. The poster represented a dream she and her mother had shared, to travel together to Italy. They'd talked at length about lazy afternoons drinking wine, sampling varieties of cuisine both would normally shun, and seeing the sights tourists were supposed to see. Angie didn't care about taking the road less traveled. She and her mother were perfectly fine with trodding a well-worn path. There was a reason people went to Venice and Florence, and visited the Vatican in Rome.

Angie had a second Italian-themed poster, this one of David, the only nude male to occupy her bathroom in quite some time. How a block of marble could become something so magnificent astounded Angie and fired her imagination. Seeing the sculpture in person had been an item on both Angie and her mom's bucket lists. Angie would have to check that item off for both of them.

Angie's dad was more a homebody than a world traveler, a polite way of calling him a workaholic. For him, a plane ride was a grand ordeal. Angie often wondered about her father's ancestry, his heritage—more than her father did, she thought. He seemed content with not knowing, resigned to the mystery. Perhaps that was why he didn't care to venture too far in this world. Everything he wanted, all he needed, existed within a fifteen-mile radius of his home.

She did the wondering for him. DeRose was a French name, and perhaps Angie's paternal grandfather was French, or maybe her father's mother kept her maiden name. Included in the basket with the baby left at the orphanage door was a card with her father's first and last name written on it, nothing more. Gabriel DeRose's past was like a block of marble that would never be carved.

Angie had her own personal history to keep carving out. She thought again about giving Tinder a try. Do it for her mother, who wanted Angie to settle down.

She settled down, all right—right on the couch with a glass of white wine and the Thai food set out on the coffee table before her. She sank into the well-defined divot on her sofa where she ate most of her meals in front of the TV. She took a bite of food, but her thoughts went to the picture she'd found in the attic, and her appetite went with it.

The small girl's sad sweet smile came to her in stunning clarity, cauterized into her memory, same as her mother's cryptic note on the back. *What will Bao find?*

Angie would eat later. She decided to call her father, who answered on the first ring. They chatted for a while, while her food went cold. It comforted her to hear him sound so strong.

"You sure you don't need company tonight?" she asked. "I can pack up my dinner and drive it over. Plenty to share."

"I'm fine, sweetheart. Honest. Walt and Louise are over and we're watching the game together. They're keeping me company."

"He's doing okay, Angie."

Angie heard Walter's powerful baritone clearly in the background. Her father had good friends to lean on, to her relief. Worrying wasn't just her father's prerogative. She turned on the Nationals game, but kept the volume down.

"Maybe tomorrow we can get together. I have some estate business to go over with you."

"Whatever you want, Dad. I'm here for you."

"I know. I'm so lucky"—his words got cut short as he became overwhelmed with emotion—"to have a daughter like you."

Angie had tears in her eyes as she looked at the photographs hanging on the wall. Some were pictures of her and Madeline, a few with Sarah Winter, as well. But the one that drew Angie's attention was a black-and-white photograph of her parents, arms draped around each other, big smiles on their faces. It was taken at Lake Anna, where her family rented a cabin at least once each summer.

Angie felt her mother's absence profoundly. Angie's life had always had holes, left by the family she never knew, but her mother's absence was a new, bigger hole. A hole shaped like the most important woman in Angie's life, a woman she could see only in pictures, thoughts, and dreams.

"I love you, Dad," Angie said and hung up. She turned up the volume on the Nats game.

Her father loved baseball, and his passion had rubbed off on her. In high school, she'd been a serviceable soccer player, but on the softball field she'd been something of a star. She was good at fielding, had quick reflexes, a fast release, and could hit for average and power. Her dad had coached her through middle school, and on Sundays the pair were often found at the batting cages over at Upton Hill.

Her dad was a stickler for technique. *Keep the shoulders back. Start the swing with the legs and the hips. Drive the front shoulder to the ball.* Those lessons got so ingrained they became reflex. When it came time for college, she could see the next level was not for her, but she played on an intramural team, where she'd met Madeline and Sarah.

What stayed from her playing days was a love for the game and a commitment to fitness. Angie tried to hit the gym at least three times a week, and she'd recently taken up yoga in an effort to win the battle between her ideal weight and the five or so pounds that crept up on her with the stealth of a panther.

No yoga now, though. Angie was too tired. And there was cold Thai food to eat.

It was the bottom of the fourth in a three-three tie when Angie's phone buzzed with a text from Madeline.

Are you watching this?

Yeah. Good game.

Not the Nats, goofball! *The Bachelor*.

Oh, no. Forgot it was on. Any good?

Good? It's a train wreck. I love it. The fangs are out.

Werewolves in bikinis, eh?

OMG! Rick just tossed Krissy into the pool.

Sticking with the Nats. Did you hear back from Sarah's mom?

Yes, confirmed. She can't wait to see us. Can't believe Sarah's been gone thirteen years.

Wow. Thirteen? Can't believe it either.

Let's text later. Abigail just pulled Rick into the bushes. Must. Watch.

Xoxo talk later.

Luv ya. You doing all right?

I'm ok. Thanks.

Ok bye xx

Every year Madeline and Angie made the drive to New Jersey to visit with Jean Winter, Sarah's mom, and share remembrances. It was supposed to be just that one year, the first year, the hardest year. It turned into an every year thing, not something that was planned. It just sort of happened, sort of evolved, and now Jean was like an aunt to the girls, like a Walt and Louise but with fewer visits.

Since Angie had no extended family of her own, her relationship with Jean Winter was something she wanted to keep and foster. The best gift Angie could give her grieving pseudo-aunt was closure. It would come only when Angie—or someone, but Angie wanted it to be her—found out what had really happened to Sarah.

People who vanished without a trace haunted the lives of those left behind. Crowds became a breeding ground for hope. Angie would see people who looked like Sarah—it could just be a way of walking, a mannerism, something very Sarah. That was because Sarah wasn't really dead. That was how Angie felt, and she could only imagine how magnified those feelings were for Sarah's mother.

Carolyn Jessup already felt the same persistent ache, and probably got flashes of hope within a crowd of strangers. Angie had to find Nadine. The likelihood of a happy reunion dimmed with each passing day.

The Nats game held Angie's interest more than the takeout. She had no trouble finding space for her leftovers. Her refrigerator was mostly empty. Any day now, a new cookbook would arrive from Barnes & Noble—something about clean eats, her most recent purchase—and Angie would peruse the pages, feeling guilty for not having the time or energy to shop and cook.

She returned to the futon when her phone rang.

"What's up, Bao?" she answered. Her pulse ticked up a notch or two.

"I think I have something on that photograph. You got a minute?"

Her pulse ticked up some more. "Yeah, sure."

"Better in person. Can you meet now?"

"Of course. Where?"

"Your place."

"Okay. What time?"

"Now. I'm downstairs."

Angie rolled her eyes. "Bao, why didn't you start the conversation with *Angie I'm downstairs. May I come up?*"

"You could have been busy. I didn't want to be presumptuous."

"Just come up." She buzzed him inside.

He had a different way of thinking about things, which was why she wanted his help to identify the girl in the photograph. Who could she be? A sister she never knew?

Bao came in wearing a gray hoodie and carrying his skateboard.

"Is that how you got here?" Angie asked.

"It's how I get everywhere." He had a studio apartment several miles from Angie's place, but his skateboard made getting around town a breeze.

Angie got Bao some water from the tap. She would have given him some wine, or a beer, but he didn't drink alcohol. A vegan and the guy who got Angie into yoga, Bao liked to have a clear head at all times. He was careful with everything he put into his body.

He set the photograph on the coffee table, and there she was—that sweet girl with the sad smile and deformed ear, wearing a lovely pink dress with white polka dots.

"So?" Angie said. "What do you got?"

"I don't know who the girl is, but I do know where this picture was taken and more important, when."

CHAPTER 14

*W*hen. Angie held her breath in anticipation.

"There are clues here," Bao said, "that tell us when this was taken, but first—" He flipped the picture over and Angie read the haunting message her mother had written on the back.

May God forgive me
IC12843488

"Some photographic paper has the brand printed on the back, like this one does."

Angie had been so focused on her mother's writing she hadn't paid attention to the wallpaper-like printing on the back. Printed in faint lettering were the words THIS PAPER MANUFACTURED BY KODAK, set at a tilt and displayed numerous times so it covered the entire back of the image.

"Kodak had four common brandings. Velox dates back to the 1940s to 1950s."

"How do you know all this?"

"I have a friend who's a photographer. I asked. I don't

get every answer from the computer. Just most of them."
Bao smiled.

Angie returned a smile. "Go on."

"Kodak Velox Paper. That watermark was used in the 1950s and 60s."

"I didn't think the photo was that old."

"It's not. This one here"—Bao's finger tapped on the watermark decorating the back of the image that read THIS PAPER MANUFACTURED BY KODAK—"came after 'A Kodak Paper,' another watermark which was from the late sixties to early seventies. Based on that, we know for sure that this image was printed between the mid-seventies to the eighties."

"Amazing."

"Now, look here." Bao flipped the image over to the picture side. "See this?" He put his finger on the poster plastered to the side of a building in the image background.

> *000*
> *DS*
> *THS*
> *'m I*
> *IN'?*

Angie had studied the poster before at her father's house. The figure in front blocked out the crucial letters, and she couldn't get any clues from it. "Yeah, I already looked at that, but couldn't make anything of it."

"Me neither. But I went to a website and put the letters into an application people use to help them with Scrabble. It creates all the words that contain those letters. For example, with the letters *T-H-S*, the application returned words like childbirths, tenths, and paths. I did it for *D-S* and got a list as well. Apostrophe *M*, I'm guessing is I'm. I'm also guessing the *I-N*-apostrophe is *I-N-G,* but there are a whole lot of words that end in *i-n-g*, right?"

"Right. And?"

"I couldn't make out the text between 000 and DS, it was just too blurry, so I wrote a little program that takes all the *D-S* and *T-H-S* words and does a search using those three zeros. I figure those zeros have to be some common number, otherwise why print it on a poster? My program ran through all word combos and the numbers one thousand, ten thousand, one hundred thousand, and one million. Manually it would have taken me forever, but my program did it all in a flash. I generated a bunch of image search URLS because that's what we're looking for. Am I right, or am I right?"

When Bao said this, he was right.

"What did you get?"

"Well, I limited the words. Based on the poster and font size, I did some calculations and I didn't think any word was greater than six letters. Also, I used only words that had *DS* and *THS* on the end. And I didn't mix the *DS* and *THS* words because there would be too many combinations. So the first search was for *one thousand, Alkyds, Poster,* then *ten thousand, Alkyds, Poster*, and so on."

"That sounds like nonsense to me."

"It's total nonsense. I was only looking at the first few rows of images for every number and word combo that got returned. It didn't take too long. I sifted through a lot of nonsense until I ran a search for *ten thousand, AIDS, Poster*."

Bao used his phone to run this exact search query. The results displayed a preview of the images, and he clicked on the first one. The image showed a black-and-white picture of a bald, middle-aged man. The words on the poster read *10,000* NEW YORK CITY AIDS DEATHS HOW'M I DOIN'?

Angie realized the words they couldn't make out because they were too small and blurry in the photograph were the most important words of all.

"At first I didn't know who the guy was," Bao said, "but I figured it out easy enough. It's a guy named Ed Koch."

Angie knew the name. "He was the mayor of New York City."

"Right on! And there's a history to this poster. A group called ACT UP made it to criticize Koch's inaction in dealing with the AIDS epidemic. 'How'm I doin?' was his catchphrase. He used to ride the subways and greet people with that slogan. I looked that up, too. So the poster was meant to be ironic."

"But now we know the city. It was New York. Nobody would hang a Mayor Koch poster in another city."

"We know more than that. We know the exact year this picture was taken. The poster was made in 1988. It could have been plastered to that building for years, but it's not all torn or faded, so I'm guessing it's pretty new in this photograph. Who knows, right? But based on the photo paper, we know roughly when the image was taken. So photo paper plus the date the poster was made, and I can tell you with one hundred percent, Bao-certified certainty that this image was taken in New York City and the year was 1988."

One of Bao's outstanding talents was his ability to tackle a problem from angles others might ignore. Angie had seen him work his magic on a number of cases, and the police who used to chase him now often thanked him for his efforts. She should not have been surprised at Bao's findings.

She gave him a big hug. "This must have been a lot of work."

"You can send my girlfriend some flowers to thank her for letting me vanish for a while."

"And I can thank you with some thank-you money. How many hours do I owe you?"

"Zero. Put this one on the house, Ange. You've done a lot for me. Least I can do this for you."

"Not happening. I'm writing you a check."

"When it's over, how 'bout you buy me a board? Polar Skate came out with a new line that'd be totally gnarly. I'm stoked we got this far, but big questions remain."

"Right. Like why does my mom have a picture of a little girl from 1988?"

"And why does she need forgiveness? Thinking out loud here. Did your mom and dad ever live in New York City?"

"No," Angie said.

"Any relatives?"

"My dad grew up in a Michigan orphanage. It's closed now. He went from foster home to foster home and ended up in California, where he met my mom. They moved from California to Virginia after the big blowout over my mom being unwed and pregnant, with me no less."

"Like whoa on the guilt."

"Like whoa, there were no stops made in New York."

"Maybe a relative you didn't know?"

"That she kept secret from my dad? I don't think so. He saw the picture. I think he'd remember a little girl with a deformed ear. Makes no sense that my mom would hide that from him."

"Well, maybe you should track down the family. Find out for yourself."

Angie grimaced at the thought. "That would break my mother's heart."

"Not to be cold and all, but your mom is gone."

Angie's gaze went to the large jade plant resting on the mantel by the window. She had taken the plant from her parents' home with a solemn vow to keep it alive, not an easy assignment given her work schedule. Angie had made arrangements with her neighbor to water the plant if necessary. It was her mother's favorite plant. She had tended it with loving care like she did all the green things in the house. Angie felt an obligation to the plant, and in a way, it echoed the obligation she felt toward her mother's history. Both had to be respected.

"My mom was adamant about having no contact with her family. Not ever. What they did to my father, what they said to her, was beyond awful. I can't just go opening doors to the past because my mother's not here to guard them. I respect her too much to do that."

"Then you may never know."

Angie gave this only a moment's thought. "There are other ways of finding out."

"Like?"

"I'll go to NCMEC and get the girl aged using age progression technology. Then I'll put the photo online. This girl would be in her thirties by now. Her friends would be on Facebook. Someone will recognize her and contact me. That way I honor my mother's wishes and still get the answers I need. And you can get that skateboard."

"Sounds like a plan. I'm still working on cracking the code." Bao turned over the picture so they could both see the cipher IC12843488 written on the back. "Maybe there's an answer hidden inside that sequence."

* * *

Three days passed and no hidden answers were found. In fact, nothing had changed, which meant Nadine was still missing.

Angie was back home, having visited with her father after work. She had another bag of takeout with her. Her phone rang. It was Mike Webb calling.

"Hey, Mike. What's going on?"

"A security guard at Union Station saw our poster and called NCMEC, and they just called me. Nadine was there. He's sure of it. The guy's name is Sean Musgrave. Good thing I canvassed with new posters. There weren't any at Union Station when I went there."

Angie's heart revved. "Where are your kids?"

"It's Thursday. They go to their mother's."

"Good. I'll pick you up in an hour."

"What? To go to DC? Musgrave won't be back at work until morning."

"Then we'll be the first ones to greet him," Angie said. "We can do a scouting expedition in the meantime. Hit up bus stations with the posters. Ask around. Maybe somebody has seen her or bought a ticket in her name. Maybe we'll get lucky."

"Fine, if Katie can keep the kids. But this can't turn into an extended stay. I've got to be back for a party on Saturday. It's a bounce house plus an obstacle course. Big job."

"Yeah, so is finding a missing girl. Be ready when I get there."

CHAPTER 15

Exhibit D: Excerpts from the journal of Nadine Jessup, pages 31–33

Mandy was a girl who showed up at the studio one afternoon and left with Ricardo. I don't know where they went, what they did, or where she came from. She was tall and thin with mocha colored skin and pretty long black hair. She wore tight jeans and had on a low cut top that left her boobs basically hanging out. Ricardo said she was another client of Macan Entertainment. I asked Mandy if she'd been in any movies and she said plenty and gave a laugh. I didn't know what that meant. I went to the bathroom and when I came out I saw Ricardo kissing Mandy. Like real kissing. He had his hands all over her ass. I don't know if he saw me, but I didn't talk after that. I went into my room and sat on the futon and looked out the window at the cloudy sky and dirty street. I had on jeans and a scoop neck sweater, clothes Ricardo bought for me because he hated everything I wore. I looked in the mirror, but I didn't look anything like Mandy. She was exotic and beautiful. Ricardo came into my room and asked what was wrong. I told him that I saw him kissing Mandy. He said so what if he did? He's an adult and he can do what he wants. I told him it made me feel jealous. He told me to grow up and then he left with her.

I remember watching TV . . . something stupid on Netflix. I remember having a burrito for dinner and making a salad. I remember wondering where the hell am I? What am I doing here? I remember getting high and then I didn't care so much about anything anymore. I think it was eleven o'clock. Ricardo had been out for most of the day and I had been cooped up inside. I didn't go out because he told me not to leave the studio on my own. He said it wasn't safe and I've been out on the streets with him enough times to know he's telling the truth. I was still upset about Mandy. I asked what he saw in Mandy that he didn't see in me. He said plenty, but I was all right. I asked if he slept with her. He told me it wasn't any of my business. I told him I'm not a dumb little girl from Potomac anymore. He laughed. I told him I wanted to quit. I told him I couldn't do it anymore. He said, "Jessie, you walk away from me now and I'll kill you." He said it joking like, ya know? But I dunno. Something about it didn't sound like a joke to me.

* * *

I was thinking about Mandy a lot. She was eating me up like acid. Was she that much prettier than me? Did she have a better body? Was she better in bed? My emotions count, too! I have feelings, but Ricardo doesn't seem to care. I cried about it, but he told me to control myself. He wanted sex, but I didn't want to do it. I wanted him to leave my room. My pictures aren't any good anyway. I'm no good at this. I'm not a model. I'm not beautiful like Mandy. I just want to go home. Now I miss home. I told Ricardo no to sex. And he grabbed my hair and yanked my head back hard. I cried out because it hurt. He said don't ever say no.

I'm stuck. Now I get it. I'm isolated from my friends. I have no phone. No money. I don't even know where the hell I am. All I have is my journal. I keep it hidden inside a slit I made in the mattress. As long as I keep a sheet over the mattress Ricardo can't see the cut I made. It's safe to put my secrets here. And my secret is this. I'm going to leave. I've decided. Even if I'm broke, I'll figure it out. I'll walk away if I have to. Nobody owns me. I'm my own person. He can have Mandy all to himself! Asshole! This whole modeling thing is BS, too. A big heap of BS. Jessica Barlow! Ha. What a joke. Baby, I'm gone. Ricardo just doesn't know it yet.

Holding off a bit. Ricardo was just so sweet to me. He made me dinner and he gave me a back rub. He told me he was sorry about Mandy. He said she's nothing compared to me. He was being stupid. He swears to me he didn't sleep with her. All they did was kiss and he said she was a terrible kisser. Nothing like me. Those were his words not mine. I didn't tell him I was planning to leave because I didn't want him to be mad at me. Guess I'll stay for a bit longer. We're going to do another photo shoot in the morning. Maybe those will be better. I think Stephen Macan knows we're living together, but I guess he didn't care. He just wants good pictures. Who knows? Maybe I killed Jessica Barlow prematurely! LOL!!!

Buggy came over after the photo shoot. He had on that stupid hat of his. Stupid jeans. Stupid bowling shirt. He had that cruel look in his eyes and reeked of cigarette smoke and marijuana. Booze, too. It was dark out when he showed up. I don't know what time exactly. He and Ricardo smoked a blunt in the kitchen. Ricardo showed him the pictures and Buggy wasn't impressed. He said I looked like a high school kid. Ricardo said for a high school girl I was broken in good and he laughed. Buggy said he'd break me in even more and then they both laughed. They talked about me like I wasn't there. Ricardo said to Buggy that he should kiss me because I was a really good kisser. Buggy came over like it was going to happen and I pushed him away. He looked at Ricardo like something was wrong. Ricardo told me not to embarrass him. Buggy went to grab me and I pushe

in Ric

that to

right. I

Buggy sa

I heard Ri

Ricardo ap

looked out t

high up. I trie

first time I rea

He asks me again about Buggy.

gross and that it's gross. He

and squeezes them hard

ask him why the wi

because this i

want to le

steps

Here's what h   , how it happened, as it
happened. Obviously, I'm still alive. I'm still here.
But I keep reliving the moment everything
changed over and over again in my mind. I have
to do something to help me process it all, so I'm
recording it here best as I remember, as if I could
somehow write it all down while I was fighting for
my life.

Ricardo knocks on the door and won't stop
knocking. I won't open it for him. He bangs on the
door with his fists. I'm on my bed hugging myself,
scared out of my mind, really freaking out.
Ricardo is pounding away, telling me open the
door, calling me puta—a whore. He says if I don't
open this door this minute, he'll kick it in and
then he'll use his belt and whip me like a mule. So
I get up from the bed and open the door. My whole
body is shaking.

Ricardo doesn't hit me though. He wants to
know why I didn't kiss Buggy like he asked me to.
He reeks of weed and his eyes are red as rubies.

...ay because he's ...grabs my shoulders ...enough to make it hurt. I ...dows are nailed shut. He says ...a bad neighborhood. I tell him I ...ve and he says go ahead and leave. He ...away and makes a path for me to the door. I ...ke a few steps. To my back he says out there I'll be mugged and raped in a matter of minutes. I hear the sirens at night, the occasional gunshots and I don't think he's lying, but I still take another step. Then he says if I walk out the door, he'll make a call that'll guarantee I'll get attacked. Guarantee it. I ask what he wants from me. Good pictures, he says. We want to make you a Macan star. Just like Mandy? I ask.

He comes at me fast and slaps me across the face. I drop to the floor. He says I better shut my mouth. He tells me not to talk back to him. He's older. He has more experience in his little finger than I have in my whole body. I'm too negative, he says. That's why the pictures aren't coming out. He's got these eyes that fire up when he's angry, redder than the bloodshot eyes of a guy high on weed, and it really scares me. He pulls me up by my shirt and gets right in my face and then without warning he just throws me to the ground. I hit the floor so hard I can't breathe. I open my mouth, but I can't get any air down. Then he climbs on top of me and puts his knees on my chest and pins me to the floor under his weight. There's no rug underneath me and it feels like my ribs are going to snap. I swear they are going to break in half. He puts his hands on my throat and starts to squeeze. I don't understand what's happening at first. I can't even explain it. It's like my body wouldn't work. I just went still. He keeps saying, you better be scared of me little girl. I'll f'ng kill you if you f with me. I'll rip your f'ing head right off. I'll go find your mama in her fancy ass house and I'll rape her and then I'll stick this knife in her throat and laugh as she bleeds to death. You want that? Do you? You think your wallet is missing? I took it you little bitch. I know where you live girlfriend, he says. I got your home address. He pulls out a knife and he puts it to my throat. It's a big blade, like you could cut a tree with it. Where did it come from? It's like he had it with him the whole time and I just didn't see it. He doesn't press down with the blade or anything, but he holds the knife to my throat for a long time. I can't stop shaking, can hardly breathe. You don't ever talk back to me, he says. You got that? You don't ask about what I do and who I do it with. I wanna screw Mandy I'm gonna do it. Maybe I'll do it and make you watch. He says that and laughs. You got that little girl? Of course I do, I finally say. At this point, I'm almost hyper-ventilating, but I'm thinking about my mom. I swear he's not lying about my wallet or what he'd do to her if I walked out. I have to keep it together. Ricardo gets off me and puts the knife away.

He leaves for a while. I'm broken, I'm weeping, I'm so alone, so lost, so confused, in my room (this room, not my room, this room) *thinking about what I'm going to write in my journal. Ricardo comes back and sits down on the futon. He apologizes. He tells me he hates when people tell him no. He can't handle it. He blames it all on the weed. He was high out of his mind when he told Buggy to kiss me, when he attacked me. He says he lied about taking my wallet, but he doesn't take back what he said he would do to my mom. I'm so confused because he says he loves me. Why would he want to hurt me? He pulls me in close and hugs me. At first I resist, but he's so upset with himself that I let him hold me. He strokes my hair and whispers in my ear that he's so sorry for everything. He didn't want to lose it on me like that. It just happens to him. Sometimes he can't control himself. He loves me so much he says. I'm his perfect girl. But warns me not to ever make him lose control again. I ask him how do I do that? He says it's simple, do everything I say, anytime I say it.*

CHAPTER 16

A ngie arrived at Mike's apartment in Falls Church at quarter to eight in the evening. She pulled up in her seven-year-old Ford Taurus, which was kind of like a cop car and a good-sized vehicle for doing those dicey transport jobs. It was also affordable. Like Mike Webb, Angie cobbled together her income. If she graphed her earnings over the years, it would look a lot like the S&P 500—plenty of peaks and valleys, but a positive trajectory over the long haul. She added to her 401(k) diligently, but was still a few twigs shy of having something that resembled a nest egg. Everything had a cost, and she refused to think of her father as a safety net.

She skimped on life insurance and long-term disability, figuring she had no dependents to look after. The idea of having a kid or two continued to tug at her, and driving a car with so much backseat room felt a little lonely at times. On occasion, she would glance in the rearview mirror and imagine car seats, with scattered Cheerios mixed in with plastic toys.

Having a kid didn't require a man, just his sperm. A few years back, she had contemplated artificial insemination; then her business had picked up, and she had something other than learning how to cook clean eats to add to the list of aspirations she wasn't fully equipped to tackle.

The only constant in Angie's life was getting older. In a spare moment, she had researched freezing her eggs—just out of curiosity, just to know. The price tag was a real eye-opener. It was ten grand to harvest them, five hundred a year for storage, and another five grand for IVF. Wasn't going to happen. It wasn't all about the money, but that was a big factor. The back seat of her Taurus would transport sullen, rage-filled teens instead of toddlers for the foreseeable future, maybe forever.

Five minutes after Angie had texted him that she had arrived, Mike Webb, wearing a light jacket, tan Dockers, and a patterned oxford shirt, came strolling out of his apartment wheeling his carry-on luggage behind him. He went to the back of her car and tapped on the trunk to get her to pop it open. He stashed the luggage, settled into the front seat, and buckled in.

"Mike, we're only going to be gone twenty-four hours. What's up with the suitcase?"

"*You* always keep a suitcase of clothes in the back of the car."

"Yeah, but that's because I may need to tail somebody for a few days and I'd look conspicuous in the same outfit. This trip is just a drive, a meeting. It's probably nothing."

Mike laughed. "Ange, I've worked for you long enough to know that it's never just nothing."

Angie told Mike about the photograph and what Bao had found out. She showed him the picture and made sure he looked at the message and the strange code written on the back. "Any thoughts on what it could mean?"

"I'm not really into cryptography. That's more a Bao thing. I could get this aged for you at NCMEC."

"Yeah, I was going to do that."

"I'll take care of it for you. Send me a copy. What's up with that ear of hers? It looks like a birth defect to me."

"Maybe she was injured."

Mike turned the picture sideways to study the part of the girl's anatomy more closely. "It's kinda freaky."

"Tell me about it," Angie said."

"What about you? Is there anybody you'd want to ask for forgiveness?"

"Yeah, Carolyn Jessup if we can't find her daughter."

Thanks to the light traffic and the late hour, they made the drive from Falls Church to DC in just under thirty minutes. Potomac, Maryland, to DC wasn't too far a ride. Just under fourteen miles; thirty to forty minutes via the Clara Barton Parkway if the traffic cooperated. A bus line ran from the suburb to the metro area, and chances were that's how Nadine left. She hadn't traveled far from home—not so unusual. Didn't make it any less danger-ous. Predators could be found in any city.

She could have picked up a Metro bus at the Mont-gomery Mall. It was about a four-mile walk from Po-tomac to the mall, a doable distance even if someone wasn't determined.

"Can you contact Metro and see about getting surveil-lance footage?" Angie asked. "I'm sure they still have it archived. Wasn't that long ago, and we know the date and relative time she would have taken off."

"You realize that Nadine could have gone to Union

Station to take a train somewhere else. You know—Philly, New York, Boston, the places she searched."

"Yeah, I know."

"So tell me again why we're here twelve hours before Sean Musgrave reports for mall security duty?"

"We're going to canvass the bus and Metro stations."

"They don't open until morning."

"Then we're going to check some of the less savory neighborhoods."

Mike groaned. "Oh great. That's why you wanted to come so early."

"She might be here."

"Or she might be in Philly, like I said."

Angie ignored him. "We'll cruise down Fourteenth Street near the old red-light district. Not optimistic though."

"What about the hotels along New York Avenue?" Mike suggested. "Then check out the fringe areas around Catholic and Gallaudet."

"Good call," Angie said. "While we're at it, let's roll by Adams Morgan, too. Maybe stake out the Cambria Hotel, The Donovan at Thomas Circle, swing by some of the clubs."

"Oh good. We'll get our groove on."

Mike wiggled his upper body in a toned-down dance jig that revealed plenty about how he'd cut a rug at a club.

"No, we got business to do."

"What kind of business can we do at a club?"

"Nadine's been gone for over a month now. She needs a place to sleep, food, a lot of amenities."

"You think she might be working the street? The girl is only sixteen!"

"Yeah. And a girl's gotta eat."

CHAPTER 17

Strikeouts all around. Mike and Angie drove around for hours, stopping only once for a bite to eat at an all-night diner in Adams Morgan aptly named The Diner. There, Mike ordered a stack of pancakes, side of bacon, hash browns, and a black coffee chaser. Angie got an egg-white omelet with spinach, tomatoes, no cheese, and a gluten-free vegan muffin.

Mike looked personally offended with her choice. "What are you doing?" he'd asked in a semi-harsh tone after the waitress left. "We're at a diner. You're supposed to order fun food."

"Egg-white omelets are fun."

"For sure they're the Cher to that vegan muffin's Sonny. I can't even believe they have vegan muffins at a place like this."

"Gluten-free vegan," Angie had corrected. "And they're everywhere now."

"No. No. Not everywhere. I'm from Willowick, Ohio, and I guarantee you our local diner has no vegan muffins on the menu. Gluten-free maybe, but definitely not gluten-free and vegan."

"Well, we have a lot of sitting and driving to do, and I don't want to feel gross. Heavy food makes me feel bloated."

"How does someone make a gluten-free vegan muffin anyway?"

"Almond meal, oat flour, maybe some agave nectar."

When Mike's coffee and Angie's lemon water arrived, he'd toasted Angie with his mug. "I take it back. That muffin sounds like the life of the party."

For about an hour, they'd gone over the map, reviewing all the places they had visited. They had seen their fair share of young working girls, but nobody who resembled Nadine.

Mike had played the lure. He'd walked the streets while Angie kept a close watch from the car. Girls came to him. *"Hey baby, looking for something, baby? Need something, sweetheart?"* He was the perfect bait, with his khaki pants and patterned oxford shirt. No undercover cop would look so lame. He'd showed the girls a photograph of Nadine, and gave Angie the thumbs-down sign after each encounter.

With luck, the security guard, Sean Musgrave, could give them a lead.

When five a.m. rolled around, Angie and Mike hit the bus counter at Union Station. She wore comfortable jeans and a loose fitting crewneck top from lululemon. Comfortable as she was, she felt as worn as her canvas sneakers. PI work, the real work, was a grind. No other way about it.

Angie tacked flyers on the pillars around the bus bays, knowing they probably wouldn't stay up. She asked the people at the ticket counter if anyone had seen Nadine or recalled someone purchasing a ticket in her name.

By nine o'clock they were both hungry again.

"How's that vegan muffin tiding you over?"

"*Gluten-free* vegan muffin," Angie said.

They fueled up at the Starbucks inside Union Station and went looking for Musgrave. At noon, they were scheduled to connect with a DC detective who'd been talking to the team at NCMEC. Tracking down a runaway was a battle fought on multiple fronts, and Angie often felt like the general trying to bring disparate armies together.

Angie's phone rang. *Carolyn Jessup.*

"Any news?" Her voice shook with longing. Carolyn knew everything Angie did, including the Musgrave lead.

"Nothing yet. We're about to meet with Sean Musgrave."

"Anything from Nadine's cell phone?"

With Carolyn's permission and the help of the phone company, Angie would be notified if any calls were made from Nadine's phone. The Find My Phone app was running, but so far there hadn't been a single ping. Mike had already contacted everyone Nadine had spoken with in the twenty-four-hour period before she'd vanished and had come up with blanks all around.

"She's not coming back, is she?" Carolyn's breathing turned heavy.

"Don't say that," Angie answered. "Until we find her, we don't give up hope. That's our rule."

"I just have a feeling, I have a really bad feeling," Carolyn said. "Last night I had this dream, this terrible dream that Nadine was floating in the house. She floated from room to room, her nightgown hanging down, but she was weightless. She looked white as the moon, and her skin was cold to the touch. I woke up screaming her name. I know it's a sign. An omen. Something horrible has happened to her."

Mike noticed Angie's puzzled expression and pantomimed the motion of drinking from a flask.

Angie shooed him away. "When I know something, I'll call. Stay strong for Nadine." She ended the call.

"What was that about?" Mike asked.

"Nothing. Just Nadine's mom being anxious, that's all. It's completely understandable."

Angie was shaken, though she didn't share any of those feelings with Mike. Something about Carolyn's dream had gotten to her. She pictured another girl floating about a room somewhere in New York City, a little girl with a sad smile and a deformed ear. Angie couldn't help but wonder if something horrible had happened to both girls.

CHAPTER 18

They met Sean Musgrave in the food court in the bowels of Union Station. He was waiting for them in front of Kelly's Cajun Grill as planned.

Musgrave was in his late twenties with a clean-shaven baby face and the solid build of a high school linebacker. He wore a white shirt with a couple official-looking patches sewn on the sleeve. Pinned to his breast pocket was a bronze star reminiscent of something a sheriff might have. With him was a swarthy fellow with a goatee, dressed in a nice suit that didn't look like it was bought at the mall.

He introduced himself as Vincent Cosco, general manager of the shops at Union Station and the guy in charge of mall security. Vincent led Angie and Mike through a locked metal door at the back of an alcove where the restrooms also were located. The shopping area's nice lighting and visual amenities were evidently saved for places where customers actually hung out. Back where cash registers didn't chime, it was a different aesthetic. The walls were bare concrete and matched the color and material of the floor. The lighting was dim but bright enough to show off the exposed ductwork, wires, and copper pipes overhead.

He took everyone to a windowless room with a coffee-maker that looked like a relic from some archeological dig, a sofa, rectangular table, and bridge chairs—all that wouldn't be picked up curbside even if they had a TAKE ME sign pinned to them—and a small fridge Angie wouldn't open if Mike double-dog-dared her.

Musgrave and Vincent sat on one side of the table, Angie and Mike on the other. She withdrew the pictures of Nadine from her bag and spread them on the table for Musgrave to study.

He looked them over, one by one, taking his time, being thoughtful. Angie knew nothing about his background, but he'd seen something, he remembered it, and he'd taken the time to contact someone who might care. That made him A-OK in her book.

"Yeah, that's her all right." Musgrave nodded.

Vincent picked up the pictures and studied the photos for himself. "You sure?"

"Yeah," said Musgrave to his boss. "It was on the second floor, between Heydari Design and Jois Fragrance. I remember it because I thought the girl looked young and might be nicking."

Vincent looked to Angie and Mike. "*Nicking* is a term we use for shoplifting."

"But she wasn't stealing?" Mike asked.

"Nah, at least I think she wasn't," Musgrave said. "A guy came up and talked to her for a while. I was watching because I had my eye on her anyway. I thought she knew him at first, but then he walked away. The girl stuck around, but then she took off after the guy. That's the last I saw her."

"And you remembered it that clearly?" Angie was dubious.

Musgrave nodded again. "Yeah. I mean, it was like a thing between them. It was . . . like a little story or something. I dunno. Guess it caught my eye and I remembered it."

A mall cop observing a young girl closely didn't give Angie the creep vibes. It was Musgrave's job, and she believed his accounting of events.

"Do you remember when you saw her?"

Musgrave's face went a little blank. "I'm not sure."

"Do you remember doing anything that day? Buying anything?"

Musgrave gave this some thought. "Oh yeah. I went to Atlas Comics and bought the new Batman book. It came that day. That was weeks ago. Dang, time flies. I wouldn't have thought it was that long ago, but it was."

"What made you remember that?" Good old Mike, always probing.

"The cover had a young girl about Nadine's age chained to a chair and the Joker was standing behind her, but all you could really see was his face. It was an awesome cover, and it stuck in my mind because of that girl."

Angie bought his explanation, no problem. She had a hard time not jumping out of her skin, though. "You wouldn't happen to have the receipt, would you?"

Musgrave pursed his lips and fished out a wallet thick as a Bible from his back pocket. He looked a little embarrassed at its girth. "I collect paper like lint. I don't really toss anything until I can't sit comfortably anymore. Silly habit."

For the next minute or so, he leafed through weeks of his life documented in the form of scrap paper. He unfolded every receipt he had stuffed in his wallet since goodness knows when and eventually handed Angie a slip of paper marked with faded blue ink. Angie confirmed it was a receipt from Atlas Comics, and the item purchased was indeed a Batman comic book. She glanced at the printed date . . . and saw it was dated six weeks ago.

"Is there surveillance footage near those stores I could look at?" It was hard to contain the excitement in her voice.

Musgrave turned to Vincent, who said, "Yeah, it's all online. We purge the data every six months for storage reasons."

"Could I see the footage, please?" Angie kept her expression as still as possible. She was trying to manage her own expectations. If this lead didn't pan out, the disappointment would hit hard.

Vincent left the room and returned carrying a laptop computer. It did not take long to open the security camera system's interface in a web browser.

"A few years back we would have had a tape library to sift through," Vincent said. "Now it's all digitized and easy to find footage. Mostly we use it for shoplifting cases, but we've certainly caught a number of other crimes on camera." He returned his focus to the laptop screen.

Angie got up so she could peer over his shoulder. Mike did the same. Part of the interface was a map marking the various locations of installed cameras.

"Okay . . . okay. So, we're looking for the camera near Heydari Design and Jois Fragrance. That would be . . . ah yeah, here. SF-R2R. That's second floor, rear, second to the right." Vincent tapped the location of the camera and entered the date March 18th. Today was the 29th day of April.

Angie said, "It would be sometime before six o'clock because that's when Sean bought the Batman comic."

Vincent shot Musgrave a slightly disapproving look. "Your shifts go to seven."

Musgrave shrugged off the rebuke. "I didn't want it to sell out. Anyway, it would be late afternoon because I bought it pretty soon after I saw her. That's why it was so fresh in my mind and stuck there."

"So let's watch from four to six. See what we see," Mike said.

Vincent cued it up. The black-and-white recording played in a window the size of a YouTube video. Taken from a high angle. the image resolution wasn't great and the playback a bit grainy, but the quality was good enough to make out faces.

"Can you speed it up?" Angie asked. The anticipation was too much.

After fifteen minutes at four times normal speed, Mike shouted, "Stop!"

Vincent froze the playback. There she was. Nadine Jessup, dressed in a pair of jeans, sneakers, and a low-cut top with a backpack slung across her shoulders.

Angie's heartbeat picked up. No feeling quite matched the adrenaline rush from closing in on a runaway. Her skin prickled and tingled. The excitement was palpable on her tongue, down her neck and arms, an energy all its own. She noted the time on the video playback. 5:15 in the afternoon. "Advance it slowly, please."

Vincent clicked a button on the interface.

Nadine moved in slow motion. After a few moments, a man carrying a bag from Heydari Design appeared in the frame.

Angie studied him carefully. Tall, handsome, balding,

but in a way that suited him. He wore a nice-looking suit, oxford shirt underneath. The black-and-white video meant she couldn't tell the color of either. He had a conversation with Nadine, but the angle was wrong for lipreading. Angie knew people who could do it if she had a better quality video. They must have been talking about shopping, because the man took out a scarf from his Heydari bag. The man and Nadine chatted for a moment, presumably about the scarf, before the man put it back in the bag.

The conversation continued. What could they be saying to each other, Angie wondered. The man took something out of his wallet—it looked like a business card—and handed it to Nadine, who took it a little apprehensively.

Angie studied Nadine's body language carefully. At first, she had seemed a little unsure, a bit defensive, but warmed up as the conversation went on. She began leaning toward him. Her arms had uncrossed and showed openness, receptiveness to whatever he was discussing with her.

At some point, Musgrave wandered into the frame and soon wandered out. Angie saw him right away, though he pointed himself out in case anyone had missed him. Something the man said to Nadine appeared to make her anxious . . . or embarrassed perhaps. She looked to the ground, shifting her weight from foot to foot. She shrugged. She studied the card he gave to her.

Who was this man? Angie wondered. What did he want with a sixteen-year-old girl? What the hell were they talking about? Angie wished the surveillance footage also captured sound. The man gestured with his hands and seemed to be asking a question of Nadine. Then he paused, took out his cell phone, and began a conversation with someone else.

Musgrave wandered back into the frame. He lingered,

appearing to notice the encounter between the older man and younger girl before he wandered away again, but they took no notice of him. The man on the phone tossed his head back, and even without sound it was obvious he gave a little laugh. Then the man put his phone away and returned his gaze to Nadine.

More conversation ensued, but the girl still looked unsure. The man's body language was harder for Angie to read. Disappointment, perhaps? The two shook hands, and the man turned around and walked away.

Angie watched with bated breath. What would Nadine do? Could this be a pivotal moment that would forever change her life?

Nadine hesitated long enough for Angie to think she was going to walk in the opposite direction. Angie's heart sank when Nadine went running in the same direction as the man.

"We need the next camera!"

Vincent checked the maps. "That's SF-R3L." After some more clicking, he got the video to load. It was like a scene transition from a movie. There was the man, walking away when Nadine came running into the frame. More conversation took place, and the man and Nadine walked out of the frame together.

"Where are they going?"

Sean and Vincent exchanged looks. Both studied the map.

"From here? I'd say the parking garage," Musgrave answered. Vincent concurred.

"Do you have cameras there?" Angie was thinking vehicle make and model, a license plate maybe, but Vincent's frown dampened her hopes.

"Light is too low there for these cameras, I'm sorry to say."

Angie gave this some thought. "We need to get pictures of this man to the DC police."

"No problem," Vincent said. "I can get that done for you today."

"Great."

From her purse, Angie fished out her car keys and handed them to Mike.

"What's this for?" he asked.

"You said you had a big bouncy house delivery."

"Yeah. So?"

"So, take my car back to Falls Church and get your work done. I'm going to stay here for a while."

"And what, pray tell, will you be doing here?"

"I think this guy is a predator," Angie said.

Mike seemed unmoved by Angie's observation. "So?"

"So, if I'm a smart hunter and I found a good feeding ground, you better believe I'm going to come back."

CHAPTER 19

Exhibit D: Excerpts from the journal of Nadine Jessup,
pages 35–37

*It was a warm spring afternoon when I left the
studio with Ricardo. Don't ask me what day or
date. I've lost track. Ricardo told me we were
moving out, so I had to get all my stuff together. I
asked him where we were going. He looked at me
and I could tell not to ask that question again. I
got this feeling that I was done. They had tried
everything to make me into Jessica Barlow. But
I'm no JBar. I'm a failure. I'm a loser like my
so-called friends think I am. It was a wake-up call
for me, what Ricardo pointed out. Their posts, the
way they talked about me. Calling me fat. Jump
off a bridge.*

*Maybe I should. Maybe I should go find a
bridge and stop being anyone's problem. Would it
hurt? I think about it. How would I want to die?
Cut my wrists? I hate blood. Maybe pills. But*

what if I just puke it all up? Jumping from a bridge . . . that freaks me out because I'm imagining how scared I'll be on the way down. Then I guess it won't matter. But I hate roller coasters. That's a funny reason not to kill yourself, but if I came to a bridge and got the opportunity, it's probably what would keep me from jumping off.

I managed to get my journal out from its hiding place in the mattress without Ricardo seeing it. Maybe he'll notice the slit I made later on. Maybe he'll think the ratty old thing had just given out. I sure hope so. I don't want him to know what I'm really thinking because I'm so messed up right now. I sometimes wish I would never wake up, that I could just die. It would be SO. MUCH. EASIER. Bye-bye world. Bye-bye. Does Ricardo love me or hate me? I just can't tell anymore. Is there even a difference? Why does love have to hurt so much?

I thought about what he said about my mom. That really stuck with me. Stuck with me like I think about a knife sticking in my throat or my mom's throat. I think about him pinning me to the ground, hovering over me. He could take me anywhere, do anything, as long as he doesn't do that again. I don't want to make him angry. I love Ricardo and he loves me, but it won't stop him from hurting me. He's like a bridge I'm standing on. I could jump off to get away from him, but I'm afraid of the pain that would follow.

* * *

We took the Cadillac. It was parked out front. Keys in it and running. Nobody is gonna mess with Ricardo. He got me something to eat at McDonald's drive-through. Then we drove to some desolate street. I didn't like that I didn't know where he was taking me, but I didn't want to be punished again so I wasn't about to say no or even ask where we were going. He stopped the car and took out a blindfold and told me to put it on. I didn't want to, but he looked at me hard, and I got scared. Then it got dark because I tied the blindfold around my head. He tightened it to make sure I couldn't see out. I felt a breeze pass by my face, but I didn't flinch. Ricardo laughed. Maybe next time I'll hit you, he said.

I thought about the old Ricardo. The one who loved me and made me feel loved. I missed him and I wondered what happened? What did I do wrong? The pictures. It was probably those damn pictures. If only I was prettier, more photogenic, the JBar he wanted me to be. What was crueler, I wondered, to never show love or to give it and then take it away?

The car turned every which way, but I was blindfolded and completely disoriented. I didn't know where we'd gone or how long we had been driving. It seemed like hours, but time has a funny way of passing when you can't see the world going by. I wondered why Ricardo wanted me blindfolded, but I wasn't about to ask him. He wasn't talking and that was my cue to stay quiet, to not make any trouble. Trouble caused me pain.

The car finally came to a stop and I heard him open his door. My heart started beating fast. I had that creepy feeling, like you get watching a horror movie. Something was going to happen. There was a reason I was blindfolded. My gut told me I was about to find out. A moment later, Ricardo opened my door and helped me out of the car. My hand was trembling and he asked what was wrong. I told him I was scared. He said, "of what?" I wanted to say of him, but I didn't want to make him mad so I said of being hurt. He whispered in my ear, do you think I would ever hurt you?

I went from outside to inside. I heard the creak of a door and the air turned stale. Someone was cooking something. Beans and rice maybe. I could smell cigarette smoke and perfume. Ricardo helped me down a short flight of stairs. Now there was a musty smell mixed with the smoke, perfume, and food. I thought of the basement at my house that had the same dank smell. I could tell I was walking on a hard surface. I heard a little splash of water under my feet when I stepped in a puddle. My heart was thundering, my body shaking.

Easy niña, Ricardo said. You fine. You fine. All is good. I take off the blindfold in a minute. You gotta work now for your food. You ready to go to work. That's what I remember him saying. I

*heard footsteps shuffling toward me. Voices
whispering. Laughs. Giggles. Get back, putas!
Ricardo yelled. A girl's voice said look at the
freshie. New meat. I like it. Someone grabbed my
ass. Nice and firm, a girl said, then laughed.*

*Ricardo dug his fingers into my arm. His nails
pinched my skin and it hurt. This was a warning,
a reminder to me that he was love and suffering,
pain and relief all rolled into one. I heard the
sound of shuffling feet. People scurried away.
Where were we? What dark world had he brought
me to? Ricardo pulled me to a stop like I was the
mule he once called me. At last, he took off my
blindfold. I blinked though I didn't have to adjust
my eyes too much because there wasn't much
light.*

*I was in a room about the size of my bedroom,
but the walls were made of wood—cheap stuff,
different types of wood all pressed together. What
else was in this room? A twin bed on a metal
frame, a wastebasket, and nothing else. No other
furniture. No windows. A small lamp plugged into
an extension cord pulled through a hole in the
wall gave off the room's only light. I heard a man
grunting. I know those noises because Ricardo
made them with me and because he made me
watch a lot of videos. It sounded like it was
coming from close by.*

*Where am I? I asked Ricardo. Your new home
he said. I don't like it here, I said. He threw me
onto the thin mattress and started to choke me.
My eyes bugged wide. He let go of my throat so I
could breathe again, but then he took out a*

lighter. He grabbed my arm hard and held the flame to my skin until the searing pain got so bad I began to scream. He covered my mouth with his hand and burned me again.

That's when Stephen Macan entered the room. He was dressed in a suit. He still looked distinguished and handsome, but there was something very cold about him. A darkness I hadn't seen in him before. He sat on the bed. The springs creaked and groaned under his weight. He told Ricardo to leave. He still had that accent I couldn't figure out. I was crying and Stephen Macan gave me some tissues. He was drinking a Coke with ice and he offered me a drink. He rubbed an ice cube over the burn on my arm. He said anytime I did something wrong from this point forward I would be burned. I started to cry harder. What do you want from me?

He told me that I worked for him now and that Ricardo wasn't my boyfriend anymore. I can't have a boyfriend. Not here. He said he tried to make something happen with the pictures, but I'm not going to be JBar. Not now, not ever. I don't have what it takes. But I still have to pay him back for all the time and energy he invested in me. I have to earn my keep, he said. I asked how I'm supposed to do that? I've never had a real job before and I don't have any skills.

The grunting sounds I heard became louder, more intense, and they distracted me. Stephen Macan grabbed my chin and turned my head to make me look him in the eyes. The coldness I saw

*made me shiver. He said my job was to make his
clients happy.*

*I told him I didn't know how to do that, but he
said I was lying. He said I took care of Ricardo
just fine. That was my training period. Now I
have to take care of others for real. My arm was
throbbing. I couldn't stop crying. I felt sick to my
stomach. I wanted to puke. Stephen Macan took
out a pack of cigarettes and a lighter. I shrank
away from the flame, but he grabbed me and
pulled me close to it. Close so my face could feel
the heat and my eyes stung from the brightness.
He put the cigarette to the flame and took a drag.
Then he gave me the smoke. I inhaled and
coughed because I took a big drag. He told me
not to take such a deep breath. He wanted me to
smoke it all because the cigarette would calm me.
It wasn't just tobacco in there, he said. He wouldn't
say what else it was, but I smoked it down
anyway and felt extremely lightheaded. Calmer.
The pain in my arm didn't go away, but it didn't
hurt as badly anymore.*

*Stephen Macan said it was time for me to go to
work. He said I belonged to him now. He called
me a piece of property he owns and said it was
time to, "earn your keep little girl."*

How? I asked.

But I knew. I knew.

*Stephen Macan got up from the bed and
opened the door to my makeshift room. Buggy
was standing there smiling a big toothy grin. He
strutted in, unbuttoning his bowling shirt. He took*

off his fedora hat and Stephen Macan took money from him. I saw this exchange. Nobody tried to hide it from me. Ricardo came back into the room. I was sitting on the bed and he leaned down and whispered into my ear to make Buggy smile or Stephen Macan will burn my face so badly my mom won't recognize me. Then he'd put me down into the hole.

What's the hole?

He wouldn't tell me. He just said, you don't ever want to go into the hole, Jessica. For a second I forgot my name wasn't Jessica. I forgot I was Nadine. Ricardo said he would wait outside for me to finish then he would take me out for lunch and take me to my new apartment. Don't I live here now? I asked. He laughed. Nah, he said, this place is for the work. Upstairs is for sleeping.

His voice sounded far away because my head was buzzing from whatever I'd just smoked. Thank God I was high. Thank God because I knew what was coming. Buggy came toward me with a giant smile on his face that put no sparkle into his black eyes.

CHAPTER 20

Day two of Angie's stakeout and already she was sick of the salads they sold in the food court. She was also sick of the lighting, the pumped-in music, the filtered air, and the echo from the din of constant chatter and footsteps. She felt like a vampire wandering the halls of the Union Station mall, going from floor to floor, store to store, looking for a tall, balding man with a handsome face and good taste in suits.

When she saw them, she tailed young, single girls because that was the bait that attracted this shark. The girls came in all shapes, sizes, and colors, but shared one common attribute—they came, and in great numbers, too. It was a Saturday, and Angie was having a hard time keeping up with the endless flow of bodies that came in and out of Union Station. Everyone there had a story and she couldn't help but wonder if some of the girls she followed were just like Nadine—naïve girls from troubled homes who fled their sad circumstances thinking they would be safer, happier on their own. Angie had been in business long enough to know they were almost always mistaken.

Mike checked in a couple times from his bouncy house party. In the background, Angie could hear what sounded like a bazillion kids making enough noise to drown out a fleet of jet airliners.

"*So any luck?*" Mike shouted into the phone.

Angie scrunched up her face as she struggled to make out what he said. "How do you stand all that racket?"

"*What?*"

Angie sighed. *I'm fine. No luck yet!* She startled a young couple walking by, who shot her an aggrieved look.

"*Did you say he's in a truck?*"

"Good-bye, Mike." Angie ended the call.

The only news she had to share was that she wasn't alone on the assignment. Vincent had circulated the man's photograph to everyone in mall security, as well as Amtrak police and the TSA and DHS security teams assigned to the station. He also sent a group e-mail to all the merchants to be on the lookout for the man in the attached photograph. He said only that the man was a suspect in an ongoing shoplifting investigation. Vincent believed that would get as much attention as the truth, and wouldn't start a panic about a possible predator running loose.

Angie trailed a willowy girl in a strappy dress into The Body Shop, and then into Papyrus, then over to Nine West. She remembered how much she hated shopping. The joy of trying on a pair of jeans just for fun was utterly lost on her. She got her high from making a break in a case, not saving 10 percent by opening a new J.Crew credit card account. Shopping to her was long lines, annoying environments, and clothes that didn't fit quite right.

By four o'clock, she was feeling low on energy, so she

got a green drink at Jamba Juice and sat in an Amtrak waiting area to recharge. She called Bao to check in.

"What's going on?"

"Just home working on that code."

"And?"

"And I've tried everything. Got some crypto guys who are better at this than me to take a few swings. There are all sorts of ciphers and codes terrorists use that we're trying."

"Bao, my mom was not a terrorist."

He gave a little chuckle. "Yeah, yeah, for sure. But the tricks are still good, so we're trying 'em all on for size."

"How's it going?"

"Slowly. It could be a substitution pattern. That's a pretty basic technique. Since we've established your mom was not a terrorist, it makes sense the code wouldn't be too sophisticated."

"What's substitution?"

"Basically it's two alphabets, and you shift one or more characters to the right or left. But these can be super tricky to crack if the alphabet is scrambled."

Angie took out the photograph, spent a moment looking at the girl's face, and turned the image over to see the words on the back. There was that code—IC12843488. Most of the coded message was numbers, which made Bao's efforts a little confusing and perhaps misplaced. "There's hardly any letters here," she said.

"Well, what if *May God forgive me* is in code?"

That made more sense. "So we think the message says one thing, but it really means something else."

"If we can figure out the key, perhaps. But we don't have a lot of text to count letter usage or help us look for patterns. That kind of makes it uncrackable."

"Is there another technique my mom could have used?"

"If I focus on the numbers, it might tell us a different story."

"What kind of story?"

Bao made a hmmm sound. "Think about a telephone keypad. A keypad has numbers associated with letters, right?"

"Yeah."

"So then it's a game of matching. Can we make any words out of the different combinations? There's also the Caesar Shift cipher." Bao was in full brain dump mode, but Angie's focus was too fragmented to let her concentrate.

She gave him a half listen, keeping her eyes out for any youngish girls traveling alone, apart from their pack. Girls who looked like they were lost among the crowd. Girls who seemed unsure of themselves. The streets were a Darwinian place, and hunters like the handsome bald guy were experts at spotting the weak ones.

Angie tried to follow Bao's description of the Caesar Shift, making a drawing on a napkin to keep up. Angie's big takeaway was that Bao had his work cut out for him.

"Keep it going, Bao. I appreciate all you're doing."

"Working hard. What's the story there?"

"Keeping my eyes open. We sent a picture of the guy from the surveillance tape to the DC police, so that'll give us extra eyes on our prize."

"Good deal. Hang tough, Ange."

"You too, Bao."

She ended the call and took a big slurp of her green juice made from kiwi, banana, mango, pineapple, green apple, spinach, and kale. She suspected this "healthy" drink had more sugar than an ice cream sundae, and damn if it didn't taste as good. She stood up and tossed away her drink.

Back to the hunt. The crowds were as plentiful as locusts. Everywhere Angie looked, she saw targets—young, vulnerable girls—but few roamed alone. Safety in numbers. Smart chicas. She didn't feel discouraged. She knew this was the place to be. She also knew that before the stakeout was over, she'd run out of clean clothes and have to go shopping after all.

CHAPTER 21

Greg Jessup might have been an absentee father, but he was not skimping on the cash when it came to finding his daughter. It was obvious after a few days that the stakeout at Union Station was going to be a long one. Angie had no other leads, and she felt confident the man on the surveillance video would eventually stalk the place again.

But when?

Angie, Mike, and Bao took shifts spending day after day at the mall, racking up per diem fees for hotel rooms and meals, without success. It was a waiting game, and she had committed to the strategy. Eventually, she would find her mystery man. It was just a matter of time.

Things at home were fine, no radical shifts in the landscape. Gabriel DeRose went to work, and Angie continued to get new cases, some of which she assigned to Mike and Bao while she took the brunt of the surveillance duty. The long-term stakeout had been her idea, so she felt obligated to take on the lion's share of the suffering. Bao continued to try and crack the code on the back of the photograph without success. Angie remained hopeful and checked in with him every day.

She called Bao after lunch, which she ate in the now dreaded food court. If she never saw another food court again, it would be too soon.

"How's it going, Bao? Making progress?" Of course, she was referring to the code.

"Working on the Flip 5-0 grind as we speak."

"Is that a type of cipher?"

"Um, no. It's kind of a skateboard move. Flip the board up and then the back truck grinds the edge."

"Hmmm. Sounds difficult."

"You know I've been trying to crack your mom's code. If I work on it anymore, I think my head is going to explode. I had to get out and skate."

Angie understood. If she didn't catch a break soon, her head might explode, as well.

The seventeenth day of the stakeout occurred on a Sunday, and it was going to be the last day of her surveillance effort. Angie was ready to try a new approach, though she had no definite plan for what that might be. Days had stretched into weeks, and the end of April became mid-May. After a dreadful night's sleep at the new Hilton Garden Inn, a block's walk from Union Station and her home away from home, she arrived at the mall before the stores opened. Nightmares had plagued her, the kind she hadn't had since childhood.

As a young girl of four or five, she had experienced night terrors. It wasn't something people talked openly about. She'd learned of her bloodcurdling screams, intense fear, and flailing limbs only by picking up snippets of conversation from her exhausted parents.

Later, when the episodes finally stopped, her parents were more forthcoming about her sleep disorder. "Remember when . . ." they'd say.

With time, they could even laugh about it.

It wasn't funny now. Angie couldn't recall a single image from her dream, but she believed the girl with the deformed ear had been a gloomy presence throughout. Perhaps Nadine had been there, as well. What stuck in Angie's mind was a feeling of suffocation. A darkness pressing down on her, something pliable and heavy she could claw at but could not clear away. Dirt, perhaps. She felt things creeping over her body, burrowing underneath her skin. It could have been bugs, it could have been fingers, because they were just feelings.

She had screamed, only without a voice. Nothing had come out, not even a hiss of air. The need to scream, to be heard, had felt as imperative as the need to breathe. Her silent yowl was the most helpless feeling she had ever known. She'd awoken with a start in a sterile hotel room and couldn't stand the thought of falling back asleep.

She'd returned to her stakeout woozy and out of sorts. Her head felt fuzzy, her body ached, and the Advil wasn't doing nearly enough. She went to the Jamba Juice to suck down an energy boost.

And she saw him. He was in line at the Starbucks, two or three storefronts down from the Jamba Juice. She recognized him by the shape of his head and his build. All of his physical characteristics were etched into her consciousness.

Angie's malaise fell away with a snap. She was wildly alert, pulse hammering. She placed her order, careful to keep watch on her mark without looking too obvious.

It made sense to her that he'd show up at this hour, when the crowds were thin. It was easier to spot the loners, the vulnerable ones. Maybe he would see a young girl traveling alone, taking an early morning train to some destination, anywhere but where she had been.

Angie's target ordered a coffee and a bagel. He stood at a counter just inside the Starbucks, leafing through the carcass of a Sunday newspaper someone had left behind. He was there for something other than reading the morning paper.

She found a seat at an Amtrak departure gate with good sight lines and watched him lazily sip from his coffee. Eventually he moved away from the counter, depositing the remains of his breakfast in the trash. Angie let him walk past her before she got up to follow.

He took the escalator up to the main shopping area and ambled along galleries just beginning to bustle with activity. He browsed store windows.

Was he looking for merchandise or searching for something else? Angie made a note of his attire in case she lost him in the growing crowd. He was dressed professionally in a gray suit jacket, white shirt, black pants, and black shoes. It was similar to what he'd worn the day he'd met Nadine.

Angie knew to avoid distractions. A turn of the head at an inopportune moment and he might be gone. Who knew when he'd return? She kept at least thirty feet back at all times, using people as shields whenever possible. Even though she was behind her target, she paced her footsteps to keep from being in sync with his. On the marble floors, the symmetry of the echo might attract his attention.

She did her best to appear like any other shopper—unhurried, browsing merchandise in store windows. She wore a drab green crew neck sweatshirt and gray pants. The clothes she kept in her car were plain, not colorful, never revealing. She never wore popular brands or anything with logos or graphics on them. Those could make people notice her. Dark, muted colors with a timeless look worked best.

She didn't bother with disguises, though she had several in the trunk of her car. Her target did not know her and wouldn't recognize her. but he would know if a stranger always seemed to be near. Angie did what others were doing, glancing at her phone as she walked and shopped, not making eye contact.

She flirted with the idea of texting Vincent, but decided not to. Mall security had no training in stealth techniques. Bringing them in risked the operation. She did pretend to call him, though, and even made up a conversation so it would look authentic.

Just be cool and casual like everyone else and this will go fine, Angie thought. Calm as she appeared, it was hard to contain her excitement. This man could lead her straight to Nadine, unless of course he drove.

She had her Ford Taurus back, having ferried Mike to Falls Church after he drove her car to Union Station. The garage had space for more than a thousand cars; the chances of Angie being parked anywhere near her target's car—if that was how he was getting around—were slim to none. He had gone to the garage on the surveillance tape, so she suspected he wasn't one for traveling by train. If she managed to get a license plate, she would consider it a victory.

Back on the ground level, her target stopped in front of H&M and browsed the window display. Angie walked right by while he went into the store. She crossed toward the main concourse, mindful to keep a thirty-foot safe distance.

Minutes later, the man with the buzzcut hair style in the gray jacket emerged carrying a small bag. Whatever he'd purchased, it hadn't taken him long to make his selection. He wandered the corridors holding the bag, and Angie remembered the Heydari bag he'd had on the day he'd met Nadine.

The man spent two hours wandering and window-shopping. Angie stayed a good thirty feet away, keeping close to the densest part of the crowd. Nothing about the man's behavior changed her thinking about his intention. He was prowling for girls, not presents. She watched him watching. His head would turn with every skirt that passed. His ears were attuned to the sounds of girls' laughter and chatter.

Angie managed to get a few pictures of him with her smartphone. Nothing worthy of a Facebook profile, but she could make out his face a little better than what she'd seen on the surveillance footage. Thus far his fishing expedition—assuming that's what it was—hadn't produced even a nibble.

Her target got lunch at Chipotle—a burrito, a bag of chips, and a soda. Angie didn't want to feel sluggish, so she grabbed a pre-made salad from Chopt, two doors down.

After lunch, the man was on the move again. Same stores, same browsing habits. Angie gave a repeat performance herself.

Forty minutes later, the man approached a girl not more than twenty who was by herself. She was tall and thin, with luxurious long brown hair, dressed in hip-hugging jeans and a formfitting top. She wore a backpack and wheeled a black suitcase behind her. Maybe the girl had just gotten off the train. She did look a bit frazzled and unsure of herself. In other words, the perfect mark.

The man walked right by the girl, but Angie could tell his gaze never really left her. Angie kept walking, too, but she stopped once her target's back was to her, sidled over to a store, and pretended to look at her phone.

The man approached the girl. He talked and she listened. He was animated and she seemed cautious, but receptive to whatever he was saying. He opened the H&M bag and Angie's breath caught when he took out a scarf. He showed it to the girl. She looked at it and nodded her head. She approved. The man smiled and put the scarf back in the bag. He went on his way. The girl remained, seemingly unsure of where she needed to go. The man took four steps, turned around, and approached the girl from behind as she headed off in the opposite direction.

Angie's body tingled with anticipation. The man tapped the girl's shoulder. She turned. Nothing registered on her face, not the slightest hint of alarm or concern. She was friendly, open to him. He took out a card from his wallet and handed it to her. She studied it. The man spoke animatedly, gesticulating. Angie pretended to browse her phone. Whatever he was explaining had some urgency. At some point, his phone rang and he took the call. The girl waited patiently for him to finish.

Angie desperately wished she could eavesdrop on the conversation. The girl smiled weakly. The man held up his hands in a gesture that reminded Angie of the phrase *now or never*. He cocked his head slightly. He waited. Then he gave the girl a faint smile, tinged with disappointment. *Ah well, your loss.* He turned on his heels and marched away from the girl. She watched him go. It looked like a repeat performance of the Nadine encounter. The man continued, but not a brisk pace. The girl hesitated.

Angie approached the girl from behind. "Go away from him, and go away fast," she said as she passed. She didn't break stride. Didn't stop to engage, but the girl heard Angie's words loud and clear.

She headed in the opposite direction. It would have been a bonus to get the business card the girl had accepted, but that would have meant stopping to engage. Engaging could have blown Angie's cover, or worse, let her target disappear. If the man was what Angie believed him to be, the card would be bogus anyway.

The man stopped and looked back. He didn't notice Angie, who took cover in a crowd. Any girl who took notice of the man's snarling face would never consider stopping to talk to him. He marched off in a huff. Angie stayed on his heels—thirty feet back, of course. Maybe he'd had enough for the day. Not every hunt was a successful one.

He took the escalator to the mezzanine level. Angie let a group go in front of her, target still in her sights.

He turned toward the parking garage. The crowds had thinned, and Angie's anxiety levels spiked. She changed her approach as she changed her stride. She was headed for her car, and he was going for his.

She fished the car keys from her purse. He either didn't notice her behind him or he didn't turn around to look. He stopped at a gleaming Cadillac Escalade. With her phone out and held in front of her at an angle, she launched her camera app and managed to snap a picture of the license plate as she passed.

He was definitely leaving. Taillights came on as he reversed out of his space and drove by Angie at a good clip. Her car was parked near the ramp on the east side of

Union Station, while he had entered from H Street. He would be long gone by the time she retrieved her vehicle.

Still, she tried. She paid at the ticket window and pulled out into traffic. The Escalade was nowhere in sight. Gone. Long gone. She pulled over where it was safe and used her phone to access the DocuFind portal.

DocuFind provided licensed private investigators with a wealth of useful data. The movies made this process look so easy. Jot down a plate, hop on a computer, and wham-o, there's your guy. A real license plate search was not as straightforward. Free websites frequently provided out-of-date or incorrect information. The DocuFind results came straight from the DMV, but *instant* was to the DMV as *animated* was to a mummy.

Angie entered the data into the website forms and submitted her request. The results could come back in an hour or a day. Soon, though, she could begin to build a profile of this man, gathering bits of his background the way a bird builds a nest, piece by piece. Date of birth, current address, criminal record, properties owned, that sort of thing. Who was this man? Did he know Nadine's whereabouts? Was Angie even watching the right person? Maybe the entire exchange between Mr. Baldy and Nadine was innocuous.

Angie was on a fishing expedition of her own. She had cast her line with a good-sized hook and some tasty bait on the end.

All she needed was a bite.

CHAPTER 22

Excerpts from the journal of Nadine Jessup, pages 38–40

I've divided my life into two periods. B.B. for Before Buggy and A.B. for After Buggy. I can't write what I did with him. I won't go there. If I wrote it down, it would be permanent and I want it to just fade away. I puked in the wastebasket after he left, I will confess that much. Ricardo came back at some point and said he'd take me out to eat, but I didn't want to go anywhere with him. I didn't want to eat either, not that it matters. I guess Ricardo didn't like my answer. He grabbed my hair and yanked it hard. I screamed because it hurt. He looked me in the eyes and said if he wanted to take me out to eat, I'd go with him. No was never an answer. Then he calmed down because he said he didn't really care what I did. He let go of my hair and I started to cry.

I asked him why he was being so horrible to me. He told me he was helping me. He was teaching me. You can't say no here. If I didn't cooperate every time something gets asked of me, I go into the hole. I wanted to know what the hole was all about, so Ricardo took me by the hand. Not in a loving way, more like a handcuff kind of way.

He pulled me out of my room. Without the blindfold I could see that I was in a basement divided into a bunch of rooms made with that cheap wood. I heard bedsprings creaking and those kinds of groans. The smell made me gag. It was that kind of smell. The corridor was narrow and the floor cement. We stopped at a kitchen area. It was filthy! I always kept the kitchen at home spotless. There was trash on the floor and piles of dirty dishes in the sink. If my mom did the cleaning, that's what our house would look like. The fluorescent lights were blinking, or maybe I was still high. I wanted to be higher. I wanted to not feel any of this. My stomach was hurting but in a strange way and somehow my body knew if I smoked a little more of what Stephen Macan gave me, the pain would go away.

There were girls sitting at the kitchen table, chain smoking cigarettes and drinking beers. A tall thin blonde girl with a strappy dress and a cocky look got up and approached me. She spoke with a thick accent that reminded me a little of the way Stephen Macan spoke.

She put her hand on my face and caressed my cheek. She said she heard about me. Knew I was the new kid and said she'll take care of me. She

*grabbed my chin and forced open my mouth. She
shoved a blue pill inside and closed my mouth for
me. She gave me a swig of her beer to swallow it
down. Then she let me have a few drags of a
special cigarette.*

*You're safe here if you do what they say.
Okay? You understand? Her exact words. I asked
her where she was from. She said Russia. She was
Natasha from Russia. But I can call her Tasha.
She said she's going to be my big sister here. She
asked me my name. I must have given her a blank
stare. I couldn't remember. What did I just smoke
and swallow? That warm feeling was coming
back. Thank God! Thank God for that feeling. I
heard Ricardo say my name was Jessica. Oh
yeah, that's right. I'm Jessica. I'm JBar . . . even
if it's only in my head, even if Stephen Macan said
that dream is over . . . if that dream was ever even
real.*

*Tasha called me pretty. She touched my hair. I
liked it. I wanted her to like me. My legs felt like
rubber, but the sick feeling in my stomach was
gone thanks to the pill. Ricardo dragged me out
of the kitchen and pulled me into the last room in
the hallway. Tasha followed us. The room was
completely empty except for a metal door cut into
the floor. Like a hatch, you know? Ricardo used a
key on a padlock that kept the door secure. Was
the lock there to keep people out or in, I wondered.
Ricardo pulled open the trapdoor and let it fall to
the ground with a bang. Tasha jumped.*

*Ricardo told me to get inside. I wouldn't
budge and his face got red because I'm not*

*supposed to say no to him. Tasha whispered in my
ear to do what he says. That's how you don't get
hurt. What happens down there? Tasha said
nothing. It's just a dark space. He wants me to get
the feeling of it so I understand. All girls go
inside once. If you're good you never go in again.
But if we mess up, if we try to leave, the hole is
where they put us. Do my job and I'll be fine.
That's what Tasha whispered in my ear, or
something like it anyway.*

*I knew our job meant Buggy and other gross
men like him. I thought I'd rather go into that pit,
so I climbed down. I was surprised because it's
not deep at all. It's a tight space and to get all the
way in I had to slide my legs out in front of me
and worked my way down onto my back. The floor
is bare earth and rocky. Painful on my hands and
knees.*

*Ricardo told me to lie down. On the dirt? I
asked. On the dirt he said. I guess my back was
sticking out the hatch door. Soon as I got flat,
Ricardo slammed the door shut and I was plunged
into darkness. I panicked and tried to sit up but
my head smacked against the metal door so hard I
got dizzy. I reached up to feel for the hatch, but
my hands scraped only the rough cement above
my head. It was as if the hatch was a magical
portal that vanished when it closed, leaving me in
this womb of darkness. I couldn't see anything.
My hands were an inch from my face and I
couldn't see them. The hole was wide, just not
deep. Maybe it was the size of the apartment
building? I didn't know. I squirmed into the*

*darkness thinking there might be another way out,
but I got worried I'd get lost down there if I went
too far. I was like a SCUBA diver going under
the arctic ice (I watched a Nature episode about
that with my dad once and it's the only way I can
explain the feeling). If I swam too far out from the
hole, I'd drown down there.*

*I didn't want to move away from the only
way out. I was suffocating on fear. I started to
hyperventilate and got all sweaty. I. Couldn't.
See. A. Damn. Thing. I mean it was pitch black,
the blackest black imaginable. I waved my hand
in front of my face, but couldn't see it. This is
what being buried alive must feel like, I thought.
There was barely any room to lift my head or my
arms. The pill Tasha gave me couldn't make the
horrible smothering feeling go away. I felt the
ceiling until I finally found the hatch. I have no
idea how long I was down in the hole before I
started banging on the door and screaming for
Ricardo to let me out. Nothing. No response. I
banged harder. Nothing again.*

*PLEASE PLEASE PLEASE, I screamed. GET
ME OUT OF HERE! OPEN UP THIS MOTHER
F'NG (INSERT EVERY CURSE WORD I
KNOW) DOOR. PLEASE! I listened. I listened so
hard my ears hurt but didn't hear a sound. Did
they leave me? Were they going to leave me
down there to die? My skin, my head, everything
buzzed strangely. Each second felt like forever.
I couldn't breathe right. My back ached from
scraping against the hard cement. I tried to lift my
legs, but I got maybe a few inches off the ground*

before they hit something hard. I think I wet my pants. Oh hell, I know I did. I was shaking beyond belief. I just kept banging on the door. PLEASE RICARDO! PLEASE OPEN UP! No more cursing. I was sweet to him. I'll do anything for you, baby, that kind of sweet. Anything. How many times did I say that? I can't remember, but it was a lot. Then I heard laughter, and finally—OH, THANK GOD, FINALLY—the door opened and light spilled in. I've never loved light more.

I couldn't catch my breath and I couldn't move, either. Ricardo said that was only five minutes and then he laughed. Five minutes! He said he keeps girls down in the hole for days with just water. Those were the longest minutes of my life. Tasha wasn't laughing. She looked sorry for me and helped pull me up. And that's the hole. Ricardo said don't break the rules and I won't go in.

After that experience, I changed my mind. I'd let Buggy screw me a thousand times before I'd go back in there.

I live upstairs in a one-bedroom apartment with Tasha. I feel so lucky that she's my room-mate. She's the only good thing about being here. The drugs aren't good, but they're necessary and they're everywhere. I'm high all the time now. It's the only way I can get through my day. Writing helps, too, I guess. I keep my diary hidden inside the futon cover, but I think Tasha knows about it. I sleep on the futon because Tasha has the bedroom. It's only fair because she has more time here, more seniority. I asked her how long she's been here and she can't really pinpoint a number. The answer though is in years. I asked her if she likes it here and she said no. I said we should leave and she pointed to the door. "Go ahead," she said. So I turned the doorknob but it wouldn't budge and that's how I found out the apartment is locked from the outside.

The apartment (other than that locked door) is a lot like the other place I lived in when I thought Ricardo was my boyfriend, back when I thought he loved me. There's a small kitchen, small bathroom, small living room with a TV, the futon (aka my bed), and an old armchair that's seen better days. The floors are wood, but pretty scratched up. We're on the third floor of an apartment complex that has a lot of units but not a lot of activity. The girls live in the upstairs units. There are bars on the window but no fire escape. Who's going to rob us? Spiderman? But then I remembered the locked apartment door and the bars made more sense.

Men don't come and go from the front entrance all day long. They go to a basement entrance in the back and their arrivals are spaced out so there's no lines or anything. The basement is where the work happens.

That's what I call it . . . the work.

*   *   *

*I found out that Natasha is eight years older
than me but she looks a lot older than that. I hope
she doesn't ever read this because I feel bad
writing it, but it's the truth. Her skin is pasty and
a bit loose. Her face looks hard like my mom's
and I know it's from drinking and smoking. I know
that I'm going to look that way too because I'm
drinking and smoking as much as she does. I
haven't seen Ricardo in a few days. He's busy.
That's all I'm told. I think he's with another girl
like Mandy . . . or maybe another me . . . another
JBar in the making, and I bet he can't get her
photos right either.*

*The girls are my family now. Tasha, Katrina,
Ashley, Nika, Daphne, Lulu, Daisy, Olyesa. Just
some of the girls I know. There's one American
who is around my age. Her name is Erin and she's
a runaway like me. Oh wait, there's also Jade.
She's older. MUCH older. Like thirties or
something, but I swear she looks older than that. I
think she's pretty though. She doesn't talk very
much. She just gets high and keeps to herself.
Maybe she knows something I don't.*

*The other girls have accents and I think
they're from Eastern Europe somewhere. Russia, I
think. That's Eastern Europe? Right? I hope Ms.
Margo doesn't read this. She's my history teacher
and I'm supposed to know this stuff. Whatever.
I'm not the sharpest knife in the drawer, as my
mother liked to say.*

*The girls, we look after each other. Doesn't
matter where we came from, if we were rich or*

poor, the color of our skin (and all the colors are represented). What matters is we're here, in this life together. This place forces fast friendships. Some of the clients can be difficult, but you can't say no to them unless you're really scared. If you do get scared then you scream, RABBIT RABBIT as loud as you can. Tasha told me people say Rabbit Rabbit at the start of a new month. I guess it's supposed to bring good luck or something. Down here it brings Casper. Casper's a big fat guy who shuttles the clients from the waiting area to the girls' rooms. Casper always wears loose black T-shirts that are as big as sails and black pants and a black baseball hat. He has lots of tattoos and so many gold chains I can't believe he can walk, let alone run, but boy, can he move fast. Nobody really messes with the girls because nobody wants to mess with Casper.

If you do scream Rabbit Rabbit you better have a good reason for calling him. If you're not getting hurt real bad, or cut, or something like that, you just have to do what's asked of you, do what the client wants.

That's the job.

There's a waiting area with a sofa, TV, and refrigerator full of beer. Buggy sometimes works with Casper, bringing clients to the girls, taking money, that sort of thing. I've seen Ricardo a few times. He's back, but I don't know where he's been and he won't say. He's been super sweet to me though, like the old Ricardo. We've had sex a few

*times. I don't even think about all the things he's
done to me. The sex means nothing. It's empty.
It's like a cough, something that happens,
something I can't control but I know will end at
some point. I don't feel anything when we're
doing it. I don't think I feel anything at all
anymore.*

*When I'm not locked in the apartment, I'm in
the room down below. I wait for the clients to
show up and do what's asked of me. I always
close my eyes during it, unless they tell me to
open them. If I have to look, I pretend it's Ricardo
on top of me and we're back in the other apartment, back when I was JBar and he was my
photographer.*

*It's become a bit of a routine, this life of mine.
Sleep. Pills. Smokes. Coffee. The room. The men.
How the hell did I get here? I keep asking myself
that question. I don't even know where I am.
Baltimore? DC? Some other city? The girls won't
tell me. They've been told not to tell me, I should
clarify. But that's okay. They're still nice to me.
I need them as friends so I don't get mad at them
for keeping it a secret. Sometimes we go out
to dinner, me and the other girls. But of course
somebody is always watching us. Ricardo, Buggy,
Casper . . . somebody is always watching.*

*The other girls all look like Tasha—hard, worn
out like the armchair in my apartment. Worn out*

*like the springs on the metal bed down below. I
get whatever money Casper doles out, which isn't
much for the work I'm doing. But I take it and I
don't complain because if I do, I might get
burned, or choked, or hit, or threatened with a
knife, or Ricardo and Casper might do all the
things they said they'd to do to my mom or my
dad if I tried to get away. What choice do I have?
I guess when I'm out to dinner with the girls I
could go to the bathroom and sneak out a back
door or something and just start running. But
what if I get caught? What if they come looking
for me? What if they catch me? I know whenever I
get back home, if I ever get home, people will ask
me why I didn't run. But what do they know?*

They've never been inside the hole.

CHAPTER 23

It was after five on Monday evening and Angie had been in her car on a stakeout for more than three hours. She'd found parking on the street with good sight lines to the front entrance of the Ashton apartments at Judiciary Square. These puppies rented for between five and ten grand a month, so whatever Mr. Tall, Bald, and Handsome did for a living, it was highly profitable.

That morning she had awoken in the same Hilton Garden Inn (no bad dreams, thank goodness) with nothing in her inbox, no name, no address, and no plan for the day. Yesterday marked two months since Nadine ran away. Angie went to the hotel lobby, where they served a continental breakfast featuring muffins the size and consistency of hockey pucks and coffee that was little more than brown colored water. The joys of her job were plentiful. She bailed on breakfast, returned to her room, showered, did some stretching and light calisthenics, and afterwards went for a walk. Her body was stiff from three sleepless nights and her stomach rumbled with hunger.

On her route, she stumbled on a Jamba Juice and put away another green smoothie.

She returned to the hotel and still had received nothing on her target, so she checked in with her father (he was doing fine, keeping busy at work), and updated Carolyn Jessup on her progress.

"So this guy has Nadine?"

Over the phone it was hard to tell if Carolyn had been drinking. It was after ten, so anything was possible. More obvious was that Carolyn's distress and worry hadn't lessened with the passing days.

"We don't know," Angie said. "I'm still trying to figure out this guy's name. It could turn out to be nothing, but it's a promising lead. I'll get back to you soon as I have more to share."

More came a few hours later when DocuFind returned a name. The vehicle matching the license plate Angie had uploaded to the search service belonged to Ivan Markovich. She spent the rest of the morning digging up information about Markovich, including a copy of his driver's license straight from the DMV. Sure enough, the picture matched the handsome guy with the buzz cut she had followed in the mall.

Using Intelisearch, a different subscription database for PIs, she ran a background check. In a few hours, she compiled a thin dossier on Markovich that included information on his parents. The best way to understand the man was to know his past, she believed.

Markovich was a thirty-five-year-old Russian American businessman who would turn thirty-six in January. His mother was from Indiana and his father from Saint Petersburg. They'd married exactly thirty-five years ago, and Angie wondered if little Ivan was already in the womb when vows were exchanged. She found court fil-

ings granting Markovich's parents a divorce only a few years after the marriage, when Ivan was five. Another record showed Markovich's mother had died two years after the divorce, but there wasn't any mention of the cause. Before divorce and death, the Markovich family had lived in Egg Harbor Township, and both Mom and Dad had W-2s from the casinos in nearby Atlantic City.

Markovich's father had a few brushes with the law— two drunken driving arrests and a couple assault charges—but served no jail time. His offspring had no criminal record and no siblings. A real estate database revealed the father sold the Egg Harbor home for a decent profit a few years after the mother died.

Angie couldn't find any trace of the family until Ivan Markovich applied for a business license to start an import-export company in the District of Columbia he called IM International. Markovich had never been married, or at least she couldn't find any marriage certificate on record. There wasn't much on his business, either. No website, no description of what he bought and sold. Either business was booming or he had another way to afford his nice car and fancy address. Maybe what he imported was young girls like Nadine, who had no experience and only one thing of value to offer.

The posh address was Markovich's only listed residence. He didn't own other property, but in terms of assets he was hardly an easy book to read. In addition to the import-export company, he was a listed founder on a reinsurance business, and had various holdings in a number of entities Angie couldn't begin to untangle without returning to her office.

Bao could, though.

He groaned after Angie explained during a phone call what she needed. "What did I ever do to you?"

"Nothing but treat me with kindness and respect. Which is why I'll treat you to a new board and a bump in pay once this case is closed."

"Promise. I'm on it even without the carrot. How's it going for you?"

"My legs hurt, my back hurts, my car stinks, I stink, I feel bloated and gross, and if I drink another green juice I might hurl."

"Guessing you're on stakeout. Still in DC?"

"That I am. I traced the handsome bald guy to a fancy apartment near Judiciary Square. I checked the garage, and he's parked there now. So I'm just waiting to see if he comes out."

Angie shook off the memories and looked up to the third floor of Swank Central where Markovich lived. He had a lovely view of a highway on-ramp, an empty lot, and a vacant office complex across the way. The kind of money he spent on accommodations might have bought him a luxury interior, but it didn't get him a scenic vista.

How he could afford such a crappy view was a question she hoped Bao could help answer.

Obtaining bank and financial records is a big no-no without a court order, but some legal maneuverings were available to her and others in her trade. UCC statements might be on file in Washington or another state if Markovich put any personal property up for collateral. There might be civil litigation, probate and corporate filings. Maybe he had something on file with the SEC. Was he invested in a nonprofit? Markovich might use shell companies for what those in the know called asset protection. Money and property could also be placed into trusts. It usually wasn't a problem to get a court order to obtain trust documents, but Angie had seen cases where a company in Delaware owned the trust, with no name attached.

The game was to erect financial barriers to keep the diggers out and the lawsuit liability to a minimum. All of it was legal, too.

She had a gut feeling about Markovich. His interaction with Nadine and the predatory behavior she'd observed at the mall had sealed it. What she needed was something concrete, something that might lead her to the young runaway.

The hours dragged on, and the waiting became tedious. Markovich hadn't left the apartment. Twice she had snuck into a nearby Starbucks to use the bathroom and got lucky. Markovich's car was still in the garage when she got back. A second set of eyes was the only way to run this stakeout, and those eyes showed up just when she needed to use the bathroom once more.

Mike Webb wore a typical outfit for him—plaid shirt with khaki pants—and was out of breath when he tapped on her car window.

She lowered her window and smiled at him. "How far away did you park?" It had to be a mile away, judging by how hard he was breathing.

"A couple blocks from here," Mike said, hands on his knees. "I ran because you said to hurry. Sorry, just have to catch my breath."

Angie arched an eyebrow. "I think we may need a fitness standard for the agency."

He held up a bag from Subway with what Angie guessed were two sandwiches inside.

"Let's start now, 'cause I'm thinking of 'fit-n-ess' this meatball sub into my mouth."

Angie laughed. "I think I saw that on some Internet meme."

"I get all my jokes recycled." His breathing less labored, Mike sat in the front seat beside Angie and fished her sandwich out of the bag.

"What are you doing?" Angie asked. "We can't both sit in the car. It's a bit conspicuous, don't you think?"

"You said you had to go to the bathroom. I was just going to hang out here until you got back. If he flees while you pee, I gotta fly, right?"

Angie returned a wink and made sure the keys were in the ignition. "Leave my sandwich on the seat. I'll be right back."

"I don't think you can call lettuce, tomato, pickles, and olives a sandwich. It's more like a salad on bread. It's like a salwich." Mike looked impressed with himself. "Hey, do you think that's trademarked?"

"I think you should stick to PI work and bouncy houses. Though I should say thanks for coming down here on such short notice. This stakeout will be a lot easier with you here."

Angie made the bathroom run, but didn't hurry. She stretched her legs and took in some fresh air. The sun had beat away the morning chill and a warm breeze carried with it all the fresh smells of spring. It was hard to trade the cloudless afternoon and scented air for the stench of her Taurus, but that was the job and she was prepared to do whatever it took.

When she returned, Mike had a strange look on his face. Angie got settled, unwrapped her "salwich," and noticed that he had devoured half of his sub. Evidently the new "fitness" program was off to a strong start.

"Got a present for you," he said.

"I was wondering what that weird look of yours was all about."

"The mother at my rental gig on Saturday has a brother who's an ENT."

"You mean EMT?"

"No, I mean ENT as in ear, nose, and throat doc. He was at the party for his nephew."

A tickle of excitement came over Angie. She thought she knew where this was headed. "And?"

"We got to talking and I mentioned I had a case involving a girl with a deformed ear. I didn't give him all the details or anything. He just told me to e-mail him the picture and while you were taking care of business just now, I got a response back."

Angie's excitement spiked higher. She had planned to follow up with a doctor on this very subject, but the Nadine search had sidetracked her. She was grateful Mike had taken the initiative. It was an important discovery. A medical issue, something possibly documented, could be useful as they tried to make a positive identification.

"What did he say?"

"He can't be definite because he would have to see the girl in his office to be sure."

"Understood. Just tell me what he said."

"Okay, okay. He said it was"—Mike glanced at his phone—"Microtia-Congenital Ear Deformity."

"What the heck is that?"

"I'll read you his e-mail. 'Hi Mike, nice to meet you at Audwin's birthday.'" Mike lowered his phone and made a look of disgust. "What's up with these names today anyway? Who names their kid *Audwin*? 'Oh what a cute little baby. I think I'll name him—Audwin.' What's wrong with—I dunno—Mike or Jack, Billy, David, or something, you know, normal."

"Different strokes for different folks," Angie said, repeating a favorite phrase of Walt Odette's. "Plenty of people would have differing opinions on your style of dress, for example."

"What's wrong with plaid and khaki? It never goes out of style."

Angie had no patience for tangents. "Is this even relevant? Who cares what the kid's name is? Read on."

Mike continued. "'The boys seemed to really enjoy the Ghost Mansion. What a hoot!'" Mike smiled at Angie. "It really is a spectacular bouncy house."

"Will you please just get to the point?"

"Easy, easy." Mike tossed his hands in the air. "I'm just reading his e-mail."

"Fine. But read the important part, will you?"

"Okay—um. 'The kids seemed to have a lot of fun. I'll definitely pass your name around—blah blah blah. Okay, here we go."

"Finally."

Mike shot Angie a sidelong glance. "'It is my best guess that the girl in the photograph has the classic Microtia. This is a congenital deformity where the external ear is underdeveloped. The condition occurs in one out of every ten thousand births. The right ear is most commonly affected, as is the case with this little girl. The angle makes it a bit difficult to make a determination with complete certainty, but the ear has a vertical skin appendage with a malformed lobule (that's earlobe). If so, the firm tissue at the upper part of the ear is a disorganized cartilaginous vestige. If you do locate this girl, please let her know that we could reconstruct the earlobe using a piece of lobular tissue from the lower end. I hope this helps. Please e-mail or call if you have further questions. Good luck in your search. Best Regards, Dave Trumbull.'"

Angie mulled over this new information. "I never heard of that before."

"Me neither," Mike said. "But now we know. So, what now?"

The answer would have to wait. A black Cadillac Escalade exited the parking garage and rolled past Angie's car. The license plate matched Markovich's vehicle.

"Now, we follow," she said.

She turned the key and the engine rumbled to life. Timing was critical. Pull out too fast and get burned, but waiting too long risked losing sight of Markovich. Angie let Markovich get down the block before she eased into the road.

They were on the move.

CHAPTER 24

Markovich was five cars ahead and easy enough to spot that Angie decided to pull over and let Mike out. He had returned to DC in his own car, a red Toyota Corolla, and it was best if they each had a vehicle on this tail. If one of them got caught in traffic or something, the other could relay location information by cell phone.

Mobile surveillance is a bit of an art form because every "how to do it right" rule comes with an exception. The amount of traffic and the environment (road conditions, traffic lights, and such) dictated how far back Angie would follow. Because of congestion, she wanted to be close. She got to within three cars of Markovich's vehicle and would try to close that gap to two or even one at the next light if possible. The basic rule was the more traffic, the closer she had to follow.

Mike was easy to spot in her rearview mirror. She got him on the phone, using hands-free calling.

"There's a major choke point up ahead," Mike said. "Intersection between H and Sixth."

Angie thanked him. Knowing ahead of time where the choke points were—places like intersections, toll roads, construction areas, basically anywhere it was possible to get stuck—was the best way to avoid getting caught in one. She pushed on the gas and weaved between a couple cars to get two cars behind Markovich.

Mike got caught at a light, but no worries. Angie continuously relayed her position to him using her cell phone.

Markovich turned left onto Massachusetts Avenue NW. Angie sped up to the intersection, but quickly decreased her speed and made the turn without burning rubber. She didn't want to give Markovich any cause to check his rearview mirror. She passed a slow-moving Nissan as she crossed over 7th Street onto K Street. Other drivers didn't care one iota if Angie was on a tail.

"Did you get your E-ZPass yet?" Angie asked.

"Um, I'm going to file an application. Definitely on the to-do list."

Angie made a *tsk-tsk* sound. "Well, do you at least have your change handy?"

"You trained me, didn't you?"

"And if I did it properly, you would have an E-ZPass." Angie didn't know if Mr. Markovich was going to take a toll road or not.

Toll roads were pretty far out of the city, mostly on the Virginia side. Either way, Angie had her E-ZPass and plenty of quarters on hand for either situation. She also had a full-frame digital SLR camera from Nikon and a digital video camera from Sony. The Polaroid CUBE, which took stills and video, was mounted to the dashboard of her car and recording the tail. One day, it could be evidence in a trial. Notes were fine, but for flawless recall, nothing beat a video recording.

When Markovich turned onto New York Avenue, heading uptown, the setting sun became a problem. The strong glare would wash out her video, and it made it difficult to keep him in sight. Things got a little better when he took a right onto 15th Street. A left would have taken her to the White House.

"I'm three cars behind him. How are you doing, Mike?"

"I got you in sight."

"Hey, you're getting better at this."

"Once I was the pupil, now I am the master."

Angie hesitated. "You really want me to say 'only a master of evil,' don't you?"

"It would be nice."

"Not going to happen."

"Dang."

Markovich crossed K Street and pulled to the curb in front of a building hidden by scaffolding. The black-painted doors to a place called Solyanka opened, releasing a bear of a man in a paisley shirt unbuttoned far enough to reveal what could have been a fur rug glued to his ample chest and enough gold chains to function as armor. He waddled toward Markovich's car.

"Mike, are you seeing this?"

"Seeing this. I can tell you Solyanka is hipster heaven for the Euro set and very Russian."

"How'd you know that?"

"Yelp."

"Good work."

Mr. Gold Chains climbed into the Escalade and drove it around the block. Markovich went into the club.

Angie didn't follow. Her guy was inside, so she found a nearby spot designated for fifteen-minute parking. A minute later, Mike drove up and honked.

Angie hung up the phone and rolled down her window. "Wait for me on the next block."

The wait lasted two hours, but since she stayed with her car, the meter maids didn't give her any hassle.

A little after seven, the sun was making its final retreat and had dappled the sky with an array of glorious colors. There hadn't been any sign of Markovich, and aside from Mr. Gold Chains, who returned on foot, nobody else had entered the club.

Angie's phone rang. "What's up, Mike?"

"I have a good parking space if you have to stretch or something."

"I'm all right for now."

"I got something else for you about our mystery girl."

"Yeah, let's have it." Angie was watching the door to the club in her rearview in case Markovich came out.

"My gal at NCMEC did an age progression on your mystery girl. She apologized for the delay getting this done. I guess there's a backlog and since yours wasn't an active missing persons case it went to the bottom of the pile. Anyway, she just sent me the results. Want to see?"

"Do I? Of course."

That was a huge development. Facial recognition might help Angie identify the girl, or perhaps social media could get the job done. Either way, knowing what the girl looked like today would satisfy a curiosity and could provide a vital clue in the search.

Angie had gotten as far as opening the e-mail from Mike when Mr. Gold Chains emerged from the club.

Mike texted to make sure she saw Gold Chains leaving. She replied that she did. She couldn't look at the girl's picture since her focus had to be on Markovich.

Soon enough, the Escalade came into view. Seconds after that, Markovich exited the club. Gold Chains held the car door for Markovich. No money was exchanged, no tip offered, and Angie suspected Markovich was a person held in high regard. He was on the move once more.

Angie got Mike back on the line. "I'm following."

"Right behind you."

She used the same techniques to follow Markovich out of DC that she had used to track him to Solyanka. He drove north, out of the District via the Baltimore-Washington parkway. From there, it was a series of highways until they got off at the Russell Street exit in Baltimore.

It was hard for Angie to focus for the hour and thirty minutes the drive took. She kept battling the urge to look at the image from NCMEC. She didn't want to give it a cursory glance. It needed to be studied, valued.

What would that little girl look like now? Where was she living? Who was she? But the biggest question loomed largest in Angie's mind. Why had her mother asked for forgiveness?

Even with Mike following, Angie refused to lose her concentration even for a moment. To do otherwise would be unprofessional and undisciplined . . . and uncharacteristic.

They followed Markovich down Martin Luther King Boulevard and onto Cathedral Street. There were some nice shops there, a little gentrified—not a hood, not that intense—but they were on the outskirts of Middle East, Baltimore, a neighborhood patrolled by the Baltimore Police Department's eastern district, and the place most responsible for the high per capita murder rate.

The Wire and *Homicide* had filmed there—which Angie wouldn't have known if Mike hadn't told her.

On Markovich's tail, Angie and Mike drove past a Zumba studio, a flower shop, and an art supply store. The sparse pedestrian traffic showed a blend of races, though white was in the minority.

Markovich pulled into the parking lot of an auto repair

place adjacent to a three-story brick apartment building that had no fire escape. But all of its windows had bars.

Angie wondered if the top floor tenants worried about a rock climber breaking in. *Those bars aren't for keeping people out*, she thought.

She came to a stop in front of a commercial printer over on the next block. It would be too conspicuous to park in front of the auto repair place where Markovich had gotten out. Using her binoculars, she watched Markovich make his way down an alley between the parking lot of the repair place and the apartment building.

She got Mike on the phone and wondered if he shared her gut feeling. "Do you think there's a rear entrance to that apartment building?"

"I was asking myself that very question. Let's watch this place for a while." He was parked on the other side of the two-way street, a few cars behind her, facing the opposite direction.

"You watch for me for a bit. I want to take a look at this girl."

From her PI work, Angie knew a great deal about age progression. It was especially tricky to do with very young children from a single photograph. Face shapes change dramatically by adulthood, making it hard to predict the changes. Variables in lighting, shadows, and expression compounded the challenge.

NCMEC was good at solving that complex problem. Its age progressions had, over the years, been instrumental in the recovery of hundreds of missing children. It was part art and part science, and the folks at NCMEC were kind to apply their expertise to Angie's case.

NCMEC could also help her with identification, since they regularly shared age-progressed images with the FBI and with thousands of police departments across the nation.

But this photo came with no parent for NCMEC progression experts to consult. Nobody could say anything about the girl's personal tastes—how she maybe loved bangs or preferred her hair short. They didn't have photos of the parents as children or of other siblings to better predict how the skull and face would lengthen. Age progression of the single photograph amounted to little more than a shot in the dark.

Angie held a breath, waiting for the image to display on her phone. And there she was.

The older version of Jane Doe had fuller lips than the original photograph. Her eyes were round and wide, but a bit more deeply set, which perhaps was why her smile still seemed a little sad. The forensic artists gave her dark brunette hair and made it long and layered. The face shape they selected was more oval than the young girl's and the nose had grown prominently.

Angie got a sense this girl was from some distinct ethnicity. *Italian,* she thought. The darker complexion seemed to go with her darker hair. She had flawless skin, which was nice to imagine, but probably inaccurate.

She was, however, very pretty, heads-turning pretty. And if anybody did give her a look, they would see a beautiful woman with one perfectly formed ear.

Angie could not take her eyes off the image. This girl was connected to some secret part of her mother's life.

Angie called Mike again. "Did you look at the rendering?"

"Of course," Mike said. "How could I not? Beautiful girl."

"It's driving me crazy not knowing."

"NCMEC will send it around. They're going to see about running it through the FBI's face recognition database."

"That would be wonderful."

"We're going to get an answer, Ange. It's just going to take time."

"Between that picture from New York City in 1988 to this one, I can't stop wondering about our girl's journey. What do you think her name is?"

"How am I supposed to know?"

"Just tell me the first name that comes to you."

"That seems a bit silly, don't you think?"

"Humor me."

"Um, all right. How about—Angie?"

"Ha-ha. Very funny," she said without a laugh.

"Well, that's the first name that came to me."

"Do it for real."

"Okay, okay. Um—Stella."

"Stella? Really. That's about as WASPY as it gets. Did you even look at the picture? This girl is Italian, or Greek, or something. I'm thinking Lydia or Carissa."

"Where the hell did you get those names from?"

"Greek girls I went to middle school with."

"Hey, hold off on naming that girl a second. You see what I see?"

Angie peered out the windshield at a thin man in a bowling shirt with a fedora hat on his head, strolling down the street with two white guys in business suits close on his heels. Street lamps illuminated details in their faces and bodies. These three didn't look like bosom buddies to Angie. Fedora Hat made no eye contact and initiated no conversation with Tweedledee and Tweedledum as he escorted them down the same alley that had swallowed Markovich.

This wasn't Angie's first rodeo. She had a pretty good sense what might be going on inside that apartment building.

"If those three are pals, I'm the Pope," Mike said.

"I was just thinking the same thing."

"You thought if those three are pals, I'm the Pope? What are the chances of that?"

"Mike, please. Not now."

"What do we do?" he asked.

"Do? We watch and wait. See if Nadine comes out."

"What about trying to get inside that building?"

"What about we might get shot."

"Good point. Police?"

"Not until I see Nadine. If this place is what I think it is, these guys could have a direct line to someone on the force."

"Ah, the Thin Blue Discount."

"I've seen it before. If this is some sort of brothel, and we're too hasty, Markovich could make the girls disappear in a heartbeat. No, this is a wait-and-see game."

"Katie's got the kids, and my next rental gig isn't until the weekend. I'm all yours until then."

"Good. 'Cause this might take a while. Nothing like a wet-wipe shower to make a girl feel beautiful."

"Hey, I don't care how badly you stink, Ange. You'll always be beautiful to me."

Angie made a smile Mike couldn't see. "You sure do know how to charm 'em. I'll give you that, Mike Webb."

An hour passed and nothing happened. Fedora Hat and Markovich hadn't reappeared. Neither had the two Tweedles in business suits.

Angie was getting restless. She called Mike. "I need to stretch my legs."

"I need to learn how to aim better when peeing into a travel mug."

"TMI, Mike. TMI."

"What does stretch really mean?"

Angie knew that Mike knew what she was really about to do. "I'll be careful!."

"I'm going with you."

"No, you watch the front of the apartment in case Nadine comes out."

"You know what I've watched? A lot of cop shows, that's what. And the partner-separating thing is never a good idea. You know what else? Forget cop shows. You might as well have a red shirt on."

"What's that supposed to mean?"

"It's a *Star Trek* thing, from the original series. The Red Shirts always get killed. It's kind of a running joke throughout the series."

Angie frowned. "A, I'm not laughing. B, I'm a lot younger than you and I've never watched any old *Star Trek* episodes, sorry to offend your inner geek again. And C, I'm just going to do some poking around. I'll be fine."

"Yeah, sure. That's what every Red Shirt says."

CHAPTER 25

Exhibit D: Excerpts from the journal of Nadine Jessup, pages 39–43

Here's what I know about this life of mine. It's big business. There's no supply and demand problem. None at all. I learned about supply and demand in my economics class. It's funny to think about economics while I'm here, doing this, this effed-up life of mine. School seems like something that happened to me a million years ago. This journal is my classroom now. It's where I can be Nadine again. You can learn by obser- vation. Mrs. Lockard taught me that in eighth grade science. So I'm observing myself, learning about me. But deep down I know Nadine is dead. Jessie Barlow took her place and went from being a future starlet to a present day slut. Harsh words, but I am what I am. I do what I do. I screw guys for money. I don't think this business (yeah, it is what it is) could exist without the Internet. The guys answer ads in places like Craigslist and Backpage and there are ways to make sure they aren't cops. I don't know what Buggy, Casper, and Ricardo do to make certain, but the only cops I've seen here are paying customers.

You can't let yourself go. You can't get fat, or too ugly, or too sick. That's what happened to Jade. Sure she was a little on the heavy side, but not fat, not by a long shot. She was older than us, too. A lot older I think. Maybe her metabolism slowed down or something. Whatever. They cut her food rations anyway. She seemed so weak all the time. Once she fainted in front of me. I begged Ricardo to give her more to eat and he slapped me hard across the face, pinned me to the floor, and put his knees on my chest. I felt like my ribs were going to snap. He told me never to speak to him like that again. I don't tell him what to do, he tells me, he tells me, HE TELLS ME!! And then he gave me one more slap just to make sure I got the message. Jade got even sicker after that. She was hungry all the time. But when they finally started feeding her again, she started to purge. Imagine that. They gave her an eating disorder. Nobody would sleep with her anymore because she was so weak and her breath stank. They tried to fix it. Tried to get her to eat and stop purging. They put her in the hole, thinking that would do it. Scare her into compliance. It got so hot down there she passed out. I saw them drag her body out. She was limp and drooling, shaking like she was

*having a seizure or something. They dragged
her to another room. I heard Casper call her
worthless. I heard Ricardo tell Buggy to deal
with it.*

I never saw Jade again.

*I now know something I didn't know before.
Stephen Macan isn't Stephen Macan. He's an
asshole and a liar. It was all a lie. Everything,
and that includes Ricardo. Without her being
there, Tasha described in perfect detail everything
about my first encounter with Stephen Macan. She
knew he asked me about a scarf for his daughter,
and that he got a phone call from his wife while I
was talking to him. Tasha told me he's done it
before. That's his thing and it was Ricardo who
made the call after Stephen signaled him and not
his wife. The scarf and the phony wife were made
up to make me feel more comfortable. It was all
a ploy. I wouldn't have fallen for a puppy in the
back of a van or somebody offering me candy, but
I sure fell for that.*

*Tasha told me Stephen's real name is Ivan
Markovich. He's a Russian and his nickname is
Stinger. We're his business. He uses guys from the
neighborhood, guys like Ricardo, Casper, and
Buggy to run his operation. A bunch of Russians
coming in and out of this building would attract
the wrong kind of attention, Tasha said. I asked
Tasha why they call him Stinger and she said,
"Isn't it obvious?" Then I laughed because his*

nickname suddenly made perfect sense to me. Nothing in my life had ever stung as hard as Ivan Markovich.

I get drugs to numb the pain—weed, booze (booze counts as a drug), cigarettes (those count too) and Oxy (that's my favorite. Hell, it's everyone's favorite). The high is almost indescribable. It's like you're in agony every moment of the day and then suddenly no more pain. The drug wears off and then pain comes back, but multiplied, way more intense than before. It's not a normal kind of physical pain. It's more like the pain of wanting the drug so badly it physically hurts. It's like the drug woke up a pain that was always inside me. It was a pain I could feel only when I wasn't high. I wanted the Oxy to make it go away. Does that make sense? I'm desperate for it and they know it.

It sure makes it easier to do what they want me to do. Rat follows maze, rat pushes lever, rat gets reward. Rat doesn't follow maze, rat gets shocked, rat disappears like Jade. Me? I stay out of the hole because I follow the maze. I do everything I'm told. Since Jade vanished I've seen a few other girls go down into the hole for one violation or another. All I know is I don't want to go back in the hole ever again. When they come out, the girls are always different. They don't talk as much. They stop looking you in the eyes. They become invisible. That's what the hole does to you. It makes you disappear. But I don't need the hole to become invisible. I just have to go outside where nobody looks at me. Maybe that's because they're afraid of Buggy and Casper who are always my escorts.

One time we were walking to the drugstore. We needed female stuff and they wanted a female to figure out what to buy. I saw a cop on our way to the store. He was about fifty, sixty feet away from us. I was thinking about breaking away from Buggy, screaming to the cop to help me when I felt something sharp poke me in the side. I might have been invisible, but that knife pressing against my back was as real as anything.

They don't let me out much anymore. That's fine. It's hard being outside. I see people on the street and they look so happy, couples and whatever, just people living their lives. One time I saw a girl about my age walking with her parents. She looked at me and I swear it was the first time I felt noticed out there. Our eyes locked for a long time. What was a girl like me doing with those two creepy men? I could tell she was trying to figure it out. Make sense of us. Good luck with that! If I can't make sense of us, what chance did she have?

Girls Like Me by Nadine Jessup

There were girls like me chained inside a
    home somewhere in Cleveland.
Held against their will by a sick man.
I saw them on the news before I became one
    of them.

I judged them. I admit it now. I judged them.
I said, Why didn't you break a window?
Why didn't you run? Why didn't you
  scream?
Because my voice was gone, I know the girls
  would say.
Because my strength was gone.
Because my courage was gone.
Because my soul was gone.
Almost everything about me was gone.
Almost.
One thing remained.
One thing.
It was hope.
My hope wasn't gone.
It never left me.
It was the blanket covering me at night as
  I slept.
Hope is what keeps me breathing.

CHAPTER 26

Angie slipped on a dark Frontrunner jacket, a wind- and water-resistant piece of athletic wear she favored, and made sure she had three things with her before leaving the relative safety of her car—her car keys (right jacket pocket), her pepper spray (left jacket pocket), and her TASER C2 (in a side holster hidden by the jacket). She loaded it with one live cartridge that had a range of fifteen feet. The law didn't require a special license, but she'd made sure she had proper training on how to use the weapon. She'd bought it three years ago for self-defense purposes only, and thankfully had never made a discharge.

Tonight she hoped to continue that streak.

Angie stretched her stiff, aching legs, scanned the area, and saw nothing troublesome. She turned and gave Mike a big thumbs-up, then gestured toward the alley. No way to see if Mike could see her, so she called him. "I'm going down that alley."

"Yeah, I figured that's what pointing to the alley meant," Mike said. "Keep that phone on. If there's trouble, call the cops."

"If there's trouble, I'm going to need my hands free to defend myself," Angie said. "I'll be fine. Back in a minute."

The alley between the brick apartment building and auto repair place was barely wide enough for two people to walk side by side. Bits of litter spotted the dirt-covered ground. Unlike the front, there weren't any windows at ground level. She came around back and gave the area a quick once-over. The two sets of buildings were nestled closely together and formed a second alleyway, too narrow for cars to pass, running perpendicular to the alley she had just left.

It was dark, but nearby street lamps provided enough light for Angie to make her way. The windows on the back of the building started at the second story. A steel fire escape stretched to the top, though it wouldn't do much good with the bars on all the windows.

She noticed concrete steps descending a few feet below ground level to a metal door. It had to be a basement entrance, and she fought the temptation to give the handle a turn. Any living quarters belowground didn't have natural light.

Angie couldn't be certain this was the building Fedora and Markovich had entered. Other buildings back there had other concrete stairs leading to other metal doors. She took another look around. The street sounds so audible on the front side of the building were absent, and the quiet unnerved her.

She hesitated, then settled on a plan and descended the concrete steps to the door that was painted some shade of green. A trickle of fear passed through her, but she pushed it aside. Her gut instinct told her *leave*. Her curiosity told her to try the handle. Angie grasped the silver knob in her right hand and gave it a turn. Locked. She put her ear to the door and gave a listen. No sound. She went back up the stairs and looked left and right. Nothing. No sign of anyone.

The perfect stillness broke when she heard the creak of a hinge directly behind her. Soon a triangle of light cut through the darkness and lit the ground at her feet. The triangle widened as the green door opened all the way. Angie spun on her heels, her eyes growing wide. The shadow of a hulking man loomed in the doorway. The sight of him momentarily stopped her breathing. Shadows and a flat-rim baseball cap hid the large man's face. He lumbered out from the entranceway, followed closely by the man in the fedora.

"Whatcha you doing back here?" The big man spoke in a deep baritone, threatening in every way.

Angie retreated a few steps, but Fedora ascended the stairs, moving with startling quickness, and wasted no time encroaching on her personal space. She thought of running, but doubted she would win a footrace. Days of surveillance work did not enhance one's physical conditioning.

Angie's next thought was of her Taser. A flick of the wrist, and she could clear her holster and get off a shot that would drop Fedora in a blink. But the big man would come at her fast and hard. She knew to control herself. An uncalculated reaction could prove costly.

Fedora looked her over, a smirk on his face. His hand reached toward her cheek, but Angie pulled away.

"Whoa, Casper, we got ourselves a real live wire here."

Casper. Nothing friendly or ghostly about him, thought Angie.

Casper moved forward, but not all the way up the stairs.

Good. Angie had a few steps on him.

"I'm looking for my friend," she said. "I think I have the wrong address."

"You have the wrong address for sure," Fedora said.

She backed up a step, but Fedora seized her wrist with the speed of a viper's strike, squeezed hard, and pulled her toward him. Off kilter, she stumbled, but soon regained balance. In the light from the open basement door, Angie noticed a beer bottle on the ground near her feet and within reach.

She twisted her arm and managed to free herself from Fedora's grasp. "Don't touch me again."

Something darkened in Fedora's eyes. He had a thin, wiry build, but Angie knew not to underestimate his strength or speed, or ignore any possible weapons. His bowling shirt was loose-fitting, and could conceal a gun the same way Angie's jacket hid her Taser.

Keenly aware that any outward signs of fear would be taken as weakness, she kept herself in check as best she could, hoping they couldn't sense the terror that smashed against her ribs. She gathered her wits.

When Fedora grabbed her wrist once again, she didn't pull away. He would have expected her to try and get free, lean back, twist her arm, that sort of thing. He seemed pleased with her submission. It was his first mistake.

"What are you protecting here?" Angie asked. The bravado in her voice surprised even her.

Anger flared in Fedora's eyes as he pulled her toward him. She went willingly.

It was his second mistake.

He put his face close enough for Angie to smell onions on his breath. "My business is none of your business." He spoke with the hint of a Latin accent. It was a hard voice, perfectly suited to the gritty Baltimore streets.

Casper propped the door open with a brick and lumbered up the stairs, taking up roost behind Fedora.

A new figure soon appeared in the doorway, this one slender, female. Not Nadine. But she could have been Nadine.

"What's going on?" the girl asked. She had an accent, too, but hers was noticeably foreign.

Angie pegged it for Eastern European and asked, "Who are you?"

It was hard to see the face because of shadows, but the girl's mannerisms were decidedly unsure. Arms folded, straddle stance with one leg forward, the other back, it appeared as if she might go in either direction.

Fedora squeezed Angie's wrist hard. "Get back inside," he snapped at the girl.

The girl shifted position and the light caught her face just right, giving Angie her first good look. She placed the girl's age somewhere between seventeen and twenty, in part because of her long straight hair and unblemished, angular face. She wore a tight blue dress appropriate for any strip club dancer.

"Are you okay?" Angie asked.

The girl hesitated. "Yes, yes. I'm fine. You should go away." The girl sank back into the basement room.

Angie knew better than to ask about Nadine. Any mention of her name could get her moved or placed in greater danger.

Fedora curled his top lip into a snarl. "This here ain't your business, *puta*."

"Then I'll go," Angie said.

"No. I don't think you will."

Angie heard a click and caught sight of a flash of steel as it unfolded from the switchblade case in his hand.

Fedora's two earlier mistakes were still in play. He had

underestimated Angie, and by keeping her close to his body, he couldn't see her hand moving. Casper didn't have a clear view, either.

With quick hands, Angie drew her weapon and fired. A square-shaped cartridge exploded from the front end of the Taser. The prongs pinned Fedora's flimsy shirt to his skin just to the right of his stomach. He moaned as if he was in the midst of a nightmare and dropped to the ground, his body shaking violently.

Casper lunged forward, hurdling Fedora's spastic form with his arms outstretched.

Angie had taken enough self-defense and martial arts classes to have one tactical doctrine drilled into reflex— if your opponent is looking you in the eyes, attack from below. Her kick was swift and on target. She caught Casper mid-stride, and her shin compressed something soft and exceedingly pliable between his legs.

He let out a howl unlike any she had ever heard and dropped next to Fedora, who was moaning incoherently on the ground. The strike had incapacitated Casper and gave Angie a chance to retrieve her pepper spray.

The canister was hot pink in color, but nothing about its contents was "girlie." Its 1.4 percent concentration of capsaicinoids, the active ingredient in chili peppers, was enough to take down a bear. Not much wind, so she didn't have to worry about blowback. She bent down and gave a blast to Casper's face.

Pepper spray, an inflammatory agent, stings the eyes and makes the skin feel like it's melting. The pain in Casper's groin was probably a tickle compared to the burn he felt. His howls continued until Angie reached for the bottle near her feet and brought it down on his head. The bottle didn't shatter, but the blow silenced the giant of a man.

She holstered her Taser, leapt over the two fallen men, and dashed down the alley at a sprinter's pace. She listened as best she could for footsteps coming up behind her. It was hard to hear anything above the blood pounding in her ears.

She spilled out of the alley, her body off-kilter, and motioned frantically for Mike to get out of there and fast. At least she hoped that was what her wild arm movements had conveyed. She didn't dare glance over her shoulder in Mike's direction, so had no way of knowing if he understood her gestures.

Angie had kept her car keys accessible and managed to fish them from her jacket pocket without breaking stride. She got the door open and the key inserted into the ignition in a matter of seconds.

Mike pulled out of his parking spot with a screech of tires and sped ahead. No wellness checks. He was learning that *go means go*. They would catch up later.

Angie started her car and jammed the steering wheel hard left. The 3.5-liter V-6 engine whined as if protesting her heavy foot on the gas pedal. She pulled out fast, no checks in her mirrors.

An approaching car slammed on its brakes and went into a skid just as Casper stumbled out of the alley.

Angie straightened the wheel and floored the accelerator once more. Her car picked up speed as she risked a check in her rearview mirror. Casper stood in the middle of the road, blocking the car that had swerved to avoid hitting her. He was in a horse stance. Hands out in front of him.

Angie heard a pop, followed by another. Gunfire, though his shots were off target because of the pepper spray. She ducked low and drove blindly for a few moments—anything more and she was sure to hit something.

She poked her head back up in time to see a right turn coming up fast.

She hit the gas when another pop sounded. Nothing shattered, but a loud *ding* suggested the metal on her car had been punctured. Her tires skidded, but she made the turn, miraculously without colliding into anything.

Angie straightened the wheel and sped away.

CHAPTER 27

Angie and Mike didn't stop driving until they were out of Baltimore. They weren't taking any chances. Getting out of the city, and fast, was the sensible thing to do.

The question remained, was Nadine somewhere inside that apartment building? Communicating via cell phone, Angie and Mike pulled into a McDonald's off I-695. The first thing Mike did was give Angie a big hug. The first thing Angie did was to check her car for bullet holes. She found one by the right rear fender. That pepper spray had probably saved her life.

Angie had briefed Mike about the two men she took down, but once seated at a table with coffees in front of them, she went over the terrifying encounter in more detail.

Mike's mouth fell open as a reverent look spread across his face. "That's like Black Widow stuff."

Angie's eyebrows arched. "A spider? I nearly got killed back there and you're comparing me to a spider?"

"No, not a spider," Mike said, almost in disgust. "More

like Natasha Romanova, expert spy, deadly assassin, KGB trained, top agent of S.H.I.E.L.D."

Angie looked a little annoyed . . . or exasperated. Either way, she had no time for his shenanigans. "Mike, is this some sort comic book thing?"

"Haven't you seen an Avengers movie?"

"No. I haven't."

He shook his head in disbelief. "You work too much, Ange. You got to get out more often. Anyway, I just compared you to Scarlett Johansson, who plays Black Widow in the movies."

Angie looked pleased. "Well, you should have just said that."

"In all seriousness, how are you doing? That was pretty intense."

Angie breathed deeply and let out a long exhale. "Yeah, I'd say. I'm going to try very hard to never have an experience like that again. But I'm okay. Really."

"What's your take on all this?"

"My take is Nadine could be there." Angie gave Mike a rundown of her thinking. They had tailed Markovich—the last person to be seen with Nadine—to an apartment building with bars on the windows and two vicious men guarding the rear entrance. Other men had been on the scene, like the two Tweedles in business suits.

But most telling of all was the girl. Impossible for Angie to know if she was being sold to men like the Tweedles, but it was certainly a possibility. What wasn't a question was the fear Angie had seen in the girl's eyes. The guards could easily explain the girl's nervousness, but what exactly were they watching over?

Mike mulled it over. "So what do we do?"

"Somehow, we have to get inside."

"Right, by calling the cops."

Angie returned a skeptical look. "Thin Blue Discount, remember? I want to know that Nadine is there before we give up control."

"Girls might be in danger and we're keeping tight-lipped? Doesn't sit well with me, Ange. Gotta be honest here."

"I get it Mike, I do. But hear me out. When I first opened my agency, I got a case with a girl a lot like Nadine. I don't talk about it because it's just too upsetting." Angie did look upset. This was picking a scab that never healed, uncovering a very dark memory. "I traced her to a motel where I thought she was being prostituted. Her name was Elise and she was nineteen. She had a drug problem and issues at home, but her parents loved her and had hired me to find her, which I did. I got recorded evidence of different men coming and going from her motel room, enough for me to call the cops. When they showed up, her pimp, a guy named Ruben McDonald, barricaded the room and refused to come out. It turned into a hostage standoff that ended up a murder-suicide."

"Jeez, Ange. I'm sorry. I didn't know."

"That's because I don't talk about it. It upsets me when I do. Maybe if I hadn't called the police, if I'd gotten to Elise somehow, if I could have talked to her, maybe I could have gotten her away from that monster. I don't know." Angie drank her coffee. "I just don't want the same thing to happen to Nadine. I want a chance to get her away from Markovich if at all possible."

Mike looked skeptical. "About you doing a stakeout . . . um, I kind of think your cover has been blown. I mean, you did tase one of those guys, and you kicked the other one in the nuts. I think they're going to remember you."

Angie chuckled. "Yeah, that's why I want you to get in there."

Mike recoiled as if he'd been the one tased. "Me? I don't want to go in there."

"Well of course you don't. And I don't blame you. I wouldn't want to go in, either. But you have to find out if she's inside."

"Hey, I'm not stripping to my skivvies, Angie," Mike said. "No way."

"Of course not. You go hang out on those streets. You find Fedora or Casper. You ask about any action. Say you're new to town. Get a conversation going."

"They'll think I'm a cop."

"Make them think otherwise."

Mike groaned. "How am I supposed to do that?"

"You show them the do-re-mi. Pay extra, but not overkill. Flash a few hundred, that should do it. Make sure you describe a girl just like Nadine. That's your type. Hopefully she's there and there's only one. You'll get alone with her. Give her my card, sneak her a burner phone and some extra cash. If you're convincing enough, I'll get a phone call. Nobody is going to check to see if you got your money's worth, believe me. You walk out of the room with a happy grin on your face, nobody will question it. The girl won't say anything, and we'll be one step closer to bringing her home."

"What if they take me to another girl? Not Nadine."

"Keep the phone and cash. Tell the girl you have a fetish that you don't like to touch, just look. It's your thing."

"You can't go to place like that and not touch. It'd be suspicious."

"I'm just saying you don't have to get undressed. Maybe dance with her. Like a little waltz."

"You want me do a waltz with a prostitute?"

"They're not prostitutes, Mike. They're victims."

Mike looked a bit ashamed of himself. "Yeah. Got it."

"I'll be nearby. If things go south, we'll get the cops there in a flash."

"So I can end up in a standoff like Elise? That doesn't sound like a good strategy."

"Let's get to her, Mike," Angie said. "If she's with those monsters, she needs our help."

Mike gave it a few seconds thought. "Okay, okay. I'm in."

"Good. We go back tomorrow. Tonight, I need wine from a box and a bad TV movie."

"Wine from a box? Might be time to take your sommelier off your Christmas card list."

"You know, I just thought of something."

"What?"

"How am I going to explain the bullet hole in my car if my dad sees it and asks?"

"That's easy," Mike said. "Tell him you drove to Baltimore."

Angie's cell phone rang. She glanced at the display and was surprised and more than a little worried to see the call was from Walter Odette. "Walt, what's going on? Is everything okay?"

"Everything is all right, but—"

Angie's stomach clenched, her chest tightened, and her throat closed. *Oh God . . . oh no. Please, please, no no . . .*

"Your dad is fine, but he's had a bit of a scare," Walt said.

Angie felt her world collapsing. A sinking sensation came on, her vision going white. "Is my dad all right?" A crack in her voice elicited an anxious look from Mike.

"Yes, yes, he's fine," Walt said. "We thought it might have been a heart attack, but the doctors aren't sure yet.

He's still in the hospital. Louise and I are with him now. We're just waiting for more tests to come back."

"Can I talk to him?" Angie's voice quavered again.

"He's being looked at right now."

"Can he talk?"

"Yes, it's not a stroke. It's nothing like what happened to your mom."

"What hospital?"

"Virginia Hospital Center, where they took your mom."

"Tell Dad I'll be there soon."

CHAPTER 28

It was evening at the DeRose house. A pale light fought its way into the TV room through a bank of windows that overlooked an expansive backyard. The yard looked neglected now that Angie's mom wasn't there to tend to the flowerbeds. Weeds had sprung up where there used to be none and the colors, always so eye-popping in spring, were notably absent.

Angie felt homesick at home, and that was something hard to get her mind around. She felt her mother's absence in the haphazard way her father stacked dishes in the cupboard (these bowls never went with those bowls); by the type of food he kept in the pantry (*Fritos? Really, Dad?*); by the laundry he had folded but left in a laundry basket in the bedroom; by the thin coat of dust collected on the pictures. Like a painting defined more by what wasn't there than what was, Angie heard her mother's voice in the silence.

It was Angie's home, but it was different now, and it would always be different.

Covered by a blanket and draped in a terrycloth robe, Gabriel DeRose reclined in his favorite chair, switched on the Nationals game, and gave Angie a big smile. He'd spent two nights in the hospital for observation and to run a bunch of tests, and today was his first day home. Already he was feeling like a new man, or so he said.

Angie didn't trust her father completely when it came to his health. He might play with the truth to safeguard his routine, that being work and Nationals games, either on the TV or at the stadium (his preference).

She'd prepared a tray with none of his favorites. She brought him hummus and carrots, cashews (unsalted), sparkling water, caffeine-free green tea, and kale chips she had baked herself.

Gabriel took a bite of a kale chip and made a face a three-year-old who tasted cod liver oil couldn't match. "Whatever this is, it's an affront to real chips everywhere. A chip is supposed to taste good."

Angie held a second kale chip up to her father's mouth. "It is good, Dad. It's just an acquired taste, that's all. And according to your doctor, you're going to need to acquire a lot of new tastes."

Gabriel looked contrite. "I was so sure I was going to die."

"The doctor said a lot of people mistake acid reflux for a heart attack. It's not that uncommon."

"Doesn't make it any less embarrassing."

"Well, you did the right thing calling me so I could get you to the hospital." Walt's baritone drew Angie's attention behind her. He enjoyed an open-door policy at the DeRose household and had let himself in through the front door. He gave Angie a big hug and peck on the cheek, and set his hand on Gabriel's shoulder and gave a squeeze. "How's our patient today?"

"Mortified," Gabriel said.

Walt picked up a prescription bottle of Nexium Angie

had set on the food tray. He read the label. "This is all they gave you?"

"That and some other . . . changes."

Walt's eyebrow arched. "Changes? Such as?"

Gabriel looked down as Angie stood akimbo, smiling at her dad.

"Such as no fatty, fried foods," Angie said. "Maybe some exercise, Dad. A little less work and little less stress."

"Who needs less stress?"

Madeline Hartsock had open-door privileges, as well. She came in and gave Angie, Gabriel, and Walt each a hug. Family was family, even if it wasn't by blood. "How are you feeling today, Mr. DeRose?"

"Just fine, thanks. And you are a thirty-three-year-old woman, my daughter's best friend, and I should be Gabriel . . . or even Gabe." Gabriel winked.

"So I guess cheese lasagna is in the fatty food category," Walt said, sounding disappointed.

"Just a little," Angie answered.

"Well, it won't break Louise's heart. More for us and maybe the Karlsons. Goodness knows they can't resist her lasagna. But hey, it's the thought that counts." Walt patted Gabriel on the shoulder and turned his attention to Angie. "And how are you holding up? Any new leads on your runaway?"

"I've got a guy on it." Angie wasn't about to bring up the scare she had down in Baltimore. Better if her father thought her job was only a tick or two less safe than an accountant's.

Talk of Nadine reminded her of the photograph of the girl. She showed Walt and her dad the image NCMEC had prepared.

"So who is this pretty woman?" Walt asked.

"This is the girl in the photograph I found in the attic," Angie said. "Aged about thirty years."

"I told you about that, Walt," Gabe said.

"Oh yeah," said Walt. "Let me see the original."

Angie got her copy and showed it to Walt. Madeline took another look, as well.

Walt held up the image of the young girl and the age progression version for comparison. "Amazing what you can do with computers these days."

Walt and Gabe were products of a different era, when a room full of computers wasn't nearly as powerful as the phone in Angie's purse, and a fax machine was something of a novelty. Her father had always worked in finance, a little staid compared to Walt's distinguished career in law enforcement. When they could speak in private, Angie would tell Walt all about the two thugs she took down and show him the bullet hole in her car. He would get a kick out of the story. It would be the opposite of her dad's reaction.

Angie and Walt frequently talked guns, police techniques, and law enforcement trends when they got the chance. He had begun his career with the Washington PD, but found his true calling when he'd joined the U.S. Marshals. He'd been with the Marshals Service for thirty years, accruing plenty of commendations and accolades along the way. He was also a wellspring of stories.

Angie enjoyed her long chats with Walt on the back deck, drinking beer and talking shop. He spoke of his marshal days with reverence. She wondered if one day she would look back on her time with DeRose and Associates with the same misty-eyed recollection. Having built the agency from the ground up, she held every expectation she would.

With his marshal days long behind him, Walt enjoyed

traveling and spoiling his five grandkids. It wasn't un-common for him to take off on lengthy solo adventures, or for him and Louise to be gone months at a time. Some-times, Angie's parents had gone with them, but her dad wasn't big on traveling. Instead, he and Walt went on local fishing trips together or blew off steam at the gun range.

Her father owned several firearms that he kept in a gun safe in the basement. As a young girl, Angie found the unfinished basement creepy, and never went down there alone. Her parents used it for storage, though her father kept an elliptical machine down there he used on occa-sion. Hopefully, he would start using it more.

"So any idea who this girl might be?" Walt asked.

"No idea at all," Angie said. "But I've got my guy Bao working on it. He's trying to figure out the code on the back."

Walt turned the image of the young girl over and read it for himself. He gave a few head scratches as if to say Bao had his work cut out for him, and handed both pic-tures back to Angie. "Well, if there's anything I can do to help, you let me know."

"Will do. I have to get back on the Nadine case soon. I think we're close. This may have to wait."

Gabriel coughed to get attention. "What do you mean by soon? I'm in need of some help here, if you hadn't no-ticed."

"Dad, you are not in a nursing home, and you're not even that sick. You just need to take better care of your-self, that's all."

"What about the Nats games? I have tickets for tomor-row night. I wanted to take you."

"I've got to get back to Baltimore," Angie said.

"I'll go with you," Madeline said.

"Hey, you didn't give me a chance," Walt said, grinning.

Gabe took a look at Madeline. "Yeah, maybe next time, Walt."

The next several hours, the four sat in the TV room and watched the Nats dismantle the Cubs. Well, Madeline, Gabriel, and Walt watched the game. Angie was busy going over e-mail, answering voice messages, and making sure the agency and her farmed-out cases continued to run smoothly. She touched base with Bao only to learn he had made more progress with his skateboard tricks than her mom's mysterious code, but it wasn't for lack of trying.

She also got in touch with Mike Webb, who was at a bar a few blocks from Angie's Alley, as he called it.

"Any luck getting inside that apartment building?"

"I haven't seen Hat Man or Casper the Hefty Ghost since you went all ninja on them," Mike said.

"Well, are you looking?"

"I'm at a bar. Of course I'm looking."

"For the men, Mike. Not a hookup."

"Oh. Well, I'm looking for them, too. I'm blending here. I'm being seen, so when I make the approach, I'll be a known entity, not some stranger who could be a cop."

"Right. What's your cover? That's a pretty crappy part of town to just hang out in."

"Restaurant consultant. And it's not that bad here. There's a couple good places to eat. A chicken joint and some gyro thing. And I got a nice hotel."

"How nice, Mike?"

"Nice."

"Mike."

"I'm away from the kids, Ange."

"Okay, okay. Just make it nice-*ish*, all right?"

"Yeah, yeah. How's your pop holding up?"

"Better, thanks. Call when you got something. And Mike, thanks for being there for me. I owe you."

Walt left during the seventh-inning stretch, but Madeline made it all the way to the ninth. "We're still on for next week, right?"

Angie slapped her own forehead. "Sarah's mom."

"Every year. She looks forward to our visit."

"I'll be there, of course," Angie said as she gave Madeline a hug. *And Sarah won't, because Sarah's dead. Sarah's body has decomposed down to the bones.* Angie kept her thoughts private, but Madeline would have agreed.

When the house was finally quiet, her father snoring softly in his chair, the e-mail queue down to something respectable, the phone calls answered, the work fires all put out, Angie got into her pajamas and read a magazine in her old bedroom, but not on her old bed. The home had been renested after Angie left for college, the furniture changed long ago, and all echoes of her childhood subsequently silenced. All echoes except for the one made by a little girl Angie didn't know, who had some connection to her and to her mother.

All this got Angie thinking about the attic where she'd found the picture in the jewelry box. She would let her father sleep in that chair a little longer, so she could return to the attic uninterrupted.

She began rummaging through boxes, plastic containers, and sundry bags, mostly filled with clothes. There was nothing of real interest, nothing until she found a container with her mother's old check registers inside. There were boxes full of registers going back years—decades, actually. Not that this surprised Angie, who knew of her mother's penchant for keeping papers because she was too busy to shred them, and never threw anything in the trash that could be used by identity thieves, even bank registers from accounts closed long ago.

It was fun and a little sad to review a lifetime of purchases. She found plenty of pedestrian entries—food, clothing, utility bills—but the more personal ones were what Angie found most touching, including all the lessons (dance, swim, horseback riding, tennis, soccer, art camps); all the home repairs; all the charitable giving, including one check for fifteen hundred dollars labeled a loan made out to Susie Banks, a close friend of Kathleen's. Aunt Susie, to Angie. All the women close to her mother were aunts to Angie, except for her real aunts, who Angie didn't know.

As Angie looked at her mother's handwriting, she thought of the words on the back of the photograph. *Forgive me.* "Forgive you for what, Mom?" she said aloud.

As she flipped through the check registers, years passing in seconds, a blur of purchases speeding before her eyes, one entry caught her eye. It was a two-hundred-dollar sum paid to MCEDC and recorded as "Microtia Gift." The gift had been made five years ago, recorded as paid on March the fourth.

Microtia was the little girl's ear deformity. Angie had looked up the condition online, but learned nothing revealing or helpful in her search for the girl's identity. Using her phone, Angie typed MCEDC into Google and found the Microtia-Congenital Ear Deformity Center in Burbank, California. From what she could tell, it looked to be the world's most prominent institute for research and surgical repair of microtia and a related condition called atresia.

Angie combed the check registers again with a different focus. The more recent check registers should be

downstairs in her mother's desk, but in these older registers she soon came upon another entry for a payment to
MCEDC, that one also made on the fourth of March, also
for two hundred dollars. She kept looking, register after
register—thirty or so registers in total, stored in a dozen
check boxes. Angie found the same entry made year after
year. The checks were always written on the fourth of March
and always for two hundred dollars, which told Angie it
was significant, though she had no idea why.

The last entry Angie found dated back to 1988. It might
have been the first entry recorded. She didn't know if other,
older registers were anywhere else in the house.

Downstairs, she rifled through her mother's desk and
found her more recent checkbook registers. She flipped
through pages, but did not have to go back very far. A little
over a month before her death, Kathleen DeRose wrote a
two-hundred-dollar check to the MCEDC on March the
fourth.

Angie sat in her mother's office chair, spun it a few
times, thinking what it could mean, knowing she would
end up calling Bao.

Angie's phone rang. She was sure it was Bao calling
her. "Were your ears ringing?"

It wasn't Bao. It was Mike. "Ange, I got a joke for
you. Three pimps walk into a bar."

Angie gasped. "They're there?"

"Mr. Fedora, Casper the Friendly Killer, and some tall,
thin, good-looking guy I hate on account of those very at-
tributes. A couple girls are with them, and they don't look
like they subscribe to *Good Housekeeping*, if you get my
drift. I'm going to strike up a little conversation. See what
happens."

"You be careful as can be."

"Hey, I'm Captain Careful, the world's dullest super-hero."

"Listen, if you can't get inside, see if one of the girls can get Nadine the burner phone and my business card. The message is we want to help. Don't play the hero, Mike. Got it?"

Mike hummed a few bars from Superman's theme song in response.

CHAPTER 29

Exhibit D: Excerpts from the journal of Nadine Jessup, pages 44–50

I am here in the basement on my bed (my bed, ha that's a good one, like I want to claim it for my own . . . mine, mine, mine). Anyway, here I am on a bed in my, oh let's call it "designated area," my cube (like where my dad's employees work) down in this bogus maze of makeshift rooms. I'm staring up at a ceiling carpeted with so much mold I want to gag, waiting for something to happen, something I don't want to have happen. I don't want another job, another man, but someone will show up because someone always shows up. To pass the time, I'm sneaking in a little journaling, but it doesn't make me feel any better. I still feel sick and dirty and disgusting. Whatever was me, the old me, I think has rotted away and now whatever I am is all that's left.

At least I have something inside me to numb the pain, something Tasha gave me, something small and blue that makes the mold on the ceiling ripple like waves and my body feel weightless and my soul feel free. I can do anything in this state of mind. Even let them use my body as an ATM for "Stinger" Markovich, Ricardo, and the others. I understand that I'm here, trapped in this situation because of me and nobody else. I could have said no to the pictures. I could have somehow not fallen for Ricardo, not trusted him, escaped from that first apartment when he gave me the chance. I could have said no to the work, no to using my body, but I didn't fight them because I was afraid—afraid of them—and now I'm a part of this. You can't separate a part from the whole without suffering, Ivan said to me. He told me you can't cut off an arm and not have it bleed.

I could try and leave this place, sure, but I know it's going to hurt if I do. Somehow it's going to hurt badly, so I'm stuck here and probably I'll stay here until I disappear like Jade, the older girl they starved until she wouldn't eat. I'll stay here until the day another girl takes my place and lies on this very bed (my bed/her bed), staring up at the same mold-covered ceiling.

I saw Ricardo for the first time in a while. He kissed me on the lips, but I played possum, acted like I was dead, didn't kiss back at all, and he didn't like it so he didn't stick around for anything more. He said he's with a new girl now and he's not going to bring her here because he loves her too much. Strange. For all the horrible things Ricardo has done to me, horrible horrible things, I thought he couldn't possibly hurt me any more than he already had.

I was wrong.

The craziest thing just happened. I mean crazy! I'm still freaking out. My heart is racing like mad and Tasha gave me something to calm me down, but I don't think it's working. I don't know what to do. I'm so happy I want to burst into tears, but I'm so scared I want to cry, as well, so I'll be back in a minute because I'm going to the bathroom to cry my eyes out and probably puke.

Miss me? Ha-ha. No, really I did leave and I really did cry, but I didn't puke. Whatever, I feel so much better, but I'm still not sure what to do or what to make of what just happened. Here's the skinny. I'm downstairs in the room (yes, that room) just chillaxin, high as a raindrop spit from a cloud (my friend Brianna used to say that) so that was good. I'm numb to this now, so I can be (as my mom would say) flippant about what it is I do to survive, though the pills help, the pills make it a whole lot easier to get the job over with. And this job was some middle-aged guy with a middle-aged belly and it was gross what he came here to do so I hated him right away. But I played with him because that's what's expected of me and the alternative is the hole.

Tasha was awake when I got back upstairs. She was making tea, something she did a lot. She had on gray sweats and a blue T-shirt and looked super relaxed which was so weird to me. This was just Tasha's life. This was her normal and I guess it was my normal, too. It was hard to get my head around that one. When we weren't downstairs being fantasy gals or release valves for these sicko Johns we wore sweats and drank tea and watched television and did Sudoku and read books and cried. Just because we are prostitutes doesn't mean we stopped having feelings.

Tasha had a funny look on her face and I asked her what was wrong. She told me she went out with Ricardo, Casper, and Buggy for drinks with a couple of the girls. I knew which ones without her having to say. Getting out of here had everything to do with how long a girl had been on the job. Like I wrote, I go out rarely, and I'm always accompanied. For the most part I'm kept indoors like a house cat. Tasha has more freedom because with more years comes more trust.

Tasha told me she was hanging out at Club 324 and some guy came up to her and started talking. Casper got all territorial (her word), but she told him to go away. It could be business, right? Then this guy starts asking questions about

me. He describes me anyway, calls me Nadine
(Tasha didn't know my real name) and he showed
her a picture of me on his phone. He told her my
mom was looking for me and she had hired him to
find me. Tasha told me she didn't say yes or no,
but the guy is persistent. He says he followed Ivan
to the apartment building. And they think I might
be with him. He thinks he knows what this place
really is. So Tasha on the sly told this guy that I'm
fine and healthy and all that, and then she gave
him the cold shoulder, but not before the guy gave
her a phone and a card of some woman named
Angie.

After this big news I'm all kind of freaked out.
Tasha poured us both a cup of tea and we sat on
the futon aka my other bed. She placed the phone
and business card on the coffee table and told me
the choice was mine. My body went hot and cold
at the same time and it had nothing to do with
being high (which I was BTW). It was the
weirdest feeling ever, I mean so surreal I can't
even begin to explain it. Tasha knew exactly what
that phone call might mean. Police. A raid. A
rescue. But what about her? This was her life
now. She had no family. No money. No relatives.
She had nothing but Casper, Buggy, Ricardo, and
Ivan. And horrible as it was, it was better than the
unknown and that's where she'd be headed, into
the unknown. No money for food, no place to live,
and nobody to supply her with pills. Believe me,
the pills were an important part of the equation.
But she said she knows what this life is, and what
it will do to me. It'll turn me into her and she

doesn't want that for me, so she gave me the phone and said the choice is mine. But what will happen to Tasha if I make that call? What would happen to me?

And that's when I started to panic. Could I just leave? Should I? What was I going to tell my mom and dad once I got home? What would they think of me when they found out what I had done? I don't belong there anymore. I belong here, right where I am.

Tasha called me her little sister. She said she'd understand if I made the call and I shouldn't worry about her. I told her how scared I was, how I was afraid of going home, afraid if I left they would find me and kill me or kill my mom and dad. If I left, they would put everyone who stayed behind down in the hole, including Tasha. I wanted Tasha to reassure me that I was over-reacting. I wanted her to tell me I had nothing to worry about, that nothing would happen to me, or to her, or to my parents. That's what I wanted her to say. Instead, she told me she understood and that she'd feel the exact same way.

CHAPTER 30

Angie left her father's house at 4:30 in the morning. She woke her dad to tell him she was going, and without delay got in her car and drove out of town. She would talk to him about the check registers later, when he was more awake and his memory could be trusted. She drove north instead of east, a long detour on her way to DC because some news had to be delivered in person.

Carolyn Jessup came to her front door dressed in a checkered bathrobe, looking half asleep. Angie had awoken her with a phone call made from Carolyn's front porch. She made the call so Carolyn wouldn't have to wait long to find out what Angie had come to share. Carolyn's hair was tangled, and her eyes, ringed with dark circles, showed the strain of her daughter's absence.

"We think we've found her," Angie said. "We believe your daughter is alive and in good health."

Carolyn's legs buckled as her eyes misted over. Angie grabbed Carolyn's arm to hold her steady.

Carolyn placed a hand to her chest. Her ragged breathing made it difficult to speak. "Where—where is she?"

"Baltimore," Angie said.

Carolyn let out a sob. "Why? Who is she with?"

"Invite me in. I'll tell you everything I know."

Soon they were seated at a kitchen table. Carolyn didn't offer Angie any tea, not even a glass of water. She only had time to get the facts.

Angie explained to Carolyn how they had followed Nadine's trail from Union Station to an apartment building in Baltimore. She told her about Mike's encounter at a bar with a woman he believed knew Nadine.

"Who does she know in Baltimore?" Carolyn asked.

Angie pulled her lips tight. Breaking news usually involved breaking hearts. "You need to brace yourself. We think Nadine is being trafficked for sex."

Carolyn made an expression Angie had seen on people who had just been shot—horror, shock, sadness, and confusion blended into one.

"She's just a girl," Carolyn said, her lower lip trembling. "She's my baby girl." Tears. "I need a drink. Excuse me a moment."

Angie waited at the kitchen table while Carolyn got the vodka from behind the cereal. *Who is she hiding it from?* Angie wondered. *Herself?*

Carolyn poured a shot of vodka into a chilled glass she got from the freezer, downed it, and then poured another. "What now?"

"Now we try to get her out of there. Safely."

"Can't she just leave?"

"It's not that easy. Your daughter is very scared."

"Who has her?"

"We think it's a Russian named Ivan Markovich. We don't know the other men involved. We're working on getting IDs. These are very bad people, Carolyn, I'm not going to lie to you. Your daughter is in danger."

"Then call the damn police and get her out of there."
Carolyn's jaw tightened as her eyes turned fierce.

"We already did. My associate Mike has gone to the
Baltimore PD and filed a report."

"And there's been no action taken?"

"No."

"Well, why not?"

"Hard to say. These things happen. They did send a
cruiser by the apartment, but that's it. Nobody is storming
the castle. It could be that the police have used the service, if you know what I mean, and some detective with
the Baltimore PD has an incentive to do nothing."

Carolyn's disgusted face said it all. Angie didn't tell
her about the runaway named Elise and the standoff and
how that police action turned out. In a way, Angie was
glad no action had been taken.

"Look, I know this is hard to hear. I do. But Mike gave
the woman a phone to give to Nadine. There's a chance
we can coax her out of there, and that's what we're going
to try and do."

"But they're going to hurt her."

"I don't think so. They want your daughter healthy so
she can . . . can . . . work for them." *Work for them.* Angie
grimaced at her turn of phrase. What else was she supposed to say? The truth, she supposed, but Carolyn was
smart enough to figure out the euphemism all on her own.

"Can you get her out?" Carolyn's hands were trembling, and the third shot of vodka didn't quiet the shakes.

"She's probably rooted. I want to give her some time
to think her options over. We believe she has a phone
now, and my card."

"Let me call her or text even." Carolyn sounded desperate, but Angie was going to hold firm.

"We're waiting for her to make the first contact."

"Why?"

"Because we can't be certain who has the phone. It could be the woman we gave it to, or Nadine, or someone else. What we don't want is for Nadine to be linked to the phone. It could be dangerous for her. Best to wait and see if she makes first contact. I'm counting on it that she will. We're going back on stakeout. When she wants out, we'll be ready to receive her. Meanwhile, we'll keep putting pressure on the police."

Carolyn stood, but her legs wouldn't hold her. She knelt and put her head in Angie's lap. Her sobs came in waves, her body convulsed in sputters.

Angie stiffened at first. Her job was to hunt, to find, to retrieve. She was a task-oriented person, goal-driven, and so she froze, unsure exactly how to comfort Carolyn in her time of grief. Then, very gingerly at first, but soon with more confidence, Angie stroked the back of Carolyn's head and shushed her the way her mother had consoled her.

"Promise me you'll bring her home," Carolyn said, her voice cracking.

Angie knew better. So much could go wrong, so many terrible things could happen. Of course she knew better. "I promise," she said, smoothing the back of Carolyn's head. "I promise."

Raynor Sinclair had followed Angie all the way from Arlington to Potomac and that amused him. Wasn't she the purported expert at tailing someone? And he was tracking Angie in plain sight, never once rousing her suspicion. She made a pit stop at her apartment before journeying to Maryland, but the detour wasn't to evade him. She had gone upstairs and came down minutes later, taking enough time to water a plant and check the mail, he supposed. There were dozens of ways Angie could have lost him if she had wanted to, but she took no counter-measures.

Highway driving made it especially easy to spot him in his Acura SUV. All Angie had to do was change speed—say, drop her speed from seventy-five miles per hour down to sixty. If she still saw his car in her rearview mirror, it would be cause for concern. With little traffic on the roads at that time of morning, he was relatively easy to spot, but she was clueless. She was focused on all the wrong things.

Good for him, bad for her.

Angie left the highway. Raynor did the same, follow-ing at a safe distance as she drove along leafy streets dot-ted with fine-looking homes, all with well-tended lawns.

They reminded him of his childhood home in Madi-son, Wisconsin. More specifically, the lawns reminded him of his father, now long dead, the man who had taught him how to grow grass and the proper way to cut it. No grass grew where Raynor lived now, a two-bedroom lux-ury apartment in DC that boasted of being a big-city sanc-tuary in the middle of everywhere.

His father had taught Raynor many things, including how to hunt. Raynor might have shunned grass for a con-crete landscape, but he still loved to hunt, and tracking Angie counted as sport.

A hundred or so yards up ahead, she pulled to a stop. Raynor pulled over as well. From his car, he watched her ascend a flight of stairs to the wide front porch of a colo-nial home. A woman came to the door, and Angie went inside. No other cars were parked curbside, so he decided to drive around the block. A check of the address told him it was Carolyn Jessup's residence. Angie's business there was perfectly justified.

He had a good idea where she'd be headed next. With only one way to get there from where he was, Raynor drove off and found parking where he could wait without being conspicuous. Eventually, he would affix a GPS tracker to the undercarriage of Angie's car so he could watch her all the time. The technology, though, didn't feel like sport. It felt like cheating.

Sport. Hunting. Raynor again thought of his father, Truman Sinclair, a stoic disciplinarian who'd corralled four sons with lies about needing only the Bible, when what he really used was his belt. Of the four brothers, Raynor, who was the youngest, was also the best hunter. He could innately judge his quarry's pace. As Wayne Gretzky famously said of the hockey puck, Raynor went not to where the animal was, but to where the animal was going to be. He could spot blood on a trail as if he possessed a hound's nose for the scent.

A memory came to him—the blur of a grouse carving through thickets.

It was a difficult shot, one Raynor's brothers and his highly skilled father would have passed on. But Raynor thought he could hit the bird, even though his backside hurt from the belt beating he'd taken the day before. Only fourteen years old, and somehow he could block out his excruciating pain to get a lock on his target.

Raynor and his father were grouse hunting by themselves.

"Quality time," his dad called it as he tightened the laces of his boots. The hunt was Truman Sinclair's way of apologizing for the thrashing he had given his son over a

stack of video games Raynor stole from the home of a neighborhood kid.

He had been at the boy's home the day of the theft, so it wasn't a stretch when suspicion fell on him. Parents exchanged phone calls, and upon returning home from his job at the insurance company, Truman Sinclair went on a hunting expedition of a different sort. In no time, he found the missing items in a shoebox stashed underneath Raynor's bed. Confronted with the evidence, Raynor had no choice but to confess. Punishment was meted out swiftly and without mercy. The belt, oh the damned belt.

Tears clung to Rainer's eyes as his father drove him to the neighbor boy's home to return the stolen items. The pain from the welts on his backside paled when compared to the agony of his humiliation. While the boy stood in the doorway of his ranch home looking smug, the mother stood behind her son as triumphant as a queen rejoicing over her enemy's head on a spike.

She wasn't rejoicing the day Raynor shoved a stick through the spokes of her beloved son's bicycle wheel as he barreled down Ridge Road. The bike stopped rolling, but the boy kept going—right over the handlebars and onto the unforgiving pavement, where he landed with a crunch. The boy suffered a cracked skull, broken leg, and a raft of internal injuries. Police never did find out who shoved a branch through the bicycle wheel. That was because while the boy lay on the ground, bleeding from the ears, Raynor set the heel of his boot on the boy's throat and swore he'd kill him if he ever told.

The kid spent two weeks in a hospital recovering. He was really never quite the same. Popular and preppy before, Smash Mouth (that's what Raynor called him) turned moody and withdrawn. At a class reunion years later, Raynor heard that Smash Mouth, then in his twenties, had *overdosed on painkillers while living in his parents' basement.*

But all that happened after the hunt; after the grouse burst from the thicket, its wings flapping wildly for flight; after Raynor pulled the trigger and peppered the bird's meaty chest with shot; after the bird went into a hapless tailspin before gravity did its job; after his father burst from their hiding place to confirm the kill. Raynor watched his father trudge through the dense grasses with a look of joy bordering on reverence.

How can he be smiling? *Raynor thought.*

Raynor's bottom bled into his underwear a full day after his beating. He had to squat to take a crap, and would have to do so for at least a week. The worst part of all was that he would get another thrashing, probably sometime soon, over something just as stupid as those video games.

Truman picked up the bird and held it up for Raynor to see. A broad smile cut his face.

But Raynor wasn't smiling. He was back on his bed, his pants down to his ankles, his teeth clenched together, waiting with dreaded anticipation for the next blow from his daddy's leather whip.

Everything went black.

But it couldn't have been all black, or he'd have missed his target. He remembered the tension against his finger as he pulled the trigger. He remembered the crack and an echo like a peal of thunder. He remembered seeing his father's neck explode, blood spewing from several holes as if pumped through a strainer, a confused look replacing the beam of pride.

* * *

Gravity took his father down, same as it did that dead bird. Eventually the police came. Raynor refused to leave his father's side. He was sputtering and crying, all very real because he was deeply upset. He loved his father, but hated what his father did to him. None of that ever came up during the investigation. He never spoke a word of the abuse. His brothers never suspected their own kin capable of murder, or they didn't share the theory if they did.

Truman Sinclair's death was later ruled a tragic hunting accident.

Raynor's punishment was the guilt he would carry for the remainder of his days. It hurt a lot less than the belt, though he accepted that he did miss his father, strange as that was to admit. He hunted as a reminder of the better times. Hunting in Virginia was damn good sport, with big game like elk, bear, and deer to bag and plenty of birds to shoot.

Raynor wasn't so lost in thought that he failed to notice Angie drive past his car. He waited a few beats before pulling out into traffic behind her. He could bag all the elk he wanted, but nothing exhilarated him quite like hunting people.

CHAPTER 31

"**B**ack at it" meant Angie was back in her car—the Taurus with a bullet hole in the rear—and Mike was in his—the little red Corolla. Angie would submit the repair bill to Greg Jessup, along with the charges for Mike's hotel room and a host of other expenses they'd racked up on this case. Angie also was back to having aching legs, a stiff back, and a bloated belly, this time from the stale bagel she ate because she couldn't find a decent meal in the neighborhood.

They were down the street from the brothel, or the *alleged* brothel as the Baltimore PD seemed to think of it. The response (or lack thereof) infuriated Angie, who put aside her fears about Elise and another murder-suicide bloodbath. She wanted more engagement from law enforcement, though it went without saying she wanted a different outcome.

She'd brought two-way radios so she and Mike could communicate without using up cell phone minutes.

"Just charge Papa Greg for the overage," Mike suggested.

"I'll handle the billing and you talk to me on the radio

from now on," Angie replied, not curt, but leaving no room for negotiation.

Mike covered one side of the busy two-way road. Angie, who was parked about a hundred yards away from him, covered the other. It was relatively easy to maintain a proper stakeout in the daylight, under the cover of heavy pedestrian and vehicle traffic. With temporary tinting to her windows, she didn't worry about Casper and Buggy spotting her.

Even so, she had no intention of being in this for the long haul. She wanted Nadine to call. Every minute, it seemed, she was picking up her phone, glancing at the display, cradling it in her hand, waiting for the vibration of text, the chime of her ringtone.

The phone finally rang, but it was her father. She went through a health check with him. He assured her he was doing just fine. She believed him enough, and told him she was back in Baltimore. Her dad sounded more worried about her than she did about him. But he was used to her job and the dangers it brought, and he accepted those dangers with the expected degree of reluctance.

What her father couldn't do was offer an explanation about the check registers Angie had discovered in the attic. "Your mother had a lot of causes she supported," her dad said.

"Yeah, but the MCEDC isn't one she ever talked about, and it just so happens they provide care for the same condition our Jane Doe has."

"Maybe your mom felt obligated to the girl somehow."

"Well, I'd say," Angie replied. "But the same amount, given on the same day each year? Don't you think that's a little strange, Dad?"

"I think the whole thing is little strange," her father said for the first time. "I don't know what to make of the picture or your mother's note on the back, or any of it. And to be honest, it's really starting to upset me."

Angie shriveled up inside. Disappointing her dad was something she strived to avoid, but upsetting him, especially now, felt like an egregious violation of their close bond. She made a fast retreat. "I'm sorry, Dad. I'm just trying to figure it out, that's all."

Her father went silent for a long time, and Angie's anxiety level spiked. Why was it she could take down two armed and dangerous men in a street scuffle, but when it came to her father, she still felt like a little girl eager to please? Some roles could be reversed, she guessed, the way a spouse could become an ex, but others were so ingrained, so deeply rooted, they were burned into the psyche as if seared with a cattle brand.

"Angie, I understand your need to pursue this," her father eventually said. "Your mom's death has been—"

Angie figured the next word would be *hard*, but a few shaky breaths interrupted him, the kind that foretold tears the way dark clouds implied rain.

"It's been difficult on us all," he eventually managed. "I don't know what to tell you about the picture and your mom's checks to that organization. All I can tell you is that your mom loved you very much. Maybe there was a secret in her past, something she kept from us both . . . from everyone, for all I know. But is it going to do you any good to find out what it was?"

That took Angie by surprise. She hadn't considered any other way to look at it. "What do you mean?"

"I mean, you have a vision of your mom, and that vision is frozen right now. She can't get any older. She can't change who she was to you, what she meant. In a way, odd as it is to think about in these terms, she's in a state of suspended animation. She's the woman who gave birth to you, who loved you, who cared for you. She's that woman. Now if you find out something about her, some secret she didn't want us to know, how is that going to change your perception of her? The way she is now is something you can't ever get back."

"I just think I should know the truth."

"Okay, okay. I get it, I really do," her father said. "But give this some consideration, if you will. Your mom is in a state of suspended animation for me as well. Don't just think about what the answers mean to you, Angie. Think about what it could do to me."

The only time Angie had ever been hit in the gut hard enough to take her breath away was when Flo Mendelssohn sucker-punched her in the eighth grade. Angie had the same creeping sick feeling in her stomach once again. Her dad had a point. Was digging into the past jeopardizing the future? What good would the answers do any of them? She had an unblemished vision of her mother, and her father had the same. Angie was living a perfectly good life. Was the truth worth knowing if it came at the expense of all her memories, of her contentment, of her dad's happiness? It was a question without an easy answer.

Angie's mind churned up various possibilities. What if her mom had led a double life, and somehow that little girl was a part of it? Could she have had an affair? Could the girl be a niece or someone of importance her mother turned her back on? What if her mother had somehow hidden a pregnancy? Angie had seen enough Lifetime movies in her day to come up with a myriad of explanations, all of them with the potential of ripping her dad's broken heart into even more pieces.

One thing was certain—she wasn't going to stop searching for answers—but now she had a new wrinkle to consider. Would the truth become a burden, a secret she would have to keep from her father?

They ended the call with usual salvos of *I love you, be careful, call if you need* . . . but something lingered, a residue Angie found unpleasant and hoped would clear with time.

The cloudless sky cast in bright sunshine had turned her car into a terrarium of sorts. She cracked a window for air, but could still sponge sweat off her body. She needed to clear her head and get a bit of fresh air.

She radioed Mike. "I'm taking a walk."

A crackle first, and then Mike said, "I'm taking orders for lunch."

"We just ate lunch."

Crackle. "No, you just ate a bagel and I had a corn muffin. That is not lunch, Ange. That's what old ladies feed pigeons. I'm getting a burger, fries, and a Coke. Good news. I'll buy and fly."

"Wait until I get back from my walk. I want to see if anything is going on inside the apartment."

Of course, going for a stroll as herself wasn't an option because Casper and Mr. Fedora might recognize her. From the trunk of her car, Angie got the box-o-disguises, as Mike had taken to calling it. She waited for a lull in foot traffic before slipping on a red wig, stylish black-rimmed glasses, and a beige trench coat she'd picked up at a thrift store. Angie adjusted her wig, using the window for a mirror.

Mike called her cell phone. "Angie, careful. There's a gorgeous redhead standing right outside your car door."

Angie rolled her eyes. "Thanks for the warning, Mike."

"Think you could get her number?"

"Mike, please."

"Okay, well, ask her if she wants a cheeseburger. My stomach is sending out Morse code."

"She wants a salad, maybe with chicken on the side if it's not from some greasy spoon."

"Tell her I'm going to Paul's Pollo Emporium."

"I thought you were getting a burger."

"I am. Paul does it all. You forget I've been here a few days now. I have the lay of the land."

"Just get me a salad, but wait to go until after I get back," Angie reminded him before ending the call. She grabbed her purse from the backseat and made sure the camera hidden in her glasses was recording.

Mike hadn't gotten any pictures of Ivan and the others. Angie hoped she might get lucky. If one of them had a warrant, it could inspire a little more attention from the police.

Then Angie went walking. She pretended to window-shop at the art supply place, but gave real consideration to trying Zumba after peering in on a class in progress. Her situational awareness sharpened once she crossed the street. She strolled in front of the auto repair place, and then came upon the alley that Ivan Markovich took to reach to the back of the apartment building. It was the same alley Casper had chased her down, though it looked a lot different during the day—far less threatening. She could still feel Casper's presence looming behind her.

When Angie came to the front of the apartment building, she considered backtracking, cutting through the alley, and going to the basement door, but decided against it. Too much risk for potentially too little reward. She decided to try to sneak a peek into one of the apartment windows instead, and maybe record some video evidence for the police. The windows weren't quite at eye level, but she noticed an overturned milk crate she could use as a step stool.

Letting go a long exhale, followed by a couple furtive glances, Angie emboldened herself to step onto a patch of dirt in front of the apartment where a small garden could have gone. She picked up the milk crate and positioned it directly underneath one of the first-floor windows. She climbed up, and her weight sank the plastic edges of the crate a couple inches into the loosely packed soil.

She craned her neck to get a look inside, but the windows were grimy, the lights were off, and the bars made it difficult to get a clear view of anything. Angie put her face closer to those rust-speckled bars when a sound drew her attention toward the front steps.

The front door came open and out stepped Mr. Fedora, hat in hand, shielding his eyes from the bright sunshine. He slipped on his shades to combat the glare and noticed Angie after she had jumped down from the milk crate. While getting down, she'd pulled out one of her earrings and tossed it to the ground, then directed her gaze to her feet. She pretended not to look at Mr. Fedora, but from her peripheral vision, saw him put his hat on his head. His swagger blossomed.

"Yo, yo, lady," he said, dirtying his brown shoes to traipse through the soil. "Whatcha you doing here?"

Angie looked up, her camera filming the man's scowl in enough detail to capture wisps of hair coating his top lip. Her heart rate accelerated, but she masqueraded her fear with confidence. "I dropped an earring. It hit the curb and bounced into the dirt. I can't seem to find it."

Mr. Fedora became the consummate gentleman. "I'll help you look, baby."

Funny how his stare seemed more focused on Angie's figure than on the ground.

"What's your name, sweetheart? They call me Buggy."

"Buggy?" Angie said, not looking up and not moving her foot where the missing earring would be found underneath.

"It's a family name," Buggy said with a laugh. "Say, you fine looking. Who you here with?"

Am I supposed to thank him for the compliment? What Angie wanted to do was hit him with her Taser again. But the weapon was in her purse and right now, unnecessary.

"I'm just on my way to meet a friend," Angie said, careful not to move her head too much because the wig wasn't fitting quite as snugly as it should.

Buggy moved in, allowing Angie's camera to film a close-up of his leering grin. She smelled beer on his breath.

"You live around here, baby? I ain't seen you before."

"Like I said, I'm visiting my friend," Angie said, maybe a little too quickly.

"Yeah? Where she at? She fine lookin' like you, Big Red?"

If Buggy understood the concept of personal space, he damn well knew he was violating hers. Angie's throat tightened as she shifted her foot ever so slightly, her mind churning for a simple answer to a simple question.

She lives down on . . . on . . . on where?

Angie had had brain freezes before, but never quite like this. She didn't know these streets, this neighborhood. She knew the apartment and the alley, nothing more. But she did remember Mike saying they were on the outskirts of east Baltimore, what was commonly referred to as "Middle East" in reference to the ever-present violence.

"She's over in west Baltimore," Angie said, hoping

being vague wasn't inviting suspicion. "But we're taking a Zumba class here."

"Come a long way to Zumba," Buggy said.

"Well, she's trying out new studios. A good instructor makes all the difference."

"Yeah, I'm a teacher. You should take my class." Buggy gyrated his hips.

Angie moved her foot and made a delighted sound. She bent down, retrieved her dirt-covered earring, and held it up for Buggy to see. She took a step in retreat.

Buggy held his ground. He seemed to be weighing the earring discovery against the Zumba story, deciding if his BS radar should be pinging loudly.

"You come back here any time you want to party," Buggy said, slipping a smoke in his mouth from a pack he kept in the pocket of his bowling shirt. He lit it and blew a waft in Angie's face that wouldn't have bothered her twenty-year-old self, but made the older version want to gag.

"What's your name, baby?"

Without hesitation, Angie said, "Kathleen." She backed away. Only one person could ever comfort her after a nightmare. It was no great surprise when she opened her mouth and spoke her mother's name.

CHAPTER 32

Exhibit D: Excerpts from the journal of Nadine Jessup, pages 51–57

Every night I went to bed telling myself tomorrow would be the day I'd make the call. Tomorrow would be my last day here. Wherever this is . . . somewhere in Baltimore, I'm told. Tomorrow I'll say good-bye to Tasha and the other girls forever and then I'd say good-bye to this chapter of my life. Every day I promised myself I would do it, but I never did. Instead, I watched the phone's battery level drop like it was my own life slipping away, down from a hundred percent to fifty. Half life. Half left. But the half remaining meant I could go another day without having to make that call. It meant I could have another day without being terrified of what Ricardo would do to me if he found out I was trying to escape, or what he would do to my mom and dad if I betrayed him. The remaining bit of

*battery meant I could put off having those fears
become a reality for at least one more day.*

*I didn't know what was going to happen when
the battery got down to ten percent . . . or five.
Would it give me strength I didn't have? Would I
just dial the number on the card Mystery Man
gave Tasha? Would I? Could I? There was a
Nadine who I believed in, a girl who I thought
had the courage to do it. But it felt like that girl
was lost somewhere in a maze of cheap rooms
down in a basement with mold clinging to the
ceiling. That Nadine was lost and I was calling
her name but hearing the echo not of my voice,
but the voice of Jessica Barlow, the girl I'd
become, whoever she is.*

*It was a stupid thing waiting to make that call.
Stupid GIRL! STUPID NADINE OR JESSICA
OR WHOEVER THE HELL YOU ARE! Doesn't
matter now what percent of the phone's battery is
left because the phone is gone. I went to check the
battery life and I couldn't find the phone in my
pillow. It's gone and if Ricardo, Casper, or Buggy
found it that means I'm probably next.*

*I'm writing to you, Tasha. Dear Tasha. I'm
writing to apologize. I'm writing to you to tell you
that I love you. To say I'm sorry. I'm sorry. I'm
sorry. I'm sorry. Sorry x10. Sorry a Million Xs.
Here's the truth, here's what happened. I
remember now. I took the phone out from its
hiding spot because I was going to make the call,*

I really was, but I wanted to get high first, and I did, but then I forgot about the phone. I just left it out on the kitchen counter and went to work downstairs. STUPID THING TO DO. STUPID!! I crashed after and when I came back up I didn't even check to see if I put the phone back where I hide it. I'll never forget the look in your eyes when Ricardo woke us that night. I'm sure I looked a million times more scared than you. But when Ricardo showed us the phone, why did you tell him it was yours? Why??? I don't know what to say except that I'm sorry. I feel super sick about it. I really do. I should have owned up to it and I didn't. You gave it to me. It was my phone, but I said nothing. And now I have to go downstairs because there's a meeting about the phone and YOU! All the girls are going to be there. I haven't seen you since Ricardo dragged you away by your hair. When I get downstairs, I'm going to tell them the truth. I'm going to tell them the phone is mine. I can't let them hurt you for something I did.

Tasha, please forgive me. Please, please, please, forgive me! I froze when I saw you with your wrists tied. When they opened the door to the hole, I said nothing. When they untied your wrists I thought they were going to let you go. I was wrong. We locked eyes and I thought I understood what was going through your mind, what you wanted me to do, which was nothing. You could have stopped it. You could have told them the phone was mine. But you didn't. You were doing this for me because you knew I couldn't take the hole. You knew I couldn't take the cigarette burns Ricardo put on your arms and legs. Somehow you knew I wasn't strong enough. I almost spoke up when the door to the hole clanged shut. I swear it's true. I almost said it was MY PHONE! MINE! But then I remembered when they put me in the hole. I didn't know I was claustrophobic until I went down there. The thought of going back into the darkness again, into that crawl space, it made me shrivel up inside.

I knew for sure I couldn't take what they did to you. I couldn't handle it. So I just watched along with the other girls while Casper and Buggy held you down and Ricardo put his cigarette to your skin. I watched and said nothing because I'm a coward. I make myself sick!! I should just curl up into a ball and die. That's what I should do. I should take a big handful of your blue specials and swallow them all and just die because I'm worthless and pathetic. That's the truth. You screamed while I stayed silent. What's fair about that?

Tasha, sweet Tasha. Here's what happened after you went into the hole. Ricardo brought all the girls into the kitchen for a "little talk." A little talk, yeah right! He was trying to scare us and he did a fine job of it, too. He told us phones were not allowed but everyone already knew the rule. He said phones were contraband. I hadn't heard that word before, but I figured out pretty quickly what it meant. It was something prisoners would try to get. Good word choice, because I guess that's what we are. Prisoners. He said if we have phones, we have to give them to him now. He said there would be no penalty if we handed them over. That's what he calls putting you in the hole and burning you with cigarettes. He calls it a penalty. No wonder I didn't run, or call that Angie lady. If I got caught doing any those things it would have been a heck of a lot worse than a "penalty," I think.

It's been a full day now—a full freakin' day. How much longer are they going to keep you down there, Tasha?

Another day gone and no you. Why won't they let you out? When Ricardo came to check me for tips I told him he should let you go. He grabbed me by my throat and told me I should mind my own business. He told me my job was to make the clients come back for more of me. He took out his lighter, lit it, and held the flame up to my face so close I could feel the heat. I tried to pull away, but he grabbed my head and pulled me closer to the flame. Then he took out a cigarette and he lit it. He blew smoke in my face and he laughed. Then he kissed me and told me he loved me. He said I was still special. The most special to him, he said. Weird as it sounds, it actually made me feel good to hear those words. Good while you were suffering on my account.

No wonder I'm so effed up.

* * *

Tasha, today I knocked on the door to the hole hoping you would knock back. You didn't. I was going to knock again, but I heard Casper coming so I had to get out of there. I wanted to shout RABBIT RABBIT because maybe that would get him to help you. Right? Wrong. Casper and Buggy just do what Ricardo tells them and Ricardo does what Ivan tells him and Ivan wants you in the hole and RABBIT RABBIT isn't going to get you out.

It's the end of day two and they still haven't let you out. Two full days in the hole. Two whole days down in the darkness! Get it? Two WHOLE days? Ha-ha. Not funny. Not funny at all. It's sick, I know. Why did I even write that? I guess 'cause I don't know what else to do. You're down there because of me, Tasha. It's my fault you're in there. I took three of your blue pills today but I still can't get high enough to stop feeling sick about it and you. I keep praying it won't be long now. That they'll let you out soon. I think of you every second of every day and I pray.
Some good that's doing.

I went to the kitchen in the basement because I was hungry. I ate a protein bar and had an apple. Believe it or not they feed us pretty well here. They want to keep us healthy so they can keep us working. Nobody wants to be another Jade so we eat what they give us, which isn't horrible.

Burritos, rice, sometimes salad. But there's always protein bars in the kitchen. I had to hurry because I had a client, or a John, or whatever you want to call him. Who cares, right? I have lots of Johns. I have lots of clients. It means nothing. They mean nothing. My body and mind separate when it's happening. They get off and I get lost. That's how it works. They come from all over, these men. They aren't all Baltimore local, I can tell you that for sure. I think most of them find us through the Internet, but what do I know.

Casper came into the kitchen to escort me to my room. I was ready to go with him when Martina—I think it was Martina—yelled out RABBIT RABBIT and Casper went to her, leaving me alone in the kitchen for a while. I looked around and saw nobody was coming. Casper was dealing with some guy who got a little rough with a girl and now he was feeling what it felt like to piss off Casper. I took the knife I used to cut the apple and hid it under my dress (a dress Ricardo bought me when I thought he loved me). I pinned the knife to my thigh by slipping it into the band of my underwear, then I tried to walk normally, but I'm sure I had a little limp. I told Casper I was going to my room. I'm a good girl who can go there all by herself. He said he'd be right there. The man he was beating up begged him to stop. I got to my bed and waited.

Eventually Casper showed up and my "John" did too.

* * *

This guy was married. He had a ring. He looked soft, like a dad who worked in my dad's office. Soft, not hard like the Baltimore boys who came down here on occasion. He may have had a daughter my age. Did he think of that while he was on top of me? Anyway, he did what the guys do, which is to make noises while they grabbed me and kissed me and whatever. I didn't let him touch my thigh though. I kept turning my body at just the right time. Turning so he wouldn't find the knife. I waited until his pants were off before I took out the knife. I didn't waste any time. I put it right to this guy's throat and told him to give me his phone. Me! Doing that! Imagine! I was shaking inside, but I tried to sound tough. GIVE ME YOUR PHONE A-Hole! I think that's what I said, A-hole, but what do I remember? I was too freaked out just holding a knife to some guy's throat. I didn't know I had it in me, but I got my inner Olivia Pope on (or maybe I was channeling Emily Thorne, or hell even Ricardo). Anyway, I was tough enough to make him scared.

He told me they took his phone from him when he got inside. I knew that was BS. I knew it because Ivan let the guys film the girls if they wanted to because it made them come back for more. The guys thought they were getting something for free, Ivan said, but it's like showing a picture of crack pipe to an addict. They'd look at a photo or video and want the real thing.

The guy was shaking, and let's just say he wasn't popping Viagra because his excitement went away like a turtle slipping into its shell. I

*pressed the knife against his throat even harder
and told him to give me his damn phone. He got
up from the bed (squeak squeak went the springs)
and I went with him. I kept the knife to his back as
he got his phone from his suit jacket pocket. I
made him do the code. I used one hand to hold the
knife and the other to look at his pictures. There
were pictures of his family and I was right. He did
have a daughter about my age and son a little
older. I told him how old I was and watched the
color drain from his face. They told me you were
nineteen, he said. They lied, I said. I opened his
Facebook app and got his wife's name and his
hometown. I told him I was keeping his phone and
I would call his wife and tell her what her hubby
was up to if he told anybody about the phone or
tried to disconnect it. I'd get another phone just
like I got this one.*

*I used the knife and cut a slit in the mattress
and stashed the phone and knife in there. The guy
was shaking. Please don't call my wife, he kept
saying. Please don't tell anyone I was here. He
said he'd lose his job. I said not to worry. I won't
tell anyone if he won't. I told him he had to go
now, but that I needed a little distraction because
I had a phone call to make. He asked what kind of
distraction. I sat on the edge of the bed and
smiled at him. Then I screamed RABBIT RABBIT
loud as I could.*

CHAPTER 33

Three days on stakeout and still no word from Nadine. This was not going as Angie hoped, and she was done waiting for something to happen. Angie sent text messages in an effort to coax Nadine out, but never got a response. She was careful not to use Nadine's name, in case the woman at the bar turned the phone over to her pimp. Angie called a number of times as well, but those calls went straight to voice mail.

Once it became obvious the stakeout would drag on, Mike got his ex to look after his kids so he could stay with Angie a while longer. He had a rental gig that weekend, but Bao coordinated the job, which meant time away from code breaking.

Angie kept in regular contact with Bao, and masked her frustration at his slow progress. He was also having a difficult time (Flip 5-0 Grind difficult, according to Bao) identifying the owner of the apartment building where they believed Nadine might be found. The property was part of the L & E Trust, whatever that was. Getting more information would involve the courts, something Angie didn't have the time or inclination for.

In the course of their conversation, Angie told Bao about the check registers. He thought the discovery was interesting, but wasn't sure what to make of it, either.

Twice the phone rang while Angie was talking to Bao. Each time, she was disappointed that the caller was another job, and not Nadine. As before, Angie farmed the jobs out to different PIs for a cut of the action. Anything that wasn't Nadine-related had to take a backseat, and this included focus on a mysterious photograph taken some thirty years ago.

"See if you can link Markovich to the building," Angie directed Bao.

To stay fresh and alert, Angie and Mike took turns sleeping in their respective vehicles. The removable window tint kept pedestrians from gawking at them while they slept or sat waiting for something to happen. When their legs got achy they took turns walking the neighborhood in disguise, though Angie never went as Big Red again. They stocked plenty of water and snacks, and kept their recording devices fully charged—standard practice during a lengthy stakeout.

Mostly what they did was wait for a break. Angie documented girls coming and going from the apartment building. Sometimes Casper and Buggy came and went through the front entrance; sometimes they took the alleyway, often while accompanying eager-looking men. What Angie never saw was any sign of Nadine or the girl who'd received the phone from Mike.

Regrettably, Angie couldn't count on the police for much of anything. She made a call to Major Chris Nuccio, who was in charge of the whole eastern district. Just getting him on the phone was an ordeal.

"I've already spoken with your officers when I went to the station to file a report," Angie said. "So now I'm telling you. I think the building is being used as brothel and that a girl reported missing from Potomac, Maryland, is being trafficked for sex at that address."

"Have you seen the girl?" Nuccio asked.

"No," Angie said.

"Any contact with her?"

"No," Angie said again. She explained the burner phone and how she and Mike had followed Ivan Markovich, the last person to see Nadine, to a building in Baltimore.

"How do you know Markovich is the last person to see her?" Nuccio asked.

"We have video of him leaving Union Station with her."

"But did you see her get into his car?"

"No."

"Have you turned the video evidence over to us?"

"I believe the security team from Union Station did so, yes. You need to watch it. In the video it looks like Nadine went with Markovich into the parking garage. Obviously, he was taking her to his car. She doesn't even have her license. Why else would she go there? We need to go at this guy."

"Where does he live?"

"DC."

"Then it's a matter for the DC police, not us. Call them."

"But I think he may own this building."

"You have proof of that?"

"No. All we know is that the building is owned by a trust."

"Then your boy is still DC's jurisdiction, not ours. Okay?"

"Not okay," Angie said. "My partner and I are here

now, outside the apartment building, documenting a lot of guys going down an alley with grouchy looks on their faces and coming back all smiles."

"Fine. We'll send a cruiser over to have a look."

"You already did that. How about you get inside?" Angie said.

"How about I need a cause for a warrant."

"I just gave you one."

"You gave me an ass-chewing from a judge. I need better."

"Okay, how about you get some people down here to help us stake out the place?"

"When East Baltimore decides to take a break from being a war zone, maybe I could spare a crew to run that kind of operation. Until then, feel free to send us what you have."

If lip biting were an Olympic sport, Angie would have medaled. She forced herself to end the call on friendly terms. She didn't think the scant police response was proof of a Thin Blue Discount, but it sure it made easy to speculate.

She radioed Mike to vent. Her conversation got cut short when her phone rang.

The call came up with a Maryland area code, but it wasn't a number Angie recognized, and that included the burner phone number she had committed to memory. She answered the call with a little flitter in her heart.

"This is Angie."

A whispered voice answered back. "My name is Nadine Jessup. I think you're looking for me."

CHAPTER 34

In light traffic, the FBI headquarters on Lord Baltimore Drive was twenty-five minutes from the apartment building where Nadine Jessup was being held. It was a square brick structure nondescript as any office park building. Angie and Mike were given special passes and taken to a conference room on the third floor, where a special planning session was already in progress.

Nadine had told Angie some of the girls were foreigners. "You have to come soon. Tasha might be dead down there for all I know," she had said, confirming what Angie already suspected. Tasha, the girl down in the hole (Nadine's label for it) was the same girl who'd taken the phone from Mike.

"You have to help her," Nadine had pleaded.

Human trafficking was a federal crime. The FBI would act, and Angie couldn't be confident that the local PD would. Things were moving forward with haste, as they should have been all along.

Normally, the FBI would have thanked Angie for her service and sent her on her way. But Nadine was scared, understandably so, and would only talk to Angie. In turn, Angie requested Mike's presence, and so there they were.

A lot had happened in the four hours since Nadine's initial phone call. A tactical team had been assembled, various warrants were being expedited, and plans were hatching with urgency. Everything moved quickly—a girl's life was in danger. Angie had had infrequent contact with Nadine since the initial phone call that set all this in motion. Nadine spoke in a whispered voice and often went silent abruptly when it was no longer safe to talk. For this reason, Angie kept her phone in her hand at all times, unsure when Nadine would have the chance to call again. Everyone here was waiting for the phone to ring again.

Every seat around the massive conference table was taken, leaving standing room only for more than twenty people from various agencies who had crammed into the room, including a team from the U.S. Marshals Service who'd arrived about a half hour ago.

Another late arrival was Terrance Hill. An assistant state's attorney in Baltimore County and the current head of the Maryland Human Trafficking Task Force, he had a kind face for managing such an unkind job and appeared to have the ear of Barbara Curtis, a seasoned FBI agent who headed the FBI's arm of the task force. In her fifties, Curtis had short hair, a thin build, and could have easily been a friend of Angie's mother. Instead, she was organizing the entire tactical response.

Introductions were made and various roles explained. Angie and Mike's stakeout had proved useful, providing images of all four suspects.

"We ran photographs of the suspects through the NCIC, our National Crime Information Computer," Agent Curtis said. "Ramon Gutierrez, who goes by the alias

Buggy, came up wanted on a federal drug offense. We've brought the marshals in on our operation as a courtesy."

Bryce Taggart made an awkward wave to the agents seated around the table. The Bureau was interested in sex trafficking, not drug offenders. The marshals had a fugitive interest in this operation and he said as much. "We have one dog to put back in the pound, you guys got at least three." Bryce understood the concern that the marshals might get in the way. Nadine couldn't care less about roles and responsibilities. She just wanted out.

Angie's phone rang. She answered immediately. "Nadine?"

"It's me."

"You're on speakerphone," Angie said. "I can take you off speaker if you want. There are a lot of people here who want to help you."

"No, no. Don't leave me. Just get here soon."

"Can we get a room layout from you, Nadine?" Agent Curtis asked. She enunciated her words as though suggesting each one mattered.

"Who . . . who was that?" Nadine asked.

Barbara Curtis rose from her seat, giving Angie a good look at the black suit and gray shirt she wore. She strode to the front of the room, put her hands on the table, and leaned her body over Angie's phone as if it was an intercom. "Nadine, my name is Special Agent Barbara Curtis and I'm with the FBI's—"

Inwardly, Angie cringed. Nadine might not even understand what she was involved in, or what *human trafficking* meant.

"I'm with the FBI," Agent Curtis repeated. "I'm organizing the group that's going to help get you out of there. We need some information if you can provide it."

"I can try. What do you need?"

For the next several minutes Nadine did her best to describe the layout of various floors. Angie got a good visual of a maze of makeshift rooms in the basement constructed out of cheap particleboard. Her heart broke for Nadine. Getting her out safely was only half the battle. The road to recovery from her ordeal would be a long one, and might last a lifetime.

Nadine was brave and composed on the phone, providing agents with the location of the entrances and exits, the details of the apartments above, and the location of the hole where Tasha would be found.

"How many men are involved?" Agent Curtis asked.

"Ivan is the head," said Nadine. "Some people call him Stinger. He speaks Russian. A lot of the girls, not all, speak Russian. Then there's Casper. He's really big and kind of protects us, and another guy named Buggy."

Angie noticed the two marshals whispering to each other at the mention of Buggy's name. One of the marshals had rugged good looks, dark hair, ice blue eyes and a jawline that could slice bread. She remembered his name was Bryce Taggart, but heck if she could recall the other guy's name.

Mike had pointed Bryce out to her soon as he'd entered the room and said, "Whatever that guy's flaw is, I bet it's a doozy."

Angie had returned a warning look, but she couldn't help but notice Bryce. If he were on Tinder, she would have certainly swiped right.

Agent Curtis asked Nadine, "Are there any other people involved? Names, descriptions, anything you can give us?"

"Well there's Ricardo. He's my . . . was my"—Nadine was having a hard time getting out the words—"he was my boyfriend." Then she started to cry and everyone, including Angie, looked dismayed at the depth of this perp's cruelty.

Agent Curtis held up a picture of a tall, thin, good-looking man. "We think this is Ricardo."

Nadine began breathing hard into the phone. "Look, I gotta go. Someone is coming."

There was a lot of noise, and Angie strained to make out some words but didn't have much success.

"Oh. Oh my God. I think they're letting Tasha out," Nadine said in a breathless whisper. "Look, I gotta go. Gotta go. I'll call when I can. But please tell me you're still coming. Please!"

"We're coming," Angie said, sounding confident. She glanced around the table at representatives from the FBI, State Police, and U.S. Marshals. For a moment she forgot she was the lowest notch on the law enforcement totem pole.

"Please, Angie. Please come."

The call ended and a heavy silence filled the room.

"Look," Agent Curtis said, "this isn't going to be a shoot-'em-up breach and clear. I don't want any of those girls leaving in body bags."

Amen, Angie thought.

CHAPTER 35

Exhibit D: Excerpts from the journal of Nadine Jessup, pages 58-60

I knew they were coming to get us. I just had to wait it out. But first Tasha. She climbed out of the hole looking like a coal miner. Her arms and face were caked with dust and dirt like she was an oversized earthworm or something. I felt so so sorry for her. And I mean not just about the vacant look in her eyes, but everything. How she went down there for me. How she suffered because of me. Went into the hole to protect me. When she climbed out, she looked really confused, like she didn't know who any of us were anymore. Ricardo took her upstairs. I had to stay down-stairs with the other girls. There was more work to do. Work as in $46, you know? We usually get upstairs around three in morning, or when the guys stop showing up, whichever comes first.

* * *

*When I got back to the apartment, I found
Tasha sitting on the edge of her bed. She had
showered. Her hair was all tangled. She had a
towel wrapped around her, but her skin was dry. I
wondered how long she'd been sitting there like
that. Looking at nothing. Doing nothing. Barely
moving. I sat down next to her and told her about
Angie and the phone call with FBI people and
how they were coming to rescue us. Tasha didn't
even react. It made me nervous so I just kept
talking, saying all these stupid things about what
I would do once I got home. How I missed my
own bed and my friends. How I was never going
to have sex again, like I was going to become a
nun or something. How I was going to do things
differently. But it felt so empty to say those things
because the words were meaningless to me.
Basically, I was trying to make Tasha feel better,
when really what I was doing was justifying what
I had done by making that phone call. Deep down
I'm honestly scared to leave. Like I don't know
what will happen to me. Will Ricardo come after
me? Screwed up, right? But scared as I was about
Ricardo, I was more so scared for Tasha. If she
hadn't gone into the hole I probably would have
just stayed here. This is my normal now.*

*Tasha had a spark once, but now it's gone. She
is gone. Extinguished like a flame. Blown out like
a wish on a birthday candle that will never come
true. Why us? That's what I want to know. Why*

*were we chosen to live a life so absent of joy?
What did we do to deserve this?*

*Now that Tasha's here—well, here but not
here, not really here, now that she's out of the
hole, now I'm questioning what I've done. Before,
it seemed urgent we get out of here. Now that
they're coming it all just seems so unreal.*

*I have no home. Let's be honest about it, my
mom and dad won't want me. Not after what I've
done, what I've become. I'm like Tasha after she
got out of the hole. Vacant and gone. And they're
still coming. The FBI will be here any minute
now. Tasha is asleep. I can hear her breathing in
the room next to mine. Angie tells me everything
is going to be fine, but I don't believe her. I told
her I was scared about fitting in back home, and
worried how people would judge me. People like
Tasha wouldn't judge me. People who knew from
experience. My poor sweet friend still hasn't said
a word. Not a single word. I got a comb from the
bathroom and I brushed Tasha's long hair for
thirty minutes straight. Tasha has such amazing
hair. I wish my hair was like hers, but it's not even
close. The only thing similar about us is that
we're both completely screwed up.*

*I can see the first bit of sunrise out Tasha's
window. I haven't slept a wink. Tasha is asleep,*

*though. My stomach is knotted. I feel so empty,
utterly lost. I'm terrified of staying here and just
as scared to leave. I thought about jumping up
and down when the police show up. Pretending I
have a gun or something. Imagining that they'll
shoot me and this will all be over. All the pain, my
dark emptiness.*

I just got a text message from Angie.

They're coming.

Ricardo is going to blame me. I know he is.

I'm sorry, Angie.

I'm so so sorry.

But I've got to undo what I've done.

CHAPTER 36

The tactical attack truck carrying Bryce Taggart bounded down rutted streets in a part of Baltimore he knew well. Plenty of fugitives wanted by the federal court system hid out in this part of the city, and it was Bryce's job to track them down. The high-profile cases—the ones Wolf Blitzer would cover incessantly—merited the Marshals Special Operations Group. But nabbing pedestrian d-bags like Ramon Gutierrez, aka Buggy, was the purview of local task forces led by guys like Bryce.

Through a rectangular window made of bulletproof glass, Bryce took in the glorious sunrise that speckled an otherwise bleak cityscape with bands of color. Early in the morning and he was dressed like Baltimore was Fallujah. He was not alone. Nine other guys were in the back of the BearCat, dressed similarly, but only three had body armor and tactical helmets marked with the U.S. Marshals stencil. For weaponry, Bryce had his M-4 long gun and Glock pistol snapped securely in its holster.

Based on Nadine's information, they'd decided to hit the building at six in the morning. Tasha was out of immediate danger and Special Agent Curtis wanted to go in with a bit of daylight. At that hour, most everyone in the house would still be sleeping and the fewest civilians would be exposed to risk. Bryce agreed with the decision.

The multistory structure made entry a bit tricky, but again thanks to Nadine, Bryce knew where to look for Buggy. Ricardo and Casper shared an apartment on the first floor. When Buggy stayed over, which happened frequently, he preferred to crash in one of the makeshift rooms in the basement. Evidently Casper snored.

The plan was to breach the front entrance with overwhelming force, with local police assigned to watch the front and rear alley. If anyone tried to escape out back, they'd enjoy a short sprint at most before the manacles came on.

Two mobile command posts had been set up, one for the Marshals and one for the FBI. The law enforcement organizations could pretend to swim in the same pool, but it didn't mean each wouldn't try to piss in the other's lane.

Glancing down the row of guys from the FBI dressed in tactical gear, Bryce smirked as he made eye contact with an agent seated on the bench across from him. "I'm surprised you guys didn't bring a second BearCat to this shindig. Heck, I expected the whole fleet." The FBI's penchant for excessive personnel deployment was good fodder for the Marshals.

"Ha-ha," the agent answered without smiling. "Very funny, Taggart."

Bryce tightened the straps on his Kevlar vest and winked. Bryce had two guys from the Marshals with him, as well as two local cops whose loyalty was to the USMS. But it was still one fewer than the FBI had brought, so ribbing was allowed.

The agent Bryce had antagonized leaned forward in

his seat. "Taggart, tell me. How does it feel to spend your career snatching low-hanging fruit like Buggy Gutierrez? I bet it gets pretty boring. If you ever grow a bigger pair, give us a call. I'm sure we can find an opening for you somewhere." The special agent grabbed his crotch.

Bryce gave it some thought, but not for long. "Aren't you guys the Blue Team?"

"Yeah, Red Team is taking down Markovich in DC."

"Blue team, now that's appropriate," Bryce said.

The agent squinted. "Why's that?"

"Because you got big blue balls, of course." Bryce followed another wink with a rakish grin, then checked the time on his Casio watch. By now the Red Team had probably stormed into Ivan "Stinger" Markovich's stylish DC residence, cuffed him, and read him his rights. His arrest was scheduled to go down around the same time as this one.

Red Team's raid would be a bit blind because they didn't have an inside source like Nadine feeding them information. She was a brave girl and proving to be a critical mission asset, which meant Angie and Mike were useful, too. Those two were parked safely inside the FBI's mobile command post, tasked with getting intel from Nadine to send back to the tactical teams.

Bryce thought about checking in with Angie just because he wanted to hear her voice again. She intrigued him. She seemed smart, ambitious, and supremely capable, and he couldn't help but notice her good looks and absence of a wedding ring. But his curiosity would have to wait until the after-bust party, which hopefully would take place at McSorley's in eight or so hours.

The truck came to a hard stop.

"Let's try to keep all our bullets in their respective guns," Bryce said.

The crotch-grabbing FBI agent said, "We'll go in first. You Marshal boys can follow."

Bryce picked up a scaled-down pump-action Remington shotgun he called Little Pig, as in the nursery rhyme "Little pig, little pig, let me come in." He grinned. "You may have the bigger pair, but I got the gun." He pushed opened the rear doors.

A rush of warm wind swept into the back of the truck. First out was Bryce. He jumped to the street and headed to the target building, followed closely by a processional of armed guys all dressed in black, wearing ear protection of some sort. Not that there was any noise to block out— not yet, anyway. Everyone kept silent as they got into position at the front door.

Bryce set the barrel of Little Pig against the door lock. His pulse hammered as his blood heated up. Anyone who said they didn't get nervous before a job like this, who didn't feel a tickle of fear, was either a psychopath or a liar, and not welcome on Bryce's team. The jump in his heart was something he had come to accept. He used it as a reminder to put his training into practice.

Bryce glanced behind him. Eleven to take down three, plus round up all the girls. Should be more than enough. Everyone looked ready to strike, so he pulled the trigger on Little Pig.

The bang echoed off into the distance as the lock shot inward at high velocity. Bryce holstered Little Pig, and used the steel toe of his boot to kick the door open. He rushed inside with his M-4 ready to spit fire. He covered the corner to his right and the nearby vicinity. His back was exposed to threats down the hallway, but he wasn't concerned. Frank Dansby, the barrel-chested marshal who came in behind him, was responsible for that sector. Trust was everything.

Bryce moved only as fast he could accurately shoot. The stack stayed tight as his team of three headed for the basement door at the rear of the hallway. There were plenty of wrong ways to clear a building, and only one way to do it right. The right way usually kept people alive. As the lead man, it was Bryce's job to provide security to the front. The number two and three men covered Bryce's left and right sides respectively. A single doorway stood at the end of the hall, just as Nadine had described.

The adrenaline rush Bryce felt couldn't fully compensate for his reduced dexterity. It seemed counterintuitive, but increased blood pressure and heart rate meant less blood flow to his extremities. His visual tracking deteriorated as his peripheral field narrowed, but he wasn't alarmed. He noticed the changes to his body, had come to expect them. The best way to control fear was to have confidence in his ability. For that reason, he trained until his response to a threat situation became a reflex.

At the door to the basement, Bryce paused. Little Pig might have awoken Buggy.

Behind him, Bryce heard the sound of a mission in progress. The first floor-apartment was being cleared. Banging on doors, lots of shouting, lots of screaming.

"Open up! Open up!"

Another bang.

The agents spoke in a clipped manner—"mission-ese," Bryce called it.

"In!"

"Clear! Clear!"

"All secure!"

"On the ground, now!"

They'd found someone. The roundup was underway.

Bryce opened the basement door slowly. He kept to the strong side of the door. His numbers two and three were there to shoot anyone who might be behind it. Nobody was there. Light from a source below leaked up to illuminate a set of concrete stairs descending to a concrete landing. Stairwells were always a tactical disadvantage. Stairwells of concrete came with the added complexity of ricochet problems.

Bryce didn't have any blindside reconnaissance devices, such as thermal imagery or infrared viewers. If Buggy were waiting for them at the bottom of the stairs, it would be a situation of who shot first and best. In that event, Bryce liked his chances. At the gun range, few were better.

On the way down, he kept close to the right wall. Clearing from top to bottom played in his favor. He had smoke and flash grenades with him, but what went down also came up, and such diversions were best avoided. When he reached the landing, he took up position toward the center of the stairs and slightly forward. Buggy wasn't waiting for them at the bottom either, but that didn't mean he was still asleep.

The two follow-on team members quickly took up positions for rear security and cover. Bryce bounded down the stairs and stepped into a narrow hallway composed of particleboard.

The Baltimore fire marshals would have a field day with this place, he thought.

Overhead fluorescents lit the dank space and a pervasive moldy smell filled the air. A few of the ceiling-mounted lights blinked to create a strobe effect down the hall.

Bryce motioned to a room directly in front of him. The two marshals at his back covered the sectors he couldn't see.

He went through a silent countdown using his fingers—*three . . . two . . . one*—then lifted the latch on the flimsy particleboard door. The black hinges didn't make a sound when the door came open.

Bryce entered first. Based on Nadine's description of the floor layout, he and his team had agreed to use the buttonhook method to clear each room.

As soon as he entered, Bryce swept a wide portion of the room's right side with his M-4 and saw no threats. Frank Dansby moved across the door and cleared the hard corner by taking the opposite area of responsibility. The third man, a six-year vet of the Marshals service named Gary Graves, watched the hallway.

Even though Nadine had told Bryce what to expect, he still found the first room depressing as hell. Light from a flea market lamp resting on a ratty nightstand helped light the room. Next to the lamp was an ashtray full of butts. Nearby, a thin mattress topped a crappy rust-speckled metal bed frame. The wastebasket was full of used tissues and condom wrappers, and there were beer cans aplenty littering the floor. They cleared the room quickly and Bryce was the first back into the hallway.

The second room was a repeat of the first. Sex traffickers weren't too big on hygiene, it seemed.

From the hallway, Bryce heard Graves shout, "Hey, you! Hold it right there!"

Bryce bolted out the room. He saw Graves pointing his M-4 at a young girl he recognized. Frank Dansby followed Bryce into the hall, and he too had his weapon aimed at Nadine. The girl had her hands up. Her whole body shook violently.

"That's Nadine!" Bryce shouted. "Stand down. Nadine, you're safe. You're okay."

The girl was sickly pale, and her eyes wide and wild. "Go now!" she cried.

To Bryce's surprise, Nadine made herself big as possible by spreading out her arms and legs. Her limbs were long enough to touch the particleboard walls on either side of her. She looked to be frozen mid jumping jack. Her shout summoned two men from a doorway behind her. The guy in front was tall and lanky and had to be Ricardo. Bryce thought the one bringing up the rear looked a heck of a lot like Buggy, but it was hard to tell as he was moving so fast.

Graves held his ground to provide cover, while Bryce and Frank charged at the fleeing men.

Desperation blossomed in Nadine's eyes as realization took hold. Big guys with big guns were coming at her and weren't going to stop. In a panic, she threw herself to one side, which happened to be in front of Frank Dansby. This left a good-sized gap for Bryce to get by. There was a brief interlude where Frank had to untangle himself from Nadine, who was screaming incoherently.

Frank might have been slowed, but Bryce and Graves went ahead unencumbered. They were the first to reach the room into which the two men had vanished. Bryce unclipped a flash grenade from his battle belt and tossed it into the room before he entered. A loud bang followed, then a puff of white smoke.

Bryce burst into the room with his gun aimed at his zone only. He knew Graves was on his heel and would cover the area to his back. Both men soon had their guns pointed at the only person they could see. Ricardo squirmed on the floor, covering his ears.

"Don't move! Don't move!" Graves yelled, while pointing the gun barrel at Ricardo's head.

It wasn't clear if Ricardo could even hear, but at least he wasn't reaching for a weapon. Frank entered the room, and Bryce didn't need to see Nadine to know that she was in the hallway and handcuffed. Unfortunately, the girl they had come to rescue had turned into a potential threat. It happened from time to time.

Bryce figured Nadine was suffering from some form of Stockholm syndrome, identifying with her captor more than her rescuers. The bigger problem was that two had entered the room, but only one was there and the missing guy was the one Bryce had come to retrieve.

A metal door, more like a hatch located in the middle of the floor, was open wide. Bryce peered inside. It looked very dark down there. He groaned. "Aw, crap."

"What?" Darby said.

"I think Buggy went down in the hole."

CHAPTER 37

Bryce shone his flashlight into the hole, while Graves secured Ricardo. The beam cut through the darkness, illuminating only a fraction of the space below. Not much height, three feet at most. It was an on-your-belly type crawl space with a dirt floor and scattered debris throughout. Unquestionably, it was a horrible place to spend a few minutes, let alone days. What these animals had done to Tasha put a new stamp on the passport of human depravity, and Bryce had seen a lot of stamps over the years.

"Hey Buggy, we know you're down there. Come on up. Let's make this easy, all right?" Bryce's voice echoed.

He didn't expect a reply. He didn't get one.

Bryce turned to Frank Dansby. "Go get Nadine, will you?"

Frank returned a nod.

Bryce hesitated to put his head in the hole again just in case Buggy decided to take a shot. But he did it anyway and scanned the crawl space a second time with the help of his flashlight. It appeared the area below the basement was the size of the apartment building's foundation. Buggy could be anywhere.

Frank brought Nadine into the room. Poor girl looked utterly terrified. Nothing about Frank's manner was hostile. He was gentle with her, but her crying still bordered on hyperventilation. They'd get her medical attention soon enough.

"Is there a way out of the crawl space?" Bryce asked.

Nadine shook her head.

Bryce put a hand on her shoulder. She shrank from his touch.

"Nadine, you're not in trouble," he said, looking her in the eyes. "I promise. I'll watch after you, but I've got to know. Is there a way out?"

Ricardo, who was handcuffed on the floor, perked up. "Shut up! Don't say a word. You guys go screw yourselves."

Bryce rolled his eyes. "Yeah, I'm trembling here, amigo. Graves, get Mr. Congeniality out of here, please. Have someone from upstairs help you. I want two guys on this P-O-S."

Nadine let out a few shaky breaths. Graves radioed for help.

Ricardo glared at Nadine with hate in his eyes. "*Puta*."

Bryce could see him getting ready to spit, so he slammed the butt end of his rifle into Ricardo's midsection. The only thing Ricardo spit on after that was his shoe.

"He can't hurt you anymore, Nadine," Bryce said while Graves dragged Ricardo out of the room.

Nadine spoke only when she felt safe to do so. "Ricardo said there's a vent he could use to get out."

It made sense. There had to be an air supply, otherwise Tasha would have suffocated. Bryce figured the light source was blocked—it was so damn dark down there. "Which way is that vent? Do you know?"

"I don't know," Nadine said. Her tears were flowing freely. "Ricardo had the only flashlight. I shouldn't have gotten in your way. I just panicked. I'm sorry. I screwed everything up."

"Is Casper upstairs or is he down in the hole?"

"Casper couldn't fit through the vent. He was going to try and hide. We had just woken up Buggy when you came downstairs. Did anyone get shot because of me?" Nadine's body slumped forward from an invisible weight resting on her shoulders.

"It's okay. Honest," Bryce said, giving her a little hug of encouragement. With her hands cuffed, she couldn't hug back.

"Frank, radio our command. Tell them to watch the alley." Bryce said this as he handed Frank his M-4 and Little Pig.

"Where you going?" Frank asked.

"Buggy is our guy. I'm going to get him." Bryce had a flashlight and his Glock. He figured that would be enough. Just to be safe, he tossed a flashbang into the hole. A loud explosion erupted from down below, somewhat muted on account of the thickness of the concrete. Buggy would have endured the full effect, and the blinding flash may have temporarily disabled him.

Bryce climbed down into the hole. He breathed in steamy, hot, poorly ventilated, stale air that his lungs couldn't clean.

Floor to ceiling the space was a tight squeeze. If he arched his back even slightly, he'd scrape it against the rough-hewn cement above. He crawled forward on his hands and knees, shimmying as though he were slipping below razor wire in some Army obstacle course. His dirt-filled mouth acted like a gritty sponge, sucking up all the moisture. The flashbang had kicked up loose soil and contributed, not insignifacntly, to the dirty, smoky mayhem. Removing his Glock from its holster, Bryce's throat tightened. If he started to cough, he wasn't sure he could stop. The impenetrable darkness ignited a mild case of claustrophobia. It wasn't a paralyzing fear, but the unpleasantness stayed with him like a persistent ache.

Bryce's biggest concern was that Buggy would find the vent, get out, and get himself a hostage. Spinning on his belly, Bryce shone his flashlight in a sweeping circle. No sign of Buggy, but Bryce saw some structural support columns made of cinder block Buggy could be hiding behind. Bryce inched forward. Clouds of dust billowed off the dirt floor, launching motes that danced lazily in his flashlight's jouncing beam. Bryce's throat tightened still more. Dirt and dust continued to seep into his lungs anyway. He held his ground and listened. Was it a breath? It sounded close by. Bryce whirled toward the noise, his flashlight beam trailing.

Nothing.

"Buggy, let's not do this." Bryce listened, but the only sound was his heartbeat thundering in his chest.

A bright flash erupted and lit the crawlspace like a bolt of lightning. A simultaneous bang preceded the familiar smell of gunpowder. A bullet whizzed near Bryce's shoulder and sank into the dark.

Bryce understood his flashlight was the problem. He cut the beam and rolled. Jagged stones dug into his skin. It was worth the pain to distance himself from the hatch opening and the secondary light source. Three more shots rang out. The noise was going to be harder on Buggy than on Bryce, who wore ear protection.

From above Frank called, "Bryce, are you okay?"

Bryce figured Frank didn't need to go down there and get shot. He chanced giving away his position to respond. "Stay back. I got this," he yelled as he rolled some more.

Another shot rang out. Had Bryce not been moving, the fourth bullet Buggy fired might have found its target. Instead, the projectile sank into the shadows like the others. But Bryce now had a general idea where to find Buggy, and he crawled in that direction.

In the darkness, Bryce heard movement, sounds of scampering as Buggy took up a new position. Bryce thought he might get lucky, but Buggy was smart enough to move away from the light seeping down from the open hatch. Bryce had to decide if he wanted to go after Buggy or make his way out and wait for reinforcements. Exiting would make him an easy target.

By going down there, Bryce essentially had committed, so he decided to go get his man. He slid forward on his belly. His tactical gear pressed unpleasantly against his chest. Jagged rocks dug into his knees and elbows. He'd been down there all of four minutes and all he wanted to do was get out.

"You're going to have do things you don't want to do to get your man," Bryce's favorite instructor at the training center had once told him. "Tracking isn't just following footprints. Any clown can do that. What makes a marshal exceptional is an innate ability to read each clue, to understand the nuances, the essence of the movement, so picture in your mind these movements and imagine them as if they were your own."

No surprise his instructor's words came back to him at that particular moment. Without his flashlight, without light from the hatch, Bryce's only option was to imagine Buggy's movements. What would he do in a similar situation? How would he think?

Fear.

It was the first word that came to Bryce's mind. Buggy would be utterly terrified. He wasn't a killer. He was a dealer. So why did he shoot? Fear. A cornered animal was a most dangerous one.

He'll move toward the wall, Bryce thought. *Search for that vent.*

But where was the wall? *Damn this darkness.* Bryce held a breath and gave a listen. A scraping noise sounded not too far away. Bryce guessed fifty feet, but it was hard to gauge distance by sound alone.

Imagine their movements as if they were your own.

Bryce took the advice to heart as he played out a scenario in his mind. For a moment, he became Buggy down in the hole with his back against the wall, both figuratively and literally.

Bryce had only a general idea of Buggy's location, but he came up with a way to pinpoint it exactly. In one hand, Bryce held his Glock, and his flashlight in the other. He rocked his body and rolled onto his back, then onto his stomach, then onto his back once more. His momentum began to pick up. Rocks bit at his flesh, then released, then bit again. As he rolled, Bryce powered on his flashlight and sent it spinning in the opposite direction.

The rolling flashlight was bait, nothing more. Bryce stopped rolling, but the world kept spinning. In the dark it was hard to regain equilibrium. Hopefully, Buggy's addled brain would think Bryce was still on the move.

Sure enough a shot rang out, aimed at the rolling flashlight. Bryce did not hesitate. He fired where he saw the flash of gunfire. A groaning sound told Bryce his aim had been true.

"Are you done shooting, Buggy?"

A second groan.

"I'm not taking chances. You toss that gun where I can see it."

Bryce rolled toward the flashlight. He heard a noise, a thud. *A gun, perhaps?*

Bryce retrieved the flashlight and directed the beam where he heard that thud. The outline was distinct enough for Bryce to make out the shape of a gun. He trained his beam on Buggy. His back, indeed, was against the wall, clutching his leg, taking in short and shallow breaths. Buggy's face was smeared with dirt turned muddy from his sweat. Bryce crawled toward Buggy, flashlight in one hand, gun in the other, his finger never leaving the trigger of his Glock. Buggy's face was filled with panic. The bleeding was brisk.

"I need a doctor," Buggy said, clutching his wound.

"Better that than a mortician," Bryce said. In the cramped quarters, Bryce managed to take out a pair of TUFF-TIES, the best nylon restraints on the market. Buggy cried out when Bryce yanked his arms to get the restraints in place. He secured another set of ties around the leg wound to form a tourniquet, and then flashed his light in Buggy's eyes.

"Ramon Gutierrez, on behalf of the United States Marshals Service, I am pleased to inform you that you are under arrest."

CHAPTER 38

Angie took the elevator to the third floor of the Mercy Medical Center where Nadine Jessup was being kept overnight for observation. Nadine's parents were en route to Baltimore and Angie wanted a few minutes alone with Nadine before they arrived. She'd also wanted Mike to come up with her. Without him, they might never have found Nadine.

Mike, being Mike, saw right away how his presence could be a negative. Even though he'd played no part in Nadine's suffering, he was still a male, and might bring back memories of all she had endured. He was headed home, back to his kids, eager to hug them extra tight.

A nurse stopped Angie in the hallway to let her know Nadine was sleeping.

"I won't wake her," Angie said, masking her disappointment. "I just want to see her."

"She's heavily sedated. I doubt she'll wake up until morning."

Angie last spoke with Nadine by phone minutes before she inexplicably interfered with the mission. In the aftermath, Nadine was rushed off to the hospital, taken by ambulance and escorted by a cadre of FBI agents. Angie hadn't had a moment to connect with her in person, but was told she was doing fine and in relatively good health.

It was important for Angie to see for herself. Peering into the room, she looked at Nadine sleeping peacefully. She wore a hospital gown and had an IV in her arm, probably to provide electrolytes for dehydration. She looked perfect, a perfect person. But beneath her flawless skin were wounds so deep they might never heal. *What had happened to her down in that basement,* Angie wondered. *Why did she turn against the people who had come to her rescue? What twisted mind games did her traffickers play?*

A lump formed in Angie's throat. The intensity of her emotions took her by surprise. She had found hundreds of runaways, but something about Nadine was special.

This was more than a job. It was a calling. The mission was over for Angie, while Nadine's road to recovery was just beginning. Angie couldn't walk that path for her.

Angie felt utterly relieved and weirdly empty now that she had nothing more to do. She wasn't Nadine's caseworker from social services or a victim-witness coordinator from the FBI. She was a retrieval specialist. Her job was to track down runaway kids and take them home. Mission accomplished. Mission over.

When Nadine's parents showed up, she would debrief them and then go home. Of course, she would be available for Nadine if she ever wanted to meet in person, if she wanted to shake hands with the woman who'd reunited her with an alcoholic mother and an absentee father. Some parts of Angie's job were hard to swallow, but that was the gig. She wasn't in the business of putting broken lives back together again.

Angie's gaze lingered on the IV in Nadine's arm. It

was the second time she had set foot inside a hospital since her mother's death and the reminders continued to be painful and sad. Time would lessen her grief, but would it heal Nadine?

Angie jumped when she felt a gentle tap on her shoulder. She whirled and saw a handsome face smiling at her. It took a moment for recall to kick in.

Bryce Taggart wore jeans, a tan blazer, and a white dress shirt underneath. He looked extremely relaxed for someone who had just gotten into a gun battle inside a crawlspace. Among law enforcement, word of his actions had spread like a California brush fire.

"Is she sleeping?" He leaned his body against the doorframe and craned his neck to take a peek inside Nadine's hospital room.

"Yes," Angie said, backing away from the door. "Soundly, thanks to whatever sedative they gave her."

Bryce extended his hand and introduced himself. "We met at the FBI briefing before the mission, but weren't formally introduced. You did great work, Angie. Top notch."

"Thanks, though word is you did pretty good yourself. I heard all about your exploits down under with Buggy."

"Yeah, well, he's where he belongs. Scratch that. He's at the Baltimore Medical Center, but soon he'll be where he belongs."

"What are you doing here?" Angie asked.

"I've got to write my report, and I needed Nadine's statement. I can get it later."

"She's been through a lot. Take it easy on her, okay? She's not going to face charges for what she did?"

Bryce shook his head. "The Feds are pretty good about viewing juveniles who are trafficked as victims. She'll be fine. You got my word."

"Glad to hear."

"Say, there's a little gathering down at McSorley's to celebrate a job well done. Care to join?"

Angie didn't have to think long. She was whole-body exhausted and eager to check on her dad. She was also eager to return to her routine, stop farming out jobs, and maybe, just maybe, help Bao crack the code on the back of the photograph. She had a lot on her mind. Drinks with a rowdy crowd at McSorley's didn't fit into the picture. "No thanks," she said, second-guessing her decision after a flash of his gleaming smile.

"How about I buy you a cup of coffee in the cafeteria?" he suggested.

That was an offer Angie couldn't refuse.

The cafeteria, except for the seating area, was closed, but the hospital offered free coffee as a courtesy. Bryce drank his black. Angie made a green tea. She expected Bryce to make some comment, but it was Mike who would have said something, a yoga joke perhaps.

She had plenty of questions for Bryce, and he didn't seem in any hurry to get to McSorley's.

"Where are the other girls?"

"We took them to different hospitals for observation. Most checked out okay, I heard. A couple were being kept overnight, but I don't know why."

"What's going to happen to them?"

"You mean after?"

"Yes, after."

Bryce leaned forward and Angie felt a little jump of excitement. He smelled a bit like mint. There was a reason minty toothpaste was so popular. Bryce had a lot of attractive features—his smile, for one; the short hair; a perfect amount of scruff; and a jawline even Mike couldn't help commenting on. But it was Bryce's eyes Angie found most alluring. It wasn't just the color, though his shade of blue was indeed striking. It was more how his eyes sparkled with a sense of adventure, but conveyed wisdom and compassion at the same time.

Something about Bryce Taggart wasn't typical of the law enforcement types she had encountered over the years. She was curious about him.

"Well, the Americans will be treated differently from undocumented foreigners. That's for starters."

"How many Americans?"

"Five out of the fifteen, including Nadine."

"Five," Angie repeated.

"These guys could make tens of thousands of dollars per week per girl," Bryce said. "It's huge business. Thirty some odd billion dollars per year according to some estimates I've seen reports estimating two hundred thousdand CSE victims in the US alone."

CSE—commercial sexual exploitation. Angie knew the acronym, but thought Bryce's figure was low. She'd heard it was more like three hundred fifty thousand children, but it might include all of North America. It certainly doesn't account for women and men over the age of eighteen. That number would be much higher.

"It's just slavery wearing a new disguise," she said, deciding not to correct his number.

"They were still grooming Nadine for more. Some of the girls were sold to dozens of men a day. Not everything took place in the basement. Some girls worked different motels in the area."

"Where did he find them? I know he got Nadine at the shops at Union Station. What about the others?"

"Not sure about the Americans. But the foreigners are

from Eastern Europe mostly," Bryce said. "Markovich must have access to a smuggling pipeline. We'll figure out how he got them here. That I'm sure of."

"That's great. But what's going to happen to the girls now?"

Not all the runaways Angie tracked down ended up being trafficked for sex, but enough did to give her experience with the cruel irony of rescue. Without their traffickers, a lot of the girls had no place to live and no means to support themselves.

"There's help out there," Bryce said. "The government might seem big and bloated, but undocumented juveniles and adults have access to pretty good resources from the Department of Health and Human Services. The Office of Refugee Resettlement, I've heard, has an outstanding program and is pretty well funded through Catholic Charities. They won't be abandoned."

"So no jail?"

"No jail."

"And Tasha? She was Nadine's lifeline in there."

"I'm guessing they're all going to apply for T Visas. It's for trafficking victims and it allows them to stay. ORR helps with that, as well."

Angie frowned. "You and I both know a lot of those girls are going to end up working in strip clubs."

Bryce shrugged. "Not saying you're wrong. We found a lot of narcotics in the apartments. I wouldn't be surprised if Nadine's hooked on something. I also wouldn't be surprised if some of the girls want a good payday to fuel their habit."

Angie was disgusted by it all. The adage "sex sells" was meaningless to most people, a slogan and nothing more. But it was real for her. It was the face of many of the kids she tracked down.

"How'd you get into this business, anyway?" Bryce asked.

Angie took a sip of her tea. Her throat was unusually dry and she wasn't sure it was from the stale hospital air. "You want the whole story or the Cliff notes?"

The twinkle in Bryce's eyes flared. "The crew at Mc-Sorley's isn't missing me."

Angie told Bryce about Sarah Winter and her friend Madeline Hartsock. She described how she'd become a PI, and Madeline a prosecutor, because Sarah's disappearance inspired them to make a difference. Angie felt comfortable opening up to Bryce. She told him about her mother's death, and her father's health problems. She shared more with him in a few minutes than she'd done with men she'd dated for months.

"What about you?" Angie asked. "Former military?"

"Why do you ask?" Bryce said. "It's my bad-assery, isn't it? I've been told I radiate it."

Angie laughed. "No, it's just that a lot of marshals come from the military. My dad's best friend was in the service." ·

"Oh yeah? What's his name? Maybe I know him."

"Walter Odette."

The name didn't mean anything to Bryce, but Walter was long retired.

"I'm not military," Bryce said. "I'm not really your typical U.S. marshal, either."

"Oh? What are you?"

"English major," Bryce said. "Poetry, in fact."

Angie could barely contain her surprise. "You're a poet?"

"No," Bryce said, holding up a finger, a gesture intended to correct her mistake. "I'm a former student of poetry. I'm actually a terrible poet. As in roses are red, violets are blue, terrible. But I can appreciate good work. Emily Dickinson, Dylan Thomas, Wordsworth, Whitman."

"I'm not too familiar with poetry. If I were to pick a poet to read, where would I start?"

"Starter poetry? I'd go with Judith Viorst."

"Okay. Which book should I buy?"

"Try *Alexander and the Terrible, Horrible, No Good, Very Bad Day.*"

Angie squinted. "Wasn't that a movie with Steve Carell?"

"Blasphemy," Bryce said. "It was a children's book first and foremost. But I did see the movie with a nephew, and it was pretty good fun."

"No kids?" Angie flushed with embarrassment. *Oh God, Angie, you really had to go there?* She wanted to slap her forehead as her face turned hot and probably red.

Bryce just smiled. "No. No Mrs. Bryce, either, in case you were wondering. I've had my opportunities, but I let them pass me by. And before you think it, I'm not afraid of commitment."

Angie gave him a crooked smile. "Well, what is it with you, then?" She'd already dipped her toe in the water. Why not dive in?

Bryce's gaze revealed nothing. "You'll have to read my poetry to find out."

"You said it was terrible."

"And that right there could explain why a handsome devil like me is still single at thirty-three." He winked.

Angie returned a laugh.

"No, the truth is I haven't met the right person. Nothing more exciting than that. There's no great drama to my joining the Marshals Service either. I grew up in Bethesda. Green yard, loving parents, an annoying sister who is now my best friend in the world. I went to college, studied poetry, and one day realized I didn't know a bit about this world. The grit. The grime. The underbelly. I knew quads and ultimate Frisbee and beer and bands like Nirvana, so after college I applied for the Marshals. Seemed like a good way to get that kind of experience. Okay, I watched *The Fugitive*, and then I applied."

Angie laughed again. If he was trying to worm his way into her good graces, he was doing a good job. "At least you admit it," she said.

"Anyway, I've been with the Marshals ever since. Worked in a lot of different cities—cue another reason I'm single—and somehow I ended up here in lovely Baltimore."

Angie held up her phone. "This usually doesn't stop ringing. My dad thinks that's the reason I'm still single. He may be right."

"Since we're on the subject, maybe I could buy you a drink sometime."

Angie liked his confidence. There was no reason to dance around attraction. People got picked up in bars and online, so why not after helping to break up a human trafficking ring?

"I live in Virginia," Angie said.

Bryce did not seem deterred. "I have this contraption called a car. I swear it makes long distance seem like nothing."

Oh, that smile.

"Yes. You can take me out for a drink some time."

"McSorley's," Bryce said, an eyebrow arched, finger pointing at the wall behind her as if to imply the bar lay just beyond.

"Sometime, but not tonight. It's been a heck of day and I've got to get home, check up on my dad. I just have to wait for Nadine's parents to show up. They'll be here soon."

"It's not going to be an easy reentry for her," Bryce said.

"Tell me about it. Her parents are the anti-Waltons."

"The Waltons? Who are they?"

Angie felt a flush of embarrassment from the joke that had fallen flat.

Bryce gave a little laugh. "I'm kidding. I know the Waltons. Good night Bobby Sue, good night John Boy, goodnight moon."

"Another of your favorite poets?"

"Margaret Wise Brown. One of the best."

Angie found Bryce refreshing. She had gone on plenty of dates where after three sips of a drink she was eyeing the door. She had the feeling she could talk to Bryce for hours and never tire of his company.

"What about the crew?" she asked. "How long will they be off the streets?"

Bryce gave the question some serious thought. It wasn't all jokes and games to him.

"The trafficking charges are going to be easy. Any girl under the age of eighteen involved in sex for money is by law being trafficked. That's years in the clink right there."

"What about kidnapping?"

"Good point," Bryce said. "None of the girls were chained up, but there were bars on the windows and most of the apartments locked from the outside. So there's a case to be made for forced confinement."

Angie's eyes turned fierce. "It's not a question there. It was forced."

"Hey, I'm on your side," Bryce said, holding up his hands. "I'm talking in the eyes of the law. You and I both know Nadine did what she believed she had to do to survive."

"How long?"

"Just my opinion, but I'd say Buggy gets twenty-five to thirty. Shooting at U.S. marshals isn't a good idea. Casper and Ricardo, this wasn't their first rodeo, so they've got the minimum fifteen coming their way. Now, Ivan Markovich is another matter entirely. Guy has no record. He'll get bail of some sort, and then it's a question of how many years they can pin on him. They'll give him twenty and he'll do fifteen. That's my best guess."

"Fifteen years for destroying all those lives."

"Nadine's still alive. It could be worse."

Angie's mind flashed on a picture of Sarah Winter. Was Sarah one of those worst-case scenarios? "Any chance Markovich gets off?"

"Not really," Bryce said.

"Why's that?"

"Because of Nadine."

"What if she won't testify?" Angie asked. "She did try to save Ricardo, after all."

"She doesn't have to testify. The FBI boys found her diary."

CHAPTER 39

Angie drove Mike from her office to the Duke Street skate park, where Bao was waiting for them. The cloudless sky was the kind of cobalt blue that made the spring and summer months seem so darn short. It had been three days since the Nadine job had come to an end and Angie hadn't spent much of that time outdoors. She'd been with her dad, who was still feeling under the weather and working from home these days, or she'd been at the office trying to put the pieces of her neglected business back together again. She had heard from Bryce, but only via text message. His texts were friendly and struck the perfect balance between *I'm interested in you* and *I'm not going to turn into a stalker*. They hadn't made an official plan to meet, but no question, he intrigued her. She had every intention of continuing their cafeteria conversation in person.

For now, text messaging would have to suffice. Bryce provided updates on the girls, and he wanted Angie to pass along a message to Nadine. Ricardo, Buggy, and Casper didn't or couldn't make bail. Those three were locked up at least until trial and there was every reason to believe they would stay incarcerated for years longer.

Ivan "Stinger" Markovich was a different story. He'd posted a half million-dollar bond, no problem there, and had only to surrender his passport. Essentially he was back to living the life of Ivan. Nadine didn't need to know everything.

The bright sunshine and warm wind brushed against Angie's skin and rejuvenated her spirits, though her time outside would have to be short. Nadine and her mother were driving down from Potomac to meet Angie in her office. The purpose of the meeting was simply to say thank you. It would be the first time Angie and Nadine had met in person, and the pending encounter left her feeling strangely anxious.

Why did Nadine touch her so deeply? Angie wondered if it had something to do with timing. After all, Nadine's case coincided with her mother's death and with the appearance of a mysterious picture of a sad little girl. Maybe, in a way, Nadine had come to represent the girl in that photograph—a lost child in need of saving. But Nadine was real, not a mysterious photograph Angie kept in her purse at all times. Unlike the girl with the misshapen ear, Nadine was someone Angie could help.

The skate park, a concrete plaza enclosed in chain-link fencing, featured a variety of well-maintained (and graffiti-free) ramps and rails. People of Bao's ilk, those who lacked a gene for fear, traversed the obstacles at a startling rate of speed, turning their boards in midair, defying gravity and in some instances logic when they nailed a perfect landing.

Angie had questioned Bao's insistence on meeting there and not at the office. His reply, "We should meet where my inspiration struck."

He wouldn't say more.

Of all the people hanging around the skate park, Mike Webb, dressed in his signature plaid and khakis, was perhaps the least hip of the bunch. Drinking coffee from a thermos didn't elevate his hipster status any. Angie wore her most comfortable attire—Converse sneakers, black drawstring pants, and a long-sleeve white jersey. She fit in more than Mike, but not by much.

Bao, wearing a baseball shirt with *THRASHER* emblazoned on the front and knee-length shorts, waved to Angie from the top of a high ramp. He descended like a missile, then used the back tail of the skateboard to bring it to a full stop five feet before taking Angie and Mike down like bowling pins.

"Yo, Ange, Mikey, so stoked you're here. This is gonna blow your minds." Bao looked like a kid with a Toys R Us gift card from Grandma.

"Happy to trek to you. What do you got?" Mike asked.

"The answer," Bao said with a gleam in his eyes. "Meet me over at the picnic tables. Gotta grab my backpack."

Moments later, he rolled over to one of several redwood tables outside the enclosure. He sat down across from Mike and Angie and powered up his computer. Mike showed his growing impatience by making "hurry up" gestures. Angie could relate; the anticipation was hard for her to take.

Bao turned his laptop screen to face them. The screen showed a website open to a page displaying a string of alphanumeric characters in the center and nothing else. Angie recognized the sequence immediately; she had it memorized, in fact.

IC12843488

"It's obvious once you know it," Bao said.

"Yeah, I'm not really loving the cryptic stuff, Bao," Mike said. "

Bao grinned and returned several nods, all in quick succession. "Right on. So here's the thing. We've been looking for the key to this code, right? The primer. Something we can use to decrypt its meaning. I mean, without the key we got nothing. Right?"

"Right," Angie agreed.

"Then you found it." Bao was looking at Angie.

"What did I find?"

"The key, the primer. The meaning!" Bao stood up from the table.

"If you leave now, I'm going to tackle you."

"No worries, bro," Bao said to Mike as he rolled his skateboard over to the fence. "I'm gonna dish it. But it was right there where it happened." Bao pointed through the fence to a ramp inside the skate park. "I was working on smoothing out my 360 Ollie Heelflip." He got a little momentum going on the blacktop and somehow launched his board into the air, spun 360 degrees, and landed back on his board.

"Bao, are we here to watch you do tricks?" Mike looked ready to make that tackle.

"No, bro, it's the number. Three sixty. Three. Six. Zero. I kept thinking about the number because I was pounding the trick and *zero* got stuck in my head. And I got thinking about the check register Angie found in the attic of her parents' house." Bao wheeled back over. "A gift made to that ear place on March fourth of every year."

Mike pretended to be awestruck. "Bao, if I had a clue what you were talking about, I would be so super impressed right now."

Bao looked to Angie, expecting her to put it together.

Angie shook her head, but then her expression changed. "Zero," she said. "Oh-three, oh-four. It's a date!" She smiled.

"Two dates, to be exact," Bao said, hitting some keys on his computer to force a web page refresh. Angie gasped. The web page now displayed two strings of numbers: the original code written on the back of the photograph, and a second string containing some dashes and few newly placed zeros.

12843488
01-02-84/03-04-88

Angie's body hummed with an electric vibration. Her wide eyes were fixated to the screen. "Bao, you know what this means? IC. You know what it is?"

"I'm right there with you, Ange," Bao answered.

Mike ran his hands through his hair. "Yeah, well, I'm a little in the dark here."

"IC is someone's initials," Angie told him.

Bao hit the space bar and the web page refreshed again. The original code was up top and the modified version down below.

IC12843488
I.C. 01-02-84/03-04-88

"Oh, I see," Mike said. "Not the letters *I.C.,* I mean. I get it now."

Angie took the photograph from her purse and set it faceup on the table. The girl with the sad smile and deformed ear seemed to be looking right into Angie's eyes, pleading with her for something. Justice, perhaps.

"The girl in this photograph," Angie said, brushing the girl's face with the tip of her finger. "We know her initials and when she was born."

"And more important," Bao added, "we know when she died."

Raynor Sinclair was parked in his Acura SUV some four hundred feet away from the picnic table at the skate park, listening to Angie's conversation with the help of a twenty-four-inch parabolic microphone dish. The attached shotgun microphone was a Sennheiser model. The MKH-8040 used a special capsule to minimize feedback and off-axis audio. The compact design made the microphone ideal for almost any application from music recording to eavesdropping.

Raynor had heard enough and made a call he felt had to be made. "She knows."

"Knows what exactly?"

"I.C."

A lengthy pause followed. "Then it's only a matter of time."

"They have the dates," Raynor said.

"I'll have to make some arrangements."

"What about me?" Raynor asked.

"You have a new focus."

"And that is?"

"Ivan Markovich made bail. I want him."

The call went dead. Just like that, Raynor had his new marching orders.

CHAPTER 40

$\mathbf{B}$ack in her office, Angie was reeling in more ways than one. The age-progressed image from NCMEC was meaningless now. It needed to be shredded. It was an insult to a little girl with the initials I.C., who for whatever reason never got a chance to blossom into the beautiful woman NCMEC's computers had invented. That girl was gone. She was dead. She had died on March 4, 1988, and for whatever reason Angie's mother had felt tremendous guilt for the tragedy.

Why?

Angie imagined a hit-and-run scenario on some rain-drenched day. Her mind's eye, conjured an image of her mother driving home from a committee meeting, a few glasses of wine over the legal limit. She imagined the *whap-whap-whap* of the windshield wipers fighting a losing battle against a deluge of water.

On the side of the road a little girl wearing a yellow rain slicker leaps into puddles, sending geysers of spray skyward. The girl giggles while Kathleen DeRose fiddles

with the wiper controls, hoping there's an even faster set-
ting. Her eyes leave the road for a few seconds at most.
But it's long enough. Her mother hears a loud, hollow
thud and the car slips into a swerve. The girl with the de-
formed ear lies faceup in a muddy bank. Red rivulets fol-
low the folds of her rain jacket and drop like a crimson
waterfall into the puddle where she had been playing.
The girl's parents are out of eyesight. It was back in the
day when children, even those as young as I.C., could run
free range.

Torrents of rain flatten Kathleen's hair as she crouches
down to feel for a pulse. Meanwhile, her pulse hammers.
Her heart lodges in her throat. The girl isn't breathing. In
contrast, Kathleen's own breath is sweet with wine. It's
obvious the girl is gone. Panic now. Kathleen compre-
hends all she is about to lose. She scrambles back into
her car and speeds away. A sound from the house where
I.C. lives cuts through the air. A scream. The anguished
cry of a mother in distress. Running down the driveway,
the mother arrives in time to see Kathleen's car racing
away. The rain is falling too hard to see the make and
model of the car, let alone get the license plate. The griev-
ing mother falls to her knees, her tears swallowed by the
rain as she cradles her lifeless child in her arms.

Angie moved on to other scenarios in which her
mother had borne witness to this girl's mysterious plight,
but for whatever reason was unable to take life-saving action. Had her mother watched I.C. drown, or burn up in a
fire, or get snatched off the street? The list of misfortunes
Angie imagined was a replay of a book she'd adored as a
child, a diabolical alphabet created by Edward Gorey
called *The Gashlycrumb Tinies*. Angie could still recall
many of the maladies from memory. Amy who fell down

the stairs, Basil assaulted by bears, and Clara who wasted away. What had happened to I.C. to cause Angie's mother to seek forgiveness?

Angie's father didn't know. She had called him on the way back to the office from the skate park. *"Do the initials I.C. mean anything to you?"*

"No. Why?"

There had been no hesitation on his part, no shift in his vocal inflection.

Angie was skilled at detecting lies, and felt certain once again that her father was not the guardian of her mother's secrets. So who was?

I is for Ida who drowned in a lake . . .

Or died on the side of a rain-soaked road.

A knock on the door drew Angie out of her head and away from her dark thoughts.

"Come in," Angie said, rising from her chair.

The door opened and Carolyn Jessup entered, followed closely by a beautiful teenage girl with straight brown hair and big brown eyes. The face was the same one adorning the missing persons poster Angie had seared into her memory, had stored in the same part of her brain where I.C.'s picture also resided.

She came out from behind her desk with her face lit up and arms open wide.

Nadine looked to her mother, but then saw the smile on Angie's face and her fleeting moment of apprehension fell away. The two embraced, and when they finally parted, both sets of eyes had filled with tears. Carolyn's eyes were red as well, and it was not long before all three were huddled together in a long group hug.

In closer proximity, Angie picked up a scent on Carolyn's breath. She wondered if the mother's eyes were red from crying or something else. Angie wasn't so naïve as to think that finding Nadine had fixed all the things that made her run away in the first place.

Nadine, as if reading Angie's thoughts, took that moment to announce she had driven from Potomac to Arlington on her learner's permit. The subtext was obvious. *Mom's too drunk to drive, but I got us here safely and I'll get us back home, too.*

And there it was again, the image of Angie's mother, impaired, driving on a rain-soaked road, heading toward a young girl in a yellow rain slicker.

"Come, have a seat," Angie said, pulling an extra chair over to her desk.

The three sat a moment looking at each other, unsure where or how to begin.

"You look so great," Angie finally said. "Really, Nadine, I'm beyond happy you're here. I can't believe I finally get to set my eyes on you."

Nadine made a slight laugh and returned a half smile. This couldn't be an easy meeting for her. Angie was a reminder of all she had endured.

From her purse, Nadine removed a gift-wrapped box and set it on the desk in front of Angie. "I brought this for you." Her soft voice sounded different without a coating of fear. The timbre was sweet to the ears, rich with innocence.

It masked horrific memories Angie wouldn't dare ask about. Details of Nadine's ordeal inside Markovich's operation were for Nadine and her therapists to sort through.

Angie smiled warmly and picked up the small package that fit into the palm of her hand. She unwrapped the shiny blue paper gently, careful not to make any tears, then lifted the lid on a cardboard box. Inside she found a second box made of wood. This box had a wind-up handle. It was much smaller than her mother's jewelry box up in the attic, the one with a hidden compartment. Right away, Angie recognized it as something from Nadine's bedroom.

She opened the top, knowing the mechanics for a music box would be found inside, and wound the handle. The notes of "Canon in D Major" chimed out. It was a tune as recognizable as "The Blue Danube."

"It's beautiful," Angie said.

"It's from my bedroom, I didn't buy it," Nadine said, sounding a bit embarrassed.

"Oh, sweetheart. If it's important to you, please I wouldn't want to take it."

"I wouldn't have been able to give it you if you didn't find me," Nadine said. "I wanted you to have something from me, something personal, not just something I bought."

Angie stood and encouraged Nadine to do the same. She embraced the girl once more.

"You're going to come through this just fine," Angie whispered in Nadine's ear. "You're so strong and I'm so proud of you." Angie gave Nadine a gentle kiss on the cheek and retook her seat.

Carolyn said, "Her father sends his thanks. Well, he sent you a bonus. That's his way."

Nadine shot her mother an aggrieved look. "Mom, please."

"Please nothing," Carolyn said with a wave. "How many times has he seen you since you've been home?"

Nadine folded her arms and looked to the ceiling. "Whatever."

"How are you doing?" Angie asked, directing her question to Carolyn.

"I'm fine," Carolyn said.

"Good," Angie said.

Reentry was a tricky process even without such massive obstacles to overcome. In most cases it was the child who had disobeyed parental rules, who had pushed boundaries and limits, who'd dealt with addiction issues. Here the roles were somewhat reversed. Nadine needed her mother sober and her father present. Those should have been the ground rules for reentry, but it wasn't Angie's place to make such demands.

"How about you, Nadine? How are you holding up?"

Nadine looked to the floor. "Yeah, it's not easy, you know. Like my friends are cool, well, some of them, but I dunno. I'm all right, I guess." She blinked rapidly and her breathing turned shallow. Sharing even a little bit of her experience was difficult.

Angie wrote something on the back of her business card and handed the card to Nadine. "I'm not sure if you still have my cell phone number, but here it is again. Call anytime. I mean it. Anytime, day or night, for any reason. Just to say hello, or talk, or vent, whatever. I'm here for you."

Nadine took the card and returned an appreciative nod. Her gaze went to Angie's walls of photographs. "What's with all the pictures?" She pointed behind Angie.

Angie turned to look at the many smiling faces framed nicely beneath glass. "Those are the runaways I've helped to find and their parents and loved ones. I'm glad you asked, because I was hoping to get a picture of you and your mom for the wall."

Angie got out her phone that had become a replacement for her camera. Carolyn and Nadine draped their arms around each other. They didn't have to put the defroster on high to get close. Angie took the picture and showed them the results.

"I look old," Carolyn said to Nadine. "You aged me."

Will you let up on her, Angie thought. She held back, though she planned on sharing her concerns with the NCMEC team that was facilitating Nadine's reentry.

Nadine, who was good at ignoring her mother's jabs, returned her gaze to the photographs hanging on the wall behind Angie's desk. "Who is that?" she asked, approaching for a closer look.

Angie saw Nadine was examining one photograph in particular. "That's my friend from college. She disappeared years ago."

Nadine got even closer. "She's pretty. What's her name?"

"Sarah Winter."

Nadine kept her gaze locked on Sarah's picture. "Sarah Winter," she repeated. "What happened to her?"

"I don't know," Angie said. "She went missing my senior year of college. I'm keeping her picture up on the wall until I find her. She'll be the only picture I'll ever take down."

"I'm glad I'm going to be on the wall now," Nadine said.

Angie took hold of Nadine's hand. "So am I, Nadine. So am I."

CHAPTER 41

It was a four-hour drive from Alexandria to Basking Ridge, New Jersey, where Sarah Winter once lived with her mother, Jean. Madeline Hartsock did most of the driving. Her SUV was roomy, and it allowed Angie to spread out and do her work.

The work involved searching (or at least trying to search) social security records for people with the initials I.C. who had been born on January 2, 1984, and who'd died on March 4, 1988. The database Angie used for her search, a product called ConnectXP, was the best on the market for locating people and researching connections.

It was an expensive tool, but one Angie had used countless times for her business. She was hoping it would solve a mystery that had begun some thirty-two years before the advent of electronic records. She wasn't having much luck. Her 4G LTE adapter gave Angie access to ConnectXP's online database, but the result set returned was too broad for the search function. It would obviously help if she had a first and last name. She had checked with Bao, but there were too many combinations for him to sift through programmatically. Angie needed more information, and was deeply frustrated by her lack of progress.

Maddy, hidden beneath her oversized sunglasses and looking cute in a scoop neck T-shirt and jeans, tried to lift Angie from her sullen mood. "How about some music?" she suggested, turning on the radio to let a pop tune blare out from the car speakers.

Angie gave a stern look. Off went the music.

"Aaaand we'll just cruise along in silence," Madeline said.

"Thank you," Angie said.

"What is the issue, if I may ask?"

Angie explained all her roadblocks.

"What about looking up I.C.'s birth certificate?"

"I looked into that," Angie said. "In New York, the physical archives start before 1910. For anything after that, I need more information—a first and last name, specifically."

"So I'm guessing Ancestry.com is out."

"Yeah," Angie said, feeling her frustration bubble once more.

"How about we let it go for now," Maddy said. "Let's focus on Jean. We're here for her and Sarah."

Angie agreed in principle, but she couldn't let it go.

The front door opened almost the same instant Madeline pulled into the driveway. Jean was waiting for the girls to show up, as she had waited for them once a year for thirteen years. Her ranch-style home was lovely, nothing too fancy, just right for a single woman who had divorced when Sarah was in high school and never remarried. For all Angie knew, Jean had never dated, either. She was very private. Happy to discuss most any topic so long as it didn't pertain to her personal life.

The home had a living room instead of a family room, a kitchen with hardwood floors instead of tile, a cat instead of a dog. Nothing about Sarah Winter's childhood home was notable, except for the absence of Sarah.

Jean had short dark hair and a kind, round face. She looked marvelous for a woman of any age, let alone someone in her late sixties. The wrinkles were there, along with other pesky signs of aging, but a Zen quality and a peacefulness from a deeper place radiated from her, making those years seem less taxing.

The women played catch-up as drinks were made— vodka tonics, as was the tradition. It was also tradition for Madeline and Angie to spend the night. Jean had two guest rooms now. The room where Sarah Winter once slept wasn't a shrine to a missing daughter anymore. Sarah's belongings had been boxed up and stowed away long ago.

In some ways—many ways, perhaps—dead was easier. At least it came with closure.

Conversation turned to talk of Angie's mother. Jean apologized for not being at the service. She'd had a funeral for a relative that unfortunately fell on the same day.

"It must have been very well attended," Jean said. "Your mother was so involved with her community."

The three women were seated in the living room, snacking on spinach and artichoke dip and White Trash Puff Balls, as Jean called them—pepperoni and cream cheese wrapped up by a Pillsbury crescent dinner roll. Years ago, Angie had been too skeptical to try it. One bite, and any apprehension fell away. There was a time for healthy eating, and it wasn't when she visited Jean Winter.

"Friends, but no family except Dad and me," Angie said.

"Your mother was an only child?" Jean asked.

"I don't actually know," said Angie. "I never knew any of her family. There'd been some kind of feud before I was born."

"A feud? What about?" Jean asked.

That's funny, Angie thought. The topic had never come up with Jean in all those years because they hadn't had any reason to broach the subject. Angie had pressed her parents for information, but it wasn't something she openly discussed with others.

"The feud was over me, I guess," Angie said. "My mom was pregnant and unmarried, and her family wasn't too keen on my dad. Some heated words were exchanged, and I guess things got a bit out of hand. My mom hadn't spoken to her family since."

Jean pursed her lips. "Such a shame. Why do we let these things get in our way? Life is too short for petty differences." She was being more candid and forthright than usual. Maybe it was the vodka talking, or maybe, with Sarah gone and almost certainly dead, she was speaking from experience.

Whatever the reason, Angie believed she was right.

The drive home usually involved a detour north to New York City. Angie wasn't big on shopping the way Madeline was, but she enjoyed the energy and the food, and sometimes they snagged last-minute tickets to a Broadway show.

This year, though, Angie asked to skip New York altogether.

Madeline couldn't mask her disappointment.

"It's the photograph, isn't it?"

"Hard to let go and have fun," Angie admitted.

"Well, now I'm pissed."

"At me?"

"No, at this damn problem of yours. It's keeping me from New York. I'm not going to let that happen."

"What do you plan to do about it?"

"I'm getting a coffee so I can jumpstart my brain. I think it's time for a fresh set of eyes on this problem."

"Whatever it takes to inspire your brilliance, I'm all for it."

Madeline pulled into a strip mall and they marched into a Starbucks. Some male eyes tracked Maddy's approach to the counter area, as male eyes often did. Angie got a black coffee and Madeline ordered something that sounded like she was speaking a foreign language. Angie was five sips into her beverage before Madeline's drink showed up with a little Mount Everest of whipped cream on the top.

"How can you drink that after those White Trash Puff Balls?"

Madeline made a wide circle with her arms that encompassed them both. "This is a judgment-free zone. Okay?" She took a big sip of her drink and spooned a finger full of whipped cream into her mouth.

"Not judging," Angie said. "I'm jealous."

Madeline handed over her straw. Angie used it to take a dollop of whipped cream for herself and then a sip of something with a delightful caramel aftertaste.

"So, any ideas?" Angie asked.

Madeline went silent for a time, thinking. "One," she eventually announced.

Angie leaned closer, her excitement showing. Madeline was as brilliant as she was beautiful, and when she had an idea, Angie listened.

"I'm all ears."

"So your mom mails a check every year to this ear place," Madeline began.

"Yes, the MCEDC," Angie said.

"Call them."

"Why?"

"Maybe Mom made the gift in I.C.'s memory," Madeline said with a smile.

Angie beamed. "Why the heck didn't I think of that?"

"Sometimes we're too close to the problem to see the solution."

Angie's moment of elation was short lived. "It's Sunday. The place will be closed."

Madeline patted Angie on the hand. "My dearest, this mystery has been waiting to be answered for over thirty years. I think it can wait one more day. And that means we can head north to New York City without even a hint of guilt to get in our way." She put away another heap of whipped cream balanced miraculously on the end of her straw and gave Angie a wink.

Tuesday afternoon, noon sharp, Angie picked up the phone and dialed the number for the MCEDC in Burbank, California. Mike and Bao were on assignment— new jobs, something other than the Nadine Jessup case. They couldn't help identify I.C. any more than Angie could.

She still felt tired from the weekend. She and Maddy had caught a three o'clock showing of *Chicago*, then poked around Rockefeller Center until after eight. Maddy had crashed at Angie's place a little after midnight and got up at 5:00 A.M. so she could get to work on time. Even though yesterday was Memorial Day, they both had had to work. Runaways and sex crimes didn't take holidays.

For Angie, the entire weekend was well worth the sleep deprivation. She had desperately needed some laughs and got plenty, along with some girlfriend advice about Bryce Taggart, who'd texted her while she and Maddy were dining at a Greek restaurant in midtown Manhattan. She thought back to the conversation.

"He wants to take me out Saturday night," Angie said to Maddy, reading Bryce's text.

"Tell him to send a selfie. I need a visual."

"I can't do that," Angie said, mortified.

"Well then, let me see his Facebook."

Angie searched Bryce Taggart's name on her Facebook app, but didn't find his profile.

"He's a U.S. marshal," Angie said. "You're a DA and have an unlisted phone number."

"Good point," Maddy said. "Plenty of creepers out there. Okay, here's my take. It would be better if you could just grab a coffee. But coming up from Baltimore for a date, we're talking commitment. You've got to plan for at least three hours. Can you handle that? Are you prepared?"

"I already had coffee with him," Angie said. "He's easy to talk to."

"And cute?"

"Yeah, he's hot."

"In that case, what are you asking me for? Much as I love you, Ange, I don't want to be Thelma and Louise: The Geriatric Years. *Go out with him."*

* * *

Angie had accepted Bryce's invitation with a text reply and was looking forward to seeing him in six days, but it wasn't the most important thing on her mind. She was too focused on the call to the ear institute. She held the picture of I.C. in her hand, while holding her breath. Her emotions vacillated between hope and dread.

A voice, noticeably softened with age, answered on the third ring, "Microtia-Congenital Ear Deformity Center. This is Dot speaking. How may I help you?"

"Yes, um, my name is Angie DeRose and I'm calling from Alexandria, Virginia."

"Yes, Angie, what can I do for you?"

Angie explained the situation. Dot listened patiently then said she would have to check the records and would get back to Angie later in the day.

Later could not come soon enough. Angie managed to catch up on paperwork and completed the expense report for Greg Jessup, who owed them quite a chunk of change for the retrieval of his daughter. Nadine hadn't called or texted since her visit to the office, but Angie thought about her all the time. She wanted to take Nadine out for lunch, just the two of them. It wasn't Angie's place to keep tabs on the girl's welfare, but she couldn't help herself. The last time she had gotten that emotionally attached to a case had brought Bao into her life.

At four o'clock in the afternoon, her phone rang.

"Yes, hello. Angie here."

"Hi Angie, this is Dot from the MCEDC."

Angie's heart began to race. A feeling of excitement covered her like a second skin.

"I'm afraid we have no record of your mother making the donation about anyone specific. I'm sorry I couldn't have been of more help."

Angie sighed aloud. She felt trapped in a giant maze, with so many dead ends she began to wonder if a way out existed.

"Now you said this was all from a photograph you found, is that correct?" Dot sounded eager to help.

"That's right," Angie said.

"Might you send it to me? I've worked here for thirty-five years. My son had the condition, and I became a volunteer and eventually an employee. Maybe I'd recognize the girl if she was ever a patient here. I couldn't give you her name, of course, but I could give her yours and maybe she'd get in touch."

"I'm afraid she's deceased," Angie said.

"Well in that case, we have nothing to lose, do we?"

Angie took a picture of the photograph and e-mailed it to Dot. It was faster than navigating her own mass of e-mails to look for the scan Mike had sent her. Dot received the image across the country about a second after Angie sent the attachment. Technology had made so many things easier, but it couldn't help her identify a girl solely by her initials and date of birth and death. It was a long shot and she knew it, but Dot had been there for years, and maybe this little girl had been a patient once.

Dot made a sound, something between excitement and shock. "Angie, I know this girl."

"You do?"

"But not because she was ever a patient here."

"I'm not following."

"Oh my," Dot said. "What is your mother's connection to her, I wonder?"

Angie wanted to scream, but managed to find the restraint. "I'm wondering the same," she said, her voice a bit shaky. "Who is she?"

"Her name is Isabella Conti. I remember her only because I and the other parents with children who had Microtia thought we might finally get some much needed attention, some real publicity, which meant more funding for the condition."

For a moment Angie couldn't breath. I.C. now had a name. *Isabella Conti*.

"Why would Isabella get you any publicity?"

"Not the girl," Dot said. "It was her father. Antonio Conti."

The name meant nothing to Angie, and she said as much.

"Back in the early eighties, Antonio Conti was a member of the Giordano crime family in New York. It was big news, a national story when Antonio Conti turned state's evidence against the Giordanos. Antonio had a wife, but I don't recall her name, and of course he had his daughter, Isabella."

"What happened to them?" Angie asked. Not a drop of moisture was present in her throat.

"Like I said, there were lots of news stories about the trial, and Isabella's picture was in the paper and on TV regularly. The reporters made several mentions about her ear. I remember this, of course, because my son, Ronnie—oh, he's Ronald now, I think I told you—had the same condition. He's forty-eight now, with three children of his own, but none of them have what he had."

"The girl," Angie said, gripping the edge of her desk, her fingers whitening from the pressure. "What happened to her?"

"I have no idea," Dot said. "After the trial, the whole family just disappeared."

CHAPTER 42

You don't come back the same from what I did. It's impossible, I think. There is no way things can return to how they were before. I see a shrink and a social worker now, and talk to these people from the FBI and NCMEC and whatever. They're just people trying to help me, but I honestly don't know if I can be helped. Everything about me is tainted with something I can't scrub off my skin no matter how many showers I take—and believe me, I've taken a lot.

I've read stuff online about people like me. People who were trafficked. That's the word for what I was—trafficked. The numbers are really mind-blowing. 21 million, I read somewhere. Something like 4.5 million people who are trafficked are also sexually exploited. Exploited or not, I consider everyone who gets trafficked for whatever reason, forced labor or forced sex, to be part of the 21 million club. But that's just a number, right? It doesn't really mean anything. I mean, let's be honest, 21 million! I've tried to imagine it, tried to wrap my brain around it. I've been to FedEx field for a Taylor Swift concert and once for some dumb football game. I think it held like, I dunno, 80,000 people. I need my calculator to do the math. 21,000,000/80,000 = 262.5 FedEx stadiums full of victims. 262.5 stadiums! Damn, it's still too big to get my mind around, so instead I focus on one number that means something to me, a number that means the most to me, in fact. I focus on the number 1. Why? Because there's 1 person named Nadine Jessup who lives in Potomac, Maryland who got trafficked for sex. That's the number that resonates for me. 1, the number that crawls into my brain every night as I try to fall asleep, thinking about the apartment I once shared with Ricardo and then the one I shared with Tasha. 1 got me caught up in that life for whatever reason. Everything that happened to me happened to only 1 person. They can eradicate (still got my vocab!) sex trafficking, I mean free all 21 million human trafficking victims worldwide and that number 1 will still be with me, following me like a shadow, sticking to me like a tattoo. Of all the victims around the globe, I might not have suffered the most, but hey this isn't a competition. The point I'm trying to make here is that I'm more than a statistic. I'm more than a success story on Angie's wall (love her BTW).

I'm a 1.

Now multiply me by 21 million.

* * *

*Oh, I should note my journal is gone so I'm
starting anew. The old one is with the police, I
guess. WTF, right?! Wrong! I'm glad they have it
if it will help put those a-holes away. Go on! Read
all my private thoughts. Read all my sinful deeds.
Go page by page and find out for yourself
everything I've done and who I've done it to.
Hell, it's not the first time I've been naked and
exposed in front of strangers.*

*The looks I get around town are a
CRAPLOAD worse than what I got when I
was with Buggy and Casper. The strangers I ran
into in Baltimore (now I know for sure that's
where I was) always looked at me like a curiosity.
What's she doing with them? That kind of
curiosity. But around here the looks I get are a
whole lot different. Sure some people eye me with
sympathy—"poor little girl" kind of thing—but
mostly what I feel is judged and dirty. They look
at me and I can just tell their minds are working
overtime trying to figure me out. But they're not
thinking about the hole, or the cigarette burns, or
the knives, or all the threats. They're thinking
what I probably would be thinking about one of
my friends if she was there instead of me. I'd be
thinking, why didn't you run? Why didn't you call
for help sooner? There's only one answer they can
come up with. I didn't want to leave.*

So Screw THEM!!!

*I wish I didn't care what anybody else thinks.
But when you're 1 out of 21 million, life can feel
pretty damn lonely.*

*   *   *

*Okay, let's talk about my mom and dad.
Nothing has changed. Mom still drinks and my
dad is still not interested in me. I spent a night at
his place and he took me out for dinner. But he
didn't know what to say to me. I swear it was like
the weirdest conversation ever! How's the fish?
Do you want another Coke? Um, yeah, okay,
Dad. . . . Is that really all he has to say to me?*

*Before all this I was just his great mistake,
right? Well, my mom was his great mistake and I
was the aftermath. I just don't get it. I'm his
daughter! Does he feel guilty because he couldn't
keep me safe or is he ashamed of me because I
slept with so many men? One thing I know for
certain, I'm not his innocent little girl anymore.
Daddies always see their daughters in a certain
light. Well, I want the lights to go out. I don't want
my dad to see me at all anymore.*

*How do I get drugs? Seriously? I don't know
how. Do I go to some street corner here in
Potomac and wait? Do I steal my mom's car and
drive back to Baltimore? Where do I get them?
Where? Believe it or not, I actually miss something about my old life. Back there, when the
business of living hurt too much, I could always
take a pill.*

*I spend most of my time in my bedroom. I feel
sort of better surrounded by my things. I say sorta
because it all looks so childish to me now. Like*

*I've outgrown everything I own. My clothes, my
books, my posters, my music, everything. It
belongs to a girl who didn't know anything about
the big bad world. Now that I know—taken a bite
of the forbidden apple kind of know—I want to get
rid of it all. The old Nadine is gone and this new
person doesn't give a rat's ass about Anna
Kendrick. This new Nadine no longer believes we
could be BFFs.*

*So that was awful. JUST AWFUL! I went over
to Sophia's house for the first time today. Her
parents were home and the way Sophia's dad
looked at me made me kind of sick. Maybe it was
all in my head. Maybe he wasn't looking at me in
that way. Maybe her dad just reminded me of the
other dads who for whatever reason forgot they
had daughters of their own.*

*Anyway, it was so awkward there I wanted to
scream. Brianna, Sophia, Hannah, Madison, we
were in Sophia's basement, all together for the
first time. Yes, I ran away, but I didn't run away
from them. I ran away from my mom mostly
because there's only so much a girl can take. But
I never wanted to leave my friends. So now we
were together again at last. But it wasn't like
before. I forgave and forgot everything Ricardo
pointed out to me. Jump off a bridge 4 real.
Calling me fat, those things. That's just girl-trash-
talk. I mean I've said mean things to them, but it
was always jokingly, and even if they were
serious I needed my friends more than anything,
so forgive and forget I say.*

For the longest time nobody said a word. We just sat on the couch drinking soda and watching some crap on MTV. I mean it's so unlike us. Before, when we were all together, you couldn't get us to stop talking. But this was awkward to the max. Sure, I got some hugs. Some, how are you doing? That kind of thing. But then it was the silent treatment. So I just blurted out—No I didn't get pregnant! No I don't have an STD or AIDS. YES I've been contacted by a bunch of people who want me to sell my story. NO I'm not selling it. YES I screwed a lot of guys! A LOT! What else do you want to know? How do we get over this? I'll tell you anything you want to know.

But here's the thing, and I think I just figured it out while I was writing this all down. They didn't want to know. Not really. They wanted it to be something they might have heard about, or saw on Law and Order: SVU, or caught a snippet of on Dateline or whatever. They didn't want it be something they could reach over and touch.

I was just too damn real for them.

Thank God Sophia came around! Thank you thank you thank you. xoxo She came over and we got honest with each other. No BS. I told her how everyone made me feel so cheap and unworthy. She apologized and we ate ice cream and well, I felt a whole lot better. Ice cream can fix anything, I swear. We must have talked for five hours straight. I told her what happened, I told everything as I could remember it, and she listened. She REALLY listened. I LOVE HER

SO MUCH!! I needed somebody and she came through. I told her about Angie and what I thought about her friend Sarah Winter. Sophia thinks I can do something to help. Make a difference in someone's life, ya know? I think Angie's wall of photographs got to me, seeing all those faces, all those lost souls reunited with the people who loved them. But what about Sarah Winter? Her picture's going to stay on Angie's wall until she's found. Ask me, I think it'll be hanging up there as long as Angie has that office. Sarah's never coming back. Without Angie's help I might have ended up just like her—someone who was never found. I need to pay it forward. That's what I think. It gives me purpose. Focus on something other than how broken I am inside. I have so many dark thoughts and dark days. I need a bit of light. If I can make a real difference in somebody's life, isn't it worth doing no matter what the cost? Sophia thinks so and I think I agree, even if it means I have to see Ricardo again.

CHAPTER 43

Raynor Sinclair parked his Acura SUV across the street from Ivan Markovich's apartment building. His muscles creaked getting out of his car. Too many hours confined, sitting and driving, had turned Raynor into a tin man. He promised himself a long vacation outdoors with his bow and arrow once this job was over.

He crossed the street, mindful to look both ways. He was mindful about everything, which was how he knew nobody was watching him or Markovich. He also knew Markovich was at home. The GPS anklet kept a reliable 24/7 vigil on his prospect.

For this meeting, Raynor went with a black suit, a black shirt underneath, and dark sunglasses. He knew he looked like a badass, but it was a fitting choice for the business he had come to discuss.

He stepped into a cool marble foyer with a fancy inlaid design fronting a mahogany reception area topped by green marble. The man seated behind the desk wore a rumpled suit and a sleepy expression. Raynor asked to be connected to Ivan Markovich in 3B. The receptionist dialed a number and handed Raynor a white landline phone.

"Who is it?" The voice on the other end sounded gruff, annoyed.

"You don't know me. But we need to talk."

A pause first, and then, "Are you police? You can talk to my attorney."

"The police don't want to help you. I do."

"Why?"

"If you have to ask, then I guess I should go."

"No. Wait. Come up."

Raynor handed the white phone back to the attendant and was soon on his way up to the third floor. Markovich was waiting at the door to let him in. He was dressed in jeans and an oxford shirt, with loafers on his feet and no socks because they didn't fit over the ankle monitor gracefully. The chains draped around his neck, same as his Rolex watch, were made of gold.

From the doorway, Raynor took a look around. He expected a bit more opulent décor—perhaps a large jade rhino or a crystal chandelier, something worthy of someone who had conceivably made millions peddling people. The place was nice enough, though. The apartment had wood throughout, and the living room visible from the doorway featured modern looking furniture favoring black leather, but the view wasn't much to behold.

Raynor believed Markovich could afford much more. *Good*. A man who was careful with his money had money to spend.

Markovich might have been somewhat frugal, but he wasn't a trusting man. He had opened the door with a Glock pistol in his hand. The G37 Gen4 was big-bore technology, a gun suitable for law enforcement, not something a first-time enthusiast would own. The choice of weaponry told Raynor plenty. Markovich was comfortable around guns and his warning look sent a message that he had pulled the trigger on a person before.

Raynor kept his sunglasses on because he wasn't about to move his hands. He also wasn't armed and wasn't worried. "You can search me for a weapon, check me for a wire, if that's your wish. I assure you I don't have any such items on me."

"Yeah? How do I know? Wires these days can be small, easy to hide." Markovich's accent was somewhat pronounced, but Raynor knew he could dial it up and down at will. Eventually it would play in Markovich's favor.

"May I take something out of my pocket?" Raynor asked.

Using his gun as a pointer, Markovich motioned him inside the apartment. He closed the door with his foot and aimed the Glock at Raynor's chest. "No tricks."

Raynor reached into his front pants pocket and removed a key with a square shaped head and an unusual tip that would fit the key ring hole on the ankle monitor. "I can take that off," he said, pointing to the GPS tracker that was part of Markovich's bail condition.

"Are you a cop?"

"I'm a friend."

"It comes off, an alarm goes off."

"No," Raynor said. "It will continue to broadcast your signal. We could move you across town and the people monitoring you will think you're still in your apartment."

"How is that possible?"

"I pay people who control the software. It's not hard."

"What is it you want?"

"May we sit? Drink?"

Markovich didn't think long. "Vodka?"

"I would have been disappointed if you had suggested otherwise."

Raynor sat on the black leather sofa and took off his sunglasses while Markovich retrieved two chilled glasses from the freezer and brought a bottle of Russian Standard out of a cabinet. Raynor took a sip of the proffered drink, appreciating the slight mineral taste and hints of caraway spice.

Markovich took a seat on the black leather chair across from him. The chair was higher off the ground than the sofa, putting Markovich in a power position. Raynor had selected his seat wisely.

"So what's this all about?" Markovich asked.

"You're going to be convicted for your crimes. You'll do twenty years minimum, but the penalty could be life." Raynor never danced around the issue with his prospects.

"How do you know?"

"Because you're guilty. Because there's plenty of evidence to convict you. You were good, but not exactly careful."

"Are you going to offer to kill the girls for me for some ridiculously high price? Is that it?"

"You're correct, but only in part. I'm here to offer you a way out that doesn't involve killing any of the girls, but it does come at a ridiculously high price." Raynor's face broke into a smile as he hoisted his glass and downed the vodka in one long, delicious gulp.

CHAPTER 44

At the office of DeRose & Associates, Angie was deep into her research on the life on Antonio Conti. The Web had a decent amount of information about Conti, just enough so she didn't have to visit the library to further her investigation.

In the world of organized crime, Antonio Conti was a soldier, a low-level operator who worked for Philip Pissano, a *caporegime*, or capo, in Dominick Giordano's notoriously ruthless crime family. The capo was a leader, head of a group of soldiers, and wielded tremendous clout and power within the organization. Conti would have been nothing but a footnote in mob history had he not been pinched on a racketeering charge related to the extortion of local businesses. His was an ill-conceived money-laundering scheme.

Because Conti already had a few priors to his name, he was looking at serious time, which certainly influenced his decision to cut a deal with the Feds. In exchange for his testimony, the DA dropped all charges against him. Branded a rat in mob circles, Conti and his family required constant police protection.

As a soldier, Antonio Conti had peddled influence with tactics of fear and intimidation. As a turncoat underworld informer, he wrought havoc and crippled the leadership of the Giordano crime syndicate. The information he revealed during his sensational trial pulled away the shroud that had blanketed the mob in secrecy. Giordano ran his organization with the sophistication of a Fortune 500 company and leveraged a network of Swiss accounts along with elaborate legal and financial maneuverings to hide their illicit activities.

While working as an informant, Conti wore a wire. He secretly recorded hundreds of hours of conversation, producing damning evidence at the trial of several high-ranking mob members including the head honcho, Dominic Giordano, and Conti's immediate supervisor, the capo Phillip Pissano. These men were not so different from the portrayals depicted in *The Godfather*. They valued loyalty and integrity above all else, cherished family, and spoke of honor, while simultaneously dealing quantities of heroin measured in tons.

They were killers who never worked on Mother's Day and abhorred the use of foul language in front of women. Their family values were in stark contrast to the brutal realities of their profession. The damage Conti's testimony had done to the crime syndicate was immeasurable. Giordano and Pissano each received life sentences and both died in prison. Other members of the mob received lengthy prison sentences including bosses, underbosses, a consigliere, and various captains and lieutenants—all taken down by the low-level Antonio Conti.

It made sense to Angie why Dot and everyone in the country, as Dot had put it, were aware of the trial. Conti's home in Williamsburg, where he lived before turning informant, was a media circus, and Conti's wife, Marie, and their only daughter, Isabella, were frequently filmed and photographed. Archived video footage showed Conti pushing his way through a phalanx of reporters on his way into the courthouse, often with his wife and daughter in tow—a daughter with a deformed right ear. Only a few photos of Isabella Conti were online, but none of them were the same as the one Angie had in her purse.

Where did that photo come from, she wondered.

The picture in the attic had been developed from a negative—had to be, because of the Kodak stamp on the back. Everything Angie had learned since making this discovery fit the narrative she had constructed. The year the photograph was taken and its location matched what she read online. Angie used Google Maps to get a street view of the Williamsburg neighborhood where Conti once lived. Many of the buildings were the same ones depicted in the photograph, though the Mayor Koch poster was long gone.

Mike Webb read the Wikipedia page over Angie's shoulder. "So he's our man. You think he and your mom had an affair?"

"She would have been in her late twenties, almost thirty back then," Angie said. "Certainly possible."

"Married to your dad for how long?"

Angie did some math in her head. "Six or seven years."

"The old seven-year itch," Mike said, in a sing-song voice.

Angie looked annoyed. "This is my mom we're talking about. Respect, please."

Mike held up his hands. "Just trying to find a connection. It would be weirdly fitting given how we profit from that sort of thing, is all." Mike held up his digital camera as reminder of the sorts of images he's paid to capture.

"Crossing a line here, Mike. You're crossing a line."
With her finger, Angie drew an imaginary line on the ground
between herself and Mike.

"I'm just saying if our business taught us anything, it's
that infidelity is pretty darn common." Mike glanced
around the office. "Say, where's Bao? I figured he'd be
here helping you with the research."

"He's gone camping with some friends. Won't be back
for a few."

"Yeah? Speaking of camping, Mr. Tad Hutchinson is
doing a little of his own in a lot of seedy motels and never
with Mrs. Tad."

Mike showed Angie the pictures he'd taken on his
Nikon D90. Angie wanted to scrub her eyeballs clean, but
the evidence would help their client retain custody of her
kids once she filed for divorce. Often in child custody
and divorce matters, the one who hired a private investigator was the one who won.

"Good work there, Mike."

"Can't crack this case, though." Mike tapped the wiki
page for Antonio Conti.

"There's a connection between Conti and my mom. I
just need to find it."

"What are the options?"

"Lovers, like you suggested," Angie said.

"What about siblings?" Mike tossed out the idea nonchalantly and watched as Angie's jaw fell open.

"But my mom's maiden name was Tyler, not Conti."

"For all you know," Mike said. "You have no connection to your extended family. I'm just saying, maybe she
and Antonio were related."

Angie gave it some thought. It would make Isabella a
cousin. "I don't know. I'll have to ask my dad."

"Any luck on the death certificate?"

"Zero," Angie said, making the same shape with her fingers. "Isabella Conti died March 4th, 1988, if you believe what my mom wrote on the back of the picture. I searched all the databases and got nothing."

"No Isabella Conti?"

"There's a record of her birth, but not of her death."

"Maybe your mom was wrong about Isabella dying," Mike suggested.

"You think the code means something else? Then Isabella might still be alive."

Mike thought it over. "No. Honestly, I don't think so. I don't have a specific reason, just a gut feeling. I think that girl is dead and I think your mom knew it."

A thought struck Angie and her face lit up. "What if she's sort of dead?"

"Oh, like a vampire," Mike said, making a fang-face with his mouth. "I like the possibility."

"No. Not like that. Like what happens when you inform on the mob"

"You get dead," Mike said.

"Or you get gone," Angie said.

It was Mike's expression that brightened. "You think they went into witness protection?"

"How else would they survive?"

"So March the fourth?"

"Maybe that's the date they all became somebody else?"

Mike gave a nod of approval. "So what now?"

Angie took out her cell phone. "Now, I call a guy I know who wants to take me out to dinner."

CHAPTER 45

The car carrying Dante Lerardi hit a pothole and bounced hard enough to send a splash of Jameson and soda onto his pant leg. "Hey!" he shouted from the backseat, holding his drink far away from his body. "Take it easy there, Pedro. This is an Armani here. Now it's all stained."

Raynor Sinclair never told Dante his real name, and Dante never asked. The sobriquet amused Raynor, who had a fair complexion and could claim only Irish and English heritage. He cracked a half smile Dante couldn't see, dug out a handful of napkins from the center console, and retrieved a fresh can of soda water from the small cooler on the passenger seat beside him.

"I'm sorry about that, Mr. Lerardi." He passed the items back to Dante with his gloved hand. "If you dab the pants with the soda, it should take out any stain."

Dante cracked open the can, dipped the napkin into the opening, and did some dabbing with a scowl on his face. "This suit probably cost more than you make in a month." He had a hard-edged voice and the clipped speaking style of a hurry-it-up Northerner.

"Again, I apologize." Raynor kept a neutral voice to

go along with his neutral expression. It wasn't easy to remain calm and composed in Dante's presence. The man had been antagonistic and boorish for most of the two-hour drive, but Raynor took the high road and acted like a true professional. He looked like a professional, too, dressed in a designer suit with a white shirt and black tie, the outfit of a chauffeur, someone who should be good at avoiding potholes. But then again, he wasn't a chauffeur.

Dante grumbled as he dabbed the wet spot, expanding against the brown fabric of his suit pants. "I look like I pissed myself. Be more careful, all right?"

"Yes, of course," Raynor said.

Dante, occupied with the stain, didn't notice Raynor glance at him in the rearview mirror, couldn't see the disdain flare in eyes hidden behind dark glasses. Once he had done enough dabbing, Dante's gaze shifted to the verdant Virginia farmland rolling past his window. "What the hell am I going to do out here? If you got me picking freakin' potatoes or something, I'll shoot you between your goddamn eyes."

Raynor cracked a half smile Dante couldn't see. "You won't have to pick potatoes."

"Yeah, I better not," Dante said, spitting out the words. He adjusted the lapels of his suit as if the act somehow bolstered his credibility as a man not to be reckoned with. "Farming is undignified." He undid a button on his silk shirt, opening the collar to expose several gold chains resting against skin artificially tanned to an unnatural shade.

"Four months ago, I was bagging ten g's a week, moving so much Big H up and down the east coast I could have made this field look like it was coated in snow. And you know what that kind of dough got me?" He ran a hand through the wisps of his remaining hair and smiled broadly enough to give a flash of his gold tooth. The brightening expression tightened the loose skin flapping beneath his chin like a turkey's wattle. "It got me a lot of play. Hotties, all fine, nubile young things. And look at me. Fifty-five, not much muscle, a threat to blow away on a windy day. You think they would have done me without the drugs and the cash? I'm talking foursomes, brother, that made my balls fall off."

Raynor said, "I'm sorry for your loss."

Dante leaned back in his seat, confused for a moment, before eventually figuring it out. "It's a figure of speech, you jackass. My balls didn't literally fall off. I'm just saying, I'm used to a certain lifestyle and this crap-ass backwoods place you're taking me to doesn't quite meet my standards."

"I can assure you, Mr. Lerardi, where you're going, you won't miss one thing from your old life."

Dante picked something out from between his teeth using a manicured fingernail. "Yeah, I better not with what I'm giving you guys. My contribution shut down most of the Big H supply coming into the ports."

"It was very helpful information," Raynor said. "I'm not going to deny you that."

"I'm just saying, I expect to be well compensated for my sacrifice."

"Oh, you will be."

"By well compensated I mean, I like redheads," Dante said. "No BS, either. I want the carpet to match the drapes, if you know what I'm saying."

In a humorless voice Raynor replied, "You're a man of very refined taste."

"Whatever," Dante said, his gaze shifting back to the window and the world zooming along outside.

"So who am I going to be anyway? I want something

badass, something that says I'm nobody's jerkoff." Whatever was lodged between Dante's teeth needed a bit more picking to get out. "What about Clint?" he suggested. "That's a badass name. Like Eastwood, but you know, something different obviously, because that'd attract a lot of attention."

"If your new name was Clint Eastwood? Yes, I think it would."

"Right. But like Clint Eastwood. Maybe Downing. Or is there a Robert Downing? You know, Iron Man."

"That's Downey, I believe."

"Iron Man is Robert Downey?"

"Yes."

"Okay, so good. What about Clint Downing?"

Raynor glanced back at his passenger. "I believe your new name is Albert Tuttle."

"Albert Tuttle?" Dante couldn't believe his misfortune. "That guy sounds like an asshole."

Thirty minutes later, the conversation hadn't much improved. Raynor was glad they were nearing their destination, or he might have done something impulsive. He turned the Cadillac onto a dirt road devoid of any structures and drove exactly 3.6 miles before he came to a stop in front of a field of sweet corn, stretching for miles along both sides of the road. The corn would be harvested late June through mid-September. By the looks of it, this field would be ready on the early side. The green stalks were already waist high.

He cut the engine. "Wait here."

Dante took one look out the window and scoffed. "Like I'd go anywhere," he said, examining his fingernails. "Just hurry it up, will ya? All this country scenery makes me itchy."

Raynor returned a polite smile, then a nod before he

climbed out of the car to unfold his tall frame, giving his muscles a needed stretch. Sunglasses shielded his eyes from the bright sunshine that slipped out from behind a puffy cloud. After he checked to see no cars were coming (though a tractor was more expected), he vanished into the corn like a scene out of *Field of Dreams*, his father's favorite movie. Every year, on the anniversary of his father's death, he watched the Kevin Costner film to honor the person he loved and hated the most.

Minutes later, the corn parted as though some massive animal were on the march, when in actuality it was Raynor driving a black four-door Chevy Silverado with off-road suspension and brand new all-terrain tires. He brought the truck to a stop in front of the Cadillac, climbed down from the cab, and opened Dante's passenger door like a good chauffeur should.

Without hesitating, Dante climbed out the back of the car and blinked away the bright sunshine before setting a pair of Tom Ford sunglasses on his face. "So that's how you do it, huh? Keep me moving. Change it up. Impressive."

"Yes, it is," Raynor said, standing by the open door of the truck's crew cab.

Dante got settled in the back while Raynor took his seat up front behind the wheel.

"So where to now, Pedro?" Dante asked.

Raynor swiveled around to present Dante with a grim smile and aimed his 92 FS Beretta at Dante's head.

Only then did it register that the back of the cab was draped completely in plastic. The clear tarp covered the seats and the wall behind Dante's head.

"Now you don't worry about potato picking or your supply of redheads." Raynor pulled the trigger and a gruesome splatter coated the plastic sheet in red.

Dante's chin fell, his chest and his body tilted slightly right, but he didn't keel over completely.

Raynor replaced his leather gloves with plastic ones so he wouldn't get the mess on his hands and took the Tom Ford glasses before he wrapped up Dante like a gory burrito. He effortlessly tossed the wrapped body into the truck's cab, covering him in a blue tarp. The body would be buried in the deep woods, in a place where Raynor enjoyed hunting, never to be found again.

It was a job well done, Raynor thought as he drove away, leaving the stolen Caddy to be found by the farmer who tended those fields.

CHAPTER 46

Angie had been to Killer E.S.P., a funky coffee shop in Old Town Alexandria where she was to meet Bryce. She liked the casual ambience and what the *ESP* stood for—espresso, sorbet, and pie. Their pies were dangerously delicious, and her stress level since making the Conti connection had summoned a craving for sugar she found impossible to resist.

It wasn't a date, not in the way it could have been when she'd accepted his invitation for a Saturday night dinner. They had business to discuss—Angie's business, to be exact.

She had spent a lot longer getting dressed for this coffee encounter than was her norm, which contradicted her belief that it wasn't an actual date.

Bryce had taken two days to call her back with news on Antonio Conti and his family. During those intervening days, she thought about Bryce quite a lot, and not just because of the research he was doing on her behalf. She wanted to see him, to impress him even, but not be overt about it.

When deciding what to wear, she'd avoided the tank

tops that pushed everything up. After several outfit changes, she went with a rare number hidden in the back of her closet—a navy blue jersey dress that hugged her curves in a flattering way. She wore her hair down so her dark locks swayed enticingly across her shoulders, and she kept the makeup to a minimum. She saw more than a few strangers noticing her as she walked to the coffee shop.

Dressed casually in faded jeans and a plaid sport shirt, the kind Mike Webb might have owned, but couldn't wear with the same panache, Bryce stood to greet Angie.

An awkward moment ensued when she stuck out her hand to shake hello and Bryce moved in for a quick hug. "We did a mission together," he said, wrapping his arms around her before she had time to pull away. "We're kind of past the handshake stage."

It happened so quickly Angie barely had time to hug him back.

They went to the counter where Angie ordered green tea and a slice of peach pie.

Bryce got the same, explaining, "I had coffee the last time I was with you."

Angie looked surprised, and found it interesting he remembered such a minor detail. "Yeah, it's good to change it up." She didn't know what else to say.

They took everything back to the table along with an assortment of napkins, forks, and knives.

"So how's Nadine?" Bryce was sweet to ask, though Angie wanted to dive right in to the meat of their meeting.

She tempered her desire. "Good, I think. We met at my office once, but I haven't really spoken to her since. I think she's adjusting. I think about her all the time, to be honest. What about the girls?"

"I don't really know," Bryce admitted. "I can barely

keep track of all the numbskulls we have to track down. But I like I said, I think they'll all be treated fairly."

Angie took a bite of her pie and savored the taste.

Bryce did the same. "Wow, you weren't kidding about this place."

"Worth the hour drive?"

"Hour and twenty with traffic," he corrected while chewing. "And yes, well worth it. Tell me about your dad. Is he feeling better?"

The question made Angie light up inside. "Yes, and thanks for asking," she said. "Though I've had a hard time not telling him about Antonio Conti."

"That's understandable. I think it was the right call to wait and see what I could dig up before you dropped that bombshell on him."

Angie's nerves rattled. She sensed the moment was at hand. What had Bryce learned? Why did he feel so compelled to share the news in person? She was good at waiting for something to happen while on stakeout, but this type of anticipation felt foreign to her.

"God, I hope my mom didn't have an affair. Did she have an affair? Oh crap, I don't think I want to know." Angie paused a beat. "I want to know. Did she?"

"I don't know," Bryce said, "and I'm not trying to be cagey or cute here. I really have no clue."

"What do you mean?"

"Listen, my job is fugitive apprehension. I'm not a witness protection specialist. Those files are safeguarded really closely, and it's not an all-access type of thing."

Angie deflated. She'd held such high hopes for this encounter.

"But I have some friends who owe me some favors," Bryce continued, "and they agreed to look for me. My contact volunteered to give them a message from you.

Obviously, he couldn't give you the Contis' new four-one-one, because their new identities are a secret."

Angie set down her fork and locked her gaze on Bryce. Her heart bubbled in her throat as her skin heated up. A thin coat of sweat crept along the back of her neck. "And? Is Isabella alive?"

Bryce let go a heavy sigh. "I don't know."

Angie's temples were pounding. She took out the picture of Isabella and put it on the table in front of him. She flipped the picture over so that he could see the code on the back. "We think this code means the date Isabella was born and the date she died, March fourth, nineteen eighty-eight."

"I can't tell you if she's alive or dead."

"Can't or won't?"

"Can't."

"Are they in witness protection or not?"

"Sort of are," Bryce said.

"Sort of?" Angie's thoughts jumbled, trying to guess how someone could sort of be in witness protection. Nothing made sense. If they had her in the program, then they should know her status, and the status of her parents.

"Conti and his family are in the system," Bryce said. "They exist. There's a record of their approval from the Chief of Witness Security and the Special Operations Unit of the OEO."

"OEO? What's that?"

"Office of Enforcement Operations at the Department of Justice. They handle the approvals. We, meaning the U.S. Marshals, can't just put people into the program. That's for the higher-ups to handle."

"So Conti and his family went in?"

"Yes. Once they're in, they're in. Then it's the job of a U.S. marshal inspector to set up the new identity, handle communications, monitor telephone calls, and such. The OEO is pretty much out of it at that point."

"Once you're approved, the government oversight is a lot less, is that what you're saying?" The picture Angie had formed in her mind was still rather fuzzy.

"Yeah, in part. Witnesses in the protection program go through rigorous psychological testing. It's a hard life, and not everyone is suited to the task. All this is predicated on a U.S. attorney sponsoring the request, and that only happens if the witness's testimony is deemed to be of real value.

"If it is, the witness is subjected to a battery of polygraphs, medical exams, and such. Applications are submitted and if approved the USMS takes over. We provide reasonable help getting the witness a job, finding them suitable housing, providing all the identity documents for family members, that sort of thing. The area of relocation is known only to the USMS. Even the case attorney doesn't know where they go."

"So who protects them? You?"

"Honestly, witness protection is a bit of misnomer. We don't provide around-the-clock protection services. It's more like witnesses are moved to a safer location and given new identities to help them live new lives. Their identities are government manufactured and as authentic as can be—new name, driver's license, and social security number. It's highly effective, but also isolating. The attorneys make it as clear as possible what a witness and the family should expect after going into the program. From what I understand, they do a good job painting a pretty bleak picture."

"Bleak in what way?"

"When you enter the program, you have to cut off all contact with your parents, your aunts, uncles, cousins, your friends, forever." Bryce paused, letting the implications set in. "Everything you know about your old life is gone and gone for good in an instant. Going back to your old life can get you killed. Usually our close monitoring of the witness ends around three months after he goes in. Then the witness is pretty much on his own."

"It sounds like a miserable life," Angie said.

"Let's just say it's not easy getting witnesses to sign up. They have to give up an awful lot."

"Yeah, like everything." Angie took another bite of pie, needing to taste something sweet. "So the Conti family, what happened to them?"

"That's the thing and the reason I wanted to see you in person," Bryce said. "According to my contact, there is no record of who the Contis became."

Angie set her fork down and her face scrunched up to show her confusion. Her brow furrowed, eyes narrowing. "What does that mean?"

"It means Antonio Conti testified against Giordano and his people and was taken into witness protection. But whoever he became—well, he and his family—they don't exist in our system. My contact couldn't explain it."

"I don't follow."

Bryce gave a solemn shake of his head. "Angie, it's the craziest thing, and I'm not surprised you're confused. I'm confused, too. Best I can explain, it's as if the entire Conti family simply disappeared, like they vanished from the face of the earth."

Angie was reeling. "What date?"

"Date?"

"When the paperwork was filed for the Contis to get into the program. When was it finalized, do you know?"

Bryce took out his phone. "I took some screen shots of the application. Let me see what's on there." He spent a minute or so going through his various pictures. "Here it is." His eyes were hard to read.

Then he took the picture of Isabella Conti that Angie had set on the table and turned it around so that the code on the back and the words *May God Forgive Me* faced her.

"Well?" The suspense was eating her alive.

Bryce said, "According these records the Conti family entered witness protection on March fourth, nineteen eighty-eight."

CHAPTER 47

*Sophia drove me to the Baltimore Central
Booking and Intake Center. Horrible building. It
looked like a castle from somebody's nightmare. I
couldn't imagine being in there for an hour, let
alone years. The beige cement walls were smooth
except for the barbed wire running underneath
the windows. We went on Sunday because that
was when they had visiting hours. I think Casper
and Buggy were being held there as well. I don't
know for sure. I didn't go to see them, only
Ricardo. But the best laid plans, right? I was
ready to face him. Ready to ask the question I
went there to ask. I got myself looking pulled
together. I went double denim with stonewashed
skinnies and a bright blue denim top, tight T-shirt
underneath. I looked cute, but not too cute. I
wanted to look good not because I wanted
Ricardo to miss me. I wanted to be something
he saw every time he dreamt of freedom.*

*   *   *

*Anyway . . . what happened? That's the
big question. I'll tell you what. NOTHING.
That's what happened. All the build up, all my
nervousness, my constant anxiety, it was ALL for
nothing. SCREW YOU BCB! Hear me? SCREW
YOU! When we got to the jail, they wouldn't let
me in to see Ricardo because I wasn't immediate
family. I guess the rule is written on the website
or something. The woman behind the plexi didn't
give a crap what I was to Ricardo. She didn't care
what Ricardo did to me, how I suffered because of
him. All she cared about was that I wasn't 18. 18
and over I could have seen him, but under? No
can do. And I didn't have a fake ID. Not 18, not
immediate family, not going to happen. That's
what the Plexi Lady said. I told the lady that in
life experience Ricardo made me a heck of a lot
older than my sixteen years. She said everyone
who comes here has got it hard and rules are
rules.*

*I was thinking about getting a fake ID. But I
didn't know how and Sophia couldn't help me
there. Well, she could help, but in other ways. She
brought some vodka from home and that calmed
me down after the BCB debacle. We were sitting
on the hood of Sophia's car taking sips of
Gatorade that wasn't just Gatorade and talking
about what to do next. This was a mission now.
I was going to get some kind of result. I had a
purpose, finally, and that's what I needed most—a
purpose. We talked it over and Sophia came up*

*with the idea, so I'm not taking the credit. I might
not be able to get in to see Ricardo, but Tasha can.*

*Dear Diary . . . ha-ha! Dear Diary. Isn't that
what your supposed to write in these things?
Deeeeaaar Diary. Hi there. I'm so screwed up.
LOL! Actually it's not a joke. I'm really messed in
the head. I want to cover all the mirrors in my
house because I get sick just looking at my
reflection. Honestly, I think of ending it some
days, slipping away into a place where I don't
have to be myself anymore. How would I do it?
I'm back to thinking about that again. Lots of
options, but I'm not going to do any bridge
jumping (sorry Madison). I think I'll go with pills.
Pills work for me. But I don't have any, so today I
tried cutting myself. Just a test, just to see how it
felt, and you know something, strangely enough it
kinda worked. Obviously I didn't kill myself, but
the pain was sooooo super intense it took the
focus off, well, my pain. When I cut, I didn't feel
anxious anymore. I felt alive, I guess. I felt like me
again. For the first time in a long time the pain
wasn't something I was creating in my head. It
was a living, pulsating thing right there on my
arm. It had a shape and texture. The blood
followed the path of my knife and it felt so good
to finally be in control of something. I got to
determine how much pain I felt, how much I bled.
Nobody else but me. Guess I'm a cutter. Looks
like I'll be wearing a lot of long-sleeve shirts from
now on.*

* * *

Pumped! I got a text from Tasha today. Wasn't hard to find her. I just had to tell my therapist that I thought it would help me if I could speak with her. I had to confront my past yadayadayada. Guess what happened? Tasha texted me about three seconds after I texted her. Actually, it wasn't total BS what I said to my shrink. I did feel better hearing from her. She was a good part of a bad experience. If I never spoke to Tasha again, I'd be left with only the bad parts.

So Tasha and I met up. Sophia (she's got her license) drove us to the Gallery at Harbor Place in Baltimore. Back to Baltimore, my old stomping grounds. Sophia had to skip school, but I didn't. I dropped out and I'll probably have to repeat 10th grade or maybe I'll just get my GED. It's hard to imagine I can ever go back to my school again. What happened to me isn't going to be forgotten by everyone over the summer.

The plan was to meet at Starbucks. I got there first and I was crazy nervous waiting for Tasha to show up. Sophia got us each a Caramel Macchiato, which is like four billion calories but it's sooooo unbelievably delicious. We chatted about things. About how bitchy Hannah, Madison, and Brianna were being. About how my dad has been sort of cool to me lately. Cool as in nice, as in acting somewhat interested in me. I slept over at his place the other day and he tucked me in, kissed my forehead like I was a kid again, and he

*even told me that he loved me. He said he was
sorry for everything I'd been through and I
believed him. Even my mom is trying to turn
things around. She's going to AA now. If she saw
my arms she'd send me to CA for sure (that's
cutters anonymous, and no Sophia hasn't seen the
scars because I keep wearing long-sleeve shirts).
When Tasha showed up, Sophia didn't know what
to do or say. I could tell she was really nervous.
Tasha wasn't a girl like us. She was a woman. She
smoked and did drugs and got paid for sex.
Instead of being embarrassed or mad, I just
laughed and grabbed Sophia's arm because I
knew what she was thinking. We're besties after
all. I told her not to be nervous around Tasha.*

    I told her I did everything she did.

    *The good part now. Tasha and I reconnected
and it was like so cathartic. We made it only a few
minutes in Starbucks before I started to cry so we
decided to take a walk. Sophia hung back 'cause
she's cool like that. She understood we needed
time alone. Tasha and I walked arm-in-arm along
the harbor. It was a beautiful day, lots of
sunshine, boats on the water, and a bunch of
seagulls dive bombing unsuspecting tourists for
their food. There was so much to do down there,
but all I wanted to do was walk and talk with
Tasha. She told me she was living at some kind of
safe house for people like us, victims of human
trafficking. Well, more for people like Tasha
because I had a safe house I ran away from. Well,
a sorta safe house. Safer now that mom is cutting*

*back on the booze. But Tasha has nothing. No
family. No real friends. No work experience. No
way to make it. They can give her all the support
in the world, but what is she really going to do
with her life? She doesn't even have a high school
degree. She can get her GED, or so she says. The
other girls don't have it any easier. When we were
back at the apartment, the food was always pretty
decent, but now Tasha gets most of what she eats
from a food pantry, and her clothes come from
Goodwill (though she looked amazing in her
jeans, heels, and this cute yellow top. That from
Goodwill? 4Real? I know where I'll be shopping!)
Tasha told me she'll probably work at a club for a
while. Yeah, that kind of club. Her plan is to save
enough money so she can go to hairstyling
school. Whatever it takes, I told her. But I did say
I'd rather see her cutting hair than twirling on a
pole at some skanky strip club.*

*Tasha held up a baggie of blue pills she
brought just for me. I lifted up my sleeve and
showed her my mangled arm. She made a face
like it was gross to look at, and put the pills back
in her purse. She got it though. I had my own way
of numbing the pain now.*

*Eventually we got down to business. I told
Tasha what I was trying to do. She thought about
it and on the spot came up with something I
hadn't ever considered. Something truly brilliant!
It was so good it made me realize my idea of
going to see Ricardo wasn't ever going to work. I
guess sometimes if you look at things from a*

*different angle what seems like big a disappoint-
ment (e.g. not getting into the prison) is really a
blessing in disguise (e.g. Tasha's idea). Of course
this whole different angle thing doesn't apply to
what Stinger Markovich did to me. There's really
no silver lining there. If I'm being honest with
myself, I'd say I wish I never met Tasha. Harsh,
but it's the truth. She's an awesome girl, don't get
me wrong, but I still wish I didn't have to know
her. I wish I didn't have to know any of them,
including Jade, the poor girl with an eating
disorder who was with us one day and gone
the next.*

*I wish I didn't have to know Jade at all.
But now my only wish is to find her.*

CHAPTER 48

On his way back to Baltimore, Bryce made a planned stop. The guy's name was Ray Anderson and he had retired from the U.S. Marshals when Bryce was still collecting Pokémon cards. Bryce and Ray had never met, but Ray's name was all over the Conti paperwork, so he figured the old-timer might be able to shed some light on the situation. Bryce wanted to do something to help out Angie, though his motives were not a hundred percent altruistic.

He was smitten, no two ways about it. Angie was the package—able, beautiful, and confident, the ABCs to Bryce's heart—but it was more than just pheromones working overtime. He felt they had a lot in common, the important things. They were cut from the same cloth. The job was a calling, a passion for each. You had to be like Angie to truly understand a woman like her, and Bryce got it. He lived it, embodied it. They were members of the same tribe, like with like.

But anything having to do with Angie would have to play out sometime down the road. It wasn't the time for Bryce Taggart's Woo Machine to go fully operational.

The Conti matter had to be resolved first. Angie needed closure, and Bryce was lucky enough to be in a position to help. Even better, he could do it without violating any laws. Well, without egregiously violating them. He was certainly skirting close to the ethical edge. Ray Anderson didn't need to know about Angie DeRose, he just needed to answer some questions from his past.

Bryce had never been to Russett, Maryland before, never had a reason to go there. Bordered by Little Patuxent River and Oxbow Lake, it was a throwback to a simpler time with modest homes, leafy streets, and neighbors known by name. Compared to Bethesda, where Bryce grew up, Russett was a speck of land with a third of the population. Ray was one of 13,000 residents, and owned a nice colonial home with blue vinyl siding and black shutters. He kept his lawn trimmed, and a small garden out front well tended.

Bryce had called beforehand, so Ray was at home and expecting him.

Ray looked a little like Bryce's dad—soft in the middle, hard in the face, with a lot of experience tucked inside the folds of his many wrinkles. He had kind blue eyes, a head of silver hair, and was dressed like Bryce in a plaid shirt and jeans. For a man in his late seventies, Ray looked robust and healthy.

Inside the house, the furniture was nice—traditional style and mostly what one would expect for a guy living off his government pension. The walls were papered with pictures of children and grandchildren.

They shook hello. Ray's hands were rough and calloused, and one finger was bandaged.

"I teach shop at the local voc-tech school," Ray explained, holding up the bandaged finger for Bryce's benefit. "Made for a good second career. But in my old age, the hammer moves faster than the reflexes."

Bryce laughed, and then he complimented Ray for having a nice place. It was how guys talked, *nice place* instead of *a lovely home*.

Ray took the compliment, said he was blessed, and then gave full credit to his wife. "You know how crazy the Marshals' life can be. Sally was the glue that kept it all together."

Eventually they settled on the screen porch overlooking a lush backyard and drank sweet tea from tall glasses filled with ice. Sally was out for the afternoon so he and Bryce had plenty of time to chat, to reminisce. Ray sounded pleased about it and Bryce took it as a signal not to jump right into the purpose of his visit.

He gave Ray time to jawbone about his second greatest love after his family—the U.S. Marshals Service. They didn't have a lot of connections in common, their careers had happened in different eras, but Ray's stories gave Bryce the sense that Ray had enjoyed a distinguished career, one that concluded with a stint on the witness protection team.

That gave Bryce the opening he sought. "I have a case I want to know if you remember."

"Ah, is this what you wouldn't discuss with me over the phone?"

"I believe important things are best discussed in person."

"And I believe when you're as old as I am, everything is important. So shoot. I'll help however I can."

Bryce gave a brief overview of Antonio Conti and his young family, who went into witness protection when Ray was forty-six, already had twenty years in the service, and would be out entirely ten years later. The name Conti didn't jump right out at him. He stared off into space a moment while collecting fragments from his past.

Using his phone, Bryce scanned his photos and showed Ray a picture of Isabella Conti. It was the one Angie had sent to him.

Ray pointed to the girl's ear as though that had triggered a memory. "Oh yeah, Conti. Mob rat. I remember now. Guess it didn't stick because I wasn't on the case for long."

"What do you mean?"

"Well, the day they were slated to go into the program I was taken off the assignment. It was kind of strange, actually."

"Strange how?" Bryce was leaning forward, hands on his knees, listening intently.

"Usually we were on a case for three or four months, at least until the witness transitioned fully into a new life. We would do check-ins, schedule phone calls, have onsite visits, that sort of thing. Conti was the first and only time I got pulled from a detail like that without any real explanation. I have no idea what happened to that family."

Ray's story sounded familiar. Nobody seemed to know what happened to the Contis. Before Bryce could ask another question, his phone rang. He saw it was a call from his fellow U.S. Marshal, Gary Graves.

"Bryce, you sitting down?"

"Yeah."

"Our boy Ivan Markovich has disappeared. He was supposed to check in with his parole officer, but no word. Went to the house and found his GPS monitor on the kitchen table and no Stinger Markovich to be found. Your ass is wanted in Washington ASAP. We're on the task force, brother. We got his boys, now we get to go and get the big man himself."

Bryce ended the call and thanked Ray for his time. He didn't have to explain the reason for his sudden departure.

Bryce and Ray were cut from the same cloth.

CHAPTER 49

When Angie arrived at the house Thursday night, she found her father watching a Nats game with Walter Odette and drinking a beer, which he'd sworn off of since his acid reflux flare-up.

Angie said, "Walt, could I have a few minutes alone with my dad?"

Both Walt and the sofa springs groaned as he rose to his feet. "Wish my ligaments came with a warranty. I could use some new ones. Gabe, I'm gonna head home. Louise is expecting me for dinner. We'll catch up later. Still up for the range this weekend?"

"For sure," Gabe said with a smile. Stashed in a gun safe down in the basement, he kept three pistols—a Glock 19, a Ruger 22/45, and a CZ 75.

Angie knew her weaponry, and her father's choices were good ones for the gun range—comfortable to shoot, with light recoil. Heavy firearms did a number on joints and muscles when firing thousands of rounds at targets. She had gone shooting with Walt and her dad plenty of times, and it was always a fun bonding experience.

Drinking beer and shooting guns; clearly her father was feeling much better.

Walt gave Angie a kiss on the cheek before he departed. "Are you okay, kiddo? You look a little tired."

"I'm fine, Uncle Walt," Angie said, but she wasn't fine, not really. She was worried about what her dad was going to say, what he might reveal.

As soon as Walt was gone, she headed to the kitchen and returned carrying a folder containing all of her research documents. She spread the documents out on the coffee table and got her father to relocate to the sofa so they could view them together. Included among the various papers was the picture of Isabella Conti.

Angie showed her father the familiar photograph. "Mom knew this little girl. She was the daughter of a mobster named Antonio Conti." She went through her findings in brief, giving her father a quick recap of Conti's tumultuous life in New York City during the heyday of the Mob in the 1980s.

After she finished, Gabriel looked at Angie with a blank expression. "Honey, I have no idea what your mother's connection is to this Antonio Conti fellow. None whatsoever."

Angie noticed a change in her father's expression, not a hint of deception, but a fearful look in his eyes. Was he thinking his wife had had an affair, had betrayed him? Angie flashed back to the conversation she'd had with her dad while on stakeout in Baltimore. The memory of Kathleen DeRose remained pristine; she still existed in that state of suspended animation.

"Don't just think about what the answers mean to you, Angie. Think about what it could do to me." Her father's words had been impactful, and yet she couldn't stop

seeking answers, no matter what the consequences of the truth might be.

"Dad, I'm sorry to keep bringing this up. Who is this girl to Mom, and why does she want forgiveness? I have to know."

Gabriel gave Angie's hand a squeeze. "I understand. I really do. And I wish I could help, but I can't."

Angie tried not to let her frustration show. Again she thought of a maze without an exit.

She made dinner for her father—chicken parm (his favorite), light on the parm (not his favorite). She was doing the dinner dishes when Bryce called with some unsettling news. Ivan Markovich was on the lam. For the moment, solving the Isabella Conti mystery wasn't Angie's top concern.

Nadine was.

Angie phoned the Jessup residence from her car. She had left her father in a hurry with a kiss good-bye and a promise to visit later in the week. Her plan was to return to her office and continue with her research, but first, Nadine. Someone had to warn her that Markovich had gone missing. Nadine wasn't at home, but Carolyn was and she sounded more lucid than the last time they'd spoken. There wasn't even the trace of a slur. They exchanged some pleasantries before Angie shared the disquieting news.

"I know," Carolyn said. "The police and some people from the FBI came by and did a wellness check."

"Are they still there?" Angie asked.

"No. They left a while ago. They're not going to stake out our place or anything. I guess because there wasn't a specific threat against Nadine. Do you think she's in any danger?" Carolyn asked.

"I don't think so," Angie said. "But I can't be certain. She should be careful. Maybe not stray too far from home."

"She and Sophia have been going to Baltimore lately," Carolyn said.

Angie almost slammed on the brakes for no reason. "Baltimore? What on earth for?"

"They've been seeing a woman named Tasha. I think she was one of the girls from the apartment."

"Yes, she was. What's Nadine doing with Tasha?"

"I don't know, and I haven't pushed her to tell me."

"Well, maybe you should." Angie regretted the words soon as they left her mouth. It wasn't her place to tell Carolyn how to parent her daughter.

"I have asked, just so you know, but I'm not being demanding about it. I don't want to push Nadine away again. And besides, I'm almost a week sober and a nasty confrontation with my daughter might upset the delicate truce I have forged between my desire and the booze. I have an AA meeting to go to right now, in fact."

"I'm sorry for what I said. It's not my place, and that's wonderful news about AA. Keep it up, Carolyn. I'm really proud of you. I mean it. And please have Nadine give me a call when she can. But tell her it's not urgent."

And it wasn't urgent. The more Angie thought about it, the more she understood the FBI's lack of response. Markovich didn't disappear to go hunting after one of his sixteen-year-old victims.

He had vanished to get away for good.

The next evening, Madeline Hartsock leaned her thin frame against the doorway to Angie's office and cleared her throat to get her friend's attention.

Angie peered out from behind a computer monitor, held up a finger—*just a moment*. The movie, a new action flick starring the ever-youthful Tom Cruise, was starting in thirty minutes and Maddy's impatient expression made it clear they were going to be late if Angie didn't stop what she was doing right then.

Angie wasn't in the mood for a movie, and regretted accepting Maddy's invitation. She was reeling from a triple whammy of disappointing news. Ivan Markovich was still missing and actively being sought by the U.S. Marshals along with other law enforcement types. Bryce's contact at the Marshals Service was in the dark about what had happened to the Contis, and had no clue who they might have become after they went into witness protection. And most discouraging of all was her father's failure to react to the name Antonio Conti. Her mother was connected to the mobster, and Angie felt certain he and her father had traveled in the same circles at some point. Frustrating. Angie had finally identified the girl in the photograph, and it didn't make a lick of difference.

Madeline glanced at her phone for the third time in a minute. "Angie, come on. Take a break, will you?"

Mike Webb appeared in the doorway behind Madeline. His sudden arrival was unannounced and unexpected. He wore gym shorts and a sweat-stained gray jersey. A blue sweatband was stretched across his head. "Mind if I use the can?"

His voice startled Maddy and caused her to jump a little. She moved aside to let Mike into the office.

"You came here just to go to the bathroom?" Angie tried to minimize the degree of her eye roll.

"I was playing pickup hoops down the street and I didn't think I could make it home, if you know what I mean."

"TMI, Mike," Angie said, motioning toward the bathroom door. "TMI."

Mike dashed into the bathroom and emerged moments later with a smile on his face.

"Better?" Angie asked.

"Much. Sorry. I didn't think anybody would be here at this hour."

"We're not supposed to be here," Madeline said with obvious disappointment. "We're supposed to be at the movies, and now I think I'm going to go by myself unless you can help unglue Miss DeRose from her computer."

"Conti?" Mike asked, knowing how overwhelming her obsessions could be.

"Yeah, Conti," Angie said.

"Maddy's right, Ange," Mike said. "Take a break. Go see a movie. Isabella isn't in any immediate danger, if you know what I'm saying."

"You think she's dead."

"If you believe the code Bao broke, then yes. She's dead."

"But it's also the same date they were supposed to go into witness protection."

"A metaphorical death is still a death," Mike said.

Maddy sighed. "Ange, remember how much fun we had in New York? Just take a breather from it all. You'll get the answers later."

New York . . .

Maddy's reference brought Angie back to their recent visit with Jean Winter. Something Jean said had been simmering in Angie's subconscious ever since. It seemed inconsequential at the time, but now Angie wasn't so sure.

Life is too short for petty differences.

Those were Jean's words, and it was also, Angie believed, a possible answer. She cringed because it was so damn obvious.

"Maddy, I'm sorry. I'm going to have to skip the movie. I'll pay for my ticket."

At the same time, Mike nonchalantly opened the top drawer of a three-drawer file cabinet and fished out a Snickers bar from one of the file folders within. He used his teeth to pry open the wrapper.

Angie frowned. "You store candy in my file drawer?"

"I thought you knew. I file it under *S*, for Snickers."

"I've been looking under *C*, for candy," Angie said with an edge.

"Come on, Angie," Maddy said. "Please go. I'm dying to see this movie."

"Say, I might go," Mike said. "What's the movie?"

"The new Tom Cruise."

"Oh yeah? Hmmmm . . ." Mike took a bite of his candy bar and chewed it slowly.

Angie didn't answer Maddy. She was too busy looking through another set of files in the cabinet compartment of her desk. She had one of her mother's death certificates in there someplace. She was sure of it.

"Hello," Maddy said. "Earth to Angie. Come in, Angie. What are you doing?"

"All these years I've respected my mother's wishes about her family," Angie said. "I never asked to speak with them. I had nothing to do with them. But Jean is right. Life is too short for petty differences."

Mike suddenly got interested. "You're going to contact your mom's family?"

"Yes," Angie said. "And I'm going to ask them about Isabella and Antonio Conti."

"Cool," Mike said. "How are you going to find them?"

Angie fished out the death certificate—a life summarized and encapsulated on a standard-size sheet of paper. It was an official-looking document, designed to be hard to forge, and authorized by the state of Virginia. On it was Kathleen DeRose's social security number. "With this," she said, holding up the certificate for Mike to see.

"A death certificate? How's that going to help?" he asked

"I'm going to get my mom's social security application," Angie said.

"What for?"

Maddy seemed to forget about the movie as she walked behind Angie's desk for a better look. Angie showed Mike and Maddy her browser window, which was open to a webpage on the Social Security Information website. The web page header read ELECTRONIC FREEDOM OF INFORMATION ACT. The sub-header read REQUEST FOR DECEASED INDIVIDUAL'S SOCIAL SECURITY RECORD. Specifically, Form SSA-711.

"Applying for a social security number requires all sorts of information about a birth, including family and employment details," Angie said. "Lucky for me, the Paperwork Reduction Act put access to all this information online."

Mike acted impressed. "How'd you know all that?"

Angie shot him a sideways glance. "We're private investigators, Mike. It's kind of our job to know these things."

Mike got the subtext. "Right," he said, acting like he knew. "I just forgot for a moment, that's all."

Angie gave him a weak smile, then returned to the web page. She was excited about her potential discovery, and felt no guilt about not heeding her dead mother's wishes in regards to their extended family.

Mike took another bite of his Snickers bar.

Angie filled in the form. She gave special attention to the required fields and selected the option to pay a sixteen-dollar fee for a computer extract of the social security card application. Angie entered her mother's name as Kathleen Eleanor DeRose, provided the date of birth, gender, and her mother's social security number. When all that was done, she took in a breath and held it. Maddy placed a comforting hand on Angie's shoulder.

"Well, this is it," Angie said, her eyes glued to the computer pointer hovering over the SUBMIT button on the web form.

In a moment, Angie's maternal grandparents would materialize on the computer extract. From there, it would be a relatively easy task to track them down or locate other relatives on her mother's side if her grandparents were dead.

Angie felt a sudden wave of sadness for all she had missed. What had been gained from keeping separate lives? Walt and Louise were fine substitutes for her blood relatives, but she craved a deeper knowledge, a connection with her past, and once more, Jean Winter's words came to her. *Life is too short for petty differences.*

Angie hit the SUBMIT button and waited. The web page reloaded, but with an unexpected red letter error message posted at the top of the form.

NO APPLICATION FOUND.

Additional prompts implied that Angie might have entered the wrong information, a mistyped number perhaps. She checked and everything was correct as documented on the death certificate, so she hit SUBMIT again, counting on it having been a technical glitch. The web page loaded again and the same error message displayed. NO APPLICATION FOUND.

Mike scratched his head. "Angie, if your mom's application doesn't exist in the system, where the heck did her social security number come from?"

He was asking the right question and Angie feared her father knew the answer.

CHAPTER 50

It was Friday night when Angie entered her father's house. She went in through the kitchen and pulled the door closed with a loud bang. The television blared from the living room, but she chose to remain rooted in the kitchen, hands clenched into fists at her sides. She took in a shaky breath that failed to calm her down. Her heartbeat continued to accelerate as her body heated up.

"Dad, I need to see you in the kitchen! Right now!" The imperative summoned her father with haste. The tenor of her voice suggested trouble. She hadn't called ahead, didn't want her father to have time to prepare an answer to the question she'd come to ask. And the answer, "I don't know," was no longer acceptable. He knew something, all right. Angie was certain of it.

Gabriel burst into the kitchen, his slippers losing traction on the tile floor. The short sprint had left him breathless and evidently without time to tie his terrycloth robe. He was dressed for bed in the usual attire, white T-shirt and striped pajama bottoms.

Angie observed the rapid rise and fall of his chest. He

had the look of someone roused roughly from a deep sleep, which at that hour was probably the case.

Gabriel fished out his glasses from a pocket on his robe and asked, "Angie, honey, what's going on? What's wrong?"

To get herself grounded, Angie took a seat at the kitchen table in the same spot where weeks ago she had shown her father the picture of a sweet little girl with a sad smile. She motioned for her father to take the seat across from her, which he did without hesitation.

To quiet the tremor of her hands, Angie kept them folded in her lap. She fell silent while her father waited patiently for her to speak. During the lull, her ears picked up on the *tick-tock* of the wall-mounted kitchen clock—a Felix the Cat model with those traveling eyes she found more creepy than cute.

Gabriel decided the silence had lasted long enough. "What is this about, Angie? Is everything all right?"

She answered her father's question by shaking her head. It took a moment before she could speak. "No, Dad, I don't think it is." A line of tears filled her lower lids and blurred her vision. She tilted her head back to hold them in place. It wasn't the time to let them go.

"No more lies, Dad," Angie said. "Who is Mom's family?"

Gabriel lowered his gaze to his lap and then slowly raised his head to reveal a contrite expression. "Why do you want to know?" His voice lacked inflection.

"Because I want to know why my mom has a social security number that seemingly materialized out of thin air."

Gabriel's eyes narrowed to slits as the creases of his brow deepened. "I don't understand. What are you getting at here?" He ran his fingers through his thinning hair and rubbed clean the lenses of his dark rimmed glasses using the cloth tie of his bathrobe.

Angie viewed both gestures as nervous tics, a subconscious reflex of a mind focused heavily on concocting an acceptable story.

"I ran Mom's social security number through an online form to get a copy of her application. I wanted to find her parents so I could ask them about Isabella Conti, but Mom has no social security application, even though she has a valid number. I don't know your family or hers, and I want to know why."

"You know the story."

Angie slammed her hand against the kitchen table, creating a clap loud enough to make her father flinch. "I know *your* story!" she bellowed, pointing at him with an accusatory finger. "Now I want the truth. Mom has a connection to a mobster and a phantom social security number. Who has that, Dad? Who? The people who need to disappear, that's who! Now, tell me the truth. I won't stop until I get it. You know me. You know how I can be."

Gabriel took in a few ragged breaths. He knew, all right. "Angie . . . I'm having a . . . a hard time breathing here."

All of the anger, Angie's inner turmoil, quieted in a blink, and her focus shifted away from questions about her mother to the health of her father. She leapt out of her chair and leaned over him, feeling his forehead with her hand. His skin felt clammy to the touch. She tuned into the fast flutter of his heart.

"Daddy, are you all right? I'm so sorry. I didn't mean to do that to you. Do I need to call an ambulance?"

Gabriel shook his head. "No, no, I'm fine," he said,

though he was still a bit breathless. "You just caught me by surprise, is all."

Angie retook her seat, but with a different attitude, no longer on the offensive. She reached across the table and took hold of her father's hands, then looked him in the eyes. "Daddy, listen to me. I love you. I don't want to upset you, but I have to know the truth. And I'm going to get the answer with your help or without it. My investigation won't be subtle. I'm going to turn over every last stone and I might attract the attention of the same people Mom was trying to hide from. I think that's what's going on here. I think Mom knew the Conti family. She was connected to them somehow and she went into hiding just like they did.

"Maybe the people Mom ran away from would come looking for you and me, if they knew where to look. I don't know. But I do know some grudges last longer than generations. Some members of the Giordano family, I bet, would love to find Antonio Conti, same as I think someone would like to find Mom and her family. I don't know who, but I won't stop looking until I get the answer. I know the relationship you had with Mom, and I know she wouldn't keep that kind of secret from you. I know it in my heart. I'll dig into your past the same as I dug into Mom's until I find someone who knows something.

"Now, you can make it safer for us both by telling me what I want to know. Don't make me go looking. Just tell me and I'll stop."

Gabriel's mouth slipped into a grimace. He rested his head in his hands, and his gaze turned distant. "Angie, please."

Angie shook her head. "You know me. You know how I can be. Who is my mother? Who is she really?"

Gabriel swallowed a breath. He looked to the ceiling, then back at Angie. "You promise you'll stop asking questions?"

"Yes, Dad," Angie said.

"It's not safe if you don't."

"I promise, Dad."

"What I'm going to say will shock you."

"Just tell me."

"Angie, sweetheart, what I'm going to tell you—well, it changes everything."

"I'm prepared for anything, Dad. Honest, I am."

"No," Gabriel said, with a slight shake of his head. "I can assure you, you're not prepared for this."

CHAPTER 51

It wasn't the kind of manhunt to which Bryce Taggart was accustomed. Instead of donning body armor and making sure Little Pig was oiled and ready for action, he manned the phones, tracked tips, and fed information to his fellow marshals working as part of the Capital Area Regional Fugitive Task Force, CARFTF for short. Teams from the SOG—Special Operations Group—were on hand and on the front lines doing the kind of fieldwork Bryce hoped to be doing when the Baltimore office volunteered him and Gary Graves for the Ivan Markovich task force.

Bryce and Graves were working out of the DC office, which was a lot nicer than his digs in Baltimore. Newer cubes, better lighting, but it still looked like an office anywhere, except that a lot of the employees carried guns. The room they shared was a cramped space with poor lighting, two phones, two laptop computers and not much else. Soon they would be moved to the official war room—a state-of-the-art command center with satellite feeds, banks of high-tech monitors, computers, the works.

But until the IT wonks got them established, they had to make do with the accommodations.

Bryce didn't think he'd be on desk duty for long. Markovich had vanished without a trace and as the hours slipped away, more marshals would be called in to assist with fugitive apprehension. The media wasn't helping to spread the word. A story about a guy jumping bail didn't carry the same weight as a prison break, so coverage had been spotty at best. Still, the tips were coming in, and Bryce was busy entering them into the tracking system while trying to figure out which ones merited a closer look.

"I'm going to get some more coffee," Graves announced, sounding a little apathetic. He wanted to be in the field, as well, but was dressed for office duty in a blue polo fronted by the U.S. Marshals insignia, black belt, and dark pants. Bryce had on the same outfit.

"If they have any more of those peanut packets, bring me one, will you?"

Bryce's desk phone rang. It was another tip on Markovich, somebody in Alaska swearing the alleged trafficker was on his charter fishing trip. That one would go to the bottom of the pile. But at least the tips were coming.

Graves returned with two coffees, but no peanuts. "They're out."

Bryce looked disappointed, an expression that changed to curiosity when a U.S. marshal Bryce didn't recognize poked his head into their small office.

"Cormack Donovan," the man said. He was a tall and thin fellow with brown hair, a boyish, clean-shaven face, and canny eyes.

Bryce didn't believe Donovan was on the Markovich task force, hadn't seen his name on any of the circulating memos, or noticed him at the multitudes of debrief meetings.

"How are you Baltimore boys adjusting to life here in DC?" Donovan asked. He had a sort of fluty voice, not exactly threatening.

"Good," Bryce said, entering more data into the system. "It's not too different."

Donovan stepped fully into the office and took a look around. "Listen, boys," he said, sitting on the edge of their worktable. "If you could put in a good word for me, let the right people know you're short-handed and could use a little help on Markovich, I'd really appreciate it. I'd like to get in on this detail, even if it means the phones." The envy came off Donovan like a bad case of BO.

"What are you supposed to be doing?" Graves asked.

"I'm actually working witness protection. I'm supposed to relocate a guy named Dante Lerardi, but I popped over here first because I'm trying to get in good with the SOC, career stuff, you know? So anything I could do to help out with their ops, I want to do it. I'd love the opportunity, if you know what I mean."

Bryce shrugged, his way of saying he understood. Witness protection wasn't as glamorous as fugitive apprehension. Marshals jockeying for position and status among the ranks wanted in on the hottest action, and it made sense Donovan wanted a seat at the Markovich table.

Instead of a firm offer, Donovan went away with high hopes and low expectations he and Bryce would work together.

By the time afternoon rolled around, Bryce was famished. He wondered if Angie was available to grab an early bite to eat. He would call only when he knew he could make it happen. He didn't want to make plans with her he'd have to cancel. Bryce played no games. He wasn't after a conquest, didn't simply want to get Angie into the sack. That kind of dating was for the younger set. He knew what he wanted and would go after her patiently and persistently, but always gentlemanly.

Afternoon turned into evening and Markovich had turned into a ghost. All leads were drying up like desert rain. It was going to be a late night, and Bryce's hopes for a dinner date with Angie were all but dashed. Not everyone at the U.S. Marshals Service working overtime was disappointed by the lack of progress.

Cormack Donovan had returned to the cramped office while Bryce and Graves were packing up their belongings to move into the war room. "Hey, guys, I just wanted to say thanks."

"You're welcome," Bryce said, not at all sure why he was being thanked, and not feeling any compulsion to ask.

"I'm on the task force now," Donovan said with a broad smile. "I figured you two put in a good word for me."

"For sure," Graves said, nodding. "We talked you up big-time."

Bryce just smiled. "What happened to your witness?"

Donovan shrugged. "I don't know. One minute I was on the Lerardi detail, and the next thing I know I'm off. I guess they got some other guy to watch him thanks to you two."

Bryce's smile retreated. He and Graves hadn't done a thing to help out Donovan, but Bryce thought it sounded a lot like what had happened to Ray Anderson all those years ago, back when he was on the Antonio Conti detail. One minute Ray had a witness to protect, and the next minute that witness was gone.

Bryce's gaze reverted to his laptop, but his focus was fractured. Donovan lingered in the doorway, motioning to someone Bryce couldn't see. Soon enough a second U.S. marshal, dressed similarly to Bryce and Graves in a polo and slacks, appeared in the doorway. He was fair-skinned, lean, fit, and tall, with an angular face and a jaw that almost came to a point. His short hair, cut military style, revealed a broad and nearly creaseless forehead. His eyes were blue and held all the warmth of stone. Without a smile, his expression was a blank.

Donovan said, "These are the Baltimore boys I was telling you about, Bryce Taggart and Gary Graves. If you want to be mad at anybody for getting me out from under your nose, blame these two."

"Last I checked, it's a temporary assignment," the man with Donovan said. "In fact, I came down here to tell your new boss just how temporary."

Donovan said, "Yeah? Well, once the SOG sees I'm the guy who brought in Markovich, I'm betting the move is going be permanent. Taggart, Graves, this is my soon-to-be ex-boss on witness protection, Raynor Sinclair."

CHAPTER 52

Buzzwords come and they go. That's the job of those words, I guess. For instance, hash tag (ya know, #) is all in right now, but I bet it's not going to mean anything to kids five years younger than me when they turn 17. Oh yeah. Happy birthday to me! I'm seventeen now. Yea me. I sure feel like I've crammed in a lot more years than that into this life-o-mine, but whatever, I'm 17 so happy birthday to me. But the buzzword thing, right? I think Human Trafficking is kind of a buzzword. I've been doing some research online and that's my big conclusion. It's sort of a fad phrase. Hot topic right now, but check with me in five years and let me know if that's still the case. My fear is some new issue is going to come along and replace it, and people won't talk about the problem anymore, and some girl is going to be trafficked just like me and because it's not a buzzword anymore she'll just think she was just a prostitute or something. #thatwouldbeashame

* * *

Here's the hard part for me. Just being honest here. I can't decide if Ricardo is really to blame for what happened to me or if I am. Did he really manipulate me into doing all those horrible things or do I just think he did so I can have someone to blame? And whenever I think that, I think, damn he's still controlling me, and that I can't win, and that's when I start to feel hopeless.

I know I'm worth more than I think I am. I know it, but it's still hard to accept it. I guess that's why they're called emotional scars. It's like having little x's scratched all over my body to mark the spot, but instead of digging up buried treasure, you'd unearth my worst nightmares.

I decided to stop cutting. And no, my shrink didn't get me to stop. I just know it's an addiction, like Tasha's little blue pills. Life isn't all one long horror show. That's what I'm starting to believe. There are good people out there, people like Sophia and Tasha, doing their best in a sometimes pretty crappy world. Where does this epiphany (thank you again SAT prep) come from, you ask? Well, Tasha came through for me yesterday. She came through BIG TIME. She called to tell me she got the information from Casper. I guess she told Casper the police were going to file charges or something unless he could prove Jade was alive. Ha! He totally bought it and Tasha is totally brilliant. So now I know where to find Jade. I guess the whole experience made me realize there is good in this world. Now I've got a chance to pay it forward. So I'm going to put down the knife for a while, stop cutting, and try and prove to myself that feeling better doesn't mean I have to make myself feel worse.

CHAPTER 53

"Just tell me," Angie said. "I'm a big girl, Dad. I can handle it."

"You've got to promise me that it's over. You and the photograph, this investigation of yours, it's done. No more digging."

"You know this girl?" Angie said, holding up the picture of Isabella Conti. Blood gushed like a rapids through her veins as she recalled her father's ominous warning. *I can assure you, you're not prepared for this.* If he did know Isabella Conti, it would mean he had lied to her, time and time again.

"No," Gabriel said. "I don't know the girl in the photograph. I promise you that's true. But I do know why your mother—well, why you couldn't get her social security application."

"Why?" Angie's jaw set tight as she placed the photo faceup on the table. Isabella's sad expression gazed up at her.

"Your mother never had one filed," Gabriel said, "at least not with that number."

Angie put her hand to her mouth. Something about

what her father said, or how he said it, triggered a thought. She came up with a reason, one inspired by her research into the Conti clan, and her theory caused her stomach to drop. "Was my mom—was she in witness protection?"

One look into her father's eyes told Angie had struck the bull's-eye.

"Not exactly," her father said. "I was. Your mom came along because of me."

Angie's head began to spin. "Wait. Then . . . then that means—"

"Yes, sweetheart. It means you're in witness protection, too. You grew up in the program, only you didn't know it."

Without warning, Angie's stomach lurched as her head began to buzz. A dizzy feeling overcame her and set the room on a tilt. "Everything is a—It's all a lie," she said, stammering. "The orphanage, your scholarship to college, meeting Mom, the fight with her family over me, it was all . . . all a lie."

Angie gasped for breath. She pushed away from the table and rushed to the bathroom, where she sent what little she'd had to eat into the toilet. Afterwards, over the porcelain sink with the water running, she gazed into the mirror, seeing a phantom of herself, a sickly pale reflection of a woman she didn't know, of someone with a secret past.

Questions peppered her like shotgun pellets. Who were her grandparents? Did she have other relatives? Were they living? Were they nearby? Why did her dad enter witness protection? Who was Angie beforehand? She had to have a different last name, something other than DeRose. What was it?

Her father was right—she wasn't prepared for this. No, not in the least.

Emerging from the bathroom on shaky legs, she used the wall to keep upright. She gazed ahead vacantly, focused on nothing at all.

Eventually, she retook her seat, but had a difficult time making eye contact with her father. "How could you do this to me?"

"What difference did it make?" Gabriel answered, reaching across the table for Angie's hand.

She pulled away from his touch.

Gabriel pushed his chair back and lowered his head. "Your story was going to be the same regardless. Either way, your mom and me were going to be the only family you knew, we were all you could ever know. What we told you was a lie, yes, but in a way, not much of one if you think about it. Your life isn't that different from the truth."

Angie forced herself to make eye contact. "How can you even say that?"

"You are a DeRose, and what matters is that you had us."

"Who—Who am I really?" Angie's voice trembled while her stomach continued with an array of somersaults.

"You're Angie."

"No, no. My birth name. What is the name on my real birth certificate?"

Angie had seen a copy of her birth certificate before, when she'd applied for a passport. The United States government had evidently manufactured the document she'd used to prove her citizenship.

Gabriel hesitated then in a quiet voice, he said, "Your birth name was Amelia. It was your mother's choice, but we both agreed to rename you Angie, because well, it reminded us of your first name."

"You mean my real name," Angie said through clenched

teeth. The quake in her voice foretold tears. "Amelia what?" Her tone was harsh.

Gabriel pulled his lips tight. "Amelia Harrington," he said, before a sob came out. A crack in the dam of long-held secrets had released a torrent of emotions. Gabriel began to cry, tears streaming down his face.

"Spare me, Dad," Angie said. "Please spare me your emotion right now. You are my dad, right?"

Gabriel's aggrieved look normally would have pained Angie, but not this time. "God, sweetheart, please. Yes, of course I'm your father."

"Don't make it sound like a given." The anger came on strong and tempered Angie's other emotions. Everything was happening so fast. In a blink, her world had inverted.

"You're my daughter," Gabriel said, his lips trembling, a pleading look cast in his watery eyes.

"Who are you?" Angie asked, fearing the answer. "Why did you have to go into hiding? What did you do?"

Gabriel's resolve took over. He knew there was no turning back now. "My given name was William Harrington. My mother was Pam Greenfield, my father Henry Harrington. Your mother was Claire Connors. Her mother was Rebecca and her father Joseph. Those are your grandparents, Angie."

"Angie," she repeated with disgust. "I'm Amelia, remember?"

"No, you're Angie DeRose. It's the only name you've ever known."

"How old was I?"

"You were just a little girl."

"How old?"

Gabriel hesitated to answer. "You were an infant."

"A baby?"

"Yes, a beautiful baby girl, who I had to protect."

"From what? What did you do?"

"I made some terrible choices," Gabriel said.

"Well, I can attest to that."

"Please, Angie, you don't understand the circumstances."

"Then enlighten me." Angie couldn't believe she was having this conversation.

Gabriel said, "As William Harrington, I was a young financial hotshot, living in New York, married to your mother and running the equivalent of a very sophisticated Ponzi scheme."

"Like Bernie Madoff?"

"Similar but a little different. You see, Madoff stole from ordinary people, while I stole from mobsters and drug dealers."

"Like Antonio Conti?"

"People who knew Conti, yes, but not from him directly."

"But you heard of him?"

"Yes, of course. But like I said, not the daughter. I didn't know her or recognize her face. I swear to you that's true."

Angie believed him. For someone like Dot at the Microtia center, Isabella Conti meant a great deal. She was a connection to her son's condition and a possible conduit to increased awareness and research funding. But for her father, Isabella was just the daughter of a man who ran in the same circles as the people he stole from.

"Did Mom know Isabella?"

"Maybe," Gabriel said. "I don't honestly know."

"What's honest about you, Dad, really?"

"What I'm telling you is the truth whether you want to believe it or not."

"So you lived in New York."

"Yes, we did. All of us, you, me, and Mom. And New York back in the eighties was a crazy place, so much money being tossed around. I got greedy, and then I got crooked, and then I got downright stupid. A friend of mine introduced me to some—well, let's call them connected fellows, and I soon became one of their trusted financial advisors. What they didn't know, and what I couldn't tell them, was that my exemplary record with stock picks was all fabricated. The statements, the returns, everything was a lie. I couldn't tell them this, of course, because it would have exposed me as a fraud, so I took them on as clients and gave them the biggest returns.

"I ended up getting more clients like them, these mafioso types. Eventually I needed to rob Peter to pay Paul, and my house of cards was teetering on collapse. I drained the bank accounts of men who threatened to skin me alive for what I did, but only after they killed you and your mother and made me watch. That was a direct threat, by the way. Not hyperbole. The only way I could protect my family was to go into hiding.

"I knew everything about their financial dealings, so I was valuable to the government. I could avoid paying for my crimes and save all our lives, but only by going into hiding after turning state's witness."

"Walter Odette," Angie said. "That's how you two became friends."

"Yes," Gabriel said. "He was my handler. He got us into the program. Relocated us from New York to Alexandria. Provided us with our new names, everything. I know you would have found all this out eventually, so that's why I'm telling you the truth. You're right, Angie. If you dig around enough, you could turn over the wrong rock. The people I stole from do not have short memories. Now, I'm counting on you. You've got to keep your promise and let this go. If we're found out, we'll both be dead."

"By who? Who will kill us?"

"With the kind of money I stole, basically anyone who had ties to my crimes. A pound of our flesh for revenge."

Angie forced herself to stand, hoping it would stop the room from spinning. It did not. "And Mom's family, your family, nobody has heard from any of us all these years?"

"No," Gabriel said. "Not once. Not ever. It's simply too dangerous."

"My God, Dad, why didn't you ever tell me?" But she knew the answer. Living as Angie DeRose had kept her out of danger. She was safely cocooned inside her phony identity. And what good was the truth, anyhow? She could have gone on living a lie and not suffered from his deception in the slightest.

She knew only what she'd been taught. She was Angie. She lived in Virginia. She was born and raised there. Her father grew up an orphan. Her mother had had a falling-out with her family. And those beliefs became rooted in her, woven deeply into the fabric of her being. Her father was right. Angie or Amelia, either way she would have ended up essentially in the same place—a girl from Virginia with no extended family to speak of. But would Amelia have become a private investigator? Would Amelia have gone to UVA? Would Amelia have become friends with Maddy and Sarah Winter? What kind of person would Amelia be?

Angie saw Amelia and the age-progressed image of Isabella Conti as one—two fictional personas existing only in a place of potential, a place of *would have been*, and *could have been*.

"Why did Mom write *forgive me* on the back of Isabella's photo?"

"I don't know," Gabriel said. "I told you everything, Angie. I swear."

She believed him, but didn't believe he was right about her life not having turned out so differently if she had grown up knowing the truth. It *was* different now. And to think, all this was because of questions she'd raised about a mysterious photograph, a photograph with a connection to her mother she still didn't understand, and perhaps never would.

But that wasn't the worst part anymore. The worst part was living with the truth. Nothing Angie had learned could change the facts of her past. It had only changed her perception of the people she loved.

"How could you do this to me?" Angie said again, pressing her hands hard against the edge of the kitchen table, readying to flee her father's home in a hurry. "How could you?"

"You still don't understand," Gabriel answered in a breathy voice. "I didn't do this *to* you. I did it *for* you."

"No," Angie said. Her father's words rang hollow. "The charade you put on let you *really* escape one life for another. You weren't hiding the truth from me, Dad. You were hiding it from yourself."

CHAPTER 54

The office, as expected, was empty when Angie showed up, though the quiet offered no respite from the noise blaring in her head. Questions rolled and tumbled about her mind with the haphazardness of a dust storm. Outside her office window, the twinkle of city lights stood like stars against a black landscape, while the outlines of nearby buildings shone beneath the spotlight of a moonbeam.

Angie sat in darkness, with only a faint light cast from the glow of her computer monitor. She had several web pages open, and searches going on in various professional databases. She wanted to learn everything she could about William Harrington and Claire Connors. When did they get married? Where? She wanted details about her grandparents. Did she have any aunts and uncles? What about cousins?

It would take time to sort through, and she needed to be patient. One hour bled into the next, and Angie hadn't made much progress. The anger remained, but as a simmer. She reflected on her life. Happy memories returned, of times with her parents at Lake Anna and Bethany

Beach, of picnics and road trips, of dance recitals and softball practices, of all the things her mom and dad would have done had she been Angie or Amelia.

The office door came open and Bao entered, rolling in on his long board, bracelets jangling rhythmically from his wrists. He wore a white T-shirt adorned with an intricate graphic design and a pair of loose-fitting jeans. His long, dark hair splayed across narrow shoulders.

"Yo, Ange, didn't know you were here. I was coming up to do some work."

"I'll be here for a bit, but feel free to join me."

Bao went to his desk and took out a laptop from the messenger bag draped across his shoulders. "My roommate is having a Magic tournament and I can't concentrate."

"Magic?"

"Yeah, it's a card game. Kind of cool. Kind of geeky, too."

Angie had known Bao was back in town. He had come back from camping early to help Mike locate another runaway girl—another potential Nadine, but this girl was named Kelsey. Angie made Mike lead on the case so she could concentrate on the Isabella Conti investigation, now in a tailspin.

"Mind if I turn on a light?" Bao asked.

"Go ahead."

The sudden brightness caused Angie to blink rapidly.

Bao glanced at her and saw what he couldn't see in the darkness. "You all right?"

Out of the darkness, Angie's raw emotions were on full display. Her agitation and anger had bubbled to the surface, where Bao could see it clearly.

"I'm fine," Angie said.

He wasn't buying it. "Come on, Ange, what gives? Is it something I did?"

"No, no, it's not you," Angie said, dabbing at her eyes with a tissue. "Of course not."

"We think we tracked Kelsey to her friend's house in Ohio, if that helps." Bao pulled his desk chair closer to Angie's.

"That's great news," Angie said, though the flatness of her voice contradicted the sentiment.

"Talk to me," Bao said. "I wanna help. Is it about the photograph?"

Angie had vowed to keep her promise to her father and stop looking for a connection between Isabella Conti and her mother. She believed that sort of investigation could get them both killed by attracting attention from the wrong sort of people. But her promise didn't mean she couldn't talk about her family secret with those she trusted the most, Bao among them. It was her burden to guard, but she felt she could share something of her story, even if only in generalities.

"You have to swear you won't tell anybody about this. Not even Mike," Angie said. "I trust you, Bao, and I could use someone to talk to. But if word got out to the wrong people, it could be dangerous to me, my dad, and anybody close to me, including you."

"You can count on me, Angie. Always and forever."

Angie believed him. She recounted for Bao carefully selected portions of what her father had told her. How her mother and father's backstory was fabricated; how she grew up in witness protection, but never knew it; how her real name was Amelia.

"Is that the Conti connection?" Bao asked.

"Let's just say I'd rather not say," Angie replied.

Sharing what little she had was cathartic on some level. The hurt wouldn't go away any time soon (or ever, perhaps), but Angie hoped it would lessen with time.

"What are you going to do now?" Bao asked. His shocked expression reminded her of someone who had just driven past a horrific car crash.

Angie settled for a vague response. "I guess I'll have to figure it out."

Bao was young. Angie hadn't confided in him for life advice as much as she did for release. His question, though, was a good one. *What now?*

Angie actually had some hands-on experience with her father's unique brand of betrayal. As an investigator, she had found kids who had been kidnapped as young children or infants by a biological parent and raised under a different identity. Was her situation so different from theirs? Over the years, she had kept in touch with some of them, and the best outcomes, from her limited exposure, were the ones where the child forgave the parent. The kids who harbored resentment needed a place to put their anger and often turned to alcohol and drugs as means of coping.

An unsettled silence took over, before Bao finally broke the spell. "Look, Ange, this is pretty heavy stuff, and well, I don't know how to make it any better."

"I know. I'm sorry to dump it all on you."

"But, I do have something to say." He seemed deeply earnest.

Angie's ears pricked up. "Yeah?"

"I was going nowhere in life until you came along. I mean I was doing drugs, I was angry all the time, a really screwed-up kid."

"And look how you turned yourself around," Angie said.

"But it happened because of you," Bao said. "Because you were there for me, and you took the time to get to know me. You introduced me to my parents, and well, I dunno."

A shrug told Angie it wasn't an easy conversation for him to have. Bao had matured tremendously since they first met, but he still suffered from trust issues. Sharing his feelings was a lot harder than showcasing his computer skills or skateboard chops.

"I'm very, very proud of who you've become," Angie said.

Bao looked pleased, but it was clear he still had more to say. "I guess my point is this. Angie or Amelia, I don't really care who you are. I just care that you're in my life, and that you were there for me, that you cared enough to help. To me your name doesn't matter, who you were doesn't matter. What matters most is that you're you, you're Angie, and I-I . . . well, I love you."

Tears came to Angie's eyes. She stood and opened her arms. Bao rose to his feet and embraced her. Then he started to cry, shoulders heaving sort of cry. He cried for his lost childhood, for the hard times, and the good ones that included his adoptive parents. Soon Angie couldn't control her own waterworks. They hugged and cried together, and she stroked Bao's long hair and told him how much she loved him.

When they broke apart, both dabbed at their watery eyes, laughing a little awkwardly.

"Sorry about that," Bao said. "It's just, you mean so much to me. I don't know what I'd do without you, but I do know where'd I be if I hadn't met you. And that's nowhere."

Angie tried to imagine life without her dad who meant so much to her, and the notion of cutting him off completely as punishment didn't sit well at all. The question was how to find a new equilibrium with her father. It took Bao to make her see the path forward more clearly.

Still, her investigative instincts continued to ping. While she had promised not to search for the Conti connection, she'd made no such offers in regards to investigating her genealogy.

"All right, you've got an Ohio girl mystery to solve, and I've got to get some work done on my own," Angie said.

"You want to be alone," Bao said.

"Ya know, I like how you just get me, Bao. I really do."

He gave her another hug, gathered up his things, and rolled away on his skateboard.

Over the course of several hours, Angie scoured the Web and various databases. She would have liked Bao's help—he was good at that sort of thing—but there was only so much information she felt safe sharing. On her own, she managed to construct a rudimentary family tree with some pretty bare branches. She scrounged up a few names, some pertinent dates, but nothing close to the photographic treasure trove she sought.

Her grandparents might very well be dead. If they did have social media profiles, none were coming up in any of their searches. Maybe because of the things William Harrington—aka Gabriel DeRose, aka Angie's dad—had done, they intentionally kept a low profile. The same could be said of her uncles, aunts, and various cousins.

Without more information to go on, Angie switched tactics and started to look into William Harrington's past. She wanted to know everything she could about her father's former life, and what had led him to the choices he had made.

On one database, Angie found documents incorporating her father's financial business. An address was on file in New York City, but it wasn't located near where Antonio Conti once resided. Still, Angie's mom and Conti could have crossed paths at some point, given the clientele her father serviced.

Bigger questions loomed. Why weren't there any articles about William Harrington? Why weren't there news reports detailing her father's Ponzi scheme? Why wasn't the trial of the mobsters he gave up to the DA covered in the local press? Maybe the deals were done secretly. Perhaps for her father's safety, arrangements were made to bury the truth. It would explain why details of his Ponzi scheme were kept out of the press.

One thing was certain. Instead of getting any answers, what Angie had were more questions for her father.

CHAPTER 55

A ngie endured a fitful night's sleep before finally surrendering to her anxiety-induced insomnia. She rose
from bed before the sun came out. Her father had called a
number of times, but she'd let his calls go to voice mail,
same as she did calls from Mike and Maddy. Angie needed
to be alone with her thoughts, painful and frustrating as
they were. She showered just after sunrise, put on her favorite pink robe, and made a pot of Trader Joe's coffee.
The first cup of the day was life-affirming and trumped
her lack of sleep and all the nagging questions about her
past.

She had left her office late, only to come home and re-
sume her hunt for information about William Harrington.
Her search was going nowhere. As Friday had turned into
Saturday, she knew come morning she would have to
make the call she had hoped not to make. It wasn't an im-
petuous decision, nor was it one she came to lightly. But
after wrestling with her options, getting answers trumped
Angie's other concerns. Bryce was a good man, and she
regretted putting him in any sort of compromising position, but he was best-equipped to help.

Angie waited until eight o'clock Saturday morning, though her restraint didn't come easy. She occupied herself with the local news. The lead story was about a house fire in McLean, not about Ivan Markovich. He wasn't the first criminal to skip bail, and the story didn't have legs. To the public, Markovich was a pimp who'd gone on the lam. They didn't understand the implications of human trafficking and why that story should have trumped a fire. Stinger being MIA meant Bryce had probably pulled an all-nighter trying to find him.

Angie was going to add to his misery.

Bryce answered her call after two rings. "Hey there. I've been thinking about you."

"Good thoughts, I hope."

"Always. I've been meaning to call, but we keep running into brick walls here and we're not getting very far with our hunt. This Stinger guy, man, I dunno. He's like a phantom or something."

"Where are you?"

"DC."

"That close? Can we meet up?"

"I would if I could. Believe me, I'd like to. How are things on your end?"

"Loaded question," Angie said. "I'm not sure you want the answer."

"Try me. Though I might have to interrupt you if the phone rings."

Angie gave Bryce an information dump, and he didn't interrupt her once.

He fell silent for a time, and then said, "I'm reeling here, Angie. I-I don't know what to say."

"Say that you'll help me," Angie replied.

"Help you how?"

"Get into the records. I want to know everything about the DeRose identity. We've got to be in there someplace."

"I'm sure you are," Bryce said.

"I want to know who my father was, what he did, what kind of deal he struck with the Feds. There's no mention of his big Ponzi scheme anywhere, or any of the mobsters he stole from for that matter, or how his information allegedly brought them down."

"FYI, that's a fast track to the unemployment line for me if I get caught."

"I'd understand if you won't help," Angie said.

"It's not a question of want to help. Of course I want to help. It's more like, holy crap. Really?"

"Yeah, tell me about it."

"Look, maybe there aren't any news reports because the information was used by the Feds, not for any trial, but just to get a sense of how these guys operated. That's worth handing a low-level Ponzi schemer a GET OUT OF JAIL FREE card. No disrespect to your dad."

"None taken, and I like your theory."

"Good. Then we're all set."

"Will you look for me, Bryce?"

He made a heavy sigh. "I have to check with my guy, but okay. No promises here. A lot depends on our pal Markovich. But I'll do what I can. What are you going to do in the meantime?"

"In the meantime, I'm going to talk to someone who might be able to shed some light on my dad's mysterious past."

Angie had open-door privileges at the Odettes' home, same as the Odettes had at her father's place. She rang the doorbell anyway. It felt like the right thing to do because she hadn't done a popover visit since her high school days.

Louise Odette opened the front door with a bright smile on her face. Her silver hair, cut just above her shoulders, wasn't styled for public viewing. Even without the benefit of makeup, she had aged gracefully, and the striking woman Walter had married more than fifty years ago was easy to see.

At eleven o'clock in the morning, she was still draped in her floral patterned bathrobe—the perfect attire for a lazy Saturday morning. Angie wore her Lands' End outfit—jeans and a white long-sleeved jersey with a fleece vest. She'd already had three cups of coffee, which in hindsight wasn't wise given her level of agitation.

"Angie, sweetie, what brings you here?"

"I was hoping to speak with Walter if he's at home."

Louise stepped back and invited Angie inside. The Odettes' home was tastefully furnished, bright and airy, very welcoming, but not at all extravagant. The color palette was whites and blues mostly, with plenty of collectables throughout—sea glass in mason jars, old watering cans, flea market treasures—all artfully arranged in wooden cases and displayed on wall-mounted shelves.

Walt was careful with his money (her dad's influence perhaps) and spent it on experiences (and grandchildren), but not things. He enjoyed traveling and it wasn't uncommon for him to be gone for months at time, sometimes with Louise, but sometimes without. The Odettes did retirement the right way, but given Angie's tax returns, she was not on pace for such adventurousness. She had better odds chasing down adulterers at seventy-five then she did taking off for a few months to soak up the Bora Bora sunshine.

"Everything all right with your dad?"

"Yeah, fine. Thanks."

"Walt's down in his workshop," Louise said, tightening the tie of her robe as she led Angie into a spacious kitchen, the heart of most any home. "Do you want some coffee?" She glanced at the kitchen clock and noticed the time. "Oh goodness me, you probably want lunch. We're not always this slow getting started, dear."

"I'm just going to have water." Angie helped herself to a glass. She knew where everything was.

"I'll go grab Walt."

Moments later, Angie and Walt were seated across from each other at the round kitchen table.

"Talk to me, Angie," Walt said.

She glanced out the window and made sure Louise was still in her garden, watering plants in her bathrobe. Angie wasn't sure if Louise was in on the secret.

"I know," Angie began. "About my mom and dad . . . and me. About our being in witness protection all these years."

Walt didn't look as shocked or surprised as she had expected. "Did your dad tell you or did you somehow figure it out on your own?"

"My dad," Angie said.

Walt returned a grim nod. "You must be in a state of shock. Look, I'm sorry, kiddo. Keeping the secret wasn't easy, but it was the job. I hope you understand."

"I do, and I don't blame you. Honest I don't."

Walt gave Angie's hand a squeeze. "Thanks. That's a huge relief. You know I love you and I'd never do anything to hurt you."

"I know. But I'm confused about something."

"I imagine you're confused about a lot."

"There's really nothing about William Harrington and his Ponzi scheme in any of the archives I've searched.

Nothing I could find about my dad turning state's evidence, either."

Birdsong filtered in through the open kitchen windows and the aroma of Louise's fresh brewed coffee tickled Angie's senses.

Walt cleared his throat and pursed his lips. "I don't know anything about that. My job was to help get your dad a new life, and that's what I did. We were close in age and, well, we just became friends. It was the only time in my career with the Marshals that ever happened to me. I really liked your dad and I empathized with his situation. You were too young to remember anything from that time. It was very tense, very scary for your parents, but I assured them it would get better with time and it did. They built new lives as new people, and we've been close ever since. I'm afraid there's not much more to the story than that."

Angie leaned forward. "But there is, Walt. How is my mom connected to Isabella Conti?"

"Who?"

Angie took the picture out from her purse and explained all she'd learned about the Contis and what she had shared with her father.

"My dad stole from the Mob, and Conti was in the Mob, and somehow this girl is connected to my mother."

"And what did your dad say?" Walt asked.

"He says he doesn't know anything. Doesn't know the girl or how my mom knew her or why she would write *forgive me* on the back of the photograph."

Walt made a *hmm* sound—it was curious to him, got him thinking. "What can I do, Angie?" He sounded earnest.

"What do you remember from that time? About my dad's business dealings. There's something there."

"Why don't you ask your dad?"

Angie looked again out the window and saw Louise bent over her nascent flower garden weeding without gloves on. The garden wasn't much to look at now, but it would be glorious in a few more weeks. Louise was quite gifted with plants.

Angie looked back at Walt. "I guess I was hoping you could tell me." For whatever reason it felt better than saying, *"I don't trust my dad to tell me the truth."*

"Tell you why there wasn't a trial?"

"It seems to me my dad got a free pass into witness protection. He committed crimes and got away with it."

"Hardly got away scot-free," Walt said. "He had to give up his entire life, his family, your mom's family. It was hardly an easy road."

Angie couldn't disagree there. "Okay. And just to reiterate, I don't hold any of this against you. You were just doing your job."

"And just to reiterate, I think of you as a niece," Walt said. "You're family to me. That's what's important. Not a name on a piece of paper."

Angie thanked him, and didn't mention that Bao had told her something similar. She got up from the table. "Well, wish me luck, Uncle Walt."

"Luck with what?"

"I'm going to take your advice and confront my dad again. And this time I'm not going to leave until he tells me the truth once and for all. I'm going to make him go through all of his business dealings until I know everything about his past, and figure out how my mom was connected to Isabella Conti."

Walt's expression changed. He looked like someone who'd just remembered where he set down his missing car keys. "You know, you got me thinking. Let me check something for you in my files. Hang on a second. No promises."

Angie agreed to wait. She drank her water and looked out at the lawn, watching Louise hard at work, thinking about her mother and how much she'd enjoyed gardening.

Angie read e-mails on her phone and the time slipped away without her noticing, but it seemed like he had been gone for a while. She held out hope for a minor miracle, a piece of paper, some sort of official document to explain the unexplainable.

But Walt returned empty-handed. "I'm sorry, Angie. I thought there might have been something in my old files, but I was wrong. My guess is your dad never had a trial. That had happened before. He gave up information and in exchange, no charges were filed."

Angie gave Walt a big hug. "A friend of mine said the same thing. Thanks for looking, but I'm not giving up. I'll figure this out with my dad, one way or another."

Walt held Angie's shoulders and looked deeply into the eyes. "I have every confidence you will."

CHAPTER 56

Home again, home again. Angie used her key to go in through the front door. The TV wasn't on, but then again the Nats weren't playing. She called out to her dad, knowing he was at home because his Lexus was in the driveway. If he happened to be taking a walk, it would be downstairs on his elliptical in the basement where he had a second television set up.

"Daddy? I need to speak with you," Angie said, setting her purse on the little desk in the kitchen that had become a catchall for odds and ends.

As she had expected, her father was at home—in the first-floor office, judging by the sound of his footsteps.

She was already rummaging through the refrigerator when he came into the kitchen. She needed a bit of food to calm what felt like a caffeine overdose, and found a bowl of egg salad on a shelf and half a loaf of bread misplaced in the drawer where the vegetables go. Her mother never would have put the bread there, though she did keep it refrigerated.

Angie took the items over to the kitchen island and

only then acknowledged her father's presence. Gabriel had on faded jeans and a denim work shirt, and looked quite relaxed, not at all like someone who had been carrying a burdensome secret for years.

Angie took down a plate from the cupboard and set it next to the food. She poured herself a glass of water. "Do you want a sandwich, Dad?"

"You're not done with this, are you?" Gabriel said.

"Nope, not even close," Angie replied. She retrieved a dull knife from a kitchen drawer and heaped some egg salad onto the bread. She spread the egg salad evenly, then cut the sandwich in two, took a bite, and chewed slowly. She washed it all down with a drink of water. "I hope you don't have plans today, because we're going to get to the bottom of this."

"Angie, please."

She took another bite, leaning against the kitchen island, acting as though she had all the time in the world. "No more, please. No more lies. Somehow your former business and Mom's former life are connected to Isabella Conti, and I'm determined to figure out how."

"I told you all I know."

"Please, Dad, that doesn't work anymore. I checked. There's nothing about William Harrington in any archives I searched. Nothing about your Ponzi scheme or the trials where you turned state's evidence. And I'm pretty good at this stuff. There should be something, but there's nothing. So either you're not giving me the whole truth or you're forgetting some key details, but either way, I'm not leaving until we sort it out."

It was a test. If he came up with the same explanation Bryce and Walt had offered, she might be inclined to believe him.

But instead of a valid explanation, Gabriel shook with anger. His face turned red and his eyes flared in anger. "I will not be spoken to this way by my daughter."

Angie refused to be rattled. She took another bite of her sandwich, chewing slowly, keeping her eyes fixed on her father, intending her actions to be interpreted as a show of defiance. "Then tell me what I want to know," she said after swallowing her bite.

"No."

"Tell me or I'm going to find the Conti family, dammit." Anger seeped into Angie's voice. "I've got a friend with the Marshals now, or did you forget? He'll help me. He'll run this up the damn flagpole if he has to. I promise you, we'll dig up whatever secret you're hiding. So let's do this on your terms, not mine. What is the connection to the Conti family and my mom? Why aren't there stories about you in the news? Why aren't you being forthcoming with me?"

Her father's face turned bright red. "Enough!" he said, stomping his foot so hard he rattled the dishes in the cupboard. He stormed over to the kitchen island, picked up Angie's plate of food, and hurled it across the room against the wall.

The plate shattered, sending jagged shards of the dish and bits of the sandwich shooting in all directions like shrapnel. Angie ducked and covered her ears, startled and scared.

"Enough!" Gabriel yelled again. "I will not be spoken to this way!"

"You're hiding something!" Angie screamed back at him, pointing her finger at his face. "What the hell are you hiding?"

Gabriel turned and stormed out of the kitchen. He

went to the TV room and turned on the television, cranking the volume.

"Talk to me, Dad."

Gabriel wouldn't respond, so Angie went back to the kitchen and cleaned up the mess.

Time passed, and Angie's hopes that her father would relent began to dim. She went into the living room and sat on the sofa. The announcer for some History Channel documentary was the only one talking.

After some time, still not having said a word, Gabriel rose from his favorite chair and Angie trailed him into the spacious first-floor office adjacent to the living room. Sun spilled inside through a bank of windows overlooking the backyard—a yard still in need of mowing.

Unwilling and unable to endure the silence a moment longer, she decided to press him again. She touched his shoulder. A connection made. "What are you hiding from me, Dad?" she asked in a gentler voice.

Gabriel kept his back to his daughter, sorting through some papers on the desk, pretending not to hear her. He was breathing hard.

"Did Mom have an affair? Am I Antonio Conti's daughter? What is it? What?"

"No," Gabriel said harshly, turning to face her. "It's none of that." His voice carried less of an edge, suggesting to Angie that he might be softening.

"Then what?" Angie's eyes were pleading as she reached for her father's hand. "It's enough. Just tell me."

Gabriel titled his head slightly and gazed at his daughter with love in his eyes. "Enough is right," he said in a quiet voice, almost to himself. "I should have known you wouldn't let it go. I had hoped, but . . . maybe it's time. Maybe all this has happened for a reason. You're safe now. That's enough for me."

"I don't understand."

Gabriel touched Angie's cheek with two plump fingers, one of which still carried his wedding ring. He set his hands on her shoulders. His back was turned to the bank of windows, and sunlight streaming in lit him in an angelic glow. Angie saw herself reflected in the lens of her father's glasses. She looked misshapen, not unlike how she felt.

"You would figure it out one way or another. I have no doubts about that. None whatsoever. But no matter what happens, no matter what I tell you," Gabriel said, "please know I love you very much, and I'm so incredibly proud of the woman you've become."

"Daddy, what is it?" Angie's chest tightened. Dread overwhelmed her.

"I'm so sorry," Gabriel said, sputtering his words as tears welled in his reddened eyes.

To Angie, it looked as though he had aged a dozen years in a matter of seconds. "Tell me, please."

Instead of her father's voice, the next sound Angie heard was a whip cracking noise, followed by the sound of breaking glass. The noise startled her. It was loud and unexpected and it sounded very close by.

Gabriel lurched forward, knocked off balance. He fell hard into Angie and his momentum carried them both to the floor where they landed in a tangled heap.

Did he have a heart attack? Angie's thoughts were reeling and her father's weight felt crushing. Using her arms and legs for leverage, she rolled her father off her body. He spilled onto his back, breathing erratically, eyes glued to the ceiling, head not moving.

"Dad, are you all right?"

Angie felt a stab of fear when her father didn't respond. On her hands and knees, she leaned over her father's face and tried to get a look into his eyes. She felt something warm and wet spread against her fingertips.

She looked behind her and saw that the floor around her father's lower back was coated in red where blood was seeping out. Her fingers were sticking into the blood.

Angie screamed and rolled Gabriel onto his stomach, seeing for the first time the hole in his denim shirt, singed around the edges as though the fabric had been burnt. Blood gushed out the hole and spread across Gabriel's denim shirt.

Angie pressed her hand against the wound, but blood pulsed through the cracks of her fingers. "Dad! Dad! Oh my God! Oh God!"

Her eyes were wide, breath shaky, body frozen from terror. She thought first about calling an ambulance, not what had caused her father to fall down bleeding. It took a moment for her fragmented thinking to gel into a sensible narrative—her father had been shot.

Movement in Angie's periphery drew her attention to a male figure lurking in the doorway. He was tall and thin with a clean-shaven face and unsettling pale blue eyes. He must have entered through the patio door. He held in his hands a high-powered rifle with an attached scope and what appeared to be a suppressor screwed into the barrel. He had more guns holstered to a battle belt secured around his black tactical pants. A black long-sleeved combat shirt and black leather boots completed his ensemble. The man's expression was a blank.

He stood five feet away, give or take, essentially point-blank range. Without uttering a word, the intruder lifted his gun and took aim, not at Gabriel, but at Angie. A bullet was coming her way, and she gritted her teeth to brace for impact and the blackness to follow. *Would it hurt?* It was human nature to fear pain, same as it was to freeze in the face of one's imminent death. The intruder's aim was high, and Angie imagined the bullet would enter through the center of her skull.

Instead of a gunshot, Angie heard her father grunt loudly.

The man's attention pivoted to Gabriel. What could have been a threat was nothing more than a bleeding man's slow roll toward the office doorway. The man trained the barrel of the rifle away from Angie and onto Gabriel, who continued his deliberate roll toward his assailant, smearing in his wake a jagged trail of blood.

Angie knew what was coming. She understood somehow what her father had intended, and she had a choice to make. She could scream, cry out for her dad, and try to plead with this killer for mercy. Or she could use the precious few seconds he had given her to strike.

Bullets spit out the barrel of the rifle with the same whip crack sound—not silent, but not at all deafening. Three shots were fired, each chambered using the rifle's bolt action. The bullets exploded Gabriel's stomach, neck, and head in that order.

The killer quickly refocused his weapon away from the bloody remains of Gabriel DeRose and back onto Angie. But Angie was no longer in the same line of sight as before. She had gone onto her stomach and crawled toward the assailant while he was busy murdering her father.

Barely able to contain her shock and horror, she'd managed to slither on her belly, traveling three feet at most. She had covered just enough distance. With her arms extended out front like giant antennae, she got to within reach of the killer's ankles. She grabbed hold, her fingers digging hard into the pliable leather of his black boots, and pulled with all her strength. The attacker got off a shot as he fell, but the bullet struck the wall behind the office desk, sending bits of plaster and drywall shooting out in various directions.

The killer fell to the floor with a hard crash. Angie heard air explode from his lungs. She was on top of him in a flash, striking him in the throat with a well-timed and well-placed punch. He gurgled and wheezed after impact. She dared not strike again and scrambled to her feet, mouth open and twisted in a silent scream. Gaining traction and balance, she raced to the front door, the closest way out.

The knob wouldn't turn, and no matter how hard she pushed and pulled, the door wouldn't budge. *What was wrong?* The killer was groaning, getting back to his feet. No way to backtrack now.

Somehow the killer must have barricaded them inside. Angie figured he had done the same to the side entrance in the kitchen. She gave only a moment's consideration to going out the kitchen window. She would have to break the glass, climb over the sink, push her way past the jagged shards to freedom. Too hard. Too much time. She imagined it would be the last act she would ever do. Angie made a different choice and rushed to the basement door in the middle of the kitchen.

She was headed downstairs, where her father used his elliptical.

And where he kept his guns.

CHAPTER 57

The Markovich search was at a standstill. Most everyone, including the team with the SOC (now with Cormack Donovan's help) were fumbling about in the dark, and not making any progress whatsoever.

Bryce had had some success, though on a completely different front. His contact, Tim Wiley, who had provided him with information on Antonio Conti, worked out of headquarters and happened to be in the building on a Saturday, helping with the Markovich effort. Bryce stopped by Wiley's office and asked him for a second favor. He needed a little digging into the DeRose identity.

After a couple minutes on his computer, Wiley looked at Bryce with a strange expression on his face. "What are you up to, Taggart?"

"Just . . . um, nothing really. Just . . . Timmy, help me out, will ya? And don't ask any questions."

"Yeah, okay," Wiley said. "But you just pinpointed a second screwed-up case with no explanation."

"What do you mean?"

"It's just like with Antonio Conti, only in reverse. I got the DeRose identity here all right—Gabriel, Kathleen, and Angie—but no clue who they were beforehand. There's absolutely nothing in the case file to tell me."

Bryce's expression became strained. He gave Wiley the name *William Harrington* to search.

"Nope. Nothing there," Wiley said. "Everything is a hornet's nest with you. Who screwed up these damn case files so badly?"

Bryce was headed for the door. "That's what I intend to find out."

It felt good to breathe fresh air again. Bryce found his car in the crowded parking lot and got settled in the driver's seat, figuring he'd head off to Alexandria once he got in touch with Angie. Another bit of unsettling news was headed her way. His call rang several times before going to voice mail. He called again and got the same result. Then he called Angie's office and someone answered, a man whose voice sounded familiar.

"DeRose and Associates. How may I help you?"

"This is Bryce Taggart. I'm looking for Angie DeRose."

"Hey Bryce, Mike Webb here. We did the job in Baltimore together. I work with Angie."

"Of course. How are you?"

"Better than you, I think. Heard our boy Markovich did a vanishing act."

"That he did," Bryce said. "And a good one at that. Sorry to be in a rush, but is Angie around? It's sort of urgent."

"No sir," Mike said. "Haven't heard from her. I left a couple messages about a runaway case we're working. It's not like her to not to call us back. If you get in touch, could you tell her to give me a call?"

"Will do. Has anybody checked her apartment?" Bryce was headed there next.

"My partner, Bao, went over to her place, but she's not at home. I'm sure she's busy with her other investigation."

"Which one? The photograph?"

"What else? It's her obsession," Mike said.

What Mike said gave Bryce an idea. As a law enforcement official, he had access to all sorts of information and could look up most anyone's address. If Angie wanted to talk to someone about the photograph, who better than her father?

CHAPTER 58

Raynor Sinclair scrambled to his feet, took an improper firing stance, and through blurred vision, got off a haphazard shot at nothing. Angie wasn't in his sight anymore, and he didn't know where she had gone.

The strike to his throat had dazed him. He believed she had only a few seconds' head start, but a few seconds in that sort of footrace could translate into minutes. He wasn't concerned about Angie getting out the front or side doors. He had stuck pennies wrapped in tape into the crack between the door and the jamb molding above and below the handle. It was a prank his brothers had pulled on him years ago, so Raynor knew from experience that the technique was extremely effective at locking someone inside. He scanned the backyard and saw no sign of her. He doubted she'd gone that way. The front door would have been his first and best choice. She was bright, exceedingly cunning, and had probably done as he would have.

The gun safe used an electronic lock from Titan, but Angie knew the code—a combination of her birthday and her parents' anniversary. An adrenaline rush like no other held at bay any emotion or thought not connected to her survival. Her father was dead, murdered in front of her eyes in the most horrible way imaginable, but she would grieve for him later. Her focus was on picking a weapon.

Angie went with the Ruger. It was light, reliable. The basement had a concrete floor with rough-hewn stone walls. Even with the light on it was dark down there . . . and dank . . . and crammed full of boxes and bins of various sizes and materials. The basement had no windows or exits. Its main purpose was for storage.

The space had nooks, such as the crawlspace underneath the stairs, where her father stored cans of paint. On the wall next to the crawlspace was where her father kept his tools—a table saw, workbench, and plenty of wrenches, hammers, extension cords, and the like—all neatly arranged on a pegboard. The heating and cooling systems, hot water tank, and electrical panels were opposite the pegboard.

Angie gathered up the gun. She checked to make sure it was loaded—it was—and took an extra magazine just in case. She hesitated then decided to take the CZ 75 as a backup, stashing that weapon into the waistband of her jeans.

At the wall by the stairs, she flicked a switch, shut off the light, and plunged the room into complete darkness. She felt along the wall, careful not to knock down any of the tools, until she found the crawlspace under the stairs. Working quickly but quietly, she moved aside a tall cardboard box full of old coats, and climbed over a stack of paint cans without knocking any over. She pulled the box in front of her, sealing herself inside as if it were a tomb.

* * *

Raynor rounded the corner and aimed his rifle into the kitchen. He saw nobody there. The side door was closed and the window over the sink was intact. Perhaps she hid in a closet or food pantry? He checked both, but didn't find her. There was another door in the kitchen he hadn't checked, and when he opened that one, he smiled.

Behind it he found a set of stairs.

Angie gritted her teeth. Her heart raced in terror and sweat coated her skin. The room seemed to be spinning. A sound from above turned her blood to ice.

Footsteps.

Raynor used a switch at the top of the stairs to turn on the basement light. No reason for him to descend into darkness. He leaned his rifle—a Model 700 SPS Tactical from Remington, with a Vortex viper 6x24 scope and a suppressor from Dakota he had threaded himself—on the wall next to the basement door. The rifle had served its purpose well, and while the subsonic ammunition didn't completely drown out the noise of the shot, it was enough for him to forgo ear protection. The usual thunderclap of the Remington was more like a car had backfired.

It had felt good in his hands, but since he wasn't familiar with the layout of the basement, the rifle's long barrel might prove a liability in a confined space. His original plan had been to use a tactical knife, a 12-inch fixed blade from Bowie, to cut Gabe and Angie's throats. But the father might have armed himself as a precaution. Angie had progressed quite far with her investigation, and Gabriel had reason to be cautious.

As for Angie, she knew her way around guns, had a license to carry, and might also be armed.

Raynor liked his skills in close-quarters combat, but he'd taken into account the two-on-one odds, plus the possibility of firearms in the mix, and decided the knife wasn't the way to go. Better to use his rifle, take up position in the backyard, which offered plenty of tall trees to hide him from the neighbors and lots of windows for sighting his targets. His plan had worked stupendously, with one notable exception.

Angie.

He had been careless with her.

He would not be so thoughtless again.

The wooden stairs groaned under Raynor's weight. It was quiet down there, but he knew his quarry was near. He could sense her the way he could that grouse on the day he murdered his father. He wouldn't let Angie get the best of him again. He would anticipate her every move, same as he did that grouse's.

In his hand, Raynor held a Glock 20 in 10mm auto—a massive piece of firepower, though without considerable recoil. He descended cautiously, surging forward, pausing frequently to scan the area for threats. Stairwells presented him with a unique tactical challenge, but his instincts told him Angie wasn't waiting at the bottom of the stairs.

His instincts were right, and he stepped into an unfinished basement with a smooth floor, but rough walls. He saw no windows, nor any doors to the outside. The duct-work, electrical wiring, and pipes running overhead were all exposed. It was an open floor plan, with lots of boxes, and lots of places for her to hide. Which way should he go?

The space was like his Remington—good on utility, short on frills. It was clean and organized with an area for exercising off to Raynor's right, and a place for storage and tools to his left. He scanned right but went left. Left offered more places to hide. The biggest mistake he could make would be to move too quickly. He inched his way forward, keeping two hands on his Glock at all times. The open area made it easy for him to slice the pie. No hallways or doors fragmented his focus. He would shoot at even the slightest bit of movement.

Sliding in front of the wall abutting the stairwell, Raynor trained his gun on the heating and cooling system in front of him. He wondered if Angie had taken refuge over there. He stepped in front of a pegboard of tools and came to a stop next to a tall cardboard box to his left. He kicked the box with his foot, not hard enough to knock it over, but with just enough force to test the weight and see if Angie might be hiding inside. She wasn't. He stepped away from the wall, stood with his back to the box, and scanned the room once more.

Angie used her ears for eyes. It sounded to her like the man was right in front of the box. In fact, she saw the box move slightly, as though he had pushed it, perhaps checking to see if she were hiding inside. Footsteps followed, but not many, one or two at most. Then a shadow blocked out what had been a sliver of light seeping in where the top of the box and the lip of crawlspace met. He was directly in front of her.

Angie leveled her Ruger. And fired.

Raynor heard a gunshot behind him, and then he felt the burn.

He fell to the floor. The sticky collision with the bullet

hadn't knocked him over. That went against the laws of physics. It was his reaction to the gunshot that sent him tumbling. The bullet had entered through his side, and could have done internal damage, but it hadn't stopped his heart. Without hesitating, he flipped onto his back and fired three wild shots aimed at the cardboard box. The noise was deafening, but not so loud as to drown out the sound of Angie's scream.

The first bullet to hit Angie struck her in the arm. The second went into her side. The third missed because she fell onto her back to minimize the chance of another hit from the fusillade. Shot placement was everything, and her would-be killer's bullet hadn't hit anything vital. She could still breathe. Her senses functioned. Her heart continued to beat. The bleeding was brisk, but not overly so. The pain, however, was intense—white hot, burning her from the inside out.

She wasn't frozen in fear, nor was she in too much pain to continue to fight. Lying on her back, she fired again. Bullets from her gun punched several holes through the cardboard and may or may not have hit her attacker. Light streamed into the crawlspace through the bullet holes in the box. Dust motes danced inside columns of brightness. The holes weren't big enough to see through, so she fired blindly again, expecting a return volley.

With his gun in his hand—a Glock pistol in .40 S&W caliber—Bryce knew something was wrong the moment he'd seen coins wrapped in electrical tape wedged between the door and the jamb molding. The coins were easy enough to remove from the outside, but it would have been impossible to do so from inside. The door was unlocked and he went right inside. Before he could even call out Angie's name, he heard a series of gunshots.

He oriented himself to the sound and soon found a set of stairs behind a door in the kitchen leading to a basement.

His heart hammered away. All the anxiety, fear, everything he'd felt while taking down Buggy, was magnified tenfold. The situation, the threat level, and the number of assailants were all unknowns.

"Angie? Are you okay?"

Bryce's call went unanswered.

"Angie, it's Bryce. Talk to me if you can?"

To his surprise, a male voice responded. "Taggart! Taggart! Raynor Sinclair, U.S. Marshals. Get down here right away. Angie's been hurt!"

The killer has a name. His name is Raynor, and he works with Bryce. These were passing thoughts. Angie's real focus was protecting Bryce.

She heard footsteps above her and screamed, "No! Don't!"

But the sound of Bryce's footsteps quickened anyway.

Raynor had moved away from the box and Angie's line of fire. He fired his weapon at the exact moment Bryce emerged from around the corner. The bullet struck Bryce in the chest, left of the heart. Shock and pain sent him to his knees. Blood painted the cement floor beneath him in drips of red. He fired off two shots, but his aim was worthless.

Raynor came forward with his gun aimed for the kill

shot. "Drop your weapon," he said, his voice even and steady despite the pain of his injury. "Do it or you're dead."

Bryce looked disoriented and off balance while placing his gun on the ground beside him.

"Now, slide your weapon over to me."

Bryce did as he was told. Raynor picked up the gun and slipped it into the waistband of his pants, wincing at a stab of pain. He approached Bryce with caution, though confident he was no longer a threat. Raynor hoisted Bryce up by his shirt collar, spun him around, and used an arm lock to the neck to keep him upright.

He pushed Bryce forward and called to Angie, "Throw out your gun and come out where I can see you, or I put a bullet through his head right now." He could hear Angie's labored breathing coming from behind the box.

"Counting to three," Raynor said. "One . . ."

More breathing.

"Two . . ."

The cardboard box came open like a hinged door. A bloody hand appeared from within and tossed out a gun. A Ruger it looked to be. The gun landed with a clatter.

"Now, you come out where I can see you," Raynor said, trying to ignore the pulsing pain in his side.

From the crawlspace, Angie slithered out on her belly, knocking over paint cans in her wake, sending them rolling across the floor like bowling pins. Her left arm appeared mangled and blood seeped out from a hole in her side where she'd been shot.

Raynor wasn't in much better shape. The pain radiating in his belly was intense, the blood loss steady. He knew he should work quickly to finish them off, but rage owned him. Angie needed to suffer for shooting him, hurting him, humiliating him.

He pointed his gun at her. "On your knees."

Angie did as she was told. "Why are you doing this?" Her voice came out shaky.

Raynor found the fear swimming in her eyes to be almost hypnotic. He rarely wounded his quarry, and so rare was the opportunity to see a living creature process death. It was a thing of profound beauty. He respected Angie greatly for her courage. But she had to die. He turned Bryce around and forced him onto his knees next to Angie. Blood continued to pour out of his body, as well. Bryce could barely lift his head, and he might have been in shock.

Raynor gritted his teeth to stave off the stabbing pain as he searched them both for any hidden weapons. He found none. They had no recourse, nothing left to do but die. He backed up three steps and aimed his Glock at Angie's head.

"You shot me," he said, breathing hard, staring Angie in the eyes. With his left hand, he unsheathed the bowie knife from a holster strapped to his boot. "Nobody hurts me. If they do, they pay for it. So I'm going to shoot you both, but I'm going to kill him quickly. You, I'm going to work on slowly, make it hurt as much possible. Any last words?"

Raynor's vision was dimming. He wasn't sure he could make Angie's suffering last as long he wanted. He needed to get to a hospital and come up with some way to explain this mess.

Angie had no last words. She refused to avert her gaze. Hatred had replaced much of the fear Raynor had seen in her eyes. He admired her even more at that moment.

Raynor adjusted his aim. "Then all that's left to say is good-bye."

A gunshot sounded with a cacophonous bang, and the

smell of blood succumbed to the overpowering stench of gunpowder.

Angie heard the bang, but instead of pain, she saw blood rise up from behind Raynor's head in a great red wave. His legs gave out and he crumpled to the floor, where she could see how a gunshot had taken apart much of his skull. Her gaze moved away from his inert form and onto the figure of a man who stood ten feet away, holding a hunting rifle in his hands.

Walter Odette.

Angie felt weightless in her body. A feeling of incredible, profound relief tempered the pain of her many injuries. For a moment, all she could feel was the joy of still being alive. Walter had come to her rescue. Of course it would have to be him. All her life, he had been there for her, playing the role of her entire extended family. He had protected her by putting her into witness protection, and here he was, all these years later, protecting her once more.

Walter had two guns on him—the hunting rifle in his hands, and slung over his right shoulder was the Remington Raynor Sinclair had used to murder her father. Angie needed to get up off her knees, desperate to hug Walter close to her. Somehow she found the strength in her legs to begin to stand.

As she started to rise, Walter set the hunting rifle on the ground and took Raynor's Remington into his hands. Then he aimed the barrel of the Remington at Angie's head and said something she simply couldn't comprehend. "This isn't the first time I killed for you."

CHAPTER 59

Angie sank back to her knees. Electric currents of pain like nothing she had ever experienced surged through her body. Bryce, also wounded, also on his knees, teetered beside her. He was too weak and dazed to speak. Though bleeding profusely, he somehow managed to keep upright and conscious.

"Uncle Walt, what are you doing?" The strain in her voice was matched only by the strain showing on Walter Odette's face.

"I'm so sorry, Angie," he said, his voice cracking, sputtering his words. "It was never supposed to have ended like this. Never. I love you and I'm so very sorry. But I have no choice."

Walter took aim once more. He had gloves on, and was going to use Raynor's gun to kill them. It was obvious Raynor would take the blame for all the murders, except for his own. Walt would get credit there—a hero neighbor who came just a little too late to prevent a tragedy. Whatever motive he would invent for Raynor's rampage didn't much matter.

Angie covered her head with her hands, expecting a

bullet that didn't come. She uncrossed her arms to look at Walter, who stood ten feet in front of her.

"Please Walter, don't do this," Angie pleaded from her knees.

Walter's finger trembled against the Remington's trigger. "May God forgive me."

Those words—so familiar to Angie—hit her like a bolt of lightning. She expected to hear a shot, and again braced herself for a pain that didn't come. Walter had hesitated once more.

She sensed a blur of motion to her right.

Leaning forward, Bryce had managed to pick up one of the paint cans Angie had knocked over, and with the grunt of a shot putter, hurled it at Walter's head. The throw was perfectly on target, and Walter used his forearm in a reflexive countermeasure to deflect what would have been a direct hit. The paint can bounced off his arm and fell to the floor with a clang. The top came off and a thick pool of turquoise spilled onto the cement.

Angie used the distraction to her advantage. What had worked before could work again.

Ignoring the pain of her injuries, fueled only by adrenaline, she fell to her right and leaned her body into the crawlspace, emerging a moment later with the CZ 75 in her hand. She had stashed the backup gun there before surrendering to Raynor. She had expected a trained professional would search her person for a second weapon, but had counted on him not searching the crawlspace.

Unlike Walter, Angie didn't hesitate to shoot. Four bullets spit out the barrel of her gun, and three punctured Walter's chest. A grunt, and he collapsed to the floor, falling onto his back, his gaze fixed to the ceiling. The Remington tumbled from his grasp and fell safely out of reach.

Angie turned her attention to Bryce. He was slumped forward, using his hand to apply pressure to the gunshot wound to his chest.

"Bryce, talk to me. How bad is it?"

Angie's own wounds continued to throb and the loss of blood made her feel lightheaded.

Bryce grunted through the pain, but managed to get out his cell phone. "I'll call 911."

Angie felt the room spinning. "What can I do to help?"

"Get . . . the . . . truth. . . ." Bryce struggled through every word. A new resolve came to him. "I'm going to be okay. I can breathe. It just hurts like a bastard. But he's not going to be here long." Bryce pointed a bloodstained finger at Walter, whose chest rose and fell with the fast action of fireplace bellows.

"No," Angie said. "I'll stay with you."

Bryce punched 911 into the phone. "I got this. You get that."

With a nod, Angie crawled over Walter, who was still breathing hard. She put her gun to his head, but took it away when he spit out a gob of blood. Instead of the barrel of her gun, she put her hand on Walter's face and gave his cheek a gentle caress.

"Tell me," she whispered in his ear. "Tell me what you and my father did. Tell me the truth before you're gone, Walter. Let it go. Give that to me, please. If you love me like you said, you'll do that one thing for me. You owe me the truth."

Tears pricked the corners of Angie's eyes. Her father was involved. His last words to her had made it clear.

"I killed people," Walter managed.

"Who?" Angie asked. "Who did you kill?"

Walter licked away some of the blood from his lips. "People—going into witness protection. . . ."

A stab of pain took away Angie's breath. She tried not to look at her bleeding, tried to center herself and her focus on the precious moment. Help would be there soon enough.

"We replaced people who were going to disappear with different people. Then we buried the records, made it . . . made it so there were no links between the old identity . . . and the new ones."

A horrible feeling came over Angie.

May God forgive me.

Walter's earlier words came back to her. *This isn't the first time I killed for you.*

"You killed the Conti family, didn't you?"

"Yes." The word seeped out of Walter's throat in a hiss.

"So that we could take over their identities."

"Yes."

"And there needed to be a little girl who I could become."

"Yes."

"I wasn't a baby when Isabella Conti died, was I?"

"You . . . and Isabella were the same . . . age. I took the picture of Isabella. . . . Your mother . . . asked me . . . for it."

Angie's father had lied when he told her she went into witness protection as an infant. He knew Angie would have made some connection to Isabella Conti if he had told the truth.

Walter was struggling even more. His breath sounds were completely erratic. Behind her, Angie could hear Bryce talking to a 911 operator, but she couldn't focus on what he was saying. She couldn't feel her gunshot wounds anymore, either.

"My mom," Angie said. "She knew."

"She did," Walter said, his voice barely a fading echo.

"Why wasn't my father's Ponzi scheme reported? Why wasn't there a trial?"

"No trial," Walter said, "because he stole money only from the Mob. Dirty money. The Mob couldn't go to the police—but they could kill him, and all of you. I"—Walter coughed up another glob of blood—"I knew there was a hit on him because I put a lot of connected guys into the program. They . . . they were still plugged into the life . . . still had their sources. One guy told me about your dad . . . I figured your dad had a lot of money . . . and he needed to disappear."

And that was enough. Angie understood it all. Walter Odette had approached her father with an offer. Pay him whatever amount of money it took, and instead of the Contis becoming the DeRose family as planned, it could be the Harringtons—William, Claire, and Amelia. They were the perfect match—like organ donors, only instead of tissue types, it was the number of people in the family and the relative ages that were a perfect match. Angie's mother knew Isabella Conti would die so that her daughter might live.

And Isabella had died all right. She'd died on March 4, 1988, the day they were supposed to enter witness protection, the day Walter Odette, a person the Contis had trusted implicitly, had murdered them all.

"You hired that man to kill me and my father," Angie said, pointing at the puddle of a man without a skull. "Why?"

But Walter's eyes were glassy. His chest no longer rose and fell to any rhythm, and the final breath had left his body.

CHAPTER 60

The memorial service for the man who was Gabriel DeRose, but wasn't, would have been more crowded had press been allowed to attend. It was Angie's wish not to turn the somber occasion into a circus. Of the several dozen or so people who came to the Silverstone Funeral Home to pay their last respects, some were friends and professional associates of Gabriel, some were friends of Kathleen, some were connected to Angie. A few introduced themselves as relatives of William Harrington.

One such relative, a cousin named Marcia Lane, approached Angie from behind. She tapped Angie's left arm, not seeing it was still in a sling. A string of apologies soon followed.

"What can you tell me about my father?" Angie asked after apologies were accepted and introductions made.

Marcia shrugged, making it clear nothing much would be forthcoming. "I heard on the news what happened and of course when they showed a picture of William, I mean your father, or Gabe, well, it triggered all sorts of memories of my cousin and his family who vanished one day without a word."

The two women exchanged contact information and made promises to meet.

Over time Angie would dive into genealogy, but she needed to mourn the loss of her father. His actions, his horrible crimes, and those of her mother, didn't erase the love she felt for her parents. And while she couldn't condone their extraordinary actions, she could give her mother one thing she'd wanted.

Forgiveness.

Angie forgave her parents while she mourned for them and for the little girl with the sad smile and misshapen ear. A girl whose fate very well could have been Angie's were it not for the terrible choice her parents had made.

Mike Webb and Bao each gave Angie a gentle hug—she'd been shot, and they were careful. For the occasion, Mike wore a semi-wrinkled beige suit, and Bao had on a long-sleeved oxford shirt buttoned to the top, crisp looking dark jeans, and his best Doc Martens. They each expressed their sincere condolences, but the conversation wasn't all about matters of life and death.

"You think you can come back to work next week?" Mike asked. "I got a big rental gig to prep for and we're really swamped. I mean, I know it's a horrible thing what happened to you and all, but honestly, Ange, the publicity has been incredible for business."

It hurt to laugh—if the bullet in her side had gone a few millimeters to the right, she'd be dead—but Angie let go a little one anyway.

Maddy, who was nearby, said, "Hey, Mike, let the girl heal and farm out the jobs you can't handle for now."

"Maybe we should hire a new full-time associate." Bao had made the suggestion on other occasions, but thought this time it might carry a bit more weight.

Angie said, "Guys, let me say good-bye to my father. Okay? We'll talk shop later."

Maddy gave Mike and Bao a look that said *I told you so*, and the three took seats in the fourth row, directly behind Carolyn, Greg, and Nadine Jessup, who had come as a family to offer their condolences.

Bryce showed up in a sharp-looking suit minutes before the service was scheduled to begin. His wounds were more severe than Angie's, and he had spent the better part of a week recovering in the hospital. He walked slowly. Like Angie, he would carry the scars of that day around with him forever.

He made his way to the front of the room where he pulled Angie aside. "I've got some new news."

She felt a jolt of excitement. A lot had happened in the two weeks since her father's cremation, not much of it good for the U.S. Marshals. Walter Odette turned out to be a very rich man. Those long vacations he took didn't even put a dent in all the money he'd made hiding people who could pay for his brand of witness protection. He had hid his wealth from Louise, so as to not attract attention, but in reality he lived a double life. His long fishing trips and other excursions were really lavish solo vacations—not exactly with the jet set, but skirting close.

Walt must have grown attached to his money, and for whatever reason he couldn't stop doing what he'd started years ago when he was a young marshal handling witness protection. When it came time for him to retire, he'd transitioned his operation to another marshal named Raynor Sinclair, who worked in witness protection and had access to the files they needed to manipulate. Questions were raised about a hunting accident that might not have been an accident. Maybe Walter learned a few things about

Raynor Sinclair and knew he was a good pick to take over the operation and rake in profits from murder.

It would take time and a lot of effort to figure out everyone Walter Odette and Raynor Sinclair had helped to hide by killing those the government had sought to protect. Their special clientele weren't people turning state's witness, but rather criminals who wanted or needed to disappear and had the means to pay. The transactions were a death sentence for those slated to go into the program. A little bit of manipulation of paperwork and files, and two sets of people disappeared—those in the program legitimately, murdered by Sinclair and Odette, and those who paid to take over the victims' government-manufactured identities. Others had been involved, and others paid off, but Odette was the mastermind and Sinclair his protégé.

Text messages between them drew a picture that clarified the last moments of Gabriel DeRose's life. Walter, panicked that Gabe was going to tell Angie the truth, ordered Raynor to make the hit. That took place while Angie was at Walter's, when she thought he was looking through his files. As best she could guess, Walter had come to the house planning to kill Raynor and the whole program would have gone dark. He may have heard what Raynor planned to do to Angie, and didn't want her to suffer. But when the time came, Walter couldn't bring himself to pull the trigger.

"Walter faked a lot of things," Angie had said to Bryce. "But his love for me wasn't one of them."

Her father had substantial assets, more than Angie realized. The money could have come from his past life, when he stole from the mob. Walter probably hadn't taken it all, just a cut. Angie had plans for the money. All of it, every last penny, would go to the Microtia-Congenital Ear Deformity Center in Burbank, California. Dot, the center's receptionist, would be shocked by the note that would accompany the gift.

Angie glanced toward the back of the room. The head of the funeral home was trying to take his cue from her when to begin. She held up a finger to ask him to wait a minute. He obliged with a nod.

"So what's this big news you have to share?" Angie asked Bryce.

He leaned in close, took hold of Angie's right hand, and put his lips to her ear. It wasn't the first time his lips were in that spot, and it wouldn't be the last. "They arrested Albert Tuttle."

Angie whispered back, "That's great. Who the heck is Albert Tuttle?"

Bryce pulled away and smiled. "Well, he was supposed to be Dante Lerardi, but Dante was murdered—and guess who took over his persona?"

Angie broke into a smile. "Ivan Stinger Markovich."

"The one and only. Back where he belongs, in jail," Bryce said.

"Hot damn. That is great news. I'm so excited to tell Nadine. But I'll wait until after."

"Speaking of after, I could use a little nursing, if you know what I mean?"

Angie kissed Bryce tenderly on the cheek. "That'll have to be later. Nadine asked me to go out with her. She has someplace she wants to take me."

"Where to?" Bryce asked.

Angie shrugged. "She won't tell me. She just said she needs my help with something."

CHAPTER 61

Why did I do it? Why did I make this my life's mission? I guess I saw too many families like Sarah Winter's out there, too many people left wondering if their kid was alive or dead. I didn't want Jade to be like Sarah—a picture hanging on a wall in limbo. Somebody loved Jade, somebody missed her, and I believed somebody wanted her to come home.

I probably should have come clean with Angie from the start, just told her what I wanted her to do, but I was afraid she'd say no. I figured if I took her, and she could see Jade, it would make her think about her friend Sarah, and she'd agree to help even if I couldn't pay.

That was my plan, anyway.

So mission accomplished. Well, in a way. The big moment happened and it was incredible and incredibly sad. You see, I don't think there are any real winners and losers here. It's not like everything is amazeballs now. That's the conclusion I've come to. It's all just stuff—it's all just things that have happened. I mean, yes, there are some losers for sure, and I'm happy to report those losers are all in jail where they're going to be for a long time. But outside of that there's me, Tasha and the other girls, Angie, my parents, Bryce (aka Angie's super cute guy), and trust me, there aren't any real winners and losers in that bunch. There's just different experiences we can choose to learn from, to grow from, or choose to let define us.

Me personally? I'm choosing to live in the light. And there is a light. I believe in it wholeheartedly. I'm not saying everything happens for a reason, but there's a reason everything happens. Does that even make sense? Ha! I mean, I guess what I'm trying to say is that I don't think I got trafficked so I could get Angie to the Lowery Motel on St. Paul Street in Baltimore. That's where Jade lived. That's where Buggy and Casper dumped her when she wasn't useful to them anymore. The Lowery is like my apartment-prison in Baltimore, only way grosser. Waaaay grosser.

On my way upstairs with Angie I kept asking myself, how did this happen? How did I end up here? I don't think God ever said, put Nadine through hell so that she may one day do this one kind thing for someone else. I think God loves me and wouldn't do anything to hurt me. But I don't think God controls it all either. Like there isn't a big book where every movement, every single thing that's said and done by every living creature

*is completely spelled out. Imagine how big that
book would be! On this day, Nadine shall leave
her shoes in the front of a closet and it is written
her mother will be half-cocked as usual and she
shall trip over those shoes. No way! That's just
not realistic (IMHO).*

*Like I said, things don't happen for a reason,
but there's a reason things happen. I wasn't
destined to meet Jade, I don't think. But I met her
because I ran away from home and because she
was addicted to drugs and had to feed her habit
any way she could. And Angie? Well, she's in the
picture because my mom wanted to find me, so she
got the best person for the job. And I wanted to
help Jade find her family, so I got the best
person for the job, too. Like I said, there's a
reason things happen. So there I was on the third
floor of this disgusting motel holding Angie's
hand.*

*Before we went in, I told Angie what this
mission was all about. I figured she might be mad,
but she wasn't. She hugged me and told me I was
a good person for even trying, and that she'd be
happy to help pro bono (which means free). She
also told me I could have been upfront with her
from the start and she would have come because
it was important to me. She's cool like that.*

*But then Angie told me not to get my hopes up.
She said drugs are hard and they make people do
and act in ways that aren't good for them (tell me
about it!). She warned me not to expect a
miracle. I told her I'd only expect nothing if I
didn't try for one.*

I'd called the manager ahead of time so I knew Jade would be at home. The manager told me Jade didn't leave her place until dark. That's when she worked the streets. That was Jade's life and it was a hard one. The old me wouldn't understand how hard. The new me understood it more than I wished to know.

Angie knocked on the door and we waited. We heard footsteps. Then the doorknob turned. And then the door opened and I froze and so did Jade. We looked at each other for the longest time. Tears came to Jade's eyes, and then to mine. Jade kept saying, Jessica, is that you? Is it really you? I had to say, yeah but I'm really Nadine because she remembered me as someone else. Jade looked like I expected her to look. The street isn't where you go to get your young on. I introduced her to Angie and I told her Angie would help her reconnect with her family. She was good at that.

Jade gave me the most heartbreaking look. "There's nobody missing me," she said. Nobody at all. No mom, no dad, no relatives. Angie still handed Jade her card, plus a bunch of numbers of support groups, and one for Narcotics Anonymous she had looked up on her phone, stuff like that. She told Jade to call anytime, that she'd be happy to help her reconnect with her family or friends or anybody she wanted help finding.

Jade wasn't interested. There was no helping her, Jade said. Maybe in another life things would be better, but not this one. Those were her exact words. We left and I felt absolutely horrible. I had wasted Angie's time and my own. Jade didn't want my help, didn't need it. My great grand purpose in life was all a bunch of BS. I had such high hopes for a happy family reunion. But instead of being a big hero, I was back to just being another sad victim of trafficking.

I cried like crazy when we got back to Angie's car. Angie didn't say anything for the longest time. She just hugged me and told me it was going to be all right. Then she said something that made me stop crying and think. She said, at least Jade has her card now. And I thought about when I got Angie's card and what it had meant to me. Without that card and phone, I had no lifeline to the outside world. I had Ricardo, Buggy, and Casper and no way out. So maybe the trip to Jade's wasn't a total waste after all. Maybe all that effort to find her was just so I could get her Angie's card. And maybe Jade would call Angie one day and maybe there'd be that happy family reunion after all.

Or maybe not. Real life isn't neat and tidy like that. It doesn't get tied up in a cute little bow. That's for fairy tales, right? But Angie had a point. We know those fairy tale ending aren't real, but we can still dream. We can still believe.

So I guess in the end I gave Jade what Angie gave me. Well, Angie didn't give it to me. I had it in me all the time, I just forgot about it for a while. It had gone dark and Angie's card sparked it right back up. Now it's in me, glowing again. And I pray it glows inside Jade, too.

It's the thing that kept me going all those dark

*days and it keeps me going now. It's what gives
me reason to believe one day Sarah Winter will
come home. It's what Jade will need if she's ever
going to get clean and leave her old life behind. If
she's ever going to call Angie for help. There's a
word for the kind of feeling I'm describing. It's an
important word for me and for 21 million
people just like me all around the world.*

The word is hope.

ACKNOWLEDGMENTS

This is one of my favorite pages to write. It's my opportunity to thank those who offered help, often in unexpected ways. In addition to my editor and agent (Meg Ruley), deepest thanks to:

Lou Bivona for putting me in touch with the right people at the National Center for Missing and Exploited Children.

Frank Conners at the U.S. Marshals Service for his invaluable insights into the work of fugitive apprehension.

Anji Pribyl MaCuk, who runs the She Spies private investigation agency (https://www.shespiespi.com/), who also became the inspiration for Angie DeRose.

The team at the National Center for Missing and Exploited Children (NCMEC) who do the hard work of keeping children safe every day of the year.

A special thanks to Leemie Kahng-Sofer for her guidance and expertise.

My mom, Judy Palmer, and Ellen Clair Lamb, who help to make sure my words ring true.

Donna Prince for helping me remember what it was like that day in the hospital.

Rebecca Scherer for always being a sounding board.

Jessica Bladd Palmer for all she does.

My kids for all they do. I'm grateful they're safe and painfully aware that not every parent can say the same about their children.

Hollis, New Hampshire

Praise for the K

"*Irresistible Force* is simply fabulous! With exhilarating action and stunning sensuality, Ayres draws you in and doesn't let go."

> —Cherry Adair, *New York Times* bestselling author

"Incredible! You'll be on the edge of your seat to see if the heroine can make it out alive."
—Catherine Coulter, *New York Times* bestselling author

"Ayres brings gritty realism and sexy heat to this romantic suspense series." —*Publishers Weekly*

"If you think dogs and romantic suspense are an excellent mix, then Ayres has just the book and new series for you. This book delivers a tasty helping of intrigue, danger, and burgeoning romance!" —*RT Book Reviews*

"Sexy, romantic, and with enough humor to keep the pages turning." —Cocktails and Books

"A steamy, exciting, suspense-filled love story."
—Clever Girls Read

"A story about a HOT cop and his K-9 partner? I was all in! And, boy, did Miss Ayres deliver! I count this book as a DEFINITE read. Cops and canines, two things near and dear to my heart!" —Charlotte's Book Review

"Pretty darn great! I can honestly say that I never put the book down once I started reading it. I'm definitely up for the next book in the K-9 Rescue series. Love this author and so glad that I discovered this great series."
—Night Owl Reviews

Also by D.D. Ayres

Irresistible Force